"Theologian and scholar Bryan Litfin has accomplished a rare feat—he has fashioned a land and time unique to any reader's experience."

JERRY B. JENKINS, author, *Left Behind* and *Riven*

"Some fiction is mere entertainment and some fiction is like a mirror in which we see ourselves and our world reflected in challenging and instructive ways. *The Sword* is a mirror of who we are at the core and what we struggle with in our nonfiction lives. Don't miss this one. It is a compelling read that is well beyond mere entertainment."

JOE STOWELL, President, Cornerstone University

"Ever wonder about a world with an 'almost-absence' of God? Theologian turned 'futurist' Bryan Litfin provides us a compelling tale of the endurance of God's amazing love—even to a distant remnant. Get your mind around *The Sword*. It could be the start of something big."

MARK ELFSTRAND, Executive Producer/Host, *Morning Ride*, Moody Radio, Chicago, Illinois

"Pulling us into the future to reveal the past, Bryan Litfin's great what-if story discovers instead what is, laying bare the tendencies of the human soul, the strategies of our adversary, and the gentle sovereignty of the eternal God. In *The Sword* discovering truth is as exciting as discovering love, for, as Litfin skillfully portrays, they are one and the same."

AMY RACHEL PETERSON, author, *Perpetua: A Bride, A Martyr, A Passion*

"The one-of-a-kind concept for this novel mixes an apocalyptic near-future with an almost medieval past. The thrilling action and romance underscores the necessity of prayer and the power of God's Word to awaken a people to have hope in a love that supersedes that which they have before known. It is refreshing to read about characters whose struggles are real and whose virtues are worthy of admiration. I cannot wait until the second book in the series hits the shelves next year."

SETH PARRISH, High School Principal, Yongsan International School of Seoul, Seoul, Korea

"*The Sword*'s thrilling, fast-paced story line draws you in and won't let you put it down. It's a swashbuckling adventure that men will love. And the character development encourages your soul, making it well worth the read. I was fascinated to discover Christianity alongside the people of Chiveis and see them experience freedom and love for the first time. It gave me a new perspective of the privilege of choosing to give one's self to God."

STACIA JOHNSTON, Wife and mother of three

"*The Sword* has something to entice every reader: action, adventure, drama, mystery, discovery and romance. Through a commanding use of descriptive language and character development, Litfin engages his readers to the point that they will feel a part of the journey themselves. Seasoned and novice readers alike will benefit from Litfin's ability to provide a thrilling adventure while at the same time giving the opportunity to ponder the theological implications and Biblical parallels held within the Kingdom of Chiveis. Boasting of an original plot set in a unique era which beckons its reader into a new world vaguely familiar with fresh twists on life, *The Sword* will leave you begging for more."

NARISSA MUIK, Vancouver, Canada

THE SWORD

CHIVEIS TRILOGY

THE
SWORD

A NOVEL

BRYAN M. LITFIN

CROSSWAY

WHEATON, ILLINOIS

The Sword

Copyright © 2010 by Bryan M. Litfin

Published by Crossway
    1300 Crescent Street
    Wheaton, Illinois 60187

Cover design: Josh Dennis

Cover illustration: Portland Studios

First printing, 2010

Printed in the United States of America

Scripture on page 7 taken from the Louis Segond Bible. All Scripture quotations are the author's translation.

ISBN-13: 978-1-4335-0925-4

ISBN-10: 1-4335-0925-3

PDF ISBN: 978-1-4335-0926-1

Mobipocket ISBN: 978-1-4335-0927-8

ePub ISBN: 978-1-4335-2301-4

Library of Congress Cataloging-in-Publication Data
Litfin, Bryan M., 1970–
 The sword : a novel / Bryan M. Litfin.
  p. cm. — (Chiveis trilogy ; 1)
 ISBN 13: 978-1-4335-0925-4
 ISBN 10: 1-4335-0925-3
 I. Title
PS3612.I865S96 2010
813'.6—dc22   2009033930

Crossway is a publishing ministry of Good News Publishers.

LB		20	19	18	17	16	15	14	13	12	11	10
15	14	13	12	11	10	9	8	7	6	5	4	3	2	1

Car je connais les projets que j'ai formés sur vous, dit l'Éternel,
projets de paix et non de malheur,
afin de vous donner un avenir et de l'espérance.
Jérémie 29:11

contents

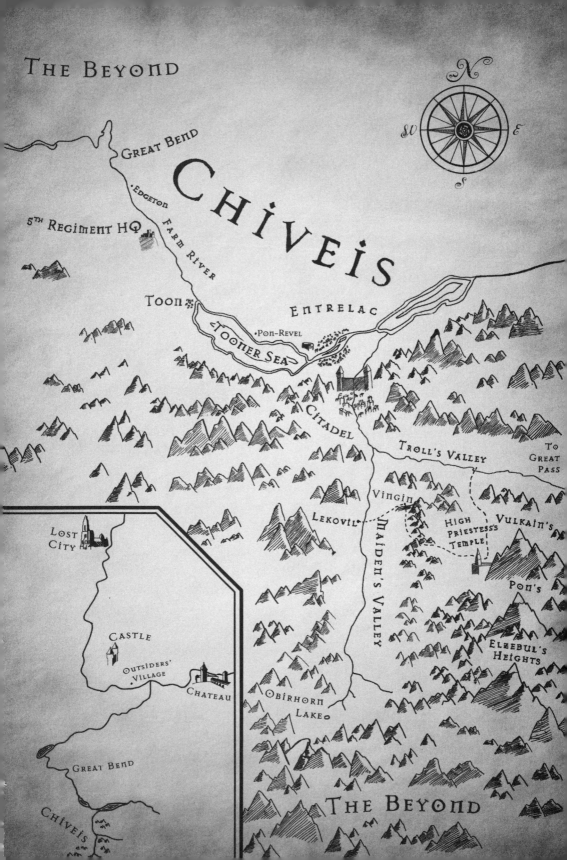

ACKNOWLEDGMENTS

I wish to acknowledge how grateful I am for my wife, Carolyn, who always supported me in the writing of this book; for my editor, Erin Healy, a consummate professional whose insights vastly improved the story; for my friends Amy Peterson and Brad Bailey, who read the entire manuscript and gave excellent advice; for the guys I commute with, Bart Bonga, David Carlson, and Chris Jones, who were a great encouragement to me from day one; and especially for Dr. Jeff Ligon, my longtime friend, who believed in Chiveis enough to go there with me in the summer of 2007.

PROLOGUE

In the year 2042, the world as we know it came to an end. The edifice of civilization proved far more fragile than anyone ever realized. One hard blow, then another—that was enough to shatter it into a million pieces.

The collapse all began with the friendly exchange of a papaya for a photograph. Some Japanese ecotourists traveled to the Brazilian rain forest to get close to nature. Unfortunately, they got a little too close. On their fourth day in the jungle, a gregarious monkey, tamed by his daily interaction with tourists, scampered up to receive a juicy prize. A lawyer from Tokyo smiled for the cameras as the monkey ate the papaya from his hand. An open cut, a little saliva—who could have predicted the devastation about to be unleashed? The deadly moment would eventually be featured on the cover of *Time*. Six months after the story ran, the magazine, like all others, ceased publication.

What the world did not know was that a malignant virus had infected the monkey population of the rain forest. A few primatologists had begun to notice a problem, but before it could be studied or contained, it made the leap from simian to human, with disastrous results.

The virus was a fatal mutation, so virulent that only a head-to-toe hazmat suit would prevent infection. It could be transmitted by direct contact or through the air. Encapsulated in a protective coating, the virus was unusually hardy, able to survive for weeks on any surface until it could infect an unsuspecting passerby. To make matters worse, its incubation period was two weeks long and symptom free. While a carrier was infecting countless others, he didn't even know he had it—until the nosebleed started. Within three days, invariably, he was dead.

That was what happened to Ken Takahashi, who had mugged with the monkey for the cameras two weeks earlier. As he sat at his desk in a Tokyo high-rise on the morning of June 20, 2042, great drops of crimson blood from his nose spattered his keyboard. A few hours later, an unrelenting headache began pounding in his temples. The fever and chills started that night. Violent vomiting and cramps like medieval torture followed, making the next two days an agony. None of the ER docs knew what to do, and so the virus claimed its first victim. When the autopsy discovered massive internal hemorrhaging, the coroner was stumped as to the reason. He called in the epidemiologist.

Soon after the Japanese tourists fell prey to the virus's exorbitant appetite for human life, citizens in capitals around the globe began reporting similar symptoms, all ending in the same horrible way. In the United States, the CDC mobilized its forces, but to little effect. The new virus was its worst nightmare come true.

Such was the beginning of the X-Virus. Though the scientific community eventually gave it a formal name, the media gave it the name that became known throughout the world. "Biohazard levels run from one to four," an epidemiologist said in a TV interview. "But this thing is just a big X to us. We have no idea how dangerous it really is."

The X-Virus fell like a spark on a dry forest. The travel boom of those days didn't help. So many people were moving around the planet that the risk of infection had multiplied exponentially. And exponential infection is exactly what occurred. People didn't know they had the virus until they had already infected thirty or forty or a hundred other people. Wherever they went during the two-week incubation period, the unwitting X-Virus carriers left a trail of invisible germs waiting for a new host to devour. It wasn't long until every doorknob, shopping cart, coin, and public handrail held a microscopic colony of death. Any breath might carry a fatal airborne pathogen.

The death toll mounted with alarming speed. In the cramped conditions of lesser-developed countries, the virus slaughtered the poor without mercy. Yet even the rich countries suffered. No one knew how to stop the viral rampage. It made its way to Aleutian natives of Alaska on supply planes. Remote African tribes picked it up from relief-agency workers. In the small world of 2042, nobody was beyond the X-Virus's reach.

Everywhere people mourned their losses. But in a twisted reprieve, their grief only lasted until their own nosebleed started, and then the mourners had something worse to think about. A macabre ritual developed that came to be called a "nose check." People habitually put their fingers to their nostrils to look for blood. When their finger came away red, they knew it was time to get right with God. Many chose suicide instead of the inevitable torment that would follow.

Global panic set in. Fear of the virus turned friends into enemies and neighbors into killers. Homes became fortresses guarded at gunpoint. Everyone hoarded food. Murder was often committed over a case of canned goods. And not without reason: food had indeed become scarce. The farmers who supplied the world's needs were being decimated along with all the rest. The means of production and distribution imploded. The wheels of industry churned to a halt as workers and executives alike abandoned their posts to run for the hills. It was a ruthless Darwinian age. But in the reign of the X-Virus, even the fittest might not survive.

When the pandemic had claimed a quarter of the earth's population, fear turned into madness. Muslim radicals were the first to go nuclear. Demagogues in Iran, Indonesia, Saudi Arabia, and Pakistan—all of which were nuclear countries in that era of proliferation—identified the plague as Allah's divine judgment on the infidels. Ideologies of hatred running in the veins of these societies coalesced into a new absolutism. The movement called itself Our Greatest Hour. Religious extremists claimed the moment in history had arrived when the superiority of Islam would be recognized. The servants of the Prophet would achieve world domination through conquest of the West. Several already tenuous Muslim governments were overthrown by mob violence and civil war. Now new fingers held the nuclear triggers.

The great powers of the world were in no position to respond with diplomatic restraint when the missiles fell from the sky. China with its Christians, India with its Hindus, the United States with its hedonists, and Europe with its neo-pagans—all were targets for Our Greatest Hour.

Beijing. New York. Washington. Paris. New Delhi. The mushroom clouds rose on the horizons over these cities, and many others.

Western governments collapsed. The rule of law gave way to the law of the jungle. In all the upheaval, a few generals from the world's superpowers seized control with a ruthless will to survive. Their response was swift and violent. Now the Muslim countries, whether or not any missiles had originated there, bore the brunt of the new warlords' revenge. With the spasmodic fury of a cornered and dying animal, the vast nuclear arsenals of the world were unleashed. No one held anything back. Even the less powerful nations, many of which had pursued clandestine nuclear programs, turned whatever weapons they had on their regional enemies. While their missiles could not crisscross the globe, they could at least exact revenge on a neighbor in some long-simmering feud. In this way, the specter of war covered all the earth.

Many experts had warned that a five-thousand-megaton nuclear war would be sufficient to eradicate human life. But now unrestrained tyrants released more than ten thousand megatons in a global omnicide. The ozone layer was destroyed, vastly increasing ultraviolet radiation on the earth. Soot, smoke, and noxious fumes darkened the sky. A radioactive cloud soared into the jet stream and snowed on the remote corners of the world. Nuclear winter descended on mankind.

Earth's temperate zones dropped below freezing for months at a time, while the cooler latitudes plunged into lethal cold. The earth fell silent under a suffocating blanket of snow. No plants could survive such extreme climatic change. Few animals did. Humanity received no new food production for two straight years. Mass starvation claimed those whom war and disease had not.

The survival of the human race was in doubt. Pregnant women, if they lived long enough to deliver, brought forth the stillborn or the deformed. Gangs of young men raped and pillaged at will. Survivors banded together to defend tribe and territory, using guns while ammunition could still be found, and clubs once bullets were no more. Genocide became the norm, spawned as it always is by unchecked power, hatred, and greed.

All the great advancements of the world fell into disuse, for who could think about such things when their bellies had been empty for days? No one was left to run the biomass power plants, or to maintain the communications networks, or to manage the companies that had seemed so necessary in the old, civilized world of commerce and trade. Titans of business were helpless against the unemployed day laborer, whose revenge was felt as the stab of a knife or the smash of a club.

The international power grid went down, plunging the earth into a new Dark Age. Night could only be chased away as man had done for all but two hundred years of his existence—by the scant comfort of a fire. Without electricity, the computers that ran the world crashed. Technological know-how was forgotten. The utopian future was not to be.

Even after the nuclear destruction ended, the X-Virus continued its murderous work for another decade or two. At last the earth's population fell so low and was isolated in such lonely clusters, that the virus could no longer spread easily. It died, fat and full, its hunger satiated.

A tiny fraction of the human race survived those evil days, but the forward march of progress had come to an end. Though the survivors carried memories of their past, the children born to them had no recollection of modern life before its collapse. Their world was an inferno of chaos and brutality and malformation. It was all they could do just to stay alive.

Nevertheless, as the years passed and the climate returned to normal, stable communities began to form. New societies arose, each with its own customs. A few visionaries even founded great kingdoms. The people of those days did not have to begin from square one, like Stone Age primitives inventing the wheel for the first time. Enough vestiges of the former world remained to give these pioneers a head start in the climb toward civilization.

The years turned into decades, and decades became centuries. Eventually the "modern" world came to be viewed as the ancient past. And so it was that in the twenty-four-hundredth year after Jesus Christ (though few on Earth knew it as such) a strange situation had emerged. The world of cars and guns and computers had become, once more, a world of horses and swords and scrolls. History had been rewound and was playing itself out all over again.

In this ancient-future world, one particular people united themselves under a king and called their realm Chiveis. It was a good and beautiful land whose snowcapped mountains provided protection and whose fields and livestock provided food. Safe in their natural stronghold, the people had everything they needed, so they didn't venture into the broader world beyond. The Chiveisi also had their own religion: they worshiped four main gods under the guidance of a high priestess. As for the gods the Ancients may have worshiped—well, who could recall such things? The books that spoke of those matters had been lost forever.

Or so it was believed.

Winter 2045

My nose has started to bleed, and so I am about to die. I am not afraid. I go into the arms of the Almighty. It isn't right for a Christian man to fear death, so I do not. I will join my beloved Yvette, whose head I cradled as she passed into eternal life a fortnight ago. Do I regret the comfort I gave her in those last hours? How could I? She gave me comfort for fifty two years. How could I withhold my love for fear of disease? O Heavenly Father, you know I have rejoiced in the wife of my youth!

All around me is death. The terrible sickness and murderous war have brought Europe to its knees. I doubt human life can continue in such car nage. The pagans hoard the food, those wicked ones! Though our beautiful city on the Rhine escaped the nuclear bombs, the dead lay on her streets, and the living flee her homes. We are so hungry! My body has wasted away. There is no sun, only the dirty skies and the icy cold. The demons laugh with wicked delight. But despite it all, hope remains!

Do not think, O finder, that I have given up my faith. Though man may perish, the Word of Dieu cannot die. I have hidden this Book in the church as a treasure for you. Only if you were led by Dieu himself could you have found it. O finder, may the Eternal One bless you. I give you a precious gift—the Sacred Scripture. Know this: the truth will set you free.

My name is Jacques Dalsace. Remember me! By the grace of Dieu, I have shared with you the gift of rebirth. Soli Deo Gloria. Amen.

PART ONE

DISCOVERY

1

The lone man deep in the woods of the Beyond knew a good sword could make the difference between life and death. Now, as the massive brown bear approached, he gripped his sword's hilt in his strong, sweaty hand and resolved to live. He had just dealt the death blow to a wild boar. Downed by heavy arrows, but still kicking and thrashing, the animal found relief in the finality of the sword's thrust. With a last squeal, the boar quit struggling and went limp. The hunter pulled his blade free of the carcass and was leaning on it to catch his breath when a rustling in the bushes signaled danger.

Turning toward the new threat, the man felt his heart jump as the enormous bear crept from the underbrush, its ears laid back, its eyes staring, its face contorted in a snarl. The hunter tightened his grip on his sword, discerning from the bear's aggressive behavior he might soon require the aid of steel. The weapon was decent, and the man was well versed in its use. All his skill at arms would be needed if the menacing bear charged.

The bear swatted the ground, huffing and barking, not backing off but steadily advancing. It was a young male, probably twice the man's weight, and its curved claws provided it with weapons it wasn't afraid to use. One swat from its paw could break a man's back or snap a limb. This animal was a predator—born to kill, to eat, to survive.

Yet for all the bear's magnificence, the man could see it wasn't in good shape. Its fur was tangled and dirty, its flanks thin despite its heavy frame—or at least thinner than they should have been in midsummer with the abundance of food. One look at the bear's face told the story: a beard of porcupine quills bristled from its cheek and eye socket. Bloody scratches framed the quills where the bear had rubbed them. The right side of its face was a festering sore oozing with pus. One eye was swollen into a bulbous lump. This bear clearly could not hunt. Yet, like the man in the forest, it, too, had resolved to live.

The man knew the bear didn't want him as prey. It wanted him to retreat, leaving behind the easy meat on the ground. *Let the bear have it!* Though pork ribs had sounded good to the man when he had taken down the boar, he had no intention of quibbling over cuisine with a wounded brown bear. Dried venison would do just fine in the campfire pot for one more night. The hunter relinquished his quarry and began to ease away, making no sudden movements or sounds.

But bears are unpredictable, especially a young male who has hardly eaten in weeks. The agonizing barbed needles had driven the creature to madness. Cold fear seized the man when he realized the tormented bear intended to vent its frustration on him. It rumbled a low growl, popped its jaws, and bunched its muscles to charge.

The man readied himself for a battle to the death. There was no chance to outrun the bear, no tree with branches low enough to climb. It was fight now or die. In some subconscious way, he realized that a sword is a poor defense against the thunderous muscles, daggerlike claws, and crushing jaws of an enraged bear. Against such power, human beings will always fail. Yet the man refused to let fear overwhelm him. Audaciously, perhaps somewhat irrationally, he prepared to confront the bear's full weight with nothing but a standard-issue soldier's sword.

With unbelievable speed, the mountain of brown fur surged toward its enemy. Ragged yellow teeth gnashed in anticipation of the bones they would crush. The man sucked in his breath, feeling the sudden rush of ice water in his veins. His stomach dropped its floor. Time slowed. It was as if he could see each drop of slobber flying from the oncoming maw, each grizzled hair standing erect on the angry face, each divot of turf kicked up by the galloping paws. Death was on its way.

As the man braced his stance for a quick dodge and thrust, chance and his body both failed him. He stepped on a loose rock, which rolled underfoot. His knee buckled in an unnatural way, and he collapsed in agony. Now, at the moment when mobility was most important, he was flat on his back with the bear nearly upon him. From the ground, the man brought up his sword in defense. Yet he understood that his already slim odds of coming out of this encounter alive had dropped sharply.

What happened next was the most surprising thing to occur so far that day. Just as the great beast was about to make its final pounce, an arrow struck its infected face like some giant usurper, the new king of all the other quills. The bear arrested its charge and threw back its head, howling from deep within its chest at this unprecedented height of pain. It reared and turned broadside. With its paw, it swiped at the arrow, snapping off the shaft but only driving the arrowhead deeper into its skull.

Another arrow flew over the man's head, slamming into the bear's ribs under its shoulder. It was a perfectly placed lung shot that buried itself all the way to the fletching. The bear dropped to all fours and started coughing up wisps of foamy blood.

There was no time to wait. The man leaped to his feet, ignoring the searing pain in his left knee. With his own roar he put his full weight behind a sword thrust to the spot where he thought the bear's heart would be. The steel found its mark and slid in deep.

The bear reacted instinctively. The back of its paw sent the man sprawling in the dust. Too dazed to move, and with the wind knocked from him, he lay motionless on his belly, trying to recover. As his awareness of danger came flooding back, he rolled over and drew his knife from his boot, ready to do final battle with the dying bear. But what he saw brought him up short. The unexpected scene eclipsed his earlier astonishment, becoming the new most-surprising event of his day. He saw a girl—a stunningly beautiful girl—with a broadhead arrow nocked in her longbow, standing over the body of the dead bear.

◆　◆　◆

The woman drew her bowstring and held the arrow in place as she approached the bear on the ground. Though it lay still, danger of this magnitude had to be treated with caution. A little blood bubbled from the bear's chest wound, staining its fur bright red. No sooner had she looked than the bubbling stopped. The bear's flanks no longer heaved, and its paws no longer twitched. Satisfied that the creature was dead, the young bow-woman turned her attention to the officer of the Royal Guard lying to the side of the clearing.

"Are you hurt?"

Though the man was on the ground, she could see he was tall and lean, with dark hair that could use a trim. A stubble on his chin indicated he had been in the field for some time. She knew from his uniform he bore a high rank in the scout force of the Kingdom of Chiveis. Yet she had to admit, he looked a little ridiculous lying there on his back.

"I'm unhurt, and also in your debt," the man answered. He made no attempt to get up, apparently content to rest on the ground after his close brush with death. "You're skilled in the use of a bow. And you have courage. The average woman would have faltered in such danger."

She lifted her chin, bothered by his mixed compliment. "I'm not an average woman."

"Obviously." The man slowly got to his feet, wincing and standing on one leg, favoring his injured knee. "So, can I ask the name of such an exceptional woman? And what are you doing out here past the edge of civilization?"

The woman considered her reply. The soldier was right: she wasn't where she was supposed to be. Royal law forbade anyone to leave the boundaries of the Kingdom of Chiveis. Though her family's fields were on the frontier, as far along the Farm River as anyone dared to live, she had journeyed even farther downstream today, where no civilian was allowed to go—into the Beyond.

"If you intend to reprimand me, remember, you'd be dead right now if not for me," she said evenly.

"Indeed, I'd be in the halls of the gods if not for your archery. But don't worry, I'm not going to report you to the authorities. I just want to know the name of the pretty girl who saved me." He raised his eyebrows and dared her to answer.

The woman decided to take him at his word. "My name is Anastasia of Edgeton. I'm the only daughter of farm folk who grow wheat along the river for the people of Chiveis." Though the guardsman had said he wouldn't report her, still, she felt defensive about violating the law and wanted to establish her family's patriotic credentials.

"What are you doing in the Beyond?"

"I left home at dawn and came here trailing a roebuck. In fact," she added defiantly, "I come here often."

"Well, Anastasia, it's a good thing you had a heavy bow with you today." He smiled, gesturing over her shoulder. "But I bet you didn't intend to take a bear for meat when you left Edgeton this morning."

The tension between them drained away. She looked at this silly figure, this handsome man on one leg, grinning at her. He was obviously accustomed to the hard ways of the wilderness. His leather jerkin was that of a man who not only ventured into the forest occasionally but lived in it for weeks at a time. Yet apparently he had a humorous side too. Her defensiveness broke, and she smiled back at him.

"It's true; I didn't expect to encounter such a fierce adversary today. But when I decide to take my quarry, I always get him. And now," she said, changing the subject, "may I have your name as well?"

"I'm Captain Teofil of the Royal Guard, the Fifth Regiment." He offered nothing else, and she knew not to inquire further.

❖ ❖ ❖

Teofil assessed the situation. On the positive side, he was alone in a secluded forest with an attractive girl. He had always managed to make the most of that situation in the past, though he doubted he would be so fortunate this time, and not just because of his injured knee. On the negative side, he was far from his horse, which he had left with his gear in a meadow a league or two away. It wouldn't be easy to hobble that distance. The negatives in the situation seemed to outweigh the positives.

He and Anastasia stood atop a bluff that loomed over the great bend in the Farm River. The river bend lay outside the formal boundary of the kingdom, though the Royal Guard did patrol the area regularly. From here, the lands of the Chiveisi stretched upstream to the southeast, where the river emerged from a lake at the settlement of Toon.

A plan began to take shape in Teofil's mind. "Anastasia, how did you come to be here?" he asked.

"As I said, I was hunting the roe deer. My village has plenty of bread, but meat is harder to obtain for those of us on the frontier."

"Right. I know you were hunting, but what I mean is, how did you travel? On foot?"

"No, in a small boat. It's at the bottom of this bluff."

"Well, I'm afraid I'm going to have to commandeer your boat in the name of the king." He meant to convey his request as a lighthearted joke, but it came out sounding more formal than he wished, like a direct order. *Teo, you always do that*, he chided himself. *You come off so cocky to people who have been nothing but kind to you.*

"My possessions are at the king's command," Anastasia replied, echoing Teo's formal tone. The veil of tension assumed its place between them again. "If you wish to make your way down to my boat, you'll have to lean on a crutch."

"Perhaps I could lean on you?" He had intended it as a legitimate option, but now he kicked himself for how presumptuous he sounded.

"I believe a wooden crutch would be more receptive to your needs, Captain," she answered with an unmistakable edge to her voice.

She moved swiftly into the forest and returned with a belt pouch, a hatchet, some hazel branches, and a handful of leather thongs. One of the sticks was in the shape of a Y, and to its top she lashed a crosspiece that could seat itself under Teo's arm. He marveled at the woman's resourcefulness. She was doing exactly what he would have done.

"How does your knee feel right now?" she asked.

"It's throbbing, actually," he said without thinking.

"You're in pain?"

"No."

"You said it was throbbing. What did you mean by that?"

"I suppose it's sort of throbbing. But the pain is minor. It's hardly worth mentioning."

Anastasia frowned and shook her head, letting out a small sigh. "Let's have a look at it."

She loosened the laces of his high leather boots so she could untuck his breeches and roll them past his swollen knee. With her long fingers she gingerly explored the joint. Teo noticed how lovely her hands were. They were the smooth hands of a lady, not rough and callused like a peasant's. Her probing touch was soft and light, except when she pressed into the tissues.

"Do any of these spots hurt?" she asked. It did, but he refused to jerk or make a sound.

Anastasia glanced up. "It seems you have something unique here, Captain—a serious injury that somehow doesn't cause pain. I'm skilled in forest remedies and healing, but it's hard to diagnose a stubborn man."

"I'm not stubborn! It just doesn't hurt that much. Not for a man like me."

"Does this hurt?" She gave his knee a hard squeeze, and he grunted in surprise.

"Aha! It seems we've finally found the tender spot." She opened her pouch and rummaged in it, then pulled out a small knife.

Teo eyed the blade in her hand. "Apparently the frontier remedies are more rigorous than those of the Citadel's doctors."

Anastasia turned up the corner of her mouth and rolled her eyes, then bent to the hem of her blue dress and began to slice off a ribbon of cloth. Teo was amazed. He realized instantly she was making a bandage wrap from the only suitable material to be found nearby. Yet he also knew that farm girls in Edgeton didn't come by their dresses easily, and they usually put great stock in such things. The garment had no doubt cost this girl several months of her earnings, with its embroidered pattern of Chiveis's white mountain-star flowers. This was, he recognized, a sacrificial act.

She wound the strip of woolen cloth around his knee, compressing it to limit further swelling. When she came to the end of the bandage, she held it with one hand, and with the other she reached to her head and loosened a hairpin. Teo noticed her hair for the first time. It was a light amber color with highlights of gold where it caught the morning sun. The style had been done up around her head in the way of girls who

31

are engaged in some strenuous task. Now when she shook her head, her blonde hair came spilling down around her shoulders in a graceful cascade. Teo realized the person in front of him was not a girl at all, but a lovely young woman. She slid the hairpin into the bandage to hold it in place.

"Anastasia," he ventured, "thank you."

"I'm only doing the king's business," she said as she handed him the crutch. "The boat is in some rushes at the inside of the river bend. It'll take you a while to make your way down the bluff. I'll meet you there later, after I collect my things." And then, like a fairy sprite, she disappeared into the forest.

◆ ◆ ◆

Anastasia arched her back and wiped the sweat from her forehead with the back of her hand, leaving a crimson smudge. She held a slimy red knife in her other hand. Bloodstains covered her dress down to its ripped hem.

The wild boar, a juvenile and not exceptionally large, had been easy to dress out. Anastasia had intended to hunt today, so she'd packed her rucksack with sharp knives and even a small bone saw. After she bled the carcass and removed the entrails, she set aside the liver, which her father especially enjoyed. When the field dressing was complete, she put the boar in a burlap sack. The hams, loins, and ribs would be welcome in her home, though she knew it would be hard work carrying the meat to her boat.

As she worked, an idea occurred to her. Perhaps Captain Teofil could stay for supper. After all, the boar was his. She should invite him to dine with her family. *What a silly idea! Ana, don't let your notions run wild like a flighty milkmaid!* She dismissed the thought from her mind.

Now that the boar was ready to be transported, Ana turned to the bear. Although bear meat didn't appeal to her palate, the young men of her village relished it. They considered it the highest cuisine, endlessly discussing how it ought to be cooked and with which spices and sauces. Ana suspected their enjoyment had less to do with the taste and more with the chance to sit around the grillfire and recount, over and over, the stories of their bear hunts. From their tall tales, one would think they had wrestled the poor beast into submission until it was hog-tied and whimpering. *Ha!*

32

What will the village boys think when I return with a load of bear steaks and a thick pelt? It was close to three years since anyone had brought bear into Edgeton. She smiled at the thought of the stir she would cause.

Ana wasn't sure how she was viewed by the young people in her hometown. Certainly she knew from the farm boys' behavior they found her attractive. It seemed she had a strange effect on them. Though all the young men sought her out, they retreated into a snail shell in her presence, stammering and gulping like adolescents holding hands on a hayride. Because of this awkward social dynamic, Ana had never been in love. That fact didn't bother her much. The boys of Edgeton were fun, and they served well enough as friends or partners to spin her in the barn dances. But she was attracted to none of them. Somehow they seemed beneath her. She frowned at this notion, for it sounded haughty as it flashed through her mind. *That's not quite right*, she thought. *It's just that I couldn't put myself in their hands and trust where they would take me.*

Bending to the bear, Anastasia slit its belly lengthwise, then made incisions up each leg and around the neck. With practiced hands, she stripped the pelt from the carcass. The chestnut fur would make a fine winter cloak. She also took the choice cuts of meat, leaving the rest for the wolves.

Of her two loads of meat, the boar looked harder to transport, so she decided to begin with it. She encountered no small difficulty hoisting it to her back, for it probably equaled half her weight. Ana was considered tall among the Chiveisi, and she liked to think of herself as strong, but her frame was slight. She didn't have the broad shoulders that would have made this a much easier task for Captain Teofil.

Winding her way down the hillside, Ana came to a place where the trail skirted a cliff face. It was no massive drop-off, but the cliff was steep and rocky, and the trail was narrow here. She didn't like the thought of negotiating the ledge with the boar on her shoulders, but there was nothing else to do if she wanted to take home the meat. An image sprang to her mind: her father broiling ribs over a grill that evening, telling Teofil, who was holding an ale in his hand, how proud he was of his only daughter.

Ana sucked up her courage and began to ease ahead. As she slid along the cliff, her foot slipped on the uneven ground. She lurched too close to the edge, gasping as she regained her balance. "I hate heights!" she cried to no one in particular as she left the place behind.

The trail brought her to the bank of the Farm River. Ana was glad to arrive at the spot where her boat was moored so she could relieve her shoulders of the heavy burden. She dropped the burlap sack into the canoe. There was no sign that the guardsman had been here. Perhaps he was hobbling around in the woods somewhere or bathing his knee in cool water upstream.

As Ana turned to ascend the bluff and retrieve the bearskin, a footprint in the mud caught her eye. Apparently the captain had been here after all. She knelt to examine the imprint. It was a boot, yet something about it seemed unfamiliar. Was this the sort of boot Teofil had been wearing? She tried to picture it in her mind. *Yes, it must have been like this.* Obviously it was his footprint, for no stranger had been observed in Chiveis in anyone's recent memory. Of course, she wasn't exactly in Chiveis at this spot.

The men of Edgeton said loners and brigands roamed the wilderness wastes, a thought abhorrent to Ana. She couldn't imagine living a solitary life in the awful expanse beyond the known world. It was one thing to venture into it occasionally to hunt, but something else entirely to abandon family and hearthfire for the yawning abyss of the Beyond. Ana knew she was different from her peers in being willing to cross the line into the wilds. What gave her a thrill would have proved terrifying to the village girls she knew—and most of the boys as well. Nevertheless, she was like all Chiveisi in her high regard for communal life. When darkness fell, she wanted to be near the safety of her loved ones. Even frontier farmers like her parents, scattering to their fields along the Farm River each day, returned to the stockaded village at night for human companionship.

Without giving Captain Teofil's boot print another thought, Ana started up the hillside to fetch her hard-earned bearskin.

❖   ❖   ❖

Rothgar fiddled with the braids in his black whiskers as he studied the actions of the girl on the opposite riverbank. Satisfied with what he had seen, he rejoined his companion, who was trying to coax the last drops of beer from a skin bag. A trickle fell on the man's chin and moistened his red beard.

"Hey, sot! Enough with your grog! We're not here to get you drunk!" Rothgar shoved his partner, causing him to inhale his drink and drop the wineskin.

"Curse you!" Red-Beard sputtered after he stopped coughing.

Rothgar ignored his partner's curse. "Listen up! That girl I saw last time is hunting in the forest again. She's making this too easy for us! And what a scrumptious piece of meat she is. Our king is gonna enjoy having her as a wife."

"What about the guardsman? He's probably still around somewhere. He had the look of a warrior."

"So what? He's on the other side of the river from us. You can take him out with your bow, and then we'll snatch the girl. He'll be no problem."

"A man like that is always a problem."

Rothgar's face contorted into a look of scorn. "Coward!"

The red-bearded man bared his teeth and cursed again. Rothgar lunged out and grabbed his partner's throat in his fist. He maintained a choking grip for several seconds, until the man's eyes bulged and his face turned purple. Finally Rothgar let go. Red-Beard leaned against a tree, gasping for breath.

"Don't you cross me," Rothgar warned with a steady gaze. "This mission is too important. The king put me in charge of the deal this time. He wants that girl bad. I don't need you messing things up."

Red-Beard gingerly rubbed his throat and winced. "I ain't meanin' to cross you. I just don't know what we're trying to do here."

"You don't need to know. Just shoot where I tell you."

"It would help if I knew more."

Rothgar frowned. "Alright, listen—I spotted that girl in the woods the last time we traded for weapons with the Chiveisi priests. When I got home, I was telling the king about her, and he got all worked up. Told me to trade for her when we returned on the summer solstice, to pay as much brimstone as it takes."

"I didn't know the Chiveisi were into the slave trade."

"They're not. They said this has to be secret. Has to look like a random kidnapping. But they want our brimstone, so they're willing to deal."

"What's so great about that stuff? It's just a useless yellow rock."

"Not to them. There's a witch who rules their land. Brimstone is sacred to her, but they don't have any hot springs to get it."

"A witch?"

"She's their High Priestess. Black hair, pure white skin. Deadly beautiful. They say every man wants her, but she wants no man."

Red-Beard guffawed. "That's 'cause she's never met me."

"Yeah, right. You can't even get a woman of your own back home." Rothgar's sneer was a challenge, but Red-Beard didn't answer.

A squirrel chattered at the two men from a branch above. It was hot. No breeze stirred the trees. Rothgar picked up the empty wineskin and pitched it at his partner. "Let's move out," he said. "We have a queen to capture."

✦　✦　✦

Teo picked his way down the bluff with the aid of the makeshift crutch. He had chosen a longer trail to the riverbank because it was less steep. Even so, the going was difficult. The day had warmed now, and exertion made sweat run from his forehead into his chin stubble. It had been a hot summer; in fact, the farmers were beginning to talk about drought. Teo progressed slowly under the intense midsummer sun.

He found himself getting frustrated. He was used to being in control of his environment, but with his knee swollen like a melon, he couldn't move at the pace to which he was accustomed. To make matters worse, he'd been forced to leave behind the pork ribs he wanted for dinner. Teo had nearly died defending his prey from a competing predator, like a wolf guarding the haunch of meat it had snatched from the pack's kill. For what? Only to leave it on a hilltop for scavengers.

Teo also hated to leave the bear steaks—they would have made good eating. He thought back to the six bears he'd taken in his twenty-eight years. The third bear had been the hardest. It moved at the last moment, so the kill shot went off mark. Wounded but still mobile, the old sow charged. That time Teo didn't fall to the ground. With a yell he charged the bear in return, driving his hunting spear into its shoulder to stop the onslaught. In the split second the bear hesitated, Teo drew his ax and severed the creature's spine. Yes, that one was definitely a tough kill. *Speaking of tough kills—how about today's? It would have been your last, Teo, if not for the girl!* He leaned on a tree to catch his breath, laughing at the absurdity of the morning's events.

Teo's mind went to Anastasia. What must she think of him? He didn't exactly cut a dashing figure, lying there on the ground as helpless as a baby. Then his attempts to banter with her had gone astray. Usually he was able to charm the women with his words, but this woman was different. She had an aloof, self-confident way about her. And she was so beautiful! Who would have guessed backward little Edgeton could produce such loveliness? Most of the farm girls Teo had seen were squat and stocky, with plain faces and dull hair—born to milk cows, not to recite lyric poetry in the aristocratic competitions back at the Citadel. In comparison to the local milkmaids, Anastasia was a goddess. Actually, she was a goddess even in comparison to the blue-blooded princesses he had known. And he had known a few of those.

Well, Teo, he said to himself, *if you had any intention of catching the girl's eye, you've ruined it already. You should put the whole affair behind you.* He resolved to do so.

Teo reached the water's edge. The little boat floated in the reeds where Anastasia had said it would be, at the inside of the great bend in the Farm River. It wasn't properly hidden, but then, its owner wasn't an army scout trained in stealth. Probably it wouldn't matter. Yet out here past the edge of civilization, in the Beyond, one ought to be watchful in all things.

The craft was a lapstrake canoe, well fashioned by some boatwright in Edgeton. The frontier people always had good boatwrights in their villages. The Farm River was their highway back to Toon at the mouth of the Tooner Sea. From there, if the need should ever arise, they could cross the sea and take refuge behind the secure walls of the Citadel. Even the courageous frontier folk, who served the Kingdom of Chiveis by raising crops out on the river where the fields were more fertile, liked to know they could escape to safety when necessary. In the mountain valleys behind the

Citadel's mighty rampart, surrounded on all sides by unscalable peaks, no intruder could break in.

Teo glanced at the bluffs above the Farm River. This particular site at the river bend always struck him as odd. He couldn't comprehend what had happened here. He understood that the Chiveisi weren't the first inhabitants of these lands. Long ago the Ancients had fought their Great War of Destruction. The remains of that ancient society could still be seen in many places—even more so in the Beyond than in Chiveis itself. A collapsed bridge here, a crumbling road there, pieces of their steel carriages left to rust over the centuries. The forest had encroached around them; hungry vines had enveloped them. Still, the shards of that long-gone civilization could often be found.

But Teo's current location seemed to be an exception. It was as if some colossal hand had eradicated the Ancients' ruins. Teo could see no remnants of their society in the vicinity. No decaying buildings protruded from the forests. And even more strange, the closer one got to the high bluff inside the river bend, the more "erased" was the evidence of the departed people. Whenever Teo came here on patrol, he marveled at how the vestiges of the past grew increasingly scarce as one approached the bluff. In what would have been an obvious location for a great city, it appeared the Ancients had left no mark. Teo knew this was unlikely. The Ancients had been far more numerous in these lands than the Chiveisi. People had no doubt lived here. What could have caused such total destruction? He would probably never know.

The long downhill hike had taken its toll on his knee, so Teo sat on the ground with his leg outstretched. While he waited for the throbbing to abate, he idly scratched the earth with a stick, loosening the soil, sifting it through his fingers. Something caught on his thumb—a rusty fishhook, its barbed point still sharp despite the intervening centuries. Teo held it up in the sun. What ancient fisherman had brought it here long ago? Did he seek to pass a lazy summer day in his favorite recreation? Was he desperate to feed his family with the day's meager catch? By what name did he call the river that Teo now called the Farm? Who was this man of the ancient past?

Looking downstream toward the Beyond, Teo let his mind imagine what was out there. He had never been that way, for he had no reason to go. Yet he couldn't help wondering what secrets lay beyond the boundaries of the known world. *Foolish thoughts! Such questions have no relevance today!* Teo shook his head. Though curiosity might be useful in his duties as a Royal Guard who patrolled the frontier, it didn't advance his other career as an ambitious young scholar at the University in Lekovil. The purpose of education, Teo had been told, was to discover utilitarian insights that could be put to good use. Leave it to the priests and monks to delve into the bigger questions of life. Scholars must avoid metaphysical speculations.

With a sigh, Teo flicked aside the fishhook. *Keep your curiosity out of sight,* he told himself. *It won't provide what you need most right now—a way home.* Perhaps practical knowledge was best after all.

Teo turned his attention to the canoe in the reeds along the riverbank. He knew it would be unwise to rush up to it as if he were on some homey stream behind the Citadel's great wall. As a guardsman of the Fifth Regiment, deployed on the outermost borders of Chiveis, he always had to be careful. Danger lurked in the Beyond. It was his job to watch for it at all times and to alert the citizenry if evacuation to the Citadel was ever needed.

From the bushes, Teo surveyed the scene. He could see a bulky sack in the bottom of the canoe, though Anastasia wasn't in sight. When all seemed clear, he scrambled to his feet with the aid of the crutch and moved closer to the boat, keeping under cover as much as possible. As he approached the little craft, he examined Anastasia's tracks in the wet mud. And then he spotted something that changed everything.

Another footprint!

Teo's mind sprang into action. The print was fresh—indubitable evidence that at least one outsider was nearby! He could only be regarded as an enemy. The Chiveisi rarely interacted with outsiders and considered all strangers hostile.

Where was Anastasia? She should have collected her belongings and arrived at the riverbank by now. Teo realized he would have to get her into the boat and out of here fast. Hand-to-hand combat was out of the question with his knee injury. If the stranger attacked, the only recourse would be escape.

"By Astrebril's beard," he muttered under his breath, "where is that girl?"

Teo assessed the situation from a strategic point of view. The safest action would be to withdraw and let the events unfold. He reminded himself he was one of the best archers in the kingdom. In fact, he was probably *the* best, though he would find out for sure at the tournament in a few months. Now, in his injured state, Teo decided he could best defend himself, if necessary, at a distance. The hunting bow over his shoulder was his only useful weapon. He retreated to a rock that provided a wide angle of view, yet was protected by cover. It had direct sight lines on the approaches to his position at the tip of the peninsula created by the U-shaped river bend. A bee buzzed near Teo's head as he settled onto the rock in the dappled sun. If outsiders were roaming nearby, he would force them to make the first move.

◆　◆　◆

The red-bearded archer grunted in surprise. "The man just disappeared! I saw him at the boat, then lost him." He stared down at the opposite riverbank, where the canoe floated at the peninsula tip. The tall Chiveisi guardsman with the dark hair was nowhere to be seen.

"Fool! I told you to mark where he went." Rothgar cuffed his partner on the back of the head.

"We'd know exactly where he was if we had stayed on that side of the river, like I suggested."

Rothgar glared at Red-Beard. "What do you know about tactics? I suppose you think we should have tied our boat alongside theirs! What's the matter? Can't you hit a target across a river?"

"I can hit anything I can see. But that soldier moves like a lynx among the trees. He's hard to follow, that one."

"How hard can it be? Didn't you just see he has a lame leg? By the gods, that's what you'll have from me if you botch this mission!"

Red-Beard scowled and uttered a profanity. The two watchers sat down to wait as the sun beat on the dry forest. Finally something moved below.

"Here comes the girl again," Rothgar said. "Let's see if she draws out the man. Ready your bow. Now we'll see if you're as skilled as they say."

"I am, and more."

The two men with braided beards watched the girl across the river bring her second load. This sack appeared to be lighter than her earlier burden. She dumped it into the canoe next to the first, slipped off her small rucksack, and bent to the water to rinse her hands.

"There's the guardsman!" Rothgar hissed. "Be ready. If you have a clean shot, take it!"

The red-bearded man nocked an arrow in his thick yew bow. Holding it lightly, he gripped the string in three fingers and drew it in a single, smooth motion. The arrow's yellow and black feathers nearly touched his lips.

On the far bank, the guardsman beckoned the woman to his side. She turned to go to him. They were still several paces apart.

"She can't be injured!" Rothgar reminded his partner. "Take the shot, quick! Take it now!" In his excitement, his feet danced, and he shook his fists.

"You're no archer, Rothgar." Red-Beard drew a breath and let the string slip from his fingers.

◆　◆　◆

It happened all at once. Teo caught a glimpse of jerky movement on the bluff across the river. In a flash of recognition, he realized it didn't belong to the natural world, but to the human. He recoiled instinctively. With a solid *thunk!* an arrow buried its head in a rotten stump where he had been standing, its yellow and black feathers quivering with the impact.

"Anastasia! Come to me!"

She obeyed immediately, running across the open space like the hunter she was, joining Teo at his side as they dropped flat in the bushes. They peered through the leaves.

"We're pinned down," she observed.

Teo looked at her. She was right, yet she didn't seem afraid. For a few

41

moments, they lay beside each other, trying to think of a way out of their predicament.

"I have a plan," Teo said at last. He slipped his knife from his boot. "Anastasia, I need some more of your skirts."

"My gown is a shredded mess already," she answered with a half-smile. "What more can it hurt?"

Teo sliced some thin ribbons from the blue material until he had about a dozen strips. He rolled over to a pine tree behind him. The bark covered the trunk in thick slabs but was falling off in a few places where the green woodpeckers of Chiveis had been working at their holes. Viscous resin oozed from the wounds in the tree. Teo smeared the cloth strips in the sticky mess until they were fully coated with an amber glaze. He drew a handful of arrows from his quiver and wrapped the cloths tightly around the shaft near the head.

Teo reached into his pocket. "Now all I need is—"

"The sticks of Vulkain!" Ana produced a small box from the pouch at her waist. Teo glanced up at her.

"How did you know?"

"I can see what you're doing plainly enough. Your plan is very clever, Captain Teofil." She had a twinkle in her eye and a slight smile on her lips. "Finally you're contributing something to the problems of our day!"

Teo met her eyes. Though she had said it in jest, it was a bold statement, much more daring than what any other girl would have said. They would have fawned over him as a dashing captain of the Royal Guard, afraid to offend him. Not this girl. Yet he had to admit: though her words stung, they were true.

Anastasia's box was filled with the little sticks made by the priests of Vulkain, one of Chiveis's three secondary deities. The divine triad reigned underneath the supreme god, Astrebril, the unyielding lord over all. Teo felt no personal devotion to any of the gods, yet he appreciated one particular attribute of Vulkain, whose special province was fire from the underworld. Vulkain's priests were masters of the yellow rock called brimstone, which they wore around their necks as an amulet. Somehow that substance could be rendered into a material that made fire. The sticks were dipped in it, and when struck against the side of the box, a flame would spring up. Teo marveled at the mysterious ways of the gods every time he lit a campfire.

With his bow in hand, Teo crept to a position in sight of the opposite bluff where he had noticed the movement of the enemy archer. "Ready?"

"Ready when you are." Ana opened the box of Vulkain sticks. "But, Captain, try not to burn down the entire forest. It's such a pretty forest."

She struck a match and held it to the cloth-wrapped arrow in Teo's bow. Immediately it crackled and sparked into a small blaze. Teo raised the burning missile to the sky and let it go. With a smoky whoosh, it arced across the river and landed near the enemy's position. Teo and Ana fired a dozen flaming arrows in rapid succession. Within minutes the opposite bank was ablaze. The tinder-dry forest, desiccated by the recent drought, took the flames into its bosom like a forbidden lover.

"Okay, let's go! Stay right beside me!" Teo threw his crutch aside and lumbered as fast as he could across the unprotected open space to the canoe, making sure he kept his body between Anastasia and the opposite bank. He half expected an arrow to come sailing out of the wall of flame, though he knew the smoke would frustrate an archer's accuracy.

Shoving the boat into the river, Teo began paddling upstream. Now he was back in control. His leg might be sorely injured, but the powerful muscles of his shoulders bore no such harm. He dug in with the paddle, and the canoe leaped forward.

"There they are! Two of them! Behind us!"

Teo turned and saw two figures on the shoreline, standing in a place the fire hadn't yet reached. He heard the whizzing sound of an arrow, followed by a splash as the missile hit the river just shy of the stern. The impact of the arrow on the water spritzed his hand. Moments later, a second arrow impaled itself in the gunwale of the canoe, and a third bounced off his paddle on its recovery stroke.

"Let me help!" Ana grabbed a paddle, adding her strength to his. Soon they rounded a curve and left their enemies behind, though they didn't dare stop. For an hour they moved quietly upstream, hugging the far bank, not wishing to make a sound lest they draw the attention of any other marauders.

Teo finally broke the silence. "Anastasia, can I ask you something?"

Ana lifted her dripping paddle and turned her head from her position in the front, awaiting Teo's question.

"May I see what you're carrying in these two giant sacks?"

Ana threw back her head and laughed. Turning again toward the front, she answered, "Sure. I think you'll be pleased."

Teo stooped and peeked inside the mouth of each burlap bag. A smile crept across his face, and he let out a long breath. With new admiration, he stared at the woman in front of him. In all the excitement, he hadn't bothered to take a good look at her. Her shredded gown was covered in blood and soil, and her tangled hair was tufted with leaves. Yet she held her head high and her back straight as she paddled toward her home. Teo's smile widened into a broad grin. And though he couldn't see her face, he was certain Anastasia was smiling too.

2

The village of Edgeton came into view as the sun's rays were beginning to angle lower in the sky. Teo noticed that when Anastasia saw the wooden dock jutting into the river, she began to paddle harder, in the knowledge she was almost home.

The town was located, as its name implied, on the edge of the Kingdom of Chiveis. Because the Fifth Regiment was permanently deployed to guard the frontier around this region, Teo knew a thing or two about Edgeton, though he had experienced little of its day-to-day life. The headquarters and barracks of the Fifth Regiment lay about a league down the river on a hill, and the soldiers communicated with the Citadel by boat or by carrier pigeon when speed was required. While the regiment's cooks and quartermasters might have had reasons for commerce with the local villagers, a captain like Teo reported directly to the Warlord, and so had little cause for interaction with the area farmers. Teo believed one of his primary duties was to protect these rustic, openhearted folk whom he admired so much. Yet it shouldn't be expected that the shepherd would mill around with the sheep.

As the canoe approached Edgeton's dock, a barrel-chested young man with no shirt roused himself from the nap he had been taking on the riverbank in the shade of his own hat. He pitched his fishing pole onto the sand and stood up.

"Anastasia! It's me—Fynn! What are you doing with the guardsman? Are you in trouble? Can I—is there—what can I do?"

Before she could answer, Teo called back, "She has no need of aid, my friend. She's with me."

Fynn didn't give up but ran along the riverbank, dodging branches, trying to stay even with the boat's progress.

"I'm in good hands, Fynn," Ana said as the canoe pulled close to the dock. Fynn joined several other young men who had been making their way to the waterfront.

"You're covered in blood, Anastasia," one of them said.

"And your hem is ripped up to your—up to there," said another, pointing at Ana's legs. His voice trailed off.

"Let me, uh, give you a hand." Fynn reached down and helped Ana onto the dock. A few snickers arose from the young men. Blushing, Fynn stepped back into the little crowd.

From the boat, Teo watched the scene unfold. Obviously the girl was beloved in her hometown. She was at peace here; this was her natural place. Her friends surrounded her with their affection, and she returned it freely. She shone as one of Edgeton's brightest constellations. In fact, she seemed to be its polestar.

Teo climbed onto the dock, leaning casually on his sheathed sword, holding his left leg as straight as he could.

"If you think she's done something wrong, guardsman, you're mistaken," Fynn said with his chin out. "She's not that type of person."

"What type of person never does any wrong?" Teo leaned forward a bit, and the men on the dock bunched together.

Ana stepped between Teo and the men and defused the tension. "My dear Fynn, Captain Teofil isn't arresting me! He has bravely escorted me from many dangers." It was only partly true, but Teo was glad she had said it.

"Fynn, could you please help me with a heavy task?" Ana rested her palm on his thick shoulder. "There are two sacks in my boat. If you could lift them out for me, I'd appreciate it."

"Of course, Anastasia!" The burly youth bent to the water and grabbed the sacks, effortlessly hauling them up. As he maneuvered for space on the crowded dock, Teo tried to step out of the way, but his injured leg buckled. He stumbled, grunting in pain.

Ana took him by the arm. "Captain Teofil, we must find you a place to rest! My house is close by. Come with me."

Teo hesitated. He knew he shouldn't delay reporting the encounter with the outsiders to his superiors, yet he was more than a little curious about Ana's home life. Perhaps a brief greeting to her parents wouldn't hurt. Convincing himself that his duty required seeing the citizen all the way to her house, Teo followed Ana up the rise toward the village. An intense ache pounded in his leg, but he ignored the discomfort and walked with a normal-looking gait.

"Oh, and by the way, boys," Ana called over her shoulder, "if you'd carry the boar meat to the butcher, I'd be so grateful. As for the bear I took today, you fellows can keep the steaks for your trouble. Thank you!"

Ana let her gaze linger a moment on their faces, their mouths making little round holes like the doors to a birdhouse. She left her friends on the dock in stunned silence. Teo smiled and shook his head at this spirited girl. *They don't make them like this in the Citadel,* he thought.

✦ ✦ ✦

The gate to the wooden stockade around Edgeton lay open, for dusk, though coming on strong, had not yet fallen. Midsummer in Edgeton was a time for long days in the fields followed by long evenings of relaxation. Teo and Ana had arrived just as one was giving way to the other. The farmers were streaming into town for an ale, a meal, and an evening with friends—in that order.

Ana's house was a modest affair. It was a chalet of rough-cut timbers with overhanging eaves, a cedar-shake roof, and numerous windows whose green shutters were flung open to catch the evening breeze. A wide balcony spanned the upper level of the building, its railing decorated with intricate carvings in a wild-animal motif. Flower boxes spilled color down the dark brown walls. Above the main door, a heraldic crest bore the image of a bear, the symbol of this frontier village. Teo guessed the home was neither the biggest nor the smallest in Edgeton. It stood at a crossroad on the main square. *That's appropriate,* he thought. *The girl is the center of this town. I wonder how many hopeful suitors have called her out to that balcony over the years?*

As they approached the home, a middle-aged couple emerged from the doorway with welcoming expressions, though Teo discerned questions behind their eyes as well. The man was well built, not paunchy as men of his age often are. The frontier men's arduous days rarely allowed them the luxury of a belly. He wore a beard, whose smattering of gray spoke more of wisdom than of feebleness. His linen shirt was tied loosely at the neck and overlaid by a vest of forest green. A wide leather belt seemed to trim his waist and broaden his shoulders. He was the quintessential Chiveisian farmer—sturdy, sober, hard working.

Ana's mother clearly was the source of her daughter's good looks. Either she was much younger than her husband or she was remarkably well preserved. In her day, she must have been quite a beauty. *No*, Teo admitted, *she's a beauty right now*. She was slim, slightly shorter than Ana, but had the same honey-colored hair. Her smile was sweet, and Teo could tell by the way she carried herself that she was the more gregarious partner in the marriage. The woman exuded charm and grace. Ana's father must be quite a man to have won her heart.

"Welcome to my home," the man said, extending his right hand to clasp Teo's. "Judging by your presence here, guardsman, and by my daughter's appearance, it seems you may have run into a bit of trouble. If you've come to her aid, you have my thanks. I am Stratetix of Edgeton, and I bid you to feel at home in our midst."

"I'm Captain Teofil of the Fifth Regiment. Thank you for your hospitality."

"Captain Teofil? Ha! Imagine that! A tournament champion in my home! The other day during our wagering, the men at the public house were debating your skills. I defended your merits, young man. In fact, I have a fair amount of steel coin resting on your shoulders."

"I'll do my best to earn you your winnings, sir."

"If you do half your best at the tournament, I think it'll be enough. I've heard how well you ride and shoot. They say you can put an arrow through a bird on the wing." Stratetix turned and gestured toward his wife. "Captain Teofil, may I introduce you to my beloved? This is Helena d'Armand of Edgeton, my bride for these past twenty-five years."

Helena stepped forward and bowed from the waist. Teo did the same.

"D'Armand?" he asked, straightening. "Are you related to Armand of Edgeton, the warrior?"

"He was my father."

"Was he indeed? He's highly regarded among the men of the Fifth. We all know the stories of how he fought at the side of the king, back in the days when battles were still waged with outsiders."

"I remember him not as a man of war but of gentleness."

"And no doubt of wisdom, too. It's said he carried great weight with the High Council and had the king's ear in all things."

"Yes, he was most wise. He taught me to value wisdom in a man above all else." Helena gestured to Teo's knee. "It appears you're wounded. Is there something we can do to make you comfortable?"

"Ah, thank you, but I have to be going."

A voice interrupted from the street. "Anastasia! Come join us! We want to hear the tale of your bear!" It was Fynn, with a gaggle of young men and women, laughing together with mugs in their hands.

Ana turned to Teo. "Captain Teofil, I wondered—that is, I believe— I believe the wild boar is your kill. The butcher will deliver it shortly. Perhaps you should rest your knee here. My father would be happy to broil the meat for our evening meal. You could discuss the hunt and politics and the things of men. It would be my honor to host you."

"Anastasia! Don't keep us waiting!" Fynn waved his empty pewter stein. "Escape from your guard and come drink with us! He can't catch you with that leg of his!" The crowd of revelers burst into laughter.

"Thank you for your kind offer," Teo said to Ana, "but unfortunately, I can't stay. I have other things to do than remain here in Edgeton."

Teo could see from the way Ana's face fell that he had said the wrong thing. Her chin dropped slowly, and she gazed at her feet for a long moment.

"What I meant is, I have important business. You know, kingdom affairs." Teo searched for the right words. "I have high-level duties. I need

to make an immediate report to the Warlord. I have to file documents."
Documents? No, Teo, that isn't it.

Ana looked up at him, her long-lashed eyes opened wide. For a moment he feared there might be tears lurking in their depths. She had such pretty eyes. They were a vivid blue, shimmering with an undertone of green.

"I certainly understand, Captain," Ana said quietly. "One must put first things first."

"Right. My professional duty is my priority. And I have friends I need to see." *Ach! Wrong again.* Teo knew it should have been his feet that got moving, but somehow his mouth did so instead. He tried to salvage the damage. "It's just that I've been in the field for some time, and I need to visit a companion of mine." *A companion? Get going, Teo!*

"For a man of your status, I'm sure a companion won't be hard to find among the highborn at the Citadel. I wouldn't want to keep you from the enjoyments of your companion." Ana bowed slightly. "I truly thank you for helping me today, Captain Teofil."

The two of them stood looking at each other. Teo wasn't sure what to say next.

Helena stepped in. "Ana, my love, your dress is ruined, and you must be exhausted. Come with me, and I'll prepare some food while you rest." She waved off the crowd of young revelers, then took her daughter by the arm. Turning to Teo, she said, "Captain Teofil, it's a pleasure to make your acquaintance. I pray the gods will fare you well."

"Thank you, Helena. It was very nice to meet you." Teo faced Stratetix. "And thank you, sir, for your welcome. But as you can see, I've encountered significant difficulties today. Things are happening that demand attention at the highest levels. I apologize, but I have to be on my way."

"Well, son, if you must leave, I understand. A man's affairs are his own. But grant me one favor, will you? Win that tournament for me! Then this old man can take a break from his labors. What do you say?" Stratetix smiled, and Teo returned the grin.

"So you'll be in attendance?"

"Of course! Me, my wife, and Ana, too. We wouldn't miss it. In fact, we have front-row seats among the Edgeton contingent. I'm sure the three of us will be cheering you on." His smile was genuine.

Teo shook the man's hand again, then turned stiffly and limped down the hill toward the dock. From there he could catch a ferry to the regimental headquarters.

As the ferryboat slipped into the current, Teo reflected on the events of his day. He had met some interesting people under some remarkable circumstances, but the most intriguing of them all was Anastasia—or Ana as her parents had called her. Teo sighed and leaned against the gunwale with his hands behind his head. *Well, I wish her the best*, he thought. *I doubt I'll ever see her again.*

◆   ◆   ◆

Ana poured water from a pitcher in her bedroom and washed her hands in the basin. "I had hoped Captain Teofil could at least stay for dinner," she said to her mother, who was emptying a kettle of boiling water into a wooden bathtub. "Offering him a meal was the least we could do."

Suddenly all the pent-up emotions of Ana's day overwhelmed her. The fierce bear, the attack by foreigners, and now Teofil's apparent indifference—it was all too much. Ana turned away from her mother, pressing the heels of her hands to her eyes. She prided herself on not being the type of woman to cry, but sometimes the tears welled up unbidden.

"I'm sure he meant no offense," Helena said. "Come now, give me your gown. At least the rag man will be happy today."

Ana studied herself in the mirror. Her hair was askew with bits of leaves and even a clump of moss stuck in it. Her gown was covered in mud and blood, and her skirt's ragged edge exposed her legs nearly up to her knees. She was sweaty and grubby, and there was a bright red blemish on her forehead.

"I've never looked so bad, Mother," she said with a sniffle. "I know I'm not fancy like the aristocrats. I'm tanned by the sun; they're pale from their ease. I'm a girl of the forest; they're dainty girls of luxury and elegance. I don't mind that. I'm content being a farm girl from Edgeton.

But sometimes a little voice nags inside my head. It's hard for a woman not to doubt herself."

"You, my love, are the most elegant woman in Chiveis. There's much more to beauty than braided hair and golden baubles and fine clothes. There is the beauty of the inner disposition—a spirit of peace."

Ana looked at her mother. Many men through the years had found her beautiful. There were even rumors that men had died over her, though Ana didn't know the details of those stories. She shrugged. "I've trusted your wisdom for twenty-four years. I suppose I shouldn't cease now."

"Then obey this wise crone's advice, and slip out of your gown and into your bath."

Ana sank into the steaming water. She felt refreshed as it washed away the grime of the day.

"You've always cherished your cleanliness." Helena's smile turned mischievous. "In fact, you consume half our supply of firewood so you can indulge in your tub!"

"The hot water is good for me," Ana countered. "It cleanses away all my cares."

"Ah, yes. So many cares for such a young one. Well, wash away your care for Captain Teofil, at least for the time being. It's part of being young to be passionate and then to be at ease."

Ana sat up in the tub. "I wasn't speaking of him, Mother! I don't care about him at all!"

"No?"

"No! Not a bit. He's—he's not my type. I'm a poet. A thinker. You know that better than anyone." Ana thought about it some more. "But Teofil—he's a rough man, a physical man of action. I doubt he's ever opened a book in his life. He's too busy riding horses or shooting arrows with his dull soldier friends. Or perhaps chasing his brainless 'companions,'" she added with a *tsk*.

"Would it surprise you to learn the captain is also a scholar at the University?"

Ana's head snapped around in her mother's direction. "You're joking!"

"I'm not. Your father knows the man's reputation very well. While I was heating your water, Stratetix told me all about him. When Captain

Teofil isn't deployed to the field, he gives lectures at Lekovil. His specialty is old scripts. In fact, he's one of the foremost experts in the Fluid Tongue of the Ancients. He can read the words of those long-lost people."

Ana glanced around her room. Its familiar furniture provided reassurance in an ever-shifting world. She sighed.

"I'll leave you now," Helena said. "When you're done with your bath, your meal will be ready. Even if the captain can't enjoy those pork ribs, at least you can. Your father has them over the grillfire now. And he said to thank you for bringing home the liver."

"I'm grateful for you, Mother. Your words are always the wisest and best."

When the door was shut, Ana lowered herself into the steaming tub until all but her face was submerged. She relaxed her mind, letting it drift. There was too much to sort through in the day's events, so she simply closed her eyes and let the hot water work its therapy on her soul.

✦　✦　✦

"Lieutenant, meet me in the map room immediately!" Teo's tone was sharp. The smooth-faced young man spun on his heel and headed up the hill.

Teo turned toward the shipmaster standing beside him on the dock. "Prepare your rowers for a night voyage. We leave for Toon and on to the Citadel within the hour. I've just been attacked by outsiders, and the Warlord will want to hear about it." The man snapped a salute and retreated toward the boathouse.

Normally Teo would have hiked to the headquarters building, but tonight his knee prevented him from making the trek, so he ordered a horse to be brought. The hilltop command center was a perfect location from which to keep an eye on the area, and it also provided easy access to the transit route of the Farm River. Teo rode up and tied the horse to the railing.

In the map room, the lieutenant stood at attention. Teo looked with satisfaction at the great map spread before him on a table. It wasn't a flat map on parchment, but a three-dimensional relief map, painted to show field and forest, moraine and glacier, river and lake.

Teo's eyes drifted to the three massive peaks at the heart of Chiveis. Each peak belonged to a god of the divine triad, while the sky belonged to the overlord, Astrebril. Chiveis was a mountain kingdom by design. If outsiders threatened, the people could find safety in the sheltered valleys. Teo admired how the mountain range presented an unbroken wall that no army could penetrate—except in one place, where the wall was breached by a cleft that led into a double-branched valley.

Past the cleft, the vales opened to the south and east, providing a suitable home for many a dairyman and goatherd. Because the two valleys were surrounded by high peaks, the only way in was through the cleft. And there, at that one vulnerable point, stood Chiveis's greatest genius. A mighty wall spanned the gap, with a single gate and imposing towers on either side to guard the entrance. The kingdom's most important buildings clung to the mountainsides behind the wall, forming a capital city known as the Citadel. No enemy had ever set foot in the Citadel; the wall was far too strong. "Our shortest wall," the people affectionately called it, for they knew their true walls were the mountains of Chiveis. Together the wall and the mountains sealed off the double valley at the heart of the realm.

Teo was well acquainted with the safe, pastoral valleys behind the Citadel's wall. When he wasn't deployed on field assignment, he spent his time at the charming academic village of Lekovil with its prestigious University. As the kingdom's primary institution of higher learning, the University stood in a dramatic location—at the foot of a waterfall that plunged down a cliff on one side of the valley.

Although Teo respected that cozy world and its snug people, he admired even more the hardy Chiveisi who dared to live beyond the Citadel's imminent protection. Teo's eyes moved from the map's mountain ramparts to the frontlands. Two lakes dominated the foreground beneath the mountain range. In the flat space between the lakes lay the upscale town of Entrelac. The lake to the west of Entrelac was the Tooner Sea, which Teo expected to cross later that night on his way to the Citadel. But first he would have to travel up the Farm River, past the fertile fields cultivated by farmers who lived in isolated villages. The last of these farm settlements was Edgeton, truly a frontier town. And beyond Edgeton was . . . the Beyond.

"Lieutenant, listen up! I want my orders followed exactly. There has been an encounter with outsiders." The young man swallowed and nodded. Teo pointed to the map in the vicinity of the river bend. "You will take a detachment at dawn to this region here. Guard these approaches here, here, and here. Watch for any signs of trouble, and await further instructions from the Citadel. The Warlord will be concerned about this. He'll send a carrier pigeon in the morning with specific orders."

"Yes, sir. I understand, Captain."

"I have one more task." Teo gestured to the meadow where he had started his day. "My horse and gear are here. Retrieve them and have a man return my things to my room."

"It will be done as you command, Captain." The lieutenant saluted and walked out.

Teo left the map room and returned to the dock. The riverboat was moored in the pale light of a rising full moon. The craft was no mere canoe, but an oaken-keeled vessel with a bank of twelve oars per side and a crew of well-muscled rowers. The men weren't happy at the prospect of an all-night row, though they were certainly capable of doing the job.

"The vessel is ready to depart when you are, Captain," said the shipmaster.

"Very good. Let's cast off."

Teo found a spot in the stern where he wouldn't be in the way of the rudderman on the starboard side. There, with a pile of ropes for a pillow, he let sleep come to him under the familiar stars of Chiveis.

✦ ✦ ✦

From the topmost windows of her temple's spire, the High Priestess could look down on all Chiveis. So high was she that even the icy summits lay within her grasp. The lands of the ignorant masses spread below her, bowing to her majesty. All the splendors of the known world were hers, the unholy queen of this earthly realm. Such glory had been granted to her by the sovereign lord: the Beautiful One, the Brilliant Star, Astrebril of the Dawn.

The room was round and barren except for a table beneath the northern window. Three other windows faced the High Priestess's realm, one in each direction of the compass. From here, everything she could see belonged to her. Astrebril had said so. But on this day, as the new dawn smeared blood across the god's great dome, the High Priestess did not look outward. What she sought could only be found within.

She gazed at the red elixir in her goblet. Light sparkled in its ruby depths. She drained it, including the dregs, in a single swallow. Then she cast the empty glass into a pit in the middle of the room. There was a soundless pause before she heard it shatter far below. Thin smoke wafted up from the fire that smoldered in the recesses of the tower's shaft. It rose into her upper room and exited through a smoke hole in the ceiling.

"It is time," said the High Priestess. "Bring me the implements."

A handsome blond eunuch glided over to the table with a leather bag. He removed four items and daintily placed them on the table: a razor, a gold saucer, a blank parchment, and an unused quill.

The High Priestess walked to the pit and stood close to its edge, her shoulders thrust forward, her arms held out behind. Wisps of smoke drifted up from the tower's belly to curl around hers. As she began to feel the elixir take effect, she swayed over the edge of the pit, experiencing a sudden desire to tumble into it, yet knowing it would be her end.

"I am ready to descend."

The eunuch turned a windlass on the wall. It lowered a horizontal iron bar from the ceiling directly over the pit. Leather stirrups hung from a chain at each end of the bar. The eunuch reached over the abyss with a hooked pole, snagged the contraption, and brought it close. He gathered the two chains and held the stirrups near the stone lip of the pit.

The High Priestess placed one foot in each stirrup and stood for a moment on the edge of death. A smile came to her lips at the expectation of ecstasy. She swung her body over the pit, standing tall in the stirrups and grasping the iron bar above her head. For a moment, she swayed there, and then the eunuch lowered her into the smoky depths.

As the world of the living disappeared, the High Priestess inhaled deeply. "Come to me, little one," she said. Soon the swirling colors and fantastic images in her mind coalesced into the form of a little imp with a deformed body and a grotesque face.

"Lead me to the one above you," instructed the priestess. In her mind's eye, the imp took her by the hand and led her to a slightly larger being. Each time she met the new and greater creature, she commanded it to lead her to the one above it.

The tenth time this happened, the High Priestess began to shake in terror. Her muscles quivered under the strain of holding herself erect in her chains. Despite the pain, the quivering in her heart terrified her even more. The being she now faced was an angel of great power.

"Who summons me?" it asked in a voice thunderous like a waterfall, beautiful and deadly.

"It is the High Priestess of Chiveis. I come—I come as a sibyl, seeking unearthly wisdom!" Her words fell out in breathy gasps as she struggled in the frame. Looking down between her legs, she could see the flicker of orange light.

The demon screamed at her. It opened its mouth wide, and a howl like all the tortured souls in hell poured into her brain. She yelled too—a bloodcurdling shriek of madness and despair and exaltation. Waves of euphoria coursed over her, convulsing her body in spasms for several seconds. At last it ended.

The High Priestess felt herself being raised from the pit. She could see no distinct images. From what seemed to be a great distance, she imagined she heard the eunuch grunting as he hooked her framework, then drew her body to the edge of the pit. She collapsed out of the stirrups onto the stone floor, where she lay inert for a long time. Her breath came in fast, shallow pants. Her ribs heaved. Her diaphragm contracted violently. Finally she gathered enough strength to crawl to the table.

The steel razor slit the priestess's palm smoothly, and she squeezed her fist. Blood seeped from her clenched fingers into the gold saucer. She dipped the new feather quill into the crimson ink and wrote unsteadily on the parchment with her eyes closed.

When her hand stopped moving, the High Priestess opened her eyes, trying to discern what she had written. In her stupor, she couldn't focus on the words. She blinked and looked again. Finally she made out the divine message: "He who comes with the sword will proclaim the god of the cross."

The words assaulted the core of her being. She let out a hiss and bolted from the room. Stumbling down a spiral staircase, the High Priestess emerged from behind a tapestry into her private chapel. The walls were adorned with idols, and an altar stood at the center of the room. Two candles burned on it, their flames adding to the red light of the dawn outside.

The High Priestess retrieved a book from a locked chest and laid it on the altar between the brass candlesticks. Deliberately, she licked her bloody palm, then gathered saliva to her pursed lips and let it fall onto the book's leather cover. The act of desecration was followed by a chanted curse. Still disoriented from her descent into the pit, the words of her liturgy came more from instinct than from conscious thought. The anathema rolled off her tongue as she denounced the god of the cross and the book that spoke of his ways. Astrebril grinned at her from an idol niche as the High Priestess stared at his magnificent, leering face.

"I will not allow it, O Beautiful One," she vowed to him. "I will not allow the Enemy to return to the world." Her heart raced at the mention of the ancient god who had been expunged from Chiveis, forgotten by its people. She glanced down at the pink gob of spittle on the book's cover. Her eyes narrowed. "On my life, my lord, I will not allow it."

The High Priestess removed three vials of yellow, white, and black powder from beneath her altar—brimstone, salt-stone, and charcoal. Though each powder was manufactured by the priests of the divine triad, only the High Priestess of Astrebril knew how to make explosive fire from all three. The mixture was her greatest secret—the awesome weapon by which the enemy god would be defeated. After pouring the finely ground powders into a mortar, she mixed them with a pestle, then struck a Vulkain stick and dropped it on the pile. Immediately a violent blaze flared up. Closing her eyes, she inhaled the acrid white smoke. A smile came to her lips.

"You smell good to me, Astrebril, my lord," she breathed.

✦ ✦ ✦

As morning dawned, Teo awoke to the sensation of rowers slowing their pace. The ship had crossed the Tooner Sea and was approaching Entrelac. Though the hour was still early, the day was shaping up into another hot one. Teo could see why the farmers were talking about drought. The grass was withering, and the vibrant colors of the flowers were fading in the midsummer heat.

Now that it was bright morning, the dazzling mountains of Chiveis had made their glorious appearance. They lifted their snow-crowned heads to the clouds, reaching into the divine heights where none but the gods Vulkain and Pon and Elzebul dared to tread. Their domination was indisputable. Only fearsome Astrebril loomed higher than these—the capricious god of the sky, the seductive god of the dawn.

The riverboat navigated into a canal built by the Ancients, then docked at a pier in the harbor at Entrelac. Teo disembarked and obtained a horse at the local army barracks. He wound his way past the upscale shops and fine chalets toward the edge of town. At last he left Entrelac and proceeded along the grand avenue that led toward the Citadel.

The fortified capital of Chiveis never failed to inspire Teo with a sense of patriotic awe. Its towering wall stretched across the cleft, linking the forested slopes that rose to become great mountains. All the important buildings of Chiveis—the opulent temples, sumptuous mansions, government offices, and even the king's own palace—lay in the flat area behind the wall or in tiers on either side. The wall was constructed of granite, and it ran for a league across the valley's narrow mouth. A churning river flowed underneath the wall through a culvert. The flow had been dammed downstream, so its water backfilled into a wide moat that lapped against the wall's mossy foundations. Traffic crossed the moat by means of a wooden causeway, guarded by a gatehouse at its outer end and by an even more imposing barbican where the causeway met the wall. The spires, ramparts, and towers of the Citadel loomed on the left and right, clinging to the hillsides and commanding a complete field of fire for the catapults and ballistae. A square flag flew from the Citadel's highest pinnacle atop the royal palace. As Teo noticed the flag's emblem of a white sword against a field of red, he was momentarily caught up in the grandeur of the kingdom he loved. "By the sword, Chiveis lives!" he exclaimed, echoing the national motto.

Teo crossed the causeway and approached the barbican in the Citadel's wall. As he passed under the portcullis, its points hanging over his head like the fangs of some giant wolf, he crossed a threshold into a less martial but no less intimidating environment. He entered a wide plaza edged with colonnades and adorned with fountains. Despite their austere beauty, Teo hardly noticed these decorative touches. Instead, like every visitor to the Citadel's majestic vestibule, he focused his gaze on the grand statue that demanded attention at the center of the square—a monumental depiction of Jonluc Beaumont.

Teo winced as he recalled his boyhood lessons in the orphanage—drilled into him with the reminder of the cane lest he forget any details—about Beaumont, the noble founder of the Kingdom of Chiveis. The latest historical scholarship suggested that about 325 years ago, Beaumont and a group of refugees came sailing down the Farm River. His earlier kingdom had been destroyed by evildoers, but with the aid of the supreme god Astrebril, Beaumont founded a new kingdom that came to be called Chiveis. It was Beaumont who envisioned the great wall across the cleft, though it was actually constructed by the succeeding generations. He also established the cult of Astrebril under a high priestess. Along with Astrebril, the Star of the Morning, Beaumont introduced the Chiveisi to the lesser triad of gods: Vulkain, the sulfurous god of the underworld; Pon, the debauched god of the forest; and Elzebul, the filthy god of dung. Historians believed Beaumont had learned the ways of these gods from the religions of the Ancients and transmitted them to the Chiveisi for pious reverence forever.

After passing through Beaumont Plaza, Teo guided his horse up the many levels of the Citadel's streets to the Warlord's Bureau. When he limped inside and informed the clerk he had come to report the presence of outsiders on the edge of the kingdom—outsiders who had attacked him—the office fell into a stir like a beehive clawed open by a foraging bear. Teo filled out the appropriate documentation and endured several inquests before bureaucrats of various ranks. Each time he told the same story: how he met Anastasia of Edgeton in the woods, found the unknown footprint, took fire from the enemy, responded with fire arrows, and made good his escape.

The interviewers from the lower echelons, all military men, took interest in the expected sorts of things: the look of the outsiders' tracks, the nature and range of their arrows, the men's physical size and appearance, their tactics, and their possible points of entry into the kingdom. But when Teo was summoned before a panel of two high-ranking officials and the Warlord himself, the questions took a different turn. The archpriest of Vulkain, an unexpected visitor at a military interrogation, sat in the middle. His pure white robe contrasted with his sallow skin as he fired questions at Teo and meticulously recorded the answers. "What was the girl doing in the woods?" he asked. "How often does she go there?" "Where does she typically travel?" "What trails does she use?" The Vulkainian priest even asked a question Teo found utterly surprising: "Is she attractive?" When Teo responded, "Probably the most beautiful woman in Chiveis," the priest nodded in a knowing way, a slight smile lingering at the corners of his mouth. He turned to the Warlord and signaled he was satisfied.

"Thank you for your time today, Captain," the Warlord said through his bushy mustache. "You are being placed on administrative leave to recuperate from your injury. I trust it won't prevent your representation of the Royal Guard at the upcoming tournament?"

"The fall equinox is three months away. I expect by then I'll be as good as new."

"Very fine. We're counting on you, Captain Teofil. Your performance will reflect on all your fellow guardsmen. You are dismissed."

Teo stood awkwardly, saluted, and hobbled from the room. But as he departed, a single question lingered in his mind: Why did the Vulkainian archpriest inquire so much about Anastasia?

◆ ◆ ◆

After the peculiar events of the day before, then the interviews today, Teo felt relieved to leave the Citadel and make his way up the valley toward Lekovil. As a part-time professor at the University, he had been assigned rooms of his own there. He looked forward to staying in this restful location for several weeks while his knee healed. Since he would arrive unexpectedly, he'd have to send messengers across the realm to gather his students for a series of lectures. Such an interruption might be inconvenient for them, but they would willingly drop their carpentry or cheese making or sheep tending to spend a few weeks studying under Teo. Parents understood that the University was their child's best chance of getting ahead in life.

Teo arrived at the intersection of the two valleys, pausing to water his horse in the frothy Chudeau River. Its gray waters tumbled downward, full of glacial silt, until they ran under the Citadel's wall into Entrelac. To his left, on the road toward the east, lay the Troll's Valley. Straight ahead to the south, on the road he was following, lay the Maiden's Valley. An abandoned stone cottage stood at the juncture of the two roads. Teo shook his head at the silly little building. Chiveisian legend said the cottage had once belonged to a priest of Astrebril who protected a royal daughter from the evil troll in the next valley. Apparently only Astrebril could protect fair maidens from danger; at least that's what mothers told their wide-eyed youngsters. *There's a fine line between folklore and religion*, Teo thought. *Both can be used to sway the masses—and both can be full of nonsense.*

The world of the gods held little appeal for Teo. As an employee of the state-run University, he was expected to tip his hat to the official religion, then get on with more practical work. His own contributions to Chiveis were primarily lexical: he translated scripts from the Ancients' language into the Chiveisian tongue so other experts could read them and perhaps find innovative applications. He wasn't supposed to waste his time investigating the belief systems of the Ancients, but to focus on their vast technological know-how. Yet Teo's curiosity sometimes got the best of him, and he found himself wondering what the Ancients believed about supernatural matters. Whenever such questions sprang to his mind, he tried to suppress them as unanswerable and irrelevant.

Shaking his head, he spurred his horse past the stone cottage into the Maiden's Valley.

Down the vale a ways, Lekovil had lost none of its bucolic charm since

Teo had last seen it. The warm sun shone on the steep-walled valley dotted with wooden chalets among the vegetable gardens and animal pastures. High above, the snowy summit of Elzebul's Height gleamed in the late-afternoon light. The mountain was the only one of the three major peaks visible from the Maiden's Valley.

The University at Lekovil stood at the base of a thin waterfall whose water spewed over the cliff's rim, struck the rock face, and shattered into a spray that sprinkled onto the plunge pool below. Teo had seen the diagrams that guided the construction of the pool in Chiveis's early days. A grassy hillock originally obscured the place where the water landed, but it had been excavated, and a pool of stone was constructed to encompass the waterfall's spray. The drops now fell on the pool's surface like rainfall on a still pond. As marvelous as this was, Teo reminded himself that the Ancients had their own marvels. They had constructed a stairway leading to a crack in the cliff face that went behind the waterfall. Visitors to the University still liked to climb up ladders to the ancient crack and walk inside the wet cliff, viewing the waterfall from behind.

Teo dismounted at the gate in the University's outer wall. It was an imposing, U-shaped wall whose two ends were set against the cliff, creating a semicircular courtyard around the plunge pool. Rooms ran along the inside of the wall, looking out on the courtyard and its pool. Teo's room was the fourth on the right from the gate.

"I'll stable your horse for you, Professor Teofil," the gatekeeper said. "Here's the key to your room. The gods be over all."

"Hail to the gods," Teo replied instinctively. He curled his finger at the gatekeeper, who had started to turn away. "Wait. Before you go, I have another assignment for you. Send messengers to my entire class roll. I'll expect my students tomorrow afternoon at my classroom."

"Your room here in Lekovil or your theater at Vingin?"

"My open-air classroom, up at Vingin. Make sure they know that."

"It will be done, Professor."

Stiff from his long day of travel as well as from his injury, Teo limped wearily to his room. Before he had passed the first door, a booming laugh welcomed him from above. It was a laugh that lifted Teo's spirits, for it came from the one man he wanted to see most right now: Maurice the

Wise, his aged mentor. *Or should I say, my "companion"?* Teo grimaced as he recalled his awkward choice of words yesterday with Anastasia.

Looking up from the courtyard's floor, Teo found Maurice smiling from the balcony of his personal rooms. He wore a richly embroidered blue robe edged with golden cord. The delicate diadem about his forehead signaled his status as a senior professor. Maurice's head was shaved bald, but a trim white goatee adorned his chin. Teo knew him as a man who loved beauty in the natural world and who abhorred anything ugly or unwise.

"My dear Teofil, nothing but the most unfortunate of accidents would suffice to drag you out of your beloved wilderness in midsummer. But judging from your ragged appearance, such an accident must have indeed occurred!" Maurice's words were spoken in the jesting tone that only a true friend can use.

"Master Maurice, your powers of observation never cease to astound me. If you can deduce from my limp, my dusty clothes, and my missing rucksack that I've met with misfortune, perhaps you'll also be able to guess that the sky is blue and the waterfall over there is wet." The rejoinder caused both men to burst into laughter.

When the laughter subsided, Maurice beckoned to Teo with his hand. "The kettle in my room is whistling for a friend to join it for tea. Come on! Walk—or should I say limp?—over this way, and we'll discuss your misadventures."

Teo obliged and soon held a soothing mug along with a plate of sausages and cheese. He settled into an upholstered settee and let out a deep sigh, then gave Maurice an elaborate account of the past two days, leaving out no detail. The convoluted story kept the old man on the edge of his seat throughout the telling, until the topic finally seemed to be exhausted.

Maurice stroked his beard and mused on the story. "Only you, Teo, could manage to get entangled in the world's two most deadly dangers in a single day."

"Wild animals and hostile enemies?"

Maurice chuckled. "No, my son, I'm talking about mortal foes and a woman's love!"

Teo snorted. "I hardly think love was involved in this escapade, Master."

"You said the young lady of Edgeton was beautiful, didn't you?"

Teo stood and walked to the window, gazing at the evening sky. "I suppose that word would apply," he said.

"When a man perceives a woman as beautiful, it proves attraction to her exists. Attraction can lead to love, and love—well, when it takes root, it can overpower even the strongest man. So you see, the most vital question then becomes, what type of woman will conquer our hero? If she be of poor quality, he'll become a slave. But if she be great, then her greatness will elevate the man to greater heights than he could ever have attained on his own."

Teo returned to the sofa, trying to understand his mentor's words.

"Be very careful, my son," said the senior professor. "Wisdom is needed here, for there is no greater catalyst for change in a man than a woman. To love a woman is to become a new kind of man, in one direction or another."

"Are you saying a woman has more power even than the gods?"

"Ah, the gods." Maurice leaned back in his leather chair. "The difference between the power of the gods and the power of a woman is this: a god holds sway over but one facet of life. For example, the forests belong to Pon, while the subterranean passages belong to Vulkain, and dirt and filth to Elzebul. Rain falls from Astrebril's dome, and there are other divine spirits who blow the various winds or stir the snows of an avalanche or fan away the heat that leaves us with winter cold. None of these events are connected, you see. Each god does as he wills."

"And what of the power of a woman?"

Maurice smiled and touched his fingertips together before his lips. "A woman holds sway over all. Teo, my son, prepare yourself in advance. The right woman can assume command of every part of your being—both body and soul. Her conquest will be total, and she will leave no province unsubdued."

"I hope that never happens to me." Teo glanced out the window again.

"It is both fearful and joyous—and not to be missed."

"I don't have much interest in either religion or love," Teo muttered. He yawned and leaned back against the embroidered pillows. For a long time, the two friends said nothing. Only the clock on the wall broke the silence with its ticking. And then, as Teo drifted off to sleep, he felt the old man draw a coverlet over him.

"Take your rest now, brave warrior," Maurice said. "You did well to protect Anastasia from danger. Fall asleep here in my rooms with her face before your mind. I suspect that out in the village of Edgeton, the reverse may also be happening tonight."

✦   ✦   ✦

In a distant forest, three men stood in the red glow of a campfire. It was the only source of light for many leagues around.

"Let me see the brimstone," ordered the archpriest of Vulkain.

Rothgar opened a canvas sack, and the Vulkainian nodded approvingly as he sifted the yellow substance with his fingers. Satisfied, the priest motioned for Red-Beard to load it onto his packhorse, then handed the reins of another horse to Rothgar. It carried the excellent steel weapons only the Chiveisi knew how to make. Rothgar picked through the saddlebags and selected a hunting knife to keep as his own. He shoved it into his belt.

The archpriest stood with his arms folded across his chest when Rothgar turned back toward him. The priest's expression was scornful. "You botched the abduction," he observed.

"*I* didn't botch it! It was my archer here." Rothgar jerked his thumb toward Red-Beard, who said nothing. "He missed the guardsman, and they got away."

"Whatever the case may be, the girl is no longer available to you," the archpriest said with a wave of his hand. "Our offer is rescinded."

"Now hold on! Our king wants that girl as a wife! You made a promise."

The archpriest sniffed. "The Chiveisi do not make promises to rabble like you. We make offers, and we are at liberty to retract them. This deal is getting out of hand. The Warlord may begin to suspect something. It's not worth the risk."

Rothgar began to feel desperate. It was bad enough to return home and face the king without the girl. Unless he could promise to fetch her at the next transaction, the king would surely demote him. Rothgar stroked his braided beard, trying to think of a way to salvage the situation.

"We'll pay double brimstone for the girl! When we come on the equinox, we'll pay double. And we'll bring a stronger force. Our men will snatch her and go."

"You failed once already. What makes you think you can succeed next time?"

Rothgar thought about it. "Maybe your people could get her for us? Knock her out. Tie her up and leave her in the woods at this spot."

"No!" The archpriest was adamant. "We will not use any violence against the girl! Someone might see it, and word could spread. The people would be outraged. It would be disastrous for the High Priestess's purposes." He tapped his finger against his lips. "There's already too much suspicion surrounding the Edgeton girl. Pick a different one. Take whomever you can find along the frontier."

"I don't want some ugly peasant! We have to have *this* girl!" Rothgar pounded his fist into his palm. "We'll pay triple!"

At the word *triple*, the archpriest cocked an eyebrow. He remained silent.

"Come on," Rothgar urged. "What do you say? Triple the brimstone." He began to think a deal might get done after all.

The archpriest exhaled and stared at Rothgar through narrowed eyes. "Alright. But the same conditions would still pertain. It would have to look like a kidnapping on the frontier. Nothing messy on our end. Just a raid from the Beyond. I know the girl's travel patterns now, so if we can find a way to alert you, we will. If not, it's up to you to capture her. Either way, no trail leads back to us, or you'll never see another Chiveisian blade again."

"Deal," Rothgar said, nodding emphatically.

The archpriest gestured toward a wooden shed in the clearing. "There will be carrier pigeons here on the equinox. You may communicate with us as usual. We will tell you how to proceed." He stepped into the stirrup and mounted his white horse, then paused to look down at Rothgar from the saddle. "If the abduction doesn't work this time, consider the deal rescinded for good. This sort of thing is dangerous for public perceptions."

Rothgar watched him leave, leading the packhorse with its load of brimstone. *"Dangerous for public perceptions,"* he mimicked in an effeminate voice after the archpriest disappeared.

Red-Beard hawked mucus and spat on the ground while Rothgar poked at the campfire. "The king isn't going to like this delay," Red-Beard said.

"Do you think I haven't thought of that, idiot?" Rothgar snatched a burning stick and hurled it at his partner, striking him in the chest. "All we have to do is tell him what happened. The king will be reasonable once we explain it."

"And what's our explanation?"

"What do you think? Gods! Your mind is as slow as your reflexes on the bowstring. We'll tell him the truth—that you missed your shot and the guardsman took the girl away."

"I don't think so! Just because you're the planner and I'm the archer doesn't mean you can pin this on me."

"Why not? I upheld my part of the task. You didn't. You should take the blame."

"I spit in your beard, Rothgar! It was your dancing around that caused the soldier to dodge. My aim was true."

"Alright, calm down. Let's do this," Rothgar said in a conspiratorial tone. "If you take the fall here, I'll make it up to you. Once we have the girl in our hands, you can have a couple of nights with her to do as you please."

"I'm not going to take the king's consort! What if she told him? He'd kill me for sure! This plan of yours is garbage. I'm not going along with it." With hands on his hips, Red-Beard glared at Rothgar.

Rothgar had reached the limit of his restraint. He drew his knife from his belt, feeling cold fury rise in his soul. "That's the last blunder you'll ever make," he snarled.

Before Red-Beard could react, Rothgar hurled the knife with a practiced hand. It planted itself in his partner's chest. For a long moment, Red-Beard stared down at it with a look of bewilderment. His eyes rolled up in his head. He sank to his knees, swayed, and landed on his side with a thump. He gurgled a few times and clawed the earth, then lay still.

Rothgar yanked his knife from the dead man's corpse. "Maybe you can finally find a woman in hell, partner!" He cocked his head and laughed at his own macabre humor. An owl fluttered from its perch in the trees. Red firelight danced among the branches as the jarring sound of Rothgar's cackle forcibly penetrated the stillness of the night.

CHAPTER

3

Teo sat by a window in the morning sunlight, eating a breakfast of soft bread, hard cheese, and fresh goat's milk. The milk and cheese no doubt came from one of the mountain dairies scattered in the pastures above the Maiden's Valley. The loaf of bread, warm and wheaty and slathered with butter, could have come from anywhere. Teo wondered if perhaps the grain might have been grown in Edgeton. His eyes drifted out the window of the University's refectory.

A priest of the Elzebulian Order interrupted Teo's thoughts. He stood over the table and peered down from under a prickly brow. "We're not accustomed to seeing you in Lekovil this time of year, Professor Teofil."

"I've experienced the misfortune of an injury in my other duties, so I've returned for recuperation. While I'm here, I'll be taking the opportunity to instruct my students."

"They arrive here later today?"

"No, not here."

There was a moment of strained silence while the men looked at each other, until the priest realized he would have to offer something more if he wanted to continue the conversation.

"You'll meet at your little theater in Vingin then?"

"It's a place that provides me a certain freedom."

"You're aware we disapprove of this, yet you continue the practice," the priest said through thin lips. Teo remained silent, giving the man no excuse to continue. He did so anyway. "There's no need for you to go clambering around in herders' villages on the remote heights. Your task is to serve your king by respecting his appointed religious experts here at the University."

"As I said," Teo answered, irritated by the pompous cleric, "I find my hillside retreat to be a place of freedom. I can immerse myself in ancient scripts without unwanted intrusions."

"Unwanted intrusions? Yes, indeed, I'm sure that's exactly what you want! But try as you might, you haven't escaped my notice, Professor Teofil. I've had my eyes on you. You pretend to be so patriotic, but I've seen how you turn up your nose at religion."

"I don't know what you're talking about."

"Don't play games with me! You sneer and mock during our ceremonies, then sneak off to some hidden corner with Professor Maurice. Neither of you is submissive to the gods. I've seen you having subversive discussions. I've overheard you ridiculing the true faith. You possess that most impious of vices—*independence*."

Teo rolled his eyes. "Independence isn't a vice. It's a stimulus to learning."

"Is that so? I believe we of the priesthood are best positioned to understand the nature of learning and the means of its attainment."

"The only thing you're in a position to understand is rote obedience to a religious system run by bossy priests." *Uh oh. That might have been too much.*

The Elzebulian stiffened, and his Adam's apple bobbed as he swallowed. His eyes narrowed. "Give consideration to your career advancement, young professor. Your free thinking doesn't bode well for you. Such rebelliousness will be counted of little esteem by those in the ruling orders." The priest tapped his pointy fingernail on the table to emphasize his ominous prediction. He leaned toward Teo, the black robes of his order hanging about his neck like the wattle of some grotesque cockerel. "The gods be over all," he whispered. When Teo didn't respond with the traditional reply, the priest whirled and marched off.

With distaste, Teo watched him go. Finishing the last slab of bread, Teo gathered some parchments and dropped them into a leather satchel. They were his notes for the history lecture he would give later that day.

Normally he would have walked to his classroom at Vingin, but considering his knee injury, he decided to ride.

Teo paused on the way out the door and glanced around the dining room at his fellow professors. Maybe the old Elzebulian was right when he suggested Teo didn't belong here. The other professors spent their time performing experiments and trying to solve man's practical problems. They dutifully cooperated with the religious authorities, then carried on with their academic work. For some reason, Teo found it much harder to be submissive. At times he regretted his involvement with an institution as hidebound as the University of Chiveis.

During Teo's teenage years at the orphanage, his sharp mind and facility for language quickly became obvious. The warders shipped him off to the University at Lekovil, where he was taught to value practical knowledge, the kind that could benefit mankind in concrete ways. He excelled at school, funding it with a military scholarship from the Royal Guard. Because of his intellectual aptitude, the University offered him a part-time lectureship when he wasn't deployed on field assignment with the Guard.

As an aspiring young scholar, Teo did his best to meet the University's expectations of obedience and pragmatism. Even so, he knew many of his academic colleagues viewed him as strange, for he openly wondered about things better left unsaid. His other career as a wilderness scout already made him something of a maverick. He certainly didn't need to exacerbate the problem by antagonizing the clergy. Yet when he was confronted by the kind of arrogant tyranny he had just encountered from the Elzebulian priest, he couldn't help but stiffen his neck. Knowing this about himself, Teo had purchased a plot of land near the pastoral community of Vingin. His private outdoor classroom on the mountainside gave him a place to study at his leisure—and to escape any disapproving eyes. He limped across the courtyard to the University's stable and called for a horse, hoping the short ride up to Vingin would distance him from the oppressive dogmatism so often found in the halls of academe.

The steep walls of the Maiden's Valley did not rise directly from the valley floor to the mountain summits. Instead the cliffs ascended to green terraces on either side, where sloping pastures of wildflowers and meadow grass provided ample forage for cows, goats, and sheep. The pastures ended at the glacial tongues and loose scree beneath the inaccessible peaks. The village of Vingin lay on one of these lush terraces, home to the herders whose livestock grew fat on Chiveisian grass. It was an out-of-the-way place, and that was just what Teo wanted.

His horse picked its way up the steep trail to the terrace on the eastern side of the valley. Soon Vingin's dark brown chalets, with their wide eaves and their window boxes overflowing with geraniums, came into view. Because it was midsummer, the cows were in the high pastures, feasting on the abundance of clover. Teo felt Vingin was, in many ways, his true home.

On a slope above town, the little theater quietly awaited the return of the students and their teacher. Teo tied his horse at the adjacent cottage and contemplated his open-air lecture hall. It was impossible to know who had first carved the stone seats out of the mountainside. The annals held no record of it. From its architecture, it was clearly Chiveisian, not Ancient. Beyond that, what more could be said?

The theater formed an intimate semicircle of stone risers that wrapped around a stage. The students sat in a curve above him as he paced back and forth on the platform. The only problem Teo could find in this arrangement was the incredible mountain vista at his back. It had a tendency to induce daydreaming.

Teo meandered among the seats of the familiar place, pulling a few weeds that had sprouted in the hairline cracks. Stretching out in the sun on one of the risers, he propped his satchel under his head and began to look over his parchments until the first students arrived.

✦   ✦   ✦

Shaphan the Metalsmith hoped to lose his name someday. Though skilled in the art of steelmongery, this wasn't the career he had in mind for himself. The hard metal was rare in Chiveis because the mountains lacked the necessary iron ore to make it. Traders in iron used to visit the kingdom, but much of the steel the Chiveisi possessed came from scavenging the remains of the Ancients. Those clever people had devised the means to forge steel implements that could resist rust over the centuries, and be reworked by smiths such as Shaphan. Precious little of it remained today, and what did survive was in high demand for the blades of weapons or for precision instruments such as clockworks. In fact, steel was so valuable, the coins of the realm were made of it. Shaphan knew the ways and habits of all metals. Yet he longed to leave his metallurgy behind and become a university scholar like Professor Teofil.

Shaphan was a well-built man of twenty-one years, with olive skin and wavy black hair that few Chiveisi could claim. On this hot day, he mopped his forehead with a rag and continued his hike up to Vingin from the valley floor. The teacher had summoned his students, and Shaphan wanted to be the first to respond. Perhaps he could engage his professor in a scholarly discourse before the rest of the students arrived.

It wasn't meant to be. As Shaphan neared the theater, he was disappointed to find several of his schoolmates already seated there.

"Where's the professor?" he asked a young woman who spun wool as her trade.

"He's in his cottage, studying. He said he'll begin class when the sun touches the western ridgecrest."

Shaphan took his seat on the front row of the theater and settled in to watch the sun make its way down Astrebril's dome. The orb hardly seemed to move, but Shaphan knew this impression was only because he was anxious to dig into the history lesson his teacher would soon provide.

At last the appointed time came. "Gather yourselves, students," called Professor Teofil as he emerged from his cottage. Shaphan readied his quill and parchment.

The day's lecture was titled "The Remains of the Ancients." Professor Teofil explained the three prevailing theories about what had happened to the buildings and artifacts of the people whose Great War of Destruction had wiped them from the face of the earth. Shaphan copied furiously as Professor Teofil explained the War Theory (that the depredations of the great war had obliterated everything), the Decay Theory (that time and weather had taken their toll), and the Scavenger Theory (that the Chiveisi had, in the intervening centuries, dismantled the remains for their personal use). Shaphan noted that the professor believed all three factors were responsible for the disappearance of the Ancients' handiwork within the boundaries of Chiveis.

Professor Teofil paused and glanced up at his students. "Of course, in the Beyond things are somewhat different," he said. Immediately a hush fell over the class. Quills stopped their scritching; ears perked up. Perhaps the professor was going to discuss the mysterious realm outside of known lands. His words carried great weight, for everyone knew he was a guardsman who sometimes set foot outside the kingdom's borders.

"In the Beyond, there are more remains of the Ancients than here in Chiveis. In fact, certain intriguing accounts in our earliest annals tell us that long ago the Chiveisi traded with wanderers in the deep forest. Those wanderers reported that great cities of the Ancients still exist—intact but entirely uninhabited. It's unlikely we'll ever know whether these reports are true. Personally, I doubt such cities exist."

Shaphan's gaze wandered over the professor's shoulder to the stupendous view of Chiveis's peaks and valleys. From his seat in the theater, he could see, far below, the wispy veil of water that plunged into the University's courtyard in Lekovil. And beyond that scene, what else? What could be found over the jagged horizon? Who had built those haunted cities of the Ancients? What inner spirit propelled them, just as Chiveis was now driven by its own citizens' turbulent desires? He lifted his quill, signaling his wish to speak.

"Yes, Shaphan?"

"Professor, you raise a fascinating topic when you speak of lost cities and ancient civilizations. I can scarcely comprehend such a thing. My question is, what abiding principles led those people along? What were their beliefs? How did they conduct their lives? I'm sure you can speak of this, if anyone can."

The professor didn't respond right away but gazed toward the far mountains. Then he turned and looked directly at Shaphan. "I can speak of no such thing," came the unexpected reply. "Let's not inquire into things that can't be known—or things that are of no real value. You're a metalworker, so I ask you, can you make a better clock spring because you understand the Ancients' beliefs? Would an awareness of their philosophies help you hone a finer blade?"

"But—"

"Mankind has few basic needs, Shaphan, and the more efficient we become at meeting them, the better it will be. That should be our goal. It's enough."

"But . . . but, Professor . . . perhaps *how to live* is more important than these things?"

Shaphan discerned an intense struggle taking place within his teacher as Teofil leaned on his lectern. His lips were pursed, and he fiddled with his parchments. Finally he looked at the class, gesturing with both hands. "Students, you tell me, can you find any practical benefit in what your classmate is asking?"

No one dared to answer, not even to say no, for none wished to become the object of the professor's criticism.

"Can you get ahead in life through ancient mystical ideas?"

Again there was silence. A large black bird soared on the thermals overhead.

"The reason for your silence is apparent. The doctrines of the Ancients bear no relevance for us today." Professor Teofil collected his parchments into a stack. "And now, students, we'll bring our investigations to an end, for it's growing late. I will expect you here tomorrow when the dawn rises above the eastern ridge."

The students gathered their materials and began to drift toward the taverns of Vingin or perhaps back to Lekovil. Only Shaphan lingered in the surrounding woods, fidgety and uncertain. Gathering his courage, he went to knock on the door of the professor's cottage.

"Who is it?"

"It's me . . . Shaphan."

There was a pause. "Alright. But make it quick."

The door opened, and Shaphan stepped into the square room. A brazier stood in a corner, unlit, for the summer evening had not yet grown chill. A cot was there too, with a straw mattress. But most of the room was occupied by cupboards full of scrolls and parchments and books. A bright lantern hung from the ceiling, and beneath it, the professor sat at a large desk. He pointed to a stool, and Shaphan took a seat.

"As you know, Professor, I didn't pay your end-of-term compensation last time around."

"It's excused, Shaphan. You're a man of humble means. To be honest,

I'm more concerned about your ill-advised questions today than your tuition payment to me."

Shaphan offered an apologetic smile. "I'd like to see if I can rectify both shortcomings." He reached into his rucksack and removed a bulky object wrapped in a cloth. "I have something for you."

As Shaphan unwrapped the gift, he was gratified to note the immediate interest his professor's face displayed. The object was a left-handed war ax with a blade of good steel and a large gemstone set in the handle. At the end of the handle was a strange little cup.

"That's a very fine battle-ax," the professor said, becoming a warrior again. "It's exactly the kind the Guard uses for parrying and counterattacks."

"Yes, I know—I've made many such axes for the Royal Guard in my work as a smith." Shaphan held up the weapon with a flourish. "But never has a guardsman had one like this!" He could see he had Professor Teofil's complete attention. "Step outside with me, and I'll show you what I mean."

In the waning light, Shaphan led his limping teacher to a tree. "I've put a cylinder inside the haft. It can be loaded with metal balls. When you press this gemstone, it moves a ball into position, and you can throw it." Shaphan pointed to a hole in the ax's end, where a ball had appeared in the cup. He cocked his arm and snapped the weapon forward. The ball bounced off the tree with a loud crack.

Teo picked up the ball, about the size of a cherry. "A weapon for near-range battle! To debilitate an enemy before he can engage."

Shaphan admired the way Professor Teofil immediately recognized the combat advantages such an ax would provide. "Yes! That was my intent! There are six balls inside. A spring pushes them up, so there's always one ready."

He handed the weapon to his teacher, who experimented with five different motions and postures. Each time, the whipping action of his arm sent the balls careening off the tree trunk.

"You're a natural! It took me days of practice to get the motion down. When you do it right, that ball's coming out fast enough to break a bone."

Teo regarded his pupil with an appraising eye. "Shaphan, your line of questions today led us down a rabbit's hole, but you've more than made up for it with this fine weapon! I'll be sure to acquaint myself with its use over the coming months. Go now to the alehouse with your friends. And, Shaphan—don't let your drinking dull your senses tomorrow and cause you to ask any more foolish questions."

The professor turned to retire to his cottage, so Shaphan hoisted his rucksack to his back. He was immensely pleased that the ax had been so well received. During the hour's walk down to Lekovil, not once did the broad grin leave his face.

◆　　◆　　◆

After finishing the morning lecture the next day, Teo dismissed his students with enough work to occupy them the rest of the afternoon and well into the evening. He rode down to Lekovil and entered the tranquil courtyard of the University. Limping to the pool, he sat on the stone wall that edged the water. The moist coolness of the waterfall's spray offset the heat of the midday sun.

Teo's spirit was troubled. He had rebuked Shaphan yesterday for his inquiries into the Ancients' beliefs. Everything in Teo's academic training told him they were foolish questions, the answers to which held no tangible benefit to mankind. Yet Teo had known Shaphan was right when he observed that learning how to live well is more important than pragmatics. Now that the idea had been stated so plainly, Teo was forced to wrestle with the implications. It meant that a scholar should be interested in spiritual insights, not just practicalities. Until now, Teo had always viewed religion as an oppressive set of rules handed down by domineering gods and enforced by pushy priests. With sudden clarity, he realized things didn't have to be that way. What if the Ancients had a religion that was attractive and easy to live by, one the Chiveisi could adopt to amend their ways? The fact of the matter was that the Ancients' beliefs were entirely unknown to the average citizen. Maybe the Ancients had something to offer with respect to religion—and if so, Teo realized it was his duty as a scholar to convey it to the masses. The notion excited him, arousing two of his most basic drives: intellectual curiosity and altruism toward the less fortunate.

Teo decided to test his radical new hypothesis. He crossed to the far side of the plunge pool where the cliff was dry because it lay beyond the waterfall's mists. A door was recessed into the cliff face, and an old man sat asleep on a stool in front of it.

"Hey, wake up!" Teo gave the man a jostle. He awoke with a shudder.

"Oh! Excuse me, Professor Teofil. Excuse me indeed. The sunshine drew me into its warmth, and I succumbed."

"Well, now's the time to awaken, O guardian of knowledge. I wish to use the Archives." Teo grinned to show he wasn't offended by the man's dereliction of duty.

The archivist withdrew a ring of keys from his belt and opened the squeaky door, then followed Teo inside. The anteroom had a low ceiling and was full of cobwebs. Seven oaken doors, each securely locked, led into the heart of the mountain. A wall sconce held a burning candle, which the man used to light a glass-enclosed lantern.

"Can't have open flames around the parchments, eh, professor? Now I'm of the mind you will be wanting the natural history section again. If I recall, that's where you left off your research last time." He began to jingle for the right key.

"I was thinking of using the Theosophical Room."

The archivist's jingling ceased, and he glanced at Teo with a strange eye. "That one's for the priests. What do you want with it?"

"My research needs take me there."

The man looked embarrassed. "Actually, sir, I have direct orders not to open that room to you."

"All the Archives are open to me. I'm a professor here."

"Begging your pardon, sir, but these orders came from very high up. They were, uh, they were specifically about you." The man fidgeted with his keys.

"And who gave you these orders contrary to the principles of our university?"

"I don't know his name. He was a tall, thin Elzebulian. Had wild eyebrows."

Teo could see he was stymied. He decided to try a different approach. "Alright then," he said. "I can look into it on another occasion, when things have been sorted out. In the meantime, I'll take my entrance to the Natural History Room."

"Very good, sir." The archivist opened the door and exited the anteroom.

Teo allowed the door to the Natural History Room to swing shut behind him. It groaned on its unoiled hinges until the latch clicked into place. The air was musty and close, suffused with the leathery smell of parchment. Teo drew it deep into his nostrils. It was a good smell—the aroma of knowledge.

In the bobbing yellow light of the lantern, Teo followed the narrow hallway past the many side rooms, each full of book cupboards. He entered the index room at the end of the hall. Long ago, diligent Chiveisian monks had created indices for the holdings in the archival collections. Some indices were well-worn favorites used by many scholars over the years. Others received little use, for they were cumbersome and not well arranged. Teo knew the better indices wouldn't contain what he sought. Even the rarely used ones wouldn't have it. He needed an index virtually no one would have used—an index of works written in the Fluid Tongue of the Ancients.

The Chiveisi understood that their speech was derived from a tongue spoken by the ancient peoples of these lands. That language had been guttural sounding, but other Ancients had spoken a language that was much more mellifluous. A handful of elite scholars could still read the lost Fluid Tongue. As a boy in the orphanage, the warders had noticed that young Teofil had a knack for language acquisition, so they sent him to Lekovil for specialized training. The fit was natural, and Teo made the Fluid Tongue of the Ancients his field of expertise.

"You are one of the few Chiveisi who can keep this forgotten tongue alive," Maurice often told him. "The gods have given you this gift for a reason." Teo continued to keep his language skills fresh—not for the sake of the gods, but because he wanted his mentor to be proud of him.

Teo spent the next half hour examining the various indices in the cramped chamber but didn't find what he needed. Sitting on a bench, he pressed his fingers to his forehead. A dead-end already? *Think, Teo!* The concentrated scent of the lamp's poppy-seed oil in such close quarters began to make him dizzy. The walls seemed to lean in on him.

An idea flashed into his mind. Perhaps a set of books somewhere else in the archives might have its own index! He went from room to room, scanning the walls. After an hour of frustration, Teo finally found what he sought: the final volume in a set of books on plant physiology was an index. The set had been printed before the Destruction, nearly four centuries ago, in the Ancients' Fluid Tongue. Teo pulled the delicate folio from the shelf. The volume was covered in dust. Clearly it had not been used in anyone's recent memory.

Now came the biggest question. Would the index have anything to say about religion? Teo knew all religious content had been purged from the archival collections by the guardian priests. Such knowledge was the private domain of the clergy. Yet he hoped something might have slipped through their censorship net. If so, it would undoubtedly be found in a book of the Fluid Tongue. Only something this obscure would have evaded the clerics' grasp.

Teo checked all the index words that might provide a clue: god, heavens, priest, vow, prayer, and so on. None of the words appeared in the index. He was about to give up when one more term came to mind. He turned to it and with a sharp intake of breath found it scrawled on the yellow page: *écriture sacrée*. His heartbeat quickened.

Finding the proper volume, Teo turned the brittle pages. The passage described a plant the Ancients had called "hyssop." He didn't know the plant, but he scanned the page and found the precise quote to which the index had pointed. Silently, he translated the text from the Fluid Tongue into his own:

About this plant, the Sacred Writing says,
"See! I have been born in sin,
and in transgression my mother has conceived me.
But you wish that truth might be deep in my heart.
Therefore make wisdom penetrate to the inside of me.
Purify me with hyssop, and I will be pure.
Wash me, and I will be more white than the snow."

That was all. The rest had to do with botanical details.

As Teo regarded the words, questions swirled in his mind. How could a newborn baby be a sinner? Before he could even begin to think through the implications of this, he heard the main door to the antechamber open as the archivist admitted another guest. Teo ripped the page from the book and stuffed the sheet into the linen shirt under his jerkin. He replaced the volume on the shelf.

Keys rattled in the lock, and the door to the Natural History Room opened as the new researcher entered. Slipping past him with a nod of greeting, Teo eased into the illumination of the brilliant sunshine. Having been in the cave for so long, the sky was too bright to gaze upon directly, and he was only able to look down at the shadows beneath his feet. Teo hurried across the stone pavement to the refuge of his mentor's room.

"Master Maurice," he called, "we have to talk. It's urgent!"

"Give me a moment, dear Teo. My old body moves nowhere near the speed it used to!"

"Ah, but your mind moves doubly fast," Teo said as the door opened and Maurice welcomed him in.

"Juniper tea?"

"Sure, if you have it. But my thoughts are racing, so let me ask you some questions while you prepare it." Teo ignored the settee where he usually sat, preferring to remain on his feet. "Master, what do you know about the religion of the Ancients?"

Maurice paused before the potbellied stove, then resumed feeding sticks into the flames and closed the little door. Still he did not answer but filled the kettle with water from a pitcher and set it on the stove to boil. Finally he turned and looked Teo in the eye.

"Why do you ask such a question?"

"I know it sounds foolish. As a matter of fact, I rebuked a student just yesterday for asking it."

"Don't rebuke your students for seeking understanding, Teo. They're a divine gift to you, to prod your mind. You owe them insight and gentleness in return."

"Then today I need that from you! I want to hear what you know about ancient philosophies."

"You have yet to answer my original question."

"Huh?" Teo realized he was too agitated to recall what it was. *Slow down*, he warned himself.

"I asked you, 'Why do you wish to know about the religion of the Ancients?'"

Teo took a deep breath. "Well, it seems I may have uncovered a piece of their Sacred Writing." He removed the torn page of the botanical book from his shirt, explaining to Maurice how he had come by it. Then he translated the text for his master, who could not read the Fluid Tongue. "Do you know what it means?" Teo asked when he had finished the translation. "The script speaks of sin and transgression. I know the terms, of course. But I don't know the Ancients' views of them."

"How come you're so interested in the Ancients all of a sudden? Haven't our priests explained things sufficiently? According to their lore, sin is the mark of the common masses. It characterizes those misguided souls who can't control themselves. But for the elite, the word doesn't apply at all. This you already know, Teo."

"Yes, and I agree with it entirely. Obviously I'm not a man of transgression, and neither are you."

"We're not?"

"Of course not! Through wisdom and skill, we've transcended all sin. But what if the Ancients knew of a way to assist those who are still mired in wickedness? I'd want to know about that."

"Why?"

"For one thing, I just want to understand it. I'm curious. You know that about me. In fact, you're the one who taught me to ask questions."

"Indeed I did." Maurice stroked his goatee. "And why else do you want to explore ancient religion?"

"I also think we could help the sinners in Chiveis find a good moral code. The people of this land are excellent folk, Master Maurice, but they need shepherds to take care of them. That's who I am—a shepherd. I provide protection for the sheep on our borders, and I feed their minds with intellectual discoveries. There aren't many people who can do the job, but those of us who can have a responsibility to carry it out."

"At any cost, Teo? Perhaps the powerful don't want ancient religion to be discovered."

"Doesn't matter. You can't go around worrying about them. You have to do what you think is right and let the chips fall where they may."

Maurice frowned at this, but the kettle whistled, and he turned to tend it. The old professor prepared the tea while Teo waited silently. As he handed over the steaming cup, Maurice's voice carried the weight of a man who perceives momentous events are at hand. Teo had never seen his mentor so grave.

"You don't know the door upon whose threshold you stand, dear Teo, son of my heart. I fear if you walk through that door, great danger will come to you. A new spirit is stirring in Chiveis. This I feel, and I can see it happening, though I don't understand it fully. I want to embrace the fresh wind that is blowing, but I fear to do so, lest I should falter."

"Whatever it may be, I'm ready to face it."

Maurice's eyes flared. "Are you indeed? Impetuous one! Are you prepared for everything to change forever?"

"If that's necessary, Master, so be it." Teo waited a long moment for a reply.

"Well then," Maurice answered, his kindly tone having returned, "all we can do is walk through the door. You must speak to a monk of Astrebril by the name of Lewth. He resides at the very nexus of these affairs, at the temple of the High Priestess. He is a trustworthy friend and shares my views on these matters. Tell him—"

Maurice the Wise paused, closing his eyes. He inhaled deeply and let out a long breath, then slipped a signet ring from his finger and handed it to Teo.

"Tell him you've been sent from me."

◆　◆　◆

The half-naked body of the King of Chiveis lay sweaty and disgusting beside the High Priestess. She glanced at him in the moonlight, his eyes closed in defeat. His discomfort and shame made her smile.

"I'm sorry," King Piair groaned in a pitiful whisper. "This . . . uh, this has never happened to me before."

"Your power is waning, Sire. I can see it ebbing from you. All the more reason to seek the invigoration of Astrebril."

"I know," the king whispered again, nodding. "I know."

The High Priestess laughed to herself. She recalled when she had first started coming to Piair's bed fifteen years ago as a nubile young priestess rising through the ranks in the Order of Astrebril. The king's beard had been darker then, and his muscle tone had been more firm. Now his wrinkled body sagged, and his whiskers were mostly gray. *But how the people of Chiveis adore him!* she thought. *They hang on his every word, bow to him in the streets, obey his royal commands.* She rolled her eyes and shook her head. If they could only see him in the dark of night: King Piair, the sovereign of the realm, reduced to a lusty old he-goat. Unable to control his desire, yet unable to release it.

Men are so weak! Who put them in charge? Reflexively, the High Priestess clenched her fists, and the stinging cut in her palm reminded her of the reason she was here. The horror of her vision came flooding back, prompting her to renew her most sacred vow: *The god of the cross will never come to Chiveis!* She shuddered at the thought and rose abruptly from the bed. It was time to act boldly against the Enemy.

The High Priestess put on her inner garment and gauzy outer robe. She thought she could feel the king's eyes watching her in the moonlight, but when she looked over her shoulder, his eyes were still closed, his expression troubled.

"I have an important matter to address with you," she said.

The king opened his eyes and stared out the window at the moon. "What is it?"

"I have received a revelation that a dangerous new religion may soon emerge in Chiveis." She paused, then took the plunge. "I want you to issue a ban against all nontraditional religions and popular gods."

"What?" Piair sat up in bed and looked at the High Priestess.

So the old man still has a little spirit worthy of a king? Ha! It won't be enough. She met his gaze. "You heard what I said. Astrebril is jealous for the devotion of the people. As king, you are obligated to preserve the true faith. Issue a ban against the superstitions of the masses. Only the Beautiful One and his divine triad deserve to be worshiped in our realm."

The king shook his head. "That idea is both illegal and unworthy, Priestess. The people of Chiveis have the freedom to follow the gods of their own choosing or no gods at all." His tone was firm.

The High Priestess slowly licked her lips. She caught the king eyeing her as she did, and she allowed his gaze to roam over her, knowing it would help her cause. Finally she spoke. "The people should bow to none but the four traditional gods of Chiveis. I warn you, Sire, Astrebril is disturbed at this encroachment from a new god. He will not be pleased with those who fail to side with him. Astrebril's fire from heaven may visit us again."

The king dropped his gaze and began to fiddle with the bedsheets as he considered his response. "Even so," he said at length, "I cannot issue a decree such as you request."

The High Priestess spun away and crossed to the other side of the room where she tugged her boots up over her slender calves. Turning back to King Piair, she regarded him for a long moment as she absently stroked the iron collar around her neck.

"Is this the end you imagine for yourself, Sire?" She put an edge into her voice.

The king didn't look up from the linen sheets he was rubbing between his fingers.

"Do you intend to spend your last years fading like a sunset? Will you stand by and do nothing until your manhood has all but deserted you?"

The king stood up from the bed and walked toward her. "You can't fight time, Priestess. Decay is inevitable."

"Is it?"

The High Priestess approached Piair until she stood very close. She traced a black fingernail along the king's bare shoulder.

"What are you saying?" he asked. "Can Astrebril stop the flow of time?"

The High Priestess caught a slight tremble in the king's voice. "No. But Astrebril has power you cannot imagine. And I can give it to you."

"If you were to pray to Astrebril, would he . . ." Piair paused.

"Would he what?" the High Priestess probed.

"Would he restore my virility?"

She caught the king's eyes and stared into them. "Perhaps. But you would have to give him something in return. I'm sure he would be pleased by the ban I just suggested."

"I might reconsider the matter, if the god showed me his favor."

The High Priestess smiled coyly. "I knew you were wise, Piair." She turned toward the door, then stopped to look back as she exited. The king stood in the middle of the room, his body droopy and pale in the moonlight. She chuckled as she closed the door behind her.

Men! They're are all the same. Kings or paupers—it doesn't matter. The male ego is like potter's clay in the hands of a skillful woman. A sense of satisfaction filled the High Priestess's soul. She knew she would get her religious ban. Not as soon as she would like, but she would get it in time. The vanity of men made it all but certain.

✦   ✦   ✦

When Teo awoke in the predawn darkness, the embers in the brazier had grown cold, and so had the cottage at Vingin. He lingered under the woolen blankets until his willpower finally overcame his lethargy. Throwing off his covers, he rose and went outside to saddle his horse under stars that had begun to fade in the night. Only the morning star glinted brightly in the blue-black sky.

Riding away from his lonely theater, Teo guided his horse up a seldom-used trail. It was the end of the week, so the students wouldn't be in session today. No one would observe his coming or going. Rising gradually through pasturelands and forests, the trail hugged the flank of the ridge above Vingin. At this early hour, the herders still slept in their warm cots, having no errand to draw them out like the guardsman who passed them unseen in the twilight.

Teo's horse followed the curve around the end of the ridge, where the trail met the tree line. Above this elevation, only grass grew, rippling like the waves of a vast sea. The dawn had broken into the ragged sky, staining the meadows red in its waxing light. As he rounded the ridge's end, Teo entered the sacred precinct of the High Priestess's temple. The alpine tundra here was open, providing expansive vistas to the distant horizons. But what truly awakened awe in Teo's heart was something much closer: the three great peaks of Chiveis had come into full view.

The one called Vulkain's Height formed a pyramid that rose to a pointed summit ever wreathed in clouds and frost. The mountain, preferring to revel in icy fastness, turned its sheer north face away from the sun. Like a hostile giant, it would gather boulders in its concave wall to hurl down on the fool who dared to approach. Pon's Height rose in the middle, and to the south of it, the peak of Elzebul reached into the sky. Between them was a tiny knob that legend said was a temple of the Ancients, though Teo didn't believe a building could be constructed so high. Snow never left these summits, even in late summer. Jumbled glaciers hung from the crags, coating the mountains in a permanent mantle of rime. Now and then, avalanches of snow and ice would slab off and go hurtling down the slopes, intent on smothering any unwelcome living thing.

These peaks, Teo marveled, were the great mountain halls of the gods of Chiveis. Nestled at their base, where the sea of grass yielded to the barren rocks and icy crevasses, lay the temple of the High Priestess. From the temple's pinnacle, her gaze could reach up, past the mighty summits, to look into the face of Astrebril himself.

You're in the lands of the powerful now, Teo reminded himself in the stillness of the morning. *You'd better watch your step.*

The Temple of Astrebril kept its secrets hidden behind an encompassing wall, though in truth it needed no wall on any but one side, for it sat against the glossy black crags of the mountain itself. The edge of Vulkain's northern face formed one protective rampart, while a steep gully dropped off behind the rear wall, flowing with frigid glacial meltwater. Another ravine fell away in front. No trail provided access to the temple except the one that climbed through the tundra toward the main gate. Teo's horse was skittish as it approached, not liking the feel of the place. The gatehouse appeared dead, and Teo would have taken the whole site as abandoned if not for the thin line of smoke curling from the High Priestess's pointed spire.

"Hail, Gatekeeper!"

No one answered. Again Teo tried, and again. At last a monk of Astrebril eased open the gate and stuck his hooded face through the crack.

"What business do you have, guardsman? You have no authority here."

"I'm not here in my capacity as a Royal Guard but as a professor at Lekovil. I seek discourse with your learned friars about scholarly things. In particular, I wish to speak to the brother named Lewth."

At that, the monk gave Teo a queer look but said nothing as he opened the gate enough for the horse to pass through. Teo dismounted, immediately noticing an unpleasant odor.

"What's that stench?" he asked as he tied his horse to a rail.

"Astrebril himself sanctifies this place with his presence," the monk answered, "but the nature of his terrible fire is not a matter to be sought by the likes of you."

The hooded figure pointed to a row of hermits' hovels along a wall. Unlike the main temple building, which seemed to be in excellent repair and perhaps even hinted at opulence inside, the huts were low and mean. No doubt the icy winds seeped in easily, making them very cold in winter.

"You will find Lewth there," the monk said, then returned to his post.

Teo approached the hut with caution. A thick fog had begun to descend, shrouding the temple in mist.

"I seek the monk named Lewth!" Teo called.

For a long time there was only silence. Then, "Who seeks him?"

"My name is Teofil, a professor at the University. I come with greetings from—from Maurice the Wise."

The monk's head appeared at the door, but Teo couldn't see his face in the depths of his cowl. "I am Lewth," he said. "We will go for a walk beyond the walls."

The monk led Teo back to the entrance, where he mumbled something to the gatekeeper about investigating natural specimens. Passing outside, Lewth marched across the sodden grass, lifting the hem of his habit above his wet sandals. Periodically he bent to inspect some flower or herb, collecting a few samples in his hand. Not until he had advanced well beyond the temple wall, so that it could scarcely be seen in the thickening drizzle, did he turn to Teo and pull back his hood to reveal his face.

"If my friend Maurice has sent you, he will have given you a specific sign."

Teo held out Maurice's signet ring, and Lewth's face lit up with approval. He was several years older than Teo and had the gaunt look of a man who fasted too much. His face was slim, with a long nose and a light beard on his pointed chin. Despite his somber manner, a lively intelligence shone in his eyes. Teo wondered what a man like this was doing in such smelly confines, bowing and scraping before the priestly hierarchy.

"I've come to discuss the religion of the Ancients," Teo said. "My master suggested you would know of this."

Lewth considered his response. "Indeed I do possess some knowledge of what you seek, Professor Teofil. I have discovered secret wisdom in my time here. All is not as it appears."

"What can you tell me?"

"That the Ancients followed various corrupt and evil religions. Our glorious founder, Jonluc Beaumont, purged Chiveis of all heresies—those of the earth worshippers and the atheistic unbelievers and many other cults. But especially those who followed the god of the cross."

"The god of the cross?"

"Yes, indeed, though I know little about the followers of this particular faith. Only the High Priestess understands their doctrines, for she has copies of their Sacred Writing. She despises the god of the cross with an abiding hatred. We monks of Astrebril are made to curse him regularly in our liturgy, though not by name. The name of that deity hasn't been revealed to us. He is an unknown god."

"Tell me even what little you know about this ancient faith, Brother Lewth, for I wish to learn of it. You have my complete attention."

A hawk called from the gloom above, and Lewth ducked his head. The sun was lost to view now, so the two men talked in the gray half-light of the swirling mist.

"Is it for academic purposes you wish to know or some other reason?"

Now it was Teo's turn to reflect on his answer. Intellectual curiosity was part of it, and so was the altruistic motive of discovering a religious path his fellow Chiveisi might find useful. Yet as Teo thought about it, he admitted there was something more basic driving him.

"I want to understand this religion because I'm skeptical about the religion of Chiveis. I'm sick of being told what to do by our gods."

Lewth hissed, and his eyes darted back and forth. "It's a bold thing you've just said, Professor Teofil. Yet in so doing, you've earned my confidence." He leaned close to Teo and began to whisper.

"You have reason to grow skeptical, young professor, you seeker of wisdom. As I said, all is not as it appears. Is the god of the cross truly evil? Or is it more evil to use weapons of burning liquid on the innocent, as the Vulkainians do? Or to make offerings of excrement to Elzebul? Or to debauch oneself in the forests of Pon? Or even—or even to call down Astrebril's curse, so that a man's house is shattered by thunder at dawn?"

"Ah! I've known that to happen. The sound of it isn't from this world. Such extreme violence can only come from the power of a god."

"Is that so?" Lewth glanced back and forth. "Come quickly with me. I'll show you something."

He led Teo to the rear of the temple, a barren place where the wall stood above a rocky meltwater gully at the dirty foot of a glacier. Drawing close to the wall, the monk revealed a slim crack where the ices of winter had broken apart the mortar. A man might even be able to slip through the opening. Lewth pointed to it.

"What do you see?"

Teo put his face to the crack. "I see a great wheelhouse. Like that at a mill, to be turned by horses. And many carts and sacks."

"Do you smell anything?"

"Yes, the sharp smell that lingers in this place is especially strong here." Teo turned toward Lewth. "What is it?"

"That I do not know, Professor Teofil. It has something to do with the High Priestess's power, but I haven't been able to figure it out. I'm hoping you will confer with your wise teacher and then at some future point perhaps you will speak with me again. However"—he leaned forward—"be very discreet."

After he had issued the warning, Lewth stepped back, but his sandal rolled on the wet gravel, and he stumbled. Teo noticed a flash of silver slip from the monk's neck. Before Lewth could prevent it, Teo seized the pendant that hung outside his cowl.

"A cross!" Teo breathed, his eyes widening. "The symbol of the Ancients' religion!"

"You shouldn't see it!" Lewth tucked the pendant away, then grabbed Teo's jerkin and pulled his face close, staring into his eyes.

"You must *never* speak of this again," he whispered, "or it will be death to us all!" He released Teo's garment abruptly, then scrambled up the slope and ran back toward the gatehouse.

Teo waited several moments to collect his thoughts. So many questions had been raised, questions to which he couldn't obtain answers right away. He hobbled around to the temple gatehouse to retrieve his horse. His knee was feeling stronger, and he was glad of that.

During the wet ride down to his cottage at Vingin, Teo was torn between two conflicting desires. Though he wanted to find out more about this ancient religion, he knew the coming weeks would require all his energy to be poured into his preparations for the great tournament on the autumnal equinox. It would take a single-minded commitment to win the dangerous competition. Yet even as Teo resolved to devote his attention to the pressing demands of horsemanship, combat training, and archery practice, he couldn't help but wonder, *Who is the god of the cross?*

CHAPTER

4

Through the window of his carriage, Teo noticed the red-haired woman slip from her royal litter and push through the crowds lining the main thoroughfare of the Citadel. Although everyone was pressing forward to cheer for Teo as a famous tournament competitor, his bodyguards wouldn't let the mob get close. However, they would make an exception for Habiloho. She was the daughter of the king. And besides, she was unbelievably good-looking.

When the lead bodyguard saw the princess step into the street, he bowed and threw open the carriage door. Teo smiled at that. The burly man, who in his days as a Royal Guard had chased down many a street thug, now hustled to oblige the whims of a petite girl. Yet Teo understood why. It wasn't only because of her red hair that Habiloho was called the Flame of Chiveis. Her temper could be fiery, and that could be dangerous because she always had the ear of her doting father.

"Welcome to my carriage, Princess," Teo said as the girl took her seat opposite him. "It's been some time since we last . . . connected." He winked at her.

"Indeed it has been a while, Teofil! And yet I believe you've grown even more handsome than when we were last together."

"And you, Habiloho—your beauty is unrivaled in Chiveis, as always."

She beamed. "I'm *truly* glad to hear you say so! All the girls are saying you'll have a prize to give out later today, and I hope to be its recipient!" She tucked her chin and looked at Teo from underneath her eyelashes.

"The prize will belong to whichever man earns it. But if it should come into my hand, I'll do my duty and award it to Chiveis's most beautiful woman."

Habiloho giggled at the thought.

The clamor of the crowd increased as the carriage entered Beaumont Plaza, packed with revelers on this holiday. Even the monumental statue of Jonluc Beaumont seemed to smile on the festivities. It was the autumnal equinox, a day to celebrate the ingathering of the harvest against the long winter ahead.

All the Citadel had turned out to cheer for Teo, a front-runner in the tournament to come later that day. Children scattered flower petals on the cobblestone pavement as the carriage bumped along, making its way to the coliseum in Entrelac outside the ramparts of the great wall. He could hear the parade of cows mooing behind him as they were led from their high mountain pastures to their winter quarters. Teo turned and looked out the rear window at the folksy Chiveisian scene. The cows' horns were festooned with wildflowers, and the matriarch of the herd carried a milking stool on her head. The animals wore their fanciest cowbells, adding to the general din.

Habiloho put her hand on Teo's thigh to recapture his attention. "Captain Teofil," she said, "I can see from your appearance you're well trained. You're so lean and hard! I'm confident you'll prevail in today's contest—and when you do, you'll choose wisely afterward."

"Only the gods can know such things, Habiloho."

"That's true, but remember, the gods can be coaxed by the arts of man. I've made a solemn vow on your behalf, Teofil. I've petitioned the great Pon for you. Perhaps he'll grant you a victory. But if he does, he'll demand an act of homage in return. All of Pon's followers will be at the revel in the forest tonight. And I want—I want you to meet me there."

Habiloho's face turned sly. She leaned close to Teo's ear, lowering her voice to a whisper, as if there were others who might hear the words her lips would speak. "You may think, brave guardsman, that the world's only mysteries lie on your distant frontiers. Don't you know? I have other mysteries at my command. Mine are a different sort, but they're no less interesting to a man like you. And"—she paused, exhaling—"I'm very willing to reveal them to you."

Teo felt the fair-skinned woman's warm breath in his ear. At that moment, the carriage shuddered to a halt. He glanced out the window. They had crossed the causeway spanning the Citadel's moat and were stopped at the outer gatehouse.

"Teo, my son!" It was Maurice.

"Let him pass!" The door to the carriage opened.

"My apologies, Princess Habiloho," Maurice said as he looked through the door. "I saw you join the captain for the ride, but I hope you won't begrudge him the company of his aged mentor. We have some matters to discuss."

Habiloho narrowed her eyes. "What choice do I have, wise professor?"

She gathered her skirts and prepared to leave. Before she alit from the carriage, she nuzzled Teo's ear again. "Provide me with a prize today, Captain," she whispered, "and I'll return the favor tonight."

Habiloho stepped from the carriage and disappeared behind the curtain of her waiting litter. The carriage started rolling as Maurice settled into the empty seat.

"I'm sorry to interrupt your conversation, Teo. Yet I'm sure there are many other men whose attentions the princess can quickly obtain."

Teo smiled at the truth of the statement.

Maurice continued, "I've come to issue you an invitation. Think of it as a pleasant distraction. A better way to spend your morning than battling your nerves in some room below the coliseum, checking your weapons over and over."

Teo looked out the window at the coliseum on the horizon. "Actually, that's exactly what I'd do if not for your invitation. What do you have in mind?"

"Let's clear our thoughts of the commonplace and the mundane. Let's allow the sublimity of lofty words to cleanse our spirits. I'm asking you to attend the poetry competition with me."

Teo considered the absurdity of Maurice's idea. To start the day with the noble art of poetry, then head to the coliseum for mayhem and violence, only to finish in the secluded forest with the opportunity for physical delights? It would be a day to remember.

"Driver!" Teo called out the window. "Take us to the recital hall!"

The carriage turned down a few side streets and stopped at the back door of the recital hall in Entrelac. It was one of the few stone buildings in town, built on a grand scale, and large enough to seat a crowd of several hundred. Teo hoped to keep a low profile as he went inside. A box seat to the side of the auditorium allowed him to stay out of view. He settled into a chair in the shadows next to Maurice.

"Any idea who's on the program today?" Teo asked.

"Yes, I obtained an updated version of the program this morning, though I seem to have misplaced it. I guess you'll have to wait until each participant comes out to take her turn." Maurice glanced at Teo with a mischievous look.

A handbell rang, and the crowd stood. Priests and monks, their wrinkled faces bearing stern expressions, filed into the hall. One of them intoned a perfunctory invocation, after which everyone was allowed to sit, though Teo hadn't risen in the first place.

The opening contestant came on stage, a rosy-cheeked girl slathered with rouge. She wore an ornate gown in the latest fashion. Accompanied by a piper, she recited her poem from memory as she plucked a harp.

"Your thoughts on the composition?" Maurice asked when it was over.

"Banal, insipid, frivolous, and superficial."

Maurice recoiled in mock surprise. "I would fear to be one of your students, receiving such severe criticism!"

"I'm capable of much worse than that."

The recital continued in the same vein, with each contestant offering a long poem set to music. Unfortunately, the poetry dealt with girlish fancies instead of epic themes. Teo glanced at the judges across from him. They seemed bored, hardly paying attention to the droning from the stage. Periodically they looked at the great clock on the wall or made a few notes on their parchments.

Teo felt himself growing frustrated as the poems spiraled down in quality. The first ones had been syrupy, but now they turned downright bawdy. Apparently it had become fashionable among the girls' well-paid literature tutors to set poems to the meter of drinking songs. The resulting lyrics dealt with first crushes and merry parties, not the great ideals upon which Chiveis had been founded. The recital dragged on. When the next-to-the-last contestant, a curly-haired girl with sparkling eye shadow, started describing the loss of her virginity, Teo decided it was time to go. He started to rise. "I think nervous pacing in a waiting room at the coliseum would be better than this," he whispered to Maurice.

"Patience," Maurice counseled, putting his hand on Teo's wrist.

Teo sighed and stared at the ceiling until the poem was finished. He'd heard more than enough and was about to head for the door again when an announcement nailed him to his seat.

"Our final contestant," the announcer said, "is a last-minute entry to the competition today. She is a new poet from one of the frontier villages. Her name is Anastasia of Edgeton."

The crowd in the recital hall broke into low murmurs. It was unusual to have a contestant from somewhere other than the aristocratic centers of Entrelac or the Citadel. Teo heard scattered comments such as "peasant girl" and "commoner" from the unsettled crowd. The judges turned to each other in whispered conversations. Everything about the scene infuriated Teo—the shoddy poems, the catty girls, the competitive parents, the snobbish judges. But all that receded when Anastasia walked onto the stage and into Teo's life again.

She carried herself with poise, standing tall, her hair bound elegantly above her head. Her scarlet gown was fitted to the waist, with a skirt that flowed behind her as she walked to the podium with her harp. An olive-skinned girl sat down nearby with a set of music pipes.

Ana stepped onto the podium and waited for the crowd to settle, but it did not. Teo sensed her uncertainty. Should she begin? Wait another moment? The chatter continued.

Teo could take no more. He vaulted the low wall of his box seat and strode toward the center aisle. A new set of murmurs arose as the audience recognized one of the tournament's favored competitors. Teo glared at the crowd, holding up his hand, palm outward. Each section of the hall to which he gestured fell silent. Finally, he extinguished the last babblers with a sharp command. He took an empty seat on the front row. The hall lay absolutely still.

Ana's regal voice announced the title of her poem: *The Turtledove Who Could Not Fly*. From its opening lines, the piece created an aura entirely different from what had come before. It was a classic ballad, written in the meter appropriate for grand themes, set to a tune preserved in musical lore from ancient times called "Amazing Grace." Ana sang the lyrics with such clear tones that the cavernous hall was filled with sweetness. The notes swirled among the stone columns, penetrating to each hidden corner. Her harp carried the story's thread forward, while the pipes provided a haunting accompaniment. Sunlight shimmered from the windows in the upper story, giving the whole place an otherworldly feel. Teo was mesmerized.

The ballad recounted the story of a lonely turtledove who had never learned the secret of flight. In rich detail, Ana painted a picture of the realm she loved so much. She heightened the pathos step-by-step as she described how the little bird traversed Chiveis and sought wisdom from various creatures but always came up short. The he-goat was too busy chasing the females. The scarab beetle only wished to roll in dung. Though the bat could fly, it was foul, lurking in subterranean caves. None of these creatures had anything to teach. Finally the dove decided to inquire from the yellow-billed chough—that glossy black bird who soared above the highest peaks. Surely it would hold the secret to flight, if anyone did. But when the dove asked for insight, the chough turned cruel, brutally pecking the smaller bird.

Ana's final stanzas formed a sad lament, filled with unrequited spiritual longing. In sorrow, the wounded turtledove looked around at its beloved, broken world and mourned for it.

You mountain-stars, so small and white,
Your blossom shines like snow.
Long have you been the folk's delight!
Why do you cease to grow?

You milch-cows who spend alpine days
With bell-decked heads bent low—

No more on clover do you graze;
No milk from you doth flow.

You summit-heights of wide renown,
Clad ever in your ice,
Take care lest you come falling down—
'Tis pride, your fatal vice!

My kingdom fair and full of light,
What darkness hath crept in?
O how can you escape this plight,
To cleanse away your sin?

The gods, they trample down upon
My beautiful Chiveis!
O who will come deliver us
From pride, our fatal vice?

I wait, alone, with longing heart
My soul begins to pine
For one who reigns o'er all to give
A prophecy divine!

As the last notes of Ana's ballad reverberated in the stillness, the spell that had fallen over the crowd lingered for a final, suspended moment. Ana stood alone on the podium, her crystalline song echoing away in the recital hall. The hint of a smile turned up her lips, and her cheeks were flushed pink. Her hand was poised gracefully at her bosom as she sought to catch her breath. She was indeed more radiant than any woman Teo had ever seen. The crowd began to rise to its feet in a spontaneous ovation—until a harsh voice rang out.

"Blasphemy!" The annoying priest of the Elzebulian Order who had confronted Teo at breakfast shouted the disparaging word into the awed silence. "I declare this poem to be blasphemy!" He stalked down the center aisle. The crowd was too stunned to speak. Everyone gaped at the turn of events.

The priest hurried to the judges' table and loomed over them with a frown on his face. The judges huddled behind their desk, conferring over their notes and whispering among themselves with their backs to the audience. Finally the crowd found its voice as a restless murmur rose to fill the awkward hush in the hall. Teo glanced at the stage. Ana was gone.

Someone yelled the name of an earlier contestant, and soon the crowd filled the recital hall with raucous shouts in support of their favorites. The agitated judges stared at each other in confusion, looking for someone to take the lead. Finally one of the judges nodded to the Elzebulian priest. He held up the victor's medal in one hand, and with the other he gestured toward the recently deflowered teenager with the pile of curls and the sparkling eyelids. She pointed to herself hesitantly and, when she received a nod from the judge, began to move forward.

No! Teo pounded his fist into his hand. *This can't be happening! How can they do this to Anastasia?* Furious, he ran backstage, looking for the only woman worthy of the prize, the woman whose poem had so stirred his heart. She was nowhere to be found. After a lengthy search, he gave up and left the hall.

Maurice met Teo at the carriage. They instructed the driver to head toward the coliseum. For a long time, they rode along in silence, each man lost in his thoughts. Teo brooded over the travesty he had just witnessed.

At last Maurice spoke up. "Whatever else we may say about today's events, Teo, one thing is certain—your Anastasia truly is beautiful."

"Yes, she is," Teo answered, looking out the window as the coliseum drew near. "She carries the true spirit of Chiveis in her soul. But apparently my kingdom can't see it."

✦   ✦   ✦

Ana felt her heart thumping in her chest as she slipped through the backstage area and out a rear door. She had known her poem was a risk. The aristocratic girls could be so unkind, not to mention the demanding judges and the fickle crowd. Ana's classic style of poetry wasn't in vogue, though she had hoped to appeal to the patriotism of the Chiveisi. *No matter,* she told herself. *I stayed true to myself. I can hold my head high.*

Where was Captain Teofil? It had been such a surprise to see him come forward with his commanding presence. He was the last person she had expected to see on the front row! She had looked for him but lost him in the tumult.

As Ana turned a corner in the alley behind the recital hall, a sallow-faced man stood in her way, making her feel uncomfortable. His face bore a leer, and his eyes held no goodwill. He made a vulgar proposition to her, but Ana turned away.

"You'll be sorry for that," he growled. "It's too bad tonight isn't the Wild Night!" Ana didn't fully understand his reference to that disgusting festival of Elzebul she despised so much.

At last she reached the main boulevard. A man's familiar voice spoke behind her: "Well done, my beloved daughter!" Ana turned to see her father, Stratetix, along with Helena holding his arm.

"Thank you, Father! Your opinion means more to me than a million judges."

He embraced her. "My opinion is that you're a woman of tranquility and courage. I couldn't be more proud," Stratetix beamed.

Glancing at her mother, Ana noticed she had tears in the corners of her eyes. Ana was moved at the sight. Though her father was proud of her achievement, only her mother had truly understood Ana's fears at taking such an artistic risk. Yet it was Helena who had most strongly encouraged Ana to write her classic poem and set it to the ancient tune. She'd carried Ana though the weeks of doubt leading up to the recital.

"I was nervous," Ana admitted, "but I knew you would be there supporting me, even if no others would."

Helena laughed. "It seems you had at least one other supporter today—Captain Teofil! It was noble of him to intervene on your behalf."

"It was! I looked for him afterward, but he was gone. I really wanted to see him." Ana's expression changed quickly. "You know—to thank him."

"Yes, love," Helena said with a nod. "I do know."

Stratetix offered one arm to his daughter and the other to his wife, steering the two women down the street.

"If you want to find the captain, I know the place to go. It's time to see whether I've put my bets on the right man. Let's hope his riding, his arm, and his bow are all strong today—for his own sake as well as for ours."

◆　　◆　　◆

Entrelac was in a festive mood. Because it was a holiday, no one was working the fields or plying the waters of the two seas. Everyone crowded the lanes, laughing and talking with friends. Acrobats, jugglers, and flame eaters in bright costumes performed their tricks for the people's amusement. A baker hawked honey buns at such a good price that Stratetix bought three, then added six more for the children playing marbles in the dirt.

"Oh my!" Ana exclaimed. "No marbles will shoot from those sticky fingers!" She pointed to their honey-covered hands, but the delighted children didn't seem to mind.

The crowds began to converge on the coliseum at the edge of town. It was a U-shaped building of stone, set on the shoreline with its open end facing the Tooner Sea. The massive structure gathered the Chiveisi in its arms for sport and drink. When the games were over, the coliseum would vomit its occupants out to a night of revelry.

Ana marveled at the arched facade of the coliseum. Idols of Pon, Elzebul, Vulkain, and Astrebril stood in each archway, for this building belonged to the four traditional gods of Chiveis. She thought about the symbolism in her poem, which the old priest had considered blasphemous. Apparently at least one person had understood her veiled critique of the state religion!

A colossal golden statue of Astrebril the Great overlooked the main gateway to the amphitheater. He was a dragon god with the bearded face of a man and the body of a serpent. Bat wings rose in covering splendor from his scaly back. His head was crowned with rays of light, symbolizing the sunrise whose daily renewal depended on him—or so it was said. Ana shivered.

As the family approached the gate, a stern Vulkainian militiaman warned them back. He gestured with his acid spray gun to indicate the reason they must wait: a parade led by the High Priestess herself was approaching the coliseum.

The priestess's open carriage was drawn by an enormous bison. The bull's horns swayed as it lumbered along, its beard hanging low, its powerful shoulders covered in a shaggy mantle of fur. The driver held a set of reins attached to a ring in the bison's slimy nose.

The archpriests of the three Chiveisian subdeities followed the carriage in procession. Each rode a horse whose coat had been dyed to match the color of its rider's order: black for the Elzebulians, bright white for the Vulkainians, and green for the devotees of Pon. Bringing up the rear, a horde of priestlings and monks trailed along on foot. Musicians banged cymbals, gongs, and drums, while flutists and harpists added to the racket.

"It's such a ridiculous scene," Ana whispered to her father.

"Guard your tongue, daughter."

With a tug of the reins, the High Priestess's carriage stopped in front of the golden statue of Astrebril. She rose from her seat and mounted a platform on the rear of the carriage, letting the crowds see her in full ceremonial regalia. They fell back in awe. The woman was beautiful, remarkably youthful in her appearance, yet old enough to have tasted the urge to wield real power. Her beauty was that of the seductress. It hypnotized the onlookers—a terrible, tangible force that reached out and gripped them hard. In the presence of the High Priestess, each man wanted her for himself. But Ana wondered, *Would he be prepared for what she would bring to his soul?*

The priestess's face was painted white, while her lips, eyes, and fingernails were colored black. She carried a brass scepter with the image of a snake engraved around it. Her straight dark hair was parted so that it swept down beside her face. Standing so close, Ana could see how truly alluring she was. The High Priestess wore a white robe that plunged at the breast, its sheer fabric clinging to her lithe body. Around her neck she wore an iron collar with a ring in it, proving she was Astrebril's slave. Ana was repulsed by the thought.

"People of Chiveis, I greet you! Today I give you the spectacles you deserve!" The High Priestess's captivating voice drew cheers and applause. "My people, hear my words! Let it be known that the contest today is more than mere entertainment. The battles of this day symbolize the battles fought in the heart of every man: Will he join the side of almighty Astrebril, or will he join with *evil?*"

"Astrebril! Astrebril! Astrebril!"

The High Priestess lifted her arms to the skies, her eyes wide with exhilaration. "And what will happen to those who dare to oppose the Beautiful One? Will it be death?"

"Death! Death! Death!" The onlookers' faces bunched up in fury, and they shook their fists in the air.

The High Priestess pointed her scepter to the statue of Astrebril, who smirked at the scene with his tongue dangling between his teeth.

"FEAR HIM!" she shouted.

An unearthly roar burst from the statue's mouth, showering flames and sparks on the people, wreathing them with acrid white smoke. Terror gripped the crowd, and everyone cowered, moaning in fear. Ana shrieked and reached for her father. His strong arm encircled her to protect her from the divine fires. Helena also clung to him. *Such an awful noise!* It was like thunder on earth, louder than anything Ana had ever heard.

"Let the spectacles begin!" The High Priestess cracked a whip, and the bison pulled her carriage through the gate into the towering coliseum.

❖   ❖   ❖

The people of Edgeton had reserved a block of good seats at the coliseum. As loyal farmers who dared to live outside the Citadel's protection, they were entitled to first pick. Ana fidgeted in the front row. She had been nervous at the poetry recital, but now the skittering in her stomach was much worse. The contestants in these games could be severely injured. In fact, many had died. *What if Teofil was to die?* The thought came to her suddenly, and it scared her, though she couldn't say why. She wanted to pray for him, but to whom?

Through the coliseum's open end, Ana stared at the deep blue water of the Tooner Sea. The wind was calm, and the lake shimmered in the sunlight. Its tranquillity stood in contrast to the fever pitch within the coliseum. The place was packed with ravenous spectators.

The first event was the horse race. An oval track had been laid out on the arena floor, and two hay bales on sturdy platforms were set up alongside as targets. The riders would have to throw their javelins into the targets as they passed by. Small catapults lined the track, ready to hurl distracting ammunition.

"There he is! Do you see the captain?" Stratetix pointed to the assembled riders as they readied their horses.

Ana spotted him immediately. Teo wore a dark blue shirt and, tucked into his high boots, riding breeches of the same color. A leather helmet was strapped around his head, scant protection against a horse's sharp hoof should he fall. *Oh, Teofil, don't fall!*

Ana put her hand on her father's arm. "It's only three laps around, right?"

"Ha! No, remember, this is the Grand Tournament. It will be six laps around, with spears at each straightaway and lots of fireballs coming at them." Ana's lip curled down at the thought.

The twelve riders led their horses to a rope stretched across the starting line. The horses stamped and snorted. At the center of the coliseum, the High Priestess stepped from beneath her awning onto a platform. As she raised her scepter above her head, a hush fell upon the crowd. No one was allowed to speak. Ana's heartbeat quickened.

The High Priestess's arm swept down, and the rope fell. The horses leaped forward at a full gallop, their riders hunched low in the saddle. A quiver of twelve javelins bobbed on the right flank of each horse. Clods of earth were kicked up underneath their furious hooves.

"A hit!" Stratetix pumped his fist. Teo's blue spear had struck the target beside the track. It was one of only five to do so. The horses rounded the first bend with Teo in the third position. On the next straightaway, he hit the target again.

One lap down, five to go! Ana felt no relief yet.

As the horses raced along, a fireball blazed into their midst. With its orange flames streaming behind, it reminded Ana of the fire arrows she and Teofil had launched at their enemies. When it smashed into the track and burst apart, two riders trying to avoid it tangled and went down, their horses tumbling in the dirt. An audible crack signaled the snapping of a foreleg. Ana winced. The crowd groaned in delight.

"Teofil hits again!" Stratetix cried. "The man can hurl a spear!"

The riders galloped around the track again and again, with Teo hitting his target each time. He maintained a position close to the front, yet never in the lead.

"The black one is making a move! Look out, Captain!" Ana's father seemed to think Teo could hear him.

A rider in black pulled alongside Teo's mount as they rounded a curve at full speed. Each began fighting with his hands, trying to shove the other man off. A rider who dislodged another from the saddle and took over his horse would score many points.

Teo seemed to be defending himself well, when suddenly the other man yanked the reins from his grip. Teo's horse lurched wildly, arching its neck, its mane flying. At that moment, the man shoved Teo hard, caus-ing him to fall to the side of the galloping horse with one foot twisted in the stirrup. Teo held the pommel with two hands, bouncing awkwardly as the horses churned forward. The other rider seized his opportunity and slammed his mount into Teo's. It shuddered at the violent impact, and one of Teo's hands fell free. He flailed, grasping the air, trying to climb back into the saddle.

Oh, hang on! Hang on! Ana clutched her skirts in her fists as she watched the deadly scene unfold.

The attacker was about to send Teo sprawling when, behind him, another competitor leaped from his horse and knocked the man in black from the saddle. The rider hit the dirt hard, cartwheeling until he smashed into a guardrail post, twisting around it in an unnatural position. There was a splotch of red on the white post. The man lay still.

Teo used the free moment to lunge upward and right himself on his horse. Stratetix and Helena cheered. Ana exhaled the breath she had been holding.

On and on the horses raced. Bodies flew as some of the riders knocked others from the saddle. Catapults hurled fireballs, taking down several more men. Teo guided his mount through the barrage, dodging and duck-ing as best he could. Yet he couldn't avoid them all. One of the bombs struck him, showering him with sparks and molten pitch.

"He's hit!" Even Stratetix was horrified. Ana gasped and gripped her father's hand.

The horses galloped madly down the final straightaway. Only three riders remained in the race. Teo swatted at the flames blazing on his shoulder.

As they drew near the final target, Teo grabbed his last javelin, ignoring his smoldering shirt. He was in second place. A rider was well ahead of him as the finish line approached.

"It's almost over!" Ana cried. *I don't care if he wins—just let it be over!*

What happened next was almost too incredible for Ana to comprehend. A fireball smashed the lead horse and sent it tumbling to the track. At the same moment, the third rider, dressed in crimson, hurled his spear toward the target but missed badly. The errant spear stabbed into the rump of Teo's mount. At a full gallop, the man in crimson jumped his horse over the fallen one, who had been in the lead. Teo felt his horse's legs give way. He kicked his feet from the stirrups and sprang toward the crimson rider in midair. Then everything was lost in a cloud of smoke.

The crowd gaped in silence. Ana closed her eyes, not daring to look.

A horse burst from the smoke. The horse belonged to the man in crimson—but its rider was the man in blue!

In a single fluid motion, Teo spun in the saddle and heaved his javelin toward the target he had long since passed. It curved in a graceful arc, planting its head in the target as Teo crossed the finish line—the last man standing. He had hit all his targets.

The crowd roared its approval.

Ana began to cry.

✦   ✦   ✦

On the sandy floor of the arena, Teo lifted his bow and drew the string to the anchor point on his cheekbone. His target was a fat apple perched on a wobbly post.

He was about to win the tournament, but his mood was sour. *What a farce this is! The crowd doesn't want to be inspired—just entertained. They'll chew me up and spit me out, just like they did with Anastasia.*

The horse race had nearly killed him. In the next event, Teo had fought a chiseled gladiator with thighs like tree trunks. Each combatant was dressed in padded armor covered by a white surcoat. Their wooden weapons had been edged with red paint to indicate where a blow had landed. Back and forth they swung ax and sword, thrusting, parrying, and hacking at each other while the crowd sated its appetite for violence. Teo was covered in bruises where the armor plates had been driven into his skin. He had bruises on top of his burns. Eventually he had managed to club his brawny opponent into submission, but for what? So the masses could be placated with spectacles? So the priestly caste could keep the populace amused?

Ana's mistreatment at the poetry competition had embittered Teo toward the people of his land. They had refused to see the beauty of her poem, either because they feared the dogmatic priesthood or because of their own vapid desires. Both reasons were inexcusable.

Teo had participated in several tournaments before, but with growing insight he had come to realize he was being manipulated. The battles he fought today weren't authentic. The whole affair was stage-managed. He longed to test himself in a real fight, like the Chiveisian warriors of old, who had defended the realm against deadly invaders.

Beyond his arrow's tip, Teo focused on the waiting apple. He was confident he could hit it. Yet in his rebellious mood, he decided to go for more.

You want spectacle? I'll give it to you!

The crowd waited for Teo to take his shot. Every eye held him in its gaze. Finally he let the arrow fly. It missed the apple, smacking into the post just underneath it. The apple wobbled and began to tumble from its perch. The crowd let out a groan.

Before the groan could die out, Teo whipped another arrow from the quiver on his shoulder and sent it slicing toward the falling apple. The arrow pierced the fruit before it hit the ground. The stunned crowd went wild.

Teo looked up at the faceless worshippers circled around him. They were from all over the kingdom—the two valleys, the Citadel, Entrelac, Toon, and the villages stretched along the Farm River. Each contingent sat together, flying its local flag as a sign of civic pride. In the distance, the late afternoon sun glinted on the Tooner Sea. Teo threw his bow to the ground. Though no one could hear him, he spoke anyway: "Beloved Chiveisi, you should aspire to more than this." He felt sad.

A gate opened, and two figures rode onto the arena floor. It was the king and the High Priestess with their respective retinues. Teo knelt.

"Rise, warrior!" said King Piair, dismounting from his stallion. "Never have I seen such strength and skill as you've displayed today!"

"I only do my duty, Sire." Teo rose and stood erect as he had been commanded.

The king looked Teo in the eye, taking his measure. Then he reached beneath his fur-lined cape and unbuckled a sword from his waist.

"Long have I wished to find a man worthy of this weapon," he said. "Do you know what I hold here?"

Teo answered that he did not. The High Priestess's horse shifted its feet.

"It is the sword of the mighty Armand! The blade is the finest steel, as keen as ever. Many battles did he fight at my side with this weapon. Now I want you to have it."

Teo swallowed. "This is a great gift, Your Majesty." The king buckled the sword of Anastasia's grandfather onto Teo's waist as the crowd cheered.

A horse was brought, and Teo swung into the saddle. The High Priestess stepped her black mare toward him, holding out a garland of white mountain-star flowers. Teo bowed his head, and she placed it around his neck. Then, unexpectedly, she traced her fingernail along the edge of his jaw. The sensation sent a shiver down his spine. "I trust," she said, her black lips whispering in Teo's ear, "you'll use that sword to serve the glory of Astrebril." Teo looked at her, uncertain as to her meaning. "Go now, Captain. Give the garland to Princess Habiloho, and make your king happy."

Teo nudged his horse forward a few steps. The people cheered, then quieted to hear his words. They knew what was coming; it was one of their favorite moments. They loved Habiloho, the Flame of Chiveis. She had been winning garlands since she was twelve. Teo saw her in the royal box, smiling as she waited. Taking the garland from his neck, he raised it high.

"Listen now, people of my heart!" he cried. "Today I do not keep this glorious prize! I give it away, that it might adorn the neck of another! I give it to the fairest flower in all of Chiveis!"

Teo whirled his horse and kicked his heels. The crowd let out a collective gasp. The horse galloped across the open expanse of the arena floor, stopping before a red and yellow flag with a bear emblem. The flag of Edgeton.

There she is!

Teo came to Ana on the front row. Her lovely mouth was open as she tried to understand what was happening. He pulled his horse close to the seating area until he was eye to eye with her. Reaching out, he took her hand in his and laid the garland in her palm.

"I choose *you*, Anastasia. You carry the beautiful spirit of Chiveis within your soul."

◆ ◆ ◆

"Who is that girl? I want any information you have!" In her private rooms beneath the coliseum, the High Priestess struggled to keep her tone civil as she addressed the priests and royal officials gathered before her. Rage gripped her dark heart, but she maintained control of herself.

The cult of Astrebril sponsored the games to please the masses and, more importantly, to manipulate the vanity of the royal family. The High Priestess understood how her blend of religion and entertainment would scratch the itches of the flea-bitten hordes. An amused populace was a docile populace. King Piair was no different. He wanted the day's narrative to climax with his pretty little daughter smiling in smug satisfaction.

Now the king would blame the High Priestess for Habiloho's disappointment. Forget about obtaining the ban on foreign religions anytime soon. It was going to take a lot of ego manipulation just to get things back to where they had started. Enraged at the setback, the High Priestess intended to make sure her plans would never go awry again. Though Captain Teofil was too popular to confront directly, the peasant girl who had stolen the prize was going to have to disappear.

A priest of Elzebul stepped forward, his eyebrows sticking up in all directions. "Magnificent One, the girl is named Anastasia of Edgeton. She's the author of a poem offered in a competition today. I was there. I thought it expressed blasphemous opinions."

At the mention of Anastasia's name, a light went on in the High

Priestess's head. *This is the same girl for whom the outsiders are offering triple brimstone!* Though she hadn't anticipated this confluence of events, it didn't surprise her. Even from a distance, the High Priestess had seen how beautiful Ana was. It made sense that the lecherous outsiders would want her as a slave and that Captain Teofil would be smitten with her as well. A smile crept into the corners of the High Priestess's mouth. She was beginning to formulate a plan—one with two advantages and no downside.

She turned to the priest of Elzebul. "Tell me about the girl's poem," she commanded. He nervously provided a synopsis. When he finished, no one else had anything to offer, so the High Priestess dismissed the useless sycophants from her presence. Turning toward a pair of Vulkainian strongmen, she pointed at the door. "You two! Go find the girl, and bring her to my chapel immediately."

The men left the room, and the High Priestess entered her underground chapel through a door behind the altar. It was here that, a few hours earlier, she had dedicated the games to the glory of Astrebril by animal sacrifice. Now she resolved to carry out the god's will through a sacrifice of a different kind. She savored the irony of her plan.

A short time later, footsteps in the hall signaled the return of the Vulkainians. They escorted a young woman between them. Her demeanor was cautious, though seemingly unafraid. The High Priestess gestured for Ana to take a seat in the pews, then waved the guards out of the room.

"Congratulations on your glorious trophy, Anastasia of Edgeton," she said smoothly. "Captain Teofil has indeed chosen well. You're exquisite."

Ana said nothing.

"Are you aware, little one, of the power your beauty gives you? Oh, it's true! Even great kings and warriors will bow to you. Learn to use your sensuality, and you can lead a man around like a bull with a ring in his nose." The High Priestess laughed as she slid to Ana's side.

"Anastasia, I've called you here to honor you. Your great beauty has won you the garland you now wear around your neck. And to show my esteem for any woman who could capture the fancy of a man like Captain Teofil, I want to offer you a favor. I hope you'll accept it."

"If I can, I will," Ana said.

"You love the deep woods, don't you? Then here's my gift. My monks are learned in the ways of nature. It would be my privilege to loan you my personal coach, to send you on a guided tour through lovely parts of the kingdom. There are some rare natural features in our realm that would astound you."

The High Priestess paused, putting her arm around Ana's shoulder, assuming a confidential air. "I know you cherish the natural beauty of Chiveis, for I've heard about your pretty poem. What a shame that even the black chough, who soars in the highest reaches of Astrebril's dome, couldn't teach the little dove to fly." The High Priestess stared into Ana's blue-green eyes. The girl pulled away.

"Anastasia, allow me to give you this gift! I'll summon a monk from my temple, a man who knows the natural world. He'll give you a tour you'll never forget! What do you say?"

Ana's voice was steady. "Thank you, Your Eminence, for your kind offer. But I'm afraid it's an offer I can't accept." Before anything else could be said, the girl ran from the room, her footsteps echoing down the hall.

The priestess sat in silence, seething. She clenched her jaw. Abruptly she picked up a wooden bench and heaved it at the altar, knocking it over with a crash. Chalices and knives clattered across the floor. Thick blood oozed from an overturned cup onto the pages of a liturgy book.

"You won't be so impudent once your new master is done with you, Anastasia of Edgeton."

✦　　✦　　✦

Ana was relieved to see her parents waiting for her outside the coliseum. Though the people of Chiveis revered the High Priestess, Ana's spirit had sensed an underlying current of evil in the woman. The experience unnerved her, and she was glad to be free. As Ana approached her parents, she noticed a tall man standing with them. *Captain Teofil!* He had cleaned up after the tournament and was back in his uniform. Ana smoothed her scarlet gown as she approached the trio.

After greeting her father and mother, she bowed to Teo. "Thank you for my prize today, Captain."

Teo returned the bow. "The prize is well deserved."

Ana smiled at him.

"Captain Teofil has asked my permission for you to join him this evening," Stratetix said. "There's a party for young people in the forest."

"The revel for Pon?" Ana felt apprehensive. The annual Pon-Revel had a reputation for decadence.

Teo nodded. "That's right! Would you be my escort, Anastasia? There's no one whose company I would enjoy more. Your poetry today—it moved me. I want to discuss it with you over good wine shared among friends."

He stepped forward and looked down at Ana with a gentle smile. His hair had been cut since she first met him in the woods, though it was still thick and unkempt in a casual sort of way. A dark lock hung loose over his face.

Stratetix spoke up. "Daughter, you may go. I'll reserve a room for you at the inn at Toon. You can retire there after the festivities are over. It's the closest town to the party. Tomorrow you can catch the riverboat home. Here are some coins." Stratetix handed Ana a pouch.

Helena agreed. "Go now and enjoy yourself. You'll be in good hands with Captain Teofil."

Ana turned toward Teo, searching his face. *I've heard many wild rumors about the Pon-Revel*, she thought. *Yet why would Teofil ask me to go if they were true? And why shouldn't I enjoy myself as the escort of such a handsome man?*

"I'd be honored to join you, Captain," she said.

◆   ◆   ◆

Princess Habiloho drew the curtains on her carriage as it pulled away from the coliseum. She didn't want to talk to anyone. She didn't want to see a living soul. She wanted to block out the entire world.

No sooner had the carriage started moving than it ground to a halt. "Why have we stopped?" she yelled up to the driver. "Get going!"

The driver opened the door and leaned in, his face apologetic. "You've been summoned." He rolled his eyes and tipped his head over his shoulder to indicate someone behind him. "The High Priestess," he whispered.

The High Priestess? What does she want with me? Habiloho stepped down from her carriage and cautiously approached the sumptuous coach parked nearby. Its door gaped open. She peeked inside.

"Have a seat."

Habiloho inhaled sharply. The voice had startled her, even though she had been expecting it. She sat down across from the High Priestess, marveling at her fair skin and perfect features.

"Welcome, Flame of Chiveis."

"It seems I don't deserve that title today, Your Eminence." The princess's voice was filled with bitterness.

"You don't? Or is it that you weren't recognized for what you truly are?"

Habiloho liked the sound of that. She turned it over in her mind.

The High Priestess changed the subject. "Do you know where Captain Teofil is now?"

"What do I care where he goes? Last I heard, he was going to the Pon-Revel."

"You're right. He's on his way there now. With Anastasia of Edgeton. I have people watching them."

Habiloho pursed her lips and wrinkled her nose as she gazed out the coach window, but she didn't speak.

"Would you like revenge?"

The question was so direct, it took a moment to register in Habiloho's mind. She snapped her eyes to the High Priestess's and asked herself, *Do I want revenge?*

"I guess so," she answered.

"Excellent." The High Priestess leaned forward. "You can obtain it, with some help."

"Help?"

"Indeed. The Captain is much stronger than you. You're not in a position to overcome him. Only Astrebril can supply the power you need."

Habiloho felt her heartbeat accelerate. *Astrebril? What does he have to do with this?* She swallowed. "What do you mean?"

The High Priestess held her captive with an intense stare. "Princess Habiloho, I'm inviting you to join the Order of Astrebril—if you are proven worthy."

The Order of Astrebril! Me? A sacred priestess?

"I . . . I don't know," Habiloho said. "I've never considered that before."

The High Priestess laughed lightly and rocked back against her cushions. She poured some wine from a decanter and handed it to Habiloho. "Of course you haven't. Let's not rush things. I'm only asking you to consider it. We should test you first to see whether it's the god's will."

"Test me?" Habiloho sipped the sweet wine. "How?"

"I have a job in mind for you. It would require you to go to the Pon-Revel tonight and speak to Captain Teofil. I can get you there ahead of him by ship. It would be the first step toward your revenge for his unbelievable cruelty to you today."

The reminder of the day's events made Habiloho's anger flare up. She clenched her jaw and spat out a curse. "That traitor," she muttered. "After all I gave to him—"

"Young princess, don't let his callous rejection today defeat you. At their core, men are weak. They can have no power over you if you don't let them. You must overcome your disappointment if you are to exact your revenge. Bide your time. Let your anger grow within your soul—let it fuel you. Tell me: do you want to hurt Teofil?"

Habiloho was taken aback. Though she had decided to take revenge on Teo, she hadn't quite thought of it as hurting him. She stared out the window as she considered her reply.

"*Do you?*" The question was urgent.

When Habiloho looked up, the High Priestess had a gleam in her eye. Though her expression was warm and inviting, the princess knew the look of raw power when she saw it. It was all there. This woman had power—in abundance.

"I do," Habiloho said firmly. "Tell me what you want from me."

✦　✦　✦

Teo and Ana left Entrelac and walked for two pleasant hours along the northern shore of the Tooner Sea while the stars came out one by one. They entered a remote area of the kingdom, uninhabited because the steep slopes made the land unsuitable for farming. The trees around them were very old. Nearby, the priests of Pon made large quantities of charcoal for sale to the people. In fact, this secret grove was sacred to the laughing, goat-horned god.

Soon the shouts of revelers came to Ana's ears. Through the trees she could see the orange glow of a bonfire sending up sparks like tiny sacrifices to Pon. But when Ana stepped into the circle of firelight, any notion that this would be an elegant soirée in a sylvan locale fled from her mind. What met her eyes was a degenerate scene. Many of the drunken revelers were naked or nearly so. Some were deeply engaged in activities that belonged only to a private setting. Ana was repelled.

"Captain Teofil, this is a place of depravity."

Teo glanced at her. "Nonsense! Come on, don't be afraid. I didn't bring you here for sensual purposes. Let's get a cup and find a place to discuss the tales of old Chiveis."

"No, Captain. I'm uncomfortable here. I don't want to be in such a sinful place."

Teo's face took on a look of astonishment. "Sinful? Anastasia, I'm no sinner. I'm not the type of person to do anything wrong!"

"A man I know once said, 'What type of person never does any wrong?'"

Teo sighed and shook his head. "What I meant by that was, we all make errors at times. But when it comes to sin—that concept is for the undisciplined masses! The term *sin* doesn't apply to righteous people like us."

"Evil loves the darkness, and it hides from the bright light. I sense such evil here."

"Are you saying I'm a sinner? An unworthy evildoer?" Teo seemed pained at the thought.

"Captain Teofil, in my experience you're a good man. But we've mistakenly come to an evil place. I want you to leave with me—now."

"I'm telling you, there's no evil here! Perhaps there are some who drink to excess or make love in the bushes. What harm is there in that? Can't we have a relaxing evening of our own? I assure you, Anastasia, I bear you no ill intent. Come on, meet my friends!" Teo turned toward the shadowy orgy.

A single dancer had taken over the center of the clearing. It was Princess Habiloho, lit by the flickering firelight. Her supple body moved in the erotic way that transfixes the eyes of men. Ana waited for what seemed like an eternity for Teo to turn around again. Instead he kept staring at the voluptuous princess.

Angry, Ana retreated into the darkness, then paused to look back. Teo still had his back to her as he watched Habiloho dance. Ana fled down a nearby path.

For a long time, she followed the trail toward Toon, her emotions raw. Every so often a rustling in the brush startled her. Though Ana was used to being in the forest, she was not often out at night. Wolves roamed this part of the realm. She would have to be careful.

"Hail, lady!" Ana's heart jumped to her throat, and she screamed in surprise.

"I mean you no harm!" A lantern was uncovered, and by its light Ana could see a monk of Astrebril atop a parked coach. "I was observing your party, and I saw you leave," he said. "The great High Priestess of my order bade me to follow you and intercept you if possible. She still holds the hope you might change your mind about her generous gift."

"No, sir. It's not a gift I can accept." Ana tried not to sound rude. No doubt the monk was only doing what he was told. But the High Priestess had an aura Ana wanted nothing to do with.

The old man descended from the coach and hobbled over with the aid of a cane. "If you won't take my mistress's tour, can I at least escort you to Toon? The deep woods of Chiveis aren't safe by night."

Ana thought it over. Clearly the old man posed no physical threat. Why not take him up on his offer? She wouldn't be accepting the High Priestess's actual gift, and it would be safer than continuing to walk alone. The hour was late, and Ana was tired. She nodded to the monk and climbed into the plush, well-appointed coach. The doors closed off the autumn chill, while a blanket and a charcoal foot warmer added to her comfort. Ana reached for the decanter of honeyed wine and poured some into a crystal cup, savoring its mellow flavor.

As the coach rocked along on its springs, Ana found herself toying with her flower garland, thinking about Captain Teofil. *There's so much nobility and strength in him, but so much foolishness and pride too!* Images of Teo swirled in her mind—his heroic race today, his vigorous combat, his incredible archery. She pictured his face when he gave her the garland, when he asked her to be his escort tonight—and also when he argued with her at the revel. He was a man of great power, though with rough edges, and many contradictions. Nevertheless, one thing had become clear: she was drawn to him.

The warmth and the wine and the rocking motion of the coach began to make Ana drowsy. She settled into the cushions and closed her eyes. *Just for a moment,* she told herself. Her head nodded. And then, though she didn't intend it, sleep took her.

✦   ✦   ✦

Ana awoke with a jolt. Everything was absolutely still. The coach had stopped. The forest was hushed. Clouds covered the moon. *Where was she! What's going on?* Her head ached.

"Driver?" No answer. The monk was gone, and so were the horses.

Ana's heart began to race, for her instincts told her danger was at hand. She opened the coach door and peeked out. The night was quiet. Slowly she eased into the darkness.

A cruel hand grabbed Ana's arm. She cried out, but the sound was muffled by the dirty sack thrown over her head.

CHAPTER

5

As a wilderness scout, Teo had trained himself to notice anything unusual, anything that didn't fit the pattern. There was nothing unusual about Habiloho's sensual firelight dance; she loved that kind of attention. But the figure lurking in the woods behind her, wearing the garb of the monks of Astrebril—that was not to be expected at the Pon-Revel.

For a long time, Teo stared at the spot where he had glimpsed the unknown man. Nothing moved. Evidently the visitor had left. It was probably of no consequence. Yet somehow it didn't seem right.

He turned. "Anastasia, I just want to—" She was gone.

Teo glanced around but didn't see her in the vicinity. He hoped she had overcome her misgivings about the party and had gone to obtain some wine. Wherever she was, she wouldn't go far—not in these dangerous forests. In the meantime, he wanted to take a closer look for clues about the mysterious visitor.

Dodging an amorous couple rolling around on a bearskin, Teo stepped out of the bonfire's circle of light into the dark forest. He stared into the shadows for a moment to let his eyes adjust, then began to scan the ground. With the firelight screened by the trees, finding tracks in the dirt was no easy task.

Teo was about to give up when he noticed a single footprint. Kneeling, he inspected it. The print was a sandal from a monk of Astrebril, like the ones Lewth had worn when Teo had visited him at the High Priestess's temple. But this man's foot was smaller, and a round dimple in the soil indicated he walked with the aid of a cane. Teo could discover nothing further, so he memorized the look of the footprint and resolved to watch for anything out of the ordinary.

He returned to the revel expecting to find Anastasia with a pair of wine cups, but she was still missing. Teo made his way to the casks of wine, nodding at friends and getting his back slapped more times than he cared to. Everyone wanted to congratulate him on his tournament victory, but he just wanted to smooth things over with the girl he'd invited to be his escort. When he finally reached the wine casks and serving tables, he didn't find her there.

Surely she—

Of course not. She wouldn't leave the party.

Or would she? Had she been that angry? Teo recalled the stern look on her face, the determination in her voice when she had said, "I want you to leave with me—now." But it was inconceivable that a young girl would set out for home by herself. These woods were infested with wolves and who knew what else. Teo couldn't imagine she would take such a risk. Yet the more he thought about it, the more he had to admit that this girl just might try it. "Anastasia, you're not like anyone I've ever met," he muttered in frustration.

Teo darted back and forth in the illuminated area of the revel, ignoring his well-wishers as he searched the crowd. With each passing moment, he grew more concerned. Even discovering Ana in the arms of some new-found beau would have come as a relief. Yet he couldn't find her anywhere. Three times he circled the clearing, calling out her name. Still no answer. Finally he was forced to acknowledge she had left the scene. But which way had she gone? There were only two options.

One trail returned the way they had come, back to Entrelac. The other trail, continuing along the lakeshore to Toon, was much more tricky. It was a winding trail, easy to lose and rarely traveled. Teo had intended to take Ana that way after the revel was over, to the inn where Stratetix had reserved a room for his daughter. Would she have chosen that unknown trail in the middle of the night? Or would she have done the more sensible thing and returned the way she had come? *Sensible? There's nothing sensible about any of this!*

Behind him a stick snapped. Teo turned around. A woman was approaching.

❖   ❖   ❖

"Good evening, Captain." Habiloho struggled to keep her tone civil, though in reality she wanted to strangle the man standing in front of her.

"Greetings, Habiloho."

"What are you doing out here in the dark woods?" She sidled closer to Teo. "Maybe that's to our advantage?"

Teo stepped back and erected an obvious barrier between them. "Enough with all that stuff, Habiloho. I'm sick of it."

Sick of it? Did he just say "sick of it"? Habiloho ground her teeth and tensed every muscle in her body. For a moment she stood there, quivering with rage in the darkness. It was all she could do to force herself to relax and not tear Teo's eyes out. She focused her mind on the High Priestess's instructions: drive a wedge between the captain and his escort.

"Have it your way, Captain," she said sweetly. "So what *are* you doing out here? Why don't you come back to the fire? Maybe we could share a cup and some old stories."

"I can't. I'm looking for someone."

Indeed. "Someone." That low-class wench from Edgeton!

"Are you looking for Anastasia?" Habiloho's eyes were wide. "She was a good choice today." The princess felt all her muscles go tense again. *Keep it together*, she told herself. *Just keep it together.*

"Have you seen her?"

The urgent way Teo asked the question was infuriating.

"I've seen her. But what's the big deal about *her*? I'm here with you right now."

"The big deal is, we had an argument, and I need to find her." Teo's frustration was spilling out. "Tell me where you saw her last!"

With sudden clarity, the situation snapped into focus. Habiloho had seen Ana moving down the trail to Toon and assumed she was playing a typical woman's game of cat-and-mouse. Offer a bit of temptation, then find a quiet place to be alone. *Not at all! These two have had a little spat!* Habiloho felt a rush of adrenaline as the pieces of the puzzle tumbled into place. This was going to be easy.

"Oh, Teofil, I'm so sorry to hear that! Now that you mention it, she did seem a little put out. But if you hurry, I'm sure you can catch her. She went that way." Habiloho pointed over Teo's shoulder. "Toward Entrelac. Keep going until you reach her. She has a good head start on you."

Teo glanced down the trail, then looked back at the princess.

"Thanks, Habiloho." He disappeared into the night.

Habiloho smiled to herself. *The High Priestess was right. Men really are stupid if you know how to push them around.*

◆ ◆ ◆

The full moon cast a silver sheen on the trail into Entrelac. Wispy clouds shrouded its face, suggesting an overcast sky might be moving in. Teo ran by what little moonlight he had, not bothering to look for tracks in a gloom that wouldn't have revealed them anyway. He hoped if he kept up his fast pace, he would reach Ana before she arrived at Entrelac.

By the time Teo reached the town, clouds covered the sky. No light gleamed off the ink-black Tooner Sea as he neared the night watchman's guardhouse.

"Hail, guardsman!" Teo slowed to a walk, panting from his run.

"Show your hands and approach slowly!" The voice was the deep baritone of a large man.

"I'm Captain Teofil of the Fifth Regiment. I seek news of a night visitor."

The watchman emerged from the guardhouse, his insignia identifying him as belonging to the Third Regiment. The lantern in his hand cast a flickering glow on his square jaw. "Aha! The great victor of the day! Well played, Captain—you made the Guard proud! As to your question, sir, no one has passed into town since I came on duty at dusk."

"A woman? Have you seen a beautiful woman?"

The man chuckled. "Yeah, I've seen plenty of those in my day."

Teo lunged at the man, grabbing his shirt in his fist and leaning into the face of the startled watchman. "You'd better listen to me, soldier! I'm in no mood for jokes! I want to know if a young woman in her early twenties, light-colored hair, has been seen anywhere around here tonight."

The watchman immediately deferred to Teo's rank. "N-no, sir! As I said, no one has come through since I went on duty."

What the . . . ? Habiloho. That liar!

Teo released his hold on the watchman's shirt. "Get me the best horse in your stable. I want saddlebags of gear and a sword. Move!"

✦ ✦ ✦

Teo hung his head and dozed in the saddle, fighting exhaustion. He had been following the remote track for several hours at a fast trot. The last time he had slept was before the tournament, and his body desperately needed rest. But he pressed on. He was even more desperate to find Anastasia.

When the horse stumbled on the dark trail, Teo awoke with a start. He reined in and dismounted. The autumn night made his breath fog. He sucked the cold air deep into his lungs to revive himself, then bent to inspect the trail. Lighting a Vulkain stick, he checked for the presence of coach tracks. The ruts were still there. *Keep going. You have to find the coach. You have to find her!*

A few hours earlier, with the aid of a lantern from his saddlebag, Teo had located Ana's foot trail on the path toward Toon. He followed it to where she had been intercepted by the monk with the cane. Ana had accepted a ride aboard his carriage, though Teo couldn't guess why. For a time, he nursed the hope that a kindly monk had simply given her a lift into town. But when the coach didn't stop at Toon, Teo's fears returned in full force.

The driver had followed an abandoned road that led behind the tilled fields along the Farm River. League after league the coach rolled on. It had even passed Edgeton without turning toward the sleeping riverside village. That was a very bad sign. *Anastasia, where are you?*

The predawn light had chased away some of the shadows when Teo

125

spotted the lonely carriage ahead in the road. He kicked his horse into a gallop, drawing his sword from its sheath, but all was still and quiet. A stream crossed the road here, and the ground was moist. Teo pulled up short so he wouldn't interfere with the tracks. Dismounting, he circled the coach as his trained eyes read the story in the soft earth.

The sandaled monk had unhitched the horses. Teo noticed he hadn't used his cane to move around this time; evidently it was a ruse. The monk had departed down a side path, leading the two horses.

Later other men had arrived. The make of their boots was foreign. *Outsiders!* Perhaps six or seven of them. Teo felt sick at the thought.

He knelt by the carriage door, where a struggle had obviously taken place. A piece of rope had been dropped to the ground, indicating some-one was bound. Among the jumbled footprints, Teo searched for the one whose presence he dreaded to find.

When he finally did, his body went cold, and his gut lurched inside of him. It was a woman's shoe print. Teo knew whose it was. His chin fell to his chest. For a long time he knelt in silence, his eyes closed.

At last he looked up. Something caught his eye. Pressed into the churned-up mud, a white flower lay crumpled and bruised. It was a mountain-star blossom, the inviolable symbol of the Kingdom of Chiveis. However, this alpine flower didn't grow in the lowlands. It must have been brought here.

Teo lifted the blossom from the mud, drawing out a string of similar flowers, all black and defiled. *The garland!* Only twelve hours ago, he had held that garland with joy and honor. Now he clenched it in his fist with rage and frustration and helplessness. Waves of an undefinable emotion washed over him as he wept on his knees in the light of Astrebril's dawn.

✦　✦　✦

The men shoved Ana along the trail, showing no mercy when she stumbled. Even so, the rough treatment from her captors wasn't the worst part. The bag over her head tormented her the most. It stank of moldy turnips, and its tight weave made breathing difficult. Ana felt as if she were suffocating.

Eventually they came to water. Ana was thrown into a boat, and the early morning sun beat down on her as she lay in the bow. The heat inside the bag became unbearable. Rivulets of sweat ran down her forehead. Her cheeks felt flushed, and her breath came in insatiable gasps.

Panic began to rise within her. Ana realized she was being carried away from Chiveis by outsiders, and the thought terrified her. In her agitation, her throat seemed to constrict. The fabric of the bag clung to her mouth, preventing her from taking a deep breath. She whimpered and squirmed in her bonds, fighting for control of herself. Everything inside her screamed for fresh air. *Help me! I'm dying!*

By an act of her will, Ana steadied her breathing. Her mind instructed her body to lie still, to grow calm, to quit thrashing. The familiar setting of Edgeton became her mental refuge, and she went there in her thoughts. She told herself the bag would be removed soon, and she would look for the right moment to escape. Until then, she would be patient. *Be strong, Anastasia. You can survive this.*

The men rowed steadily for what seemed like hours. The sun's blaze grew more intense. Thirst clawed at Ana's throat, but she couldn't think about that. She could only concentrate on getting enough air, one breath at a time. Sweat stung her eyes, annoyed her nose, salted her lips. Eventually the brown shadows of the bag began to deepen into the blackness of oblivion. Ana let unconsciousness come to her, preferring it to her present torture.

✦   ✦   ✦

"A bird approaches, Your Holiness." The archpriest of Vulkain stared from a window in the High Priestess's lofty temple. His robes were dazzling white, bleached by the power of the yellow rock whose mysteries he knew so well.

The High Priestess crossed to the window, and the Vulkainian yielded to her. She saw the pigeon growing larger against the midday sky. It landed on the sill, and the High Priestess gathered the little bird into her hand, stroking its feathers with her long, black fingernail. "Well done, faithful messenger," she whispered to it. Removing a tiny piece of paper from its leg, she returned the pigeon to a cage.

"What news of our transaction, my queen?" asked the archpriest.

The High Priestess unrolled the paper. Her tongue moistened her lips as she read. She smiled, experiencing deep satisfaction in the knowledge that, many leagues away, her sovereign will was being carried out. Her power knew no boundaries. From a nearby table, she poured a glass of wine, sipping it slowly, enjoying it.

"The secret transaction has gone well?"

"Yes. Your Vulkainians report success. They have concluded the trade with the outsiders. Several sacks of brimstone have been obtained in exchange for weapons."

"Good. And what of the girl?"

The High Priestess laughed, throwing back her head and swallowing the remaining wine. She refilled her glass, then poured another and offered it to the man who led the Vulkainian Order. He was useful to her. His brimstone was one of her most important commodities.

"The girl is theirs," she said, handing over the glass. "Our clients are satisfied with the transaction. They have received good weapons and a harem slave for their lord. We have received the sacred yellow stone—and we've eliminated the girl who ruined my games. Never again will that pretty one compete for the people's affections."

"Does the Warlord suspect us? He's always so observant."

"He observes, but he doesn't see!" The High Priestess curled her lip in a sneer. "He knows nothing of our brimstone transaction, nor of our deal for the girl. He thinks the outsiders have been raiding for slaves along the frontier. We'll simply claim they attacked my coach by night. The driver ran off, and they managed to capture the girl."

"The driver knows otherwise. He may talk."

"I've already had him executed for cowardice."

The archpriest choked on his wine. He glanced at the High Priestess, and she noticed how he instinctively backed away from her. She moved toward him, staring into his eyes. "More wine?" she asked with an innocent smile.

The archpriest shook his head. He turned toward the window and gazed at the horizon. "The Warlord will send troops after the girl," he said at length.

"He will not!" The High Priestess's retort was sharp. "Not without Astrebril's blessing. My soothsayers will seek the will of the god, and I'm quite certain Astrebril will forbid such a rash decision. Our troops shouldn't be sent to their doom in the Beyond just for one farmer's daughter." She smiled to herself, delighting in her ability to dominate the men who supposedly led Chiveis.

"In that case, the girl's life will be one of abject suffering from now on."

"Indeed. The men of the northern river are cruel and lascivious. They'll use her roughly. But such are the sacrifices that must be made for the glory of Astrebril."

✦ ✦ ✦

At the frontier headquarters of the Fifth Regiment, Teo removed a slip of paper from a carrier pigeon's leg. His frustration had mounted through the afternoon as he waited for messages to be exchanged with the Citadel. With each passing second, Ana slipped farther away. Yet it was his duty to report her abduction to the Warlord and await orders. He expected that a rescue operation would be organized immediately. A fast team of elite warriors could catch up to her and bring her home. But when Teo unrolled the paper, he was stunned at what he read:

TO: Cpt. Teofil, 5th Reg.
FROM: Warlord's Bureau
Regret to receive grievous news of citizen abduction. Warlord has ordered doubling of frontier guard contingent. Urge all citizens to remain behind walls until further notice. HP has taken auspices regarding your request; omens UNFAVORABLE. Permission to pursue abductee DENIED. Remain at your post. Emissary will arrive soon to debrief you.

Teo crumpled the piece of paper and threw it to the floor of the pigeon roost. The orders made him want to rip his insignia from his jerkin in shame. He ground his teeth and clenched his fists, turning his knuckles white. *The "abductee" has a name—Anastasia!* Were the faceless military bureaucrats willing to sacrifice her just because the High Priestess said the divine omens were unfavorable? Was Anastasia's young life expendable in the eyes of the gods?

Curse the gods of Chiveis to damnation!

The blasphemy was appalling, but Teo didn't care. He took a deep breath. Firm resolve steeled his mind. He marched from the room and entered a building across the courtyard.

"Quartermaster! Attention!"

The slim man, who hadn't seen Teo enter, jumped at the sharp order. "At your command, sir," he said, saluting and standing erect.

"Prepare an expedition pack, provisioned with rations for an extended mission. Leave one compartment empty. I will fill it myself."

"Yes, sir. And will you need weapons, sir?"

"Only a quiver of arrows. Meet me at the dock right away!"

While his pack was being prepared, Teo went to his personal quarters, where he found an oblong package awaiting him on the bed. It was the sword of Armand, given to him by King Piair at the tournament. Teo had arranged for it to be delivered here for safekeeping. He strapped the sword to his waist, noticing its lightness in comparison to a guardsman's standard-issue weapon. He knelt before his footlocker and withdrew the battle-ax Shaphan had made for him. While training for the tournament over the past several months, Teo had practiced the flicking motion that fired the balls from the ax. He belted it on his hip, its haft close to his hand. From a case in the corner, he removed his favorite bow, a heavy recurve shortbow made of yew. Last, he slid a long hunting knife into his boot. Now he was a fully armed soldier in the scout force of Chiveis.

At the dock, Teo's supplies were ready. He loaded everything into a canoe, then pushed away from the pier and slipped into the Farm River, heading downstream. The vessel sat light and tight on the water, and in a few minutes he was at Edgeton's dock.

A pall of grief covered the town. News of the kidnapping had spread quickly throughout Chiveis. Many people had fled to the comforting safety of the Citadel. Those who remained were in shock. Windows were shuttered, shop doors were latched, and the few people who plied the streets kept their eyes on their feet.

Teo approached the home of Stratetix and Helena. It was closed up, but he could hear voices inside and the sound of weeping. For a moment he hesitated at the door. Guilty thoughts tugged at him. What if he hadn't taken Ana to the Pon-Revel? What if he had complied with her wish to leave, as a gentleman should have done? No doubt he could have prevented her abduction. How could he now look her parents in the eye? He bowed his head. There was only one way to atone for his mistakes.

Teo's knock silenced the voices inside. After a pause, the door opened. It was Stratetix. His face was grim, but when he saw Teo, he brightened a bit.

"Captain Teofil, come in!"

Teo took one step inside, feeling unworthy to intrude any farther. A crowd of mourners stared at him, anxious to learn of any new developments.

"What word of a rescue, Captain? Does the Warlord plan to go after my Ana? Surely the Royal Guard is being mobilized as we speak." Stratetix's voice held a desperate edge. He was clinging to a slim thread of hope, knowing the thread could break at any moment and all would be lost. Teo pitied the depth of his suffering.

"I'm sorry to report: the gods have been consulted, and they've decreed that no expedition will be sent. The High Priestess has forbidden it."

Stratetix's shoulders sagged. "No," he murmured. "That can't be . . . it's wrong . . ." With his eyes closed, he staggered back and collapsed into a chair. He hung his head, gripping his skull in his hands.

Helena approached Teo, looking at him with the red-rimmed eyes of a mother bearing great pain. "I had thought Ana would be safe with you," she said. It wasn't a rebuke, only an observation, yet the statement fell on Teo's shoulders like the weight of a millstone.

"My lady, I . . ." There were no appropriate words.

"It's alright, Teofil," Helena said, putting her hand on Teo's shoulder. "I know you grieve with us. These events were not your fault."

Teo stared at this beautiful woman, a woman who by all rights should have slapped his face and thrown him out the door. Yet in the midst of her own crushing loss, she had found the strength to offer comforting words to the guilty. Teo was awed. *What grace she has!*

"If I may . . . I, uh . . . I've come to collect some of your daughter's things."

Helena was startled. "Captain, we aren't prepared to part with any mementos yet. Our grief is too raw."

Teo felt his face redden. "No, I'm sorry. I misspoke." He waved his hand. "What I meant was, I've come to retrieve some necessary things. A bedroll, warm clothing, suitable boots. Things she will need."

The house had fallen silent. Every face stared at Teo as if he were a raving lunatic. Stratetix raised his head from his hands.

"What are you talking about, young man? You said no expedition is to be sent. She's lost to us forever."

"No," Teo said firmly. "She isn't lost. I'm going after her on my own. I will find her in the Beyond, and I will bring her back."

The crowd let out a collective gasp. No one in the room had even begun to contemplate what Teo was suggesting. The Chiveisi didn't venture into the Beyond. Though the Royal Guard might patrol the edges of the kingdom, to single-handedly mount a rescue operation in the vast unknown was unheard of. The Beyond was an unnavigable wasteland, a dead zone where no one dared to go—and from which no one ever returned.

"Captain, some would call this madness." Helena's voice was steady, though tinged with deep emotion. "As for me, I don't call it that. I call it courage, the kind of courage that hasn't been seen in a soldier of Chiveis for many years. You remind me of the men of old. Men whom I once knew. In fact"—she paused, looking down at Teo's side—"you remind me of the man who once bore that sword."

Teo followed Helena's eyes to the sword at his hip. It had belonged to her father, Armand. He withdrew it from its sheath and held it up, the fine steel blade glittering in the light. Stratetix approached and stood at Helena's side.

"I swear to you," Teo said, "on the memory and honor of this sword—I swear to bring Anastasia back to this home or die in the attempt. There is no other call on my life than to return your daughter to you." Another murmur rippled through the crowd.

Stratetix looked Teo in the eye and clasped his shoulder with a firm grip. Hope had returned to him once more. "My wife and I thank you for this, Teofil." Helena nodded. They embraced Teo, tears running down their cheeks.

Ana's parents promised to meet Teo at the dock when their daughter's supplies were ready, so Teo took his leave and made his way to the water. As he waited there, a familiar figure approached from within the stockade. It was the burly young man named Fynn.

"So, guardsman, I hear you're going into the Beyond? You must know you're throwing your life away on an impossible quest."

"You wouldn't go after her?"

"It's a futile mission! One death will be added to another. By all the gods, no, I wouldn't go."

"You don't love her?"

Fynn's face crumpled in anger. He leaned toward Teo, pointing with his finger, though he didn't step any closer. "I *did* love her! But now is the time for *mourning*. She's as good as dead."

"If there's a chance she might be saved, I intend to go."

"That's not love! It's a fool's mistake."

"I think the greatest love is the one that takes such risks."

Fynn stood there, quivering. With a swat of his hand, he turned and headed back into town.

When Stratetix and Helena arrived at the dock, they carried a hastily prepared bundle. It contained a woman's fur-lined cloak, a field tunic, leggings, and high, warm boots. A few other necessities had been added to the bundle, which Teo wrapped in a bedroll and stuffed into the empty compartment of his heavy pack. He loaded it into his boat and untied the mooring rope. The married couple stood hand in hand as the canoe left Edgeton's dock.

"I'll pray for you, Teofil," Helena said.

"Why bother? The gods of our land said I shouldn't go. They're evil."

"I know. Chiveis is forsaken." Helena bowed her head.

Teo nodded and turned to his paddling. He fixed his eyes downstream and dug into the water with his strong arms. The canoe glided swiftly into the current.

✦ ✦ ✦

Ana was only dimly aware that the bag had been taken off her head. But when the bucket of cold water doused her, the shock yanked her into full consciousness. She sat up, coughing and sputtering, trying to understand what was happening. The laughter of cruel men surrounded her.

Where am I?

Slowly the facts solidified in her fogged brain. She was in a boat. She was far from Chiveis. Her wrists were bound. The ropes were stained red with her own blood, their chafing sting more intense now that water had been splashed on them. No matter. At least she could breathe. Ana inhaled deeply, reveling in the pleasure of taking a lungful of air.

A man stood over her, grinning maliciously and holding an empty bucket. Apparently he was the leader, for he wasn't rowing like the six other men. Ana recoiled into the boat's high prow, craving the meager security of the oaken planks at her back.

The man with the bucket set it down and lifted a lumpy sack. His thick black beard was braided into two plaits. Unsure of what the man intended as he stared down at her, Ana wanted to avert her eyes, but a voice inside her mind said, *Do not show weakness. Do not show fear.* She forced herself to gaze up at him. *Whatever may happen,* Ana told herself, *I will not give these men the pleasure of breaking my spirit.*

The black-bearded man grunted something at her, but his dialect was strange, and she didn't catch the word. He held up his bag. The other men stopped rowing and turned in their seats to see what would happen. The leader rummaged in his bag and pulled out a loaf of hard bread.

Hungry? Is he asking whether I'm hungry? Ana realized she was famished. When had she last eaten? She couldn't recall. She had lost her sense of time. All she knew was, yes, she was desperately hungry.

Ana nodded at the man. Saliva flooded her parched mouth, and her stomach rumbled at the thought of food. The man with the black beard held out the loaf to her. She raised her bound hands and took it from him.

Lifting the tough bread to her mouth, she began to tear off a bite with her teeth.

A rough palm smacked Ana hard across the chin. It wasn't a direct blow to her head, but it hurt. Worse, the blow sent the loaf flying into the water. The men in the boat burst into laughter, especially the leader, who thought his action had been particularly funny. Ana saw the loaf bobbing in the river, receding in the boat's wake. The men guffawed and slapped their thighs.

Ana rose to her feet, saying nothing, staring at the men with an accusing look in her eye. She could taste blood where her lip was split. One by one, the men quit laughing, until every eye in the boat was upon her.

With as much dignity as she could muster, Ana stood straight, with her shoulders back and her chin lifted. Deliberately, she spat her half-chewed bite of bread onto the floorboards. Then she seated herself in the bow and turned her back on the seven silent men.

❖   ❖   ❖

The burnt trees stood there, mocking him.

As Teo rounded the great bend in the Farm River, all the memories came flooding back. He looked up at the bluff to his left, where he had been attacked by the bear. He had fallen to the ground that day, expecting to be mauled—until, at the last possible moment, arrows came flying out of nowhere. Teo remembered his surprise at seeing a young woman standing there with a bow in her hand. *She was so beautiful.*

"What does that have to do with anything?" he asked himself aloud. Teo shook the thought from his head. *Remember, you're doing this because you owe it to Anastasia—and her parents. Don't let affection start clouding your thoughts, Teo!*

The burnt trees on the right continued to mock him in silence. The day he had set them afire with flaming arrows, he was the victor. The outsiders were thwarted. But it was only a temporary win. Now, just a few months later, the outsiders had what they wanted—Anastasia was in their filthy hands. What were they doing to her right now? Teo grunted at the thought, straining to chase it from his mind. It was too horrible to contemplate.

Ferocious anger welled up inside him, and he began to paddle like a man gone insane. Stroke after stroke, he dug in hard, attacking the river as if it, rather than the men who traveled it many leagues ahead, were his enemy. Sweat dripped from his forehead. Even when dusk began to fall, Teo didn't let up. He maintained his swift and angry pace for a long time, until his arms ached with the exertion and his lungs cried for a break.

When the moon rose round and full, Teo felt he had experienced a divine blessing. If the light held, he could continue paddling. *Maybe the gods aren't all bad. Perhaps I should give them one last chance.* "Gods of Chiveis," he prayed, "make the weather favorable to me."

But the moonlight didn't last. Soon tendrils of mist began to curl from the water. Before long, a fog had settled on the river. Teo could continue no farther.

He ran the canoe onto a little beach. Wrapping himself in his cloak, he tumbled into a dry place under the roots of a fallen tree.

"I'm finished with religion," Teo declared to the darkness. "From now on I rely only on myself!" He fell into a fitful sleep, full of horrible dreams, yet none as nightmarish as the fears for Ana's safety that plagued him by day.

❖   ❖   ❖

Having wept all they could, Stratetix and Helena lay side by side on their bed. The light of a full moon shone through the window. Helena noticed how bright it made the bedchamber. A thought occurred to her. "That moon—" she began.

"I know. I've thought of it too. It's shining on our little girl somewhere out there tonight."

"Unless . . ." Helena sighed and let that unthinkable thought drop away.

For a long time, neither said a word. Stratetix broke the silence. "Captain Teofil is strong and brave. He'll find her and bring her back to us."

"He can do it if anyone can. There are few like him in Chiveis. But, oh, the Beyond is so vast. Can one man succeed in such a task?"

"Perhaps we should pray to the gods."

Helena knew her husband wasn't highly religious. He had a spiritual side, yet the state cults had never held much appeal for him. She considered her reply to his suggestion. Wisdom was needed.

"My husband, to which god should we pray?"

"To Astrebril," Stratetix answered. "He's the most powerful."

"I think not."

Stratetix sat up on one elbow. He leaned closer to Helena, and she felt comforted by his warm presence and familiar smell. This was a man she trusted completely. He took care of her, and his decisions were prudent. Nevertheless, she was prepared to shake up his thinking if she must.

"Why do you say that?" he asked.

"Because I can no longer serve the gods of Chiveis. They don't love us. Obviously they don't love Ana. They abandoned her to the Beyond! They don't really want to know us or to be known. All they want is the obedience of slaves. Empty rituals. They're wicked, Stratetix—wicked! All of them. And most of all, the name you just mentioned."

Stratetix sucked in his breath. "Who then can we serve?"

Helena collected her courage—the courage to say aloud what she already knew in her heart. "There must be another," she said at last. "There has to be! He's lost in our annals perhaps. But he must be out there somewhere. Perhaps the Ancients knew of him. I don't know. But there's one thing I'm certain of."

Stratetix glanced at his wife, meeting her eyes. "What?"

"He's good."

Stratetix rolled back onto his pillow with a deep sigh. Tears came to him again, and he pounded his fist on the bed, venting his helplessness and fear. Helena took his other hand in hers. With a choking voice, Stratetix groaned in prayer. "Good God, if you're there and you are truly good, then look upon a father's suffering. Look upon a virgin daughter tonight! Evil men have her, and I can do nothing. Don't let them hurt her! Oh please, Good God, have mercy! Bring my Ana back to me!" His words dissolved into weeping. Helena was crying too, for the emotion of the moment had overcome her.

Good God, Helena asked in her heart, *would you come to us?*

✦   ✦   ✦

With a few twigs and the aid of a Vulkain stick, Teo got a tiny fire going. He was on the river before dawn with a mug of chicory coffee to take the edge off the chill. Strangely, he felt guilty about it. Surely Anastasia had no such comfort this morning; why should he? Teo reminded himself he would need all his strength in the coming days.

The river widened into a narrow lake, then closed down again. The banks were wooded and monotonous, giving Teo a feeling of isolation in the hushed emptiness of the Beyond. Around noon, the river entered a town of the Ancients. Teo could see the ruins of their haunted buildings protruding from the trees. No doubt there was steel to be found in the forest near here, but he had no time to scavenge.

At a sandy spot along the riverbank, the outsiders had beached their boat for the night. From the size of the imprint left by the keel, Teo estimated the boat had six or eight oars. He circled the place, looking for tracks. There were a few boot marks from the men and the remains of a campfire, but he couldn't find a print from Ana's shoe. Teo experienced a moment of doubt. How could he possibly find her in such vastness?

He cast a wider circle around the campsite. Something in the trees caught his eye—a steel carriage of the Ancients. Though it was rusted and decayed, Teo knew it had once been a sleek, self-propelled vehicle. Many such carriages had been discovered in the early days of Chiveis, but enterprising scavengers had long since dismantled them for their precious scrap metal. For that reason, Teo had never actually seen one, though he had read about these ancient conveyances that didn't have to be pulled by a horse. "How did a people so clever manage to kill themselves off?" he wondered aloud.

Teo peered inside the carriage's decrepit framework. The pilot's wheel was embossed with an emblem—a circle divided into white and blue quarters. Three ancient letters could still be read: B, M, and W.

A slight depression in the ground and the matted grass indicated someone had taken shelter next to the vehicle. Bending to examine the place, Teo glimpsed a piece of scarlet fabric tied to the carriage's frame. His heart skipped a beat. *Ana's gown!* He remembered how regal and demure she had looked in that gown as she walked to the stage at the poetry recital. She had also worn the dress to the tournament and then to the Pon-Revel. She wore it even now, as wicked sinners abused her, carrying her away from everything she knew and loved. And yet she was smart enough to leave a marker for anyone who might be trailing her. Teo admired the woman's spirit.

With renewed energy, he ran to his canoe and shoved off. The river became straight as he left the town behind, heading due west. Soon it emptied into an inland sea similar to the two lakes of Chiveis. Where the river met the sea, the Ancients had dammed it, causing the water to flow through a building of some kind. Today the dam was in disrepair, so water gushed through it and over it. The uneven water levels and the hazardous obstruction certainly would prevent large ships from passing. This must be why outsiders had never approached Chiveis in substantial numbers on the Farm River. Only small boats could be portaged between the lake and the river.

Teo had no trouble carrying his canoe and rucksack down to the lake. *Where to go next?* The oblong lake stretched away to the northeast and southwest.

The outsiders made the decision easy when Teo spied their ship on the northeast horizon. Unlike the little boat he had been following, this was a large sailing vessel with a square woolen sail and many oars. Though the ship was still far off, Teo estimated it would carry fifty men. He would have to be stealthy.

Hugging the shoreline to blend into the background, Teo followed the ship, always keeping it in sight, yet never getting too close. Though it didn't appear to be hurrying, its natural speed was much faster than his canoe, so Teo had to expend great effort to keep up. The afternoon wore on. As evening approached, the ship turned toward land for the night. Teo hid his canoe in an inlet, then hoisted his pack and circled around to where the outsiders were camped.

A cooking fire had been lit by the time Teo reached the spot.

Several ragged, wild-haired trappers were gathered there, haggling over furs with the outsiders. The crewmen bustled around, loading crates onto the ship. With its shallow draft, the vessel could be drawn close enough to the shore for the men to wade back and forth. The carved prow rose into the night, its fierce, demonic face alive with hatred as the orange glow of the campfire danced on it.

As Teo scanned the busy scene, he spotted her. *Anastasia!*

She sat in the midst of the camp on a log, her hands bound. A bag was over her head, but he could not mistake the red dress. A guard sat next to her, holding a rope tied around her neck. As Teo watched, the guard jerked it roughly, pulling her backward onto a sharp stone. The guard laughed as Ana struggled to sit up.

An immense surge of anger swept over Teo. For a moment he gripped his sword's hilt, ready to fly into battle, but he forced himself to stay calm and think things through. Mortal danger was everywhere. Only by the most careful planning would he and Anastasia survive. There was no chance to rescue her in a situation like this. The realization dawned on Teo that he would have to follow his enemies to their destination. Once they had relaxed and let down their guard, he would strike.

The outsiders' chieftain was an ugly man with a bushy black beard. Teo knew he was the chieftain not only by his arrogant demeanor but because he had his own goatskin tent set up to the side of the camp. He and another man stood near it, examining a parchment and pointing in different directions. Obviously, the outsiders' navigator was discussing a map with his chief. Teo desperately wanted to see the map to spy out the lay of the land. When the dinner bell rang, the chieftain pitched the map into his tent and headed toward the fire with a bowl in his hand. Teo decided to seize the opportunity.

Sneaking up to the tent from the rear, he slipped inside. A bed was covered in furs, and a wooden chest sat in a corner with a knife jabbed into the lid. A wineskin and a lantern hung from the ceiling. The map lay on the bed. Teo stared at it, trying to burn its landmarks into his mind. For a moment he lost awareness of his surroundings as he attempted to memorize the map's features. Then, with a start, he heard someone approaching. *Fight? Suicide!*

Hide? Where?

Teo scrambled.

The tent flap opened, and the chieftain walked in.

Teo watched the man's boots from his hiding place under the bed. He held his breath. The chieftain opened the cork on the wineskin and took a long, gurgling drink. He belched. Then he took something from the chest and left.

Teo slid from under the bed. The chieftain's wineskin and knife were gone with him. *That was too close*, Teo told himself as he reached the shadows of the forest.

From what he had discerned on the map, the journey to the outsiders' home would take several days. Teo realized it would be impossible to keep up with the ship once it began to travel in earnest. He needed another plan.

Late that night, when the camp had quieted down, Teo crept along the beach to the six-oared boat he had been following for two days. It was tied to the stern of the larger ship by a thick hawser. Now that the boat was no longer needed for exploratory forays, it would be towed home. Its oars had been stowed, and it was loaded with cargo. A tight goatskin tarp covered it.

Teo unfastened a corner of the tarp and slipped into the darkness. He opened a crate and emptied most of its furs into a sack, which he stuffed in a corner. After tying down the tarp from underneath, he hid his pack under some extra rope, then crawled inside the crate and shut it behind him. The long trip to the outsiders' home would be a trial of endurance in the cramped boat, especially during the day when Teo would have to stay out of sight. Yet surely his level of discomfort would be nothing compared to what Ana was enduring right now.

"I'll come to you soon, Anastasia," he whispered. He only wished she could hear his promise.

◆　◆　◆

Ana wanted to resist. She had been staying strong, keeping her spirits up, holding onto her fragile dignity. But now, at last, her strength had fled.

THE SWORD

Five days had passed since she was captured—or was it six? In all that time, she had eaten only a few crusts of bread and some moldy cabbage.

Yet it wasn't the lack of food or even the harsh mistreatment that finally wore her down. It was the awful realization that she wasn't going to escape. No one from Chiveis was coming after her. A platoon of guardsmen wouldn't come riding to her rescue. She would never go home again.

Earlier that day, Ana had arrived at the outsiders' settlement, a riverside town whose main hall was perched on an island midstream. Cobblestone bridges reached to the island from both sides of the wide, green river. A cluster of wooden huts lined each shore.

The black-bearded man—whose name, Ana discovered, was Rothgar—had marched her triumphantly from the docks to the island hall. She was met there by the ladies of the town, who ushered her to a private room, where she was made to bathe. They washed her gown and insisted on applying makeup to her face. Ana trembled at this strange welcome. She hoped it was some bizarre custom among these people. But deep in her heart she feared she knew the reason for their womanly attention.

Rothgar had come for her then. He took her to a great banquet hall lit by a candle chandelier dangling from the ceiling and a stone fireplace. A rope tied to an iron ring on the mantel raised and lowered the chandelier. In the shadowy corners of the room, hordes of feasting men were already deep into their cups. The only women present were the serving wenches, many of whom were providing much more than food and drink.

Ana had been led to the king, an obese man with a gold crown around his stringy white hair. He leered at her with a mouth whose teeth had been knocked out in some forgotten battle. The king groped her, then resumed his feasting when Ana recoiled. Rothgar hurled her to the ground.

Now Ana sat dejected on the floor. It was all too much. The loss of her home, her parents, everything she cherished. She had been treated cruelly at every turn. She knew what awaited her tonight when the king was ready to take his pleasure. Undernourished and emotionally spent, she had come to the end of her strength. Ana felt droplets running down her face. She did not realize for several seconds that they were her own tears.

A jester entered the room, and a shout went up as all eyes turned toward him. He was dressed in a ridiculous oversized robe, and his face was covered by a grotesque mask. The mask wore a fool's expression: its bulbous eyes were crossed, and a pink tongue dangled from its mouth. The men in the hall erupted in cheers.

The jester hauled Ana to her feet by her armpits. With exaggerated actions, he made sport of her as he enacted a crude and lusty courtship. Pretending to be her suitor, he pawed at her, then grew threatening when she resisted. The men egged him on, beating the tables with their palms. The jester pulled Ana close to his leering mask, holding her as if to dance at an elegant ball, only to trip her when she wasn't looking. The crowd roared. Even the serving wenches were laughing. At last, finished with his bawdy performance, the jester exited the hall.

The feast continued with more raucous laughter and crude antics. The men relieved themselves into buckets, not bothering with modesty. Dogs licked vomit from the filthy flagstones. Disgust overwhelmed Ana as she lay crumpled on the floor at the king's feet.

After a while, the jester returned to the room and strode toward Ana. A hurrah arose from the men as they toasted him with their flagons.

More mockery. More cruelty. Will it never end?

The figure in the grotesque mask lifted Ana from the floor. In a stupor, she stumbled around again while he pretended to dance with her.

The jester picked up a bucket filled with urine. He moved toward Ana, threatening to douse her with its foul contents.

Please, no. Not that!

The jester leaned close to Ana. Then, for the first time, he spoke to her.

"Anastasia, be ready! It's Teofil! I've come for you."

Ana lifted her head. She was too stunned to speak.

Teofil—here? How?

In a sudden rush, hope flooded her soul.

He had come for her!

6

Through the eyeholes in the jester's mask, Teo caught the expression on Ana's face—tentative, uncertain, hardly daring to hope. He hurt for what she had endured over the past several days. Although she had been cleaned up, she didn't look well. She was gaunt in the cheeks, and her weakened movements told Teo her ordeal had taken a heavy toll. Like a rabbit caught by a pack of wolves, she had been preyed on, made sport of, and wounded by the evil men in the room.

Despite her abuse, though, Ana still had spirit. Teo could see a spark of defiance remaining in her. Even in her diminished state, she fought against the men's attempts to degrade her. Ana's plight aroused Teo's protective instincts, fueling him with burning anger and cold courage. It was time to make war.

The raucous catcalls intensified as Teo and Ana swirled around one another, playing out their mock dance before the lusty crowd. As they stepped close, Ana leaned toward Teo and whispered, "I'm ready, Captain."

Maneuvering Ana in front of the fireplace, Teo pretended to threaten her with the bucket of filth. The feasting men urged him on, thrusting forward as they spouted encouragement. Even the king was calling for his new consort to be doused. Intense male aggression dominated the room.

Teo acted swiftly. He ran at Ana, but she dodged him. Without stopping, Teo hurled the bucket's contents into the fireplace. The fire went out with a loud hiss as an acrid cloud of steam billowed into the hall. In the same motion, Teo swept his ax from his baggy sleeve and brought it down hard on the ring to which the candle chandelier was tied. The ax severed the knot as steel rang against iron. The chandelier plunged to the floor, its candles extinguished. Shouts and confusion cluttered the sudden darkness in the feasting hall.

Teo threw the jester's mask to the floor. "Anastasia! I'm here!" He extended his hand in the dark.

"I'm with you!" Teo felt Ana's body next to his. Wrapping his arm around her, he stumbled toward the door. Tables and chairs overturned everywhere as drunken men careened around, shoving and cursing each other.

The door to the hall opened as Teo and Ana ran toward it. A man with a lantern barred the way, holding a spiked club. Teo clicked the gem-stone on his ax and sent a steel ball flying at him. The outsider dropped his lantern, which shattered in a cascade of burning oil. The man fell to the ground, moaning. Teo and Ana hurdled his writhing body and escaped into the night.

In a stable around the corner, Teo had a horse saddled and packed with his gear. It was a big animal, and tonight it would have to prove its strength. Teo shed the jester's robe and buckled on his sword.

"Just one horse?" Ana asked as she gathered her skirts and swung into the saddle.

Teo looked up at her with an amused expression. "Should I stroll around town and find us another?"

"Look out!" Ana pointed behind him.

Two armed men burst through the door. With his ax, Teo parried the first man's slashing blow, then thrust his sword deep into the man's abdomen. Before the other assailant could get into position, Teo kicked him hard in the chest and sent him sprawling into a pile of tack. Ana urged the horse forward. Teo leaped onto a hay bale, then into the saddle in front of her. His feet found the stirrups, and he galloped from the stable with Ana clinging to him.

The banquet hall had caught fire. Flames licked its wooden sides and thatched roof. In the dancing yellow light, Teo guided the horse through the trees on the island until he found the bridge to the south bank. Lanterns illuminated its length. He had started across when he heard

Ana's urgent voice in his ear: "Archers! Ahead!" At the same moment, a barrage of arrows landed on the cobblestones around him. Teo wheeled the horse and galloped in the opposite direction, along the bridge to the north.

"We're heading away from home," Ana said.

"Home is overrated. Hang on!" Ana tightened her arms around Teo's chest.

Men had gathered at the end of the bridge, blocking the way with their spears. Teo leaned to the side of the bridge and grabbed a heavy lantern from a pole. As he charged the spearmen, he hurled the lantern into their midst. The sudden blaze forced them to draw back. Sword in hand, Teo thundered through the opening, slashing at his enemies. He dodged through the alleys of the riverside village until he reached the forest. The men's shouts receded, and then Teo and Ana were enveloped by the Beyond.

✦   ✦   ✦

How long they rode through the forested hills, Teo couldn't say. It seemed like several hours. He sensed they were wandering northwest, though he had no specific destination in mind. Of one thing he was certain: he needed to find shelter right away.

It was a windy night. Rain began to fall in big, slow drops, then the downpour intensified, accompanied by thunder and lightning. Despite the chill, Teo was encouraged by the knowledge their tracks would be washed away. Yet he knew he couldn't keep Anastasia exposed for much longer. She had begun to shiver.

"Captain?" Ana's voice was faint. "I'm feeling weak. I think—"

Her grip on his chest loosened, and she started to slip from the horse's back. Teo swung around and caught her before she could fall. He slid to the ground and took the trembling girl into his arms. Setting her feet lightly on the ground, he dug into his saddlebags with one hand while he supported her with the other. She hung on his neck to stay upright. Teo pulled out her winter cloak and wrapped it around her chilled body, with the hood covering her dripping hair. He lifted her back into the saddle and climbed behind her, holding her close for warmth. She murmured in her delirium and rocked gently as they rode along. Teo kept her from falling with his arm around her slim waist.

In the driving rain, a bolt of lightning illuminated the woods for a moment. Teo glimpsed a man-made structure on a rocky outcrop above them. He couldn't tell what it was, but he believed it would offer shelter from the elements. He turned the horse uphill.

The building was a fortress of some kind. As Teo approached, he discerned it was very old. In fact, he guessed it predated the time of the Ancients' great war by many centuries. Now its towers were crumbling, and its walls lay open to any intruder. The forest had encroached. Nevertheless, the dilapidated castle would provide protection from the wind and rain.

Teo let the horse pick its way forward in the dark. By the intermittent lightning flashes, he could see they had entered a stone courtyard that once served as the castle's outer defense. Up the cobbled path they climbed, toward an inner keep with two square towers. The wind was less ferocious here, but Teo sensed that even better shelter lay ahead. They crossed a deep moat on an old bridge, then slipped through an arched passageway into the protected heart of the castle.

Most of the chambers in the ruins were open to the sky, but Teo found one that had managed to keep its low ceiling. He led the horse into it, knowing the animal's body heat would warm the space. While Ana shivered in the saddle, Teo unfurled her bedroll and laid it on top of his own to create extra thickness on the stone floor. Ana tumbled from the horse into his arms, and he carried her limp form to the bed, covering her securely.

As he turned to go outside to gather firewood, he heard Ana speak in a soft voice. "Teofil . . . thank you for coming for me."

"I always will," he answered without thinking. The inexplicable reply puzzled him, and he felt embarrassed as the words left his mouth. He shook his head at the strange statement. Hunching into his cloak, he walked into the cold rain that fell upon the lonely castle.

✦ ✦ ✦

Ana awoke with a scream. A man loomed over her with malicious intent. Hysterical, she beat him with her fists, crying, "No! No! No!"

"It's okay, Anastasia, you're safe! It's me—Teofil! You're safe!"

Awareness of her surroundings gradually returned. Ana's eyes came into focus, and she looked up to see Teofil kneeling at her side. The kind expression on his face, the weight of his hand on her shoulder, and the confirmation that she was no longer with the outsiders—these things caused a jumble of feelings to rush through her mind. Relief overcame her, and also gratitude for what this man had done.

"I'm sorry. I—I must have had a nightmare."

"You've been living a nightmare. But it's over now."

"Are we safe?"

"For now, yes. And I intend to make that permanent. Until then, you need to recover your strength."

"Where are we?"

"In a very old castle. I believe it was built by an early generation of the Ancients, long before the ones who destroyed their world. The last of the Ancients didn't build stone fortresses like this."

Ana swiveled her head and examined the room. A campfire cast a soft glow on the bare walls. Nearby, the horse blew through its nostrils and clicked its hoof against the stone floor. Ana burrowed under her blankets, experiencing a sense of security she had never expected to enjoy again. "It's warm in here," she said. "I feel much better already."

"You've slept for several hours. It's the middle of the night, but I imagine you're hungry. I've made you something." Teo moved from her bedside to the fire, returning with a small cookpot. She sat up in her bedroll and took the pot from his hand. It was melted cheese garnished with slivers of dried meat. Ana decided even her mother's cooking had never smelled so good. Teofil set down some bread chunks and his knife.

"Captain, how are my parents?" Ana speared a piece of bread and dipped it in the cheese.

"They're worried about you, of course. They grieve for you. Yet they took comfort when I swore to them—" Teofil glanced away.

"What did you swear?" Ana waited for an answer. The campfire crackled and sent up sparks.

"I swore I would bring you back or die in the attempt."

For a long time, neither said anything. At last Ana asked, "Why?"

She noticed Teofil studying her face. Was he searching for an answer to her question? Or did he hesitate to give an answer he already knew? Sitting so close to him, Ana became suddenly aware of his masculine strength. He had a strong, square jaw, and his wide shoulders lent him an aura of power. His hands were the capable hands of a man who knew how to make good things happen. Ana looked him in the eyes and did not break off her gaze.

Teo ended the moment. He stood up, laughing to himself. "I guess I owed you one! You saved my skin from the bear that time. Now we're even!"

Ana felt there was more to say than this but decided to let the matter drop. "How did you find me?"

"I caught up with you at the camp on the lake where the outsiders were trading with trappers. I knew I couldn't snatch you from the camp— you were too heavily guarded. So I hid in the cargo boat for three days, coming out only at night. When we reached the settlement, I waited until dark, then followed the sound of feasting. I sneaked into a stable and prepared a horse for our escape. Then I climbed onto the stable's roof and looked through a window. I saw the men in the banquet hall. That jester was tormenting you."

Ana shivered at the mention of her ordeal. She chewed on her bread and cheese, reluctant to speak, yet wanting to hear the full story.

"It angered me," Teo said, pacing around the firelit chamber with his fists clenched. He seemed to be reliving the events as he spoke. "I was furious. Battle rage overtook me. I couldn't wait any longer. The jester came into the alley to drink from a flask, and I decided on a plan."

"What happened to him?"

"Let's just say he will jest no more."

Ana sucked in her breath at Teofil's words. "You were bold to act when you did. It wasn't an opportune time."

"Yes and no. Certainly it wasn't the secretive approach. But since all the men were drunk, I took a risk. Besides, it was my last chance."

"What do you mean?"

Teofil came and knelt at Ana's side. "You're tired, Anastasia, and you need to finish your food. We can talk of your hardships another time."

"It *is* hard to speak of," she acknowledged, "but it feels better to talk about it than to keep it inside. Why was it your 'last chance'?"

Teofil sighed. "My last chance until you would be—"

"What?"

"Ravished."

The word seemed to embarrass the young captain of the Royal Guard. Ana was touched by his awkward concern for her. Somehow it seemed out of character for such a rugged man. And yet she had always known he had this softer side. Unfortunately, his tenderness was too often hidden by bravado.

"Thank you, Teofil, for considering my purity. I remain untouched."

"Then your parents will be relieved. And I'm very glad I acted when I did."

"Well, Captain, if you hadn't come in time, I was prepared to use this." Ana withdrew a tiny dagger from her neckline.

Teo's eyes widened. "Do you always carry a knife hidden on your body?"

Ana tilted her head and glanced at Teo from the corners of her eyes. A smile played at her lips. "Perhaps I'll let you think so," she said with a wink.

❖　❖　❖

The sun didn't rise that morning but only lightened the mist that shrouded the ancient castle. Ana was asleep again. *Good. She needs the rest.*

Teo faced the age-old dilemma of any hunted quarry: flee at top speed, or go into hiding? He had chosen the latter option out of necessity, but now their lack of movement made him uncomfortable. He knew searchers would start combing the forest at first light. He felt trapped.

At the castle's highest point, a square tower loomed into the sky. Teo guessed it would provide a good vantage point. He wanted to get above the fog to survey the surrounding terrain, so he hiked up to its base. The tower entrance was barred by a door, but its rusty hinges suggested it could easily be pulled out. When he gave the door a yank, however, it wouldn't budge. Retrieving a coil of rope from his gear, he hitched his horse to the ancient door. It was no match for the horse's strength, and it burst off its hinges at the first pull.

Teo entered and peered upward, examining the tower's hollow core. The sound of bats reached his ears from above, and their pungent guano covered the floor. A wooden staircase lined the interior wall. Teo tested the first step, then the next. The staircase felt strong enough. He decided to try it.

As Teo climbed, he began to regret his decision. The higher he went, the less stable the staircase felt. To fall here would mean serious injury, if not death. Yet he was almost to the top. Teo was debating whether to keep going or turn back when the landing he was standing on collapsed.

He dived forward, grabbing the steps ahead, clinging to the crumbling wood while his feet dangled over empty space. A colony of bats burst from their roost, swirling around Teo with high-pitched squeaks and fluttering wings as he desperately tried to claw his way up. With a lunge, he scrambled onto the wobbly staircase and bounded up the final steps to the safety of the roof.

Out in the sunlight, he immediately realized that his gamble, though far too risky, had paid off. The tower's top did protrude from the mist, providing a view of the black forest that extended for many leagues in every direction. White wisps clung to the low places, and a ribbon of fog lined the river by which he had arrived at the outsiders' village.

Teo was especially glad to get a bird's-eye view of the river's course. He knew the outsiders' settlement lay to the south. There the river flowed east-to-west, but it made a right turn as it curved around in a northerly direction, not far from his current position. If he could somehow cross the river, perhaps he could lose his pursuers and get beyond their territory. He decided to pack up and make for the river.

The damaged stairs were no longer an option, so Teo pulled the coil of rope from his shoulder, tied it to a merlon in the tower's battlement, and slid to the ground. He hated to leave some of the rope's length behind, but there was nothing else to do, so he cut it and stowed the remainder in a saddlebag. He found Ana awake in the stone hall. She had prepared coffee and a morning porridge.

"Feeling better?" he asked.

"Much better, now that I've taken some food. Rothgar wasn't much of a host."

"Rothgar?"

"The chieftain with the braided beard."

"Oh, right. I saw him. A cruel man."

"Someday he'll get what he deserves." Ana smiled ruefully, and Teo was encouraged to hear the spirit in her voice.

"Anastasia, are you well enough to travel? I'm afraid if we stay here any longer, we'll be discovered."

"Yes, I can travel. Where will you take us?"

"I want to cross the river. I have a plan."

"It seems you always do, Captain. Have something to eat, and then let's go."

While Teo wolfed down a breakfast, Ana saddled the horse. Even with two riders, the horse was in the mood to step out. Teo followed a trail to the northwest, knowing it would eventually intersect the river. From time to time they crossed roads of the Ancients, including a wide highway for steel carriages. Immediately after that, they reached the river.

Teo dismounted and helped Ana from the saddle. She was still wearing her red gown, which was ill-suited to riding. He emptied the horse's saddlebags and began to repack the contents into his rucksack.

"We're continuing on foot?"

"That's my plan. We'll make the outsiders think we're on this side of the river but we'll secretly swim across it. We might shake them off our trail. It will be much harder to track us on foot."

"Not if they have dogs."

Teo looked at Ana. He hadn't considered that possibility. "Let's hope they don't."

Gathering stones from the riverbank, Teo lashed them to the saddle and filled the saddlebags to mimic his weight for anyone reading their tracks. "That's about right for me," he said, then began to add weight for a second rider. Ana discerned what he was doing and gathered some small stones of her own. Teo hoisted a final rock and wedged it on top.

Ana cleared her throat. Teo glanced at her. She had her hands on her hips, eyebrows arched, an indignant expression on her face.

"What's the matter?"

Ana removed the big stone and dropped it to the forest floor. "Do you really think that one's necessary? I'm a hard-working farm girl, not a lazy urban princess!" Teo burst into laughter and nodded his head in agreement.

With a flask of lantern oil, Teo moistened the horse's tail thoroughly. He had just started to rummage through his rucksack when Ana handed him something else: a box of Vulkain sticks. Taking it from her hand, they exchanged smiles, as a memory passed between them.

Teo lit the match and ignited the horse's tail. With a slap on its rump, he sent it galloping into the forest. "That should throw them off," he said. "Now, Anastasia, take off your gown."

"Pardon me?"

"I said, 'Take off your gown.'" Teo gestured to the river. "We have to swim."

"I know what you meant, Captain. Even so, you shouldn't say those words to me in that commanding tone."

Before Teo could reply, Ana moved into the bushes. Teo tsked and shook his head as he removed his leather jerkin and linen shirt. He heard a splash, followed by a high-pitched gasp as Ana hit the cold water. After retrieving her shoes and gown, Teo set everything on a log, which he pushed ahead of him as he swam across the river.

Ana reached the western bank a moment before Teo and stood there shivering. She had stripped to her chemise, which clung to her as she emerged from the river. Teo averted his eyes. When he reached the far bank, he dug into the rucksack and removed a dry shift and the riding outfit Ana's mother had packed. He turned his back to her and held it out.

Ana walked closer to him. "A moment ago, you rudely ordered me to undress. Now you turn away with chivalry. You seem confused, Captain, as if you're unsure who to be."

"I know who to be. It's just that, well, you're nearly naked in that shift."

"You've never seen a woman's figure before?"

"Of course I have."

"Then is there something wrong with mine?"

"N-no—definitely not," Teo stammered, thrown off-balance by the bold question.

"So you're tempted to look, yet you don't. How come you're acting like such a gentleman now?"

Teo searched for a reply. "I guess I'm just trying to give you your privacy."

"You didn't seem to have such convictions when you were gawking at Princess Habiloho."

"What? When did I gawk at Habiloho?"

"At the Pon-Revel. You couldn't take your eyes off her at the bonfire."

"Is that what this is about? You thought I was ogling another girl when I had asked you to be my escort?"

Ana said nothing.

"Would it relieve you to know I was staring *past* her, trying to assess the danger of a certain monk of Astrebril lurking in the woods? And my assessment was a lot more accurate than yours—you got into his coach!"

There was a pause. Teo heard Ana's bare feet padding toward him on the sand. He felt the urge to turn around as she approached but held himself still. Ana stood close behind him. She put her wet hand on the bare skin of his shoulder. Teo inhaled sharply. His heart was beating rapidly, and he felt a strong emotion, though he couldn't say what it was.

"Captain, I'm sorry," Ana whispered. "I misjudged you. I do believe you're a gentleman. And that's what I want you to be." She snatched her outfit from his hand and disappeared into the forest.

✦ ✦ ✦

Rothgar crept through a thicket with two warriors. The Chiveisian fugitives weren't far away now. Obviously they were terrified, for they had galloped wildly through the forest for a long time, until their horse had to slow down. A whinny from the trees ahead told Rothgar he was close. Signaling to his two partners, he prepared to charge.

The men burst into the clearing with battle cries and drawn swords. The horse snorted and shied away as they looked around in bewilderment. Rothgar immediately understood what had happened. The horse's burden of stones and its burnt tail told him everything he needed to know. It was a clever trick, and that enraged him all the more. He snatched a rock from the horse's back and hurled it at one of his comrades. "You fool! The demons take you! Who made you a tracker?"

An hour later, the men stood along the riverbank again. "Here's the woman's shoe-print," the tracker said to his chieftain. "And here's the man's boot. It looks like they swam across. We missed it the first time."

"No, *you* missed it." Rothgar's tone was contemptuous.

"Two ships approach!" shouted the other warrior, peering upstream. "They're ours."

Rothgar hailed the cargo ships as they pulled close to the eastern bank. Each vessel held six horses amidships. "What news of the king?" Rothgar called.

The pilot of the lead ship shouted an answer: "He's badly burned and in great agony. He'll carry the scars the rest of his life. He wants the criminals to suffer even worse pain."

The two men on the bank glanced at each other, then looked to their chief. Rothgar nodded to them. They all knew of the king's sadistic cruelty. He would exact revenge of the most horrific kind. Whoever delivered that opportunity to the king would be well rewarded.

Rothgar ordered all the supplies and gear transferred to the lead ship, along with eight of the horses. "Proceed downstream to the Lost City," he instructed the pilot. "Hold the bridge there. Whatever you do, don't let the runaways get across! Kill them if you must, but take them alive if you can. The king will want to watch them be tortured."

The second ship, now lightened of its load, was ordered to patrol the river and seek the Chiveisian fugitives.

"You men will come with me!" Rothgar pointed to the three best warriors. "We'll take horses and hounds, and we'll run our quarry down. Blood will be spilled before the day is over!" The men erupted in cheers.

"Chief! Look here!" The tracker approached from the underbrush. "I think I've found something to help us!" He brought his discovery to Rothgar—a pair of women's stockings and garters.

A smile grew in the depths of Rothgar's shaggy beard. "Ha! She's a frisky one—mating in the bushes like a hind and leaving her stockings in the dirt!"

Rothgar carried the find to the hounds in their cages. He opened the doors and let out the excited dogs. When he held Ana's hosiery to their noses, they began to sniff the earth and bay in anticipation of the hunt.

"It'll be a merry chase, men!" Rothgar exclaimed. "I'll have that whore to myself tonight, and when I'm done, you can have what's left!" A malignant sneer darkened his face. "Believe me, it won't be much."

◆ ◆ ◆

Ana felt vulnerable as she changed out of her wet chemise into dry clothes. She was relieved to put on her outfit, not only for modesty's sake, but also because her new garments were much more practical. Over her dry chemise, Ana wore an ivory tunic decorated with gold trim. The tunic, with fitted sleeves and a belt that gathered it at the waist, fell to the middle of her thighs as a short skirt. She donned woolen leggings of dark brown, which would allow her to walk or sit astride a horse with greater ease. She also pulled on a pair of high boots—much better than the shoes she had selected when she had thought her day would involve only poetry and games. In her tunic and leggings, Ana looked more like a peasant traveler than a lady. But given her current circumstances, she didn't mind that look at all.

"I'm not used to seeing you like that," Teo said when she returned.

Ana smiled. "I'm quite versatile, you know. I wear gowns whenever I can and a tunic when I must."

"You make a lovely vision in both."

"A courteous word," Ana answered with a nod. "Thank you, Captain Teofil."

Hiking west through the forest, Teo and Ana crossed a narrow shipping canal on an accumulation of debris and fallen logs, then came to an overgrown road. Teo stooped to examine it. The highway, still visible underneath the layer of organic material, was made of the black stone the Ancients always used. Though now severely deteriorated, it was still flecked with the white paint that had marked its surface.

"The Ancients were excellent engineers," he said. "Their roads cut straight across the countryside instead of meandering around. We could travel quickly on this old roadbed."

"Which direction—north or south?"

"Chiveis is to the south, but so is our enemy's territory. We could try going that way, but we might run into searchers. Or we could strike north and establish some separation from them."

"Wherever you go, I'll follow."

Ana had no sooner uttered those words when she heard a distant sound that sent a wave of terror coursing through her body. Her mouth dropped open, and she saw Teo's eyes widen as the sickening realization dawned on him as well. *Hounds!* They were approaching from the south.

For a moment, the pair stood absolutely still, trying to comprehend this new threat. Then Teo uttered a single word: "Run!"

Driven by fear, Ana sprinted north on the road with Teo at her side. Her breath started coming in gasps, but she kept running, desperate to lose her pursuers. Yet part of her knew it was futile. The baying of the hounds grew nearer.

They rounded a bend in the road and were forced to halt. Thorns blocked the way ahead. The hounds were close now. Ana panted heavily, her hand on her chest, trying to regain her breath. She felt Teo grip her arm, and she knew what it meant. The pack of dogs had emerged onto the road behind them, followed by four men on horseback. Teo and Ana stood exposed. The men looked directly at them, pointing and shouting.

Even at a distance, Ana recognized one of the men: Rothgar! Her stomach lurched. She would rather die than fall back into his filthy hands. Putting her finger to her bosom, she felt the dagger clipped to her chemise. She had stolen it from one of her captors with a specific purpose in mind. Teofil had thought it was for self-defense, but she knew it was inadequate for that. In her heart Ana resolved—as a last resort—to use the knife for its true purpose. On herself.

◆　　◆　　◆

Teo saw everything with the clarity that comes only in the most desperate moments. He was alone in a remote forest with nowhere to run or hide.

It would be a battle to the death. And if he died, what would happen to Anastasia? *Torment, degradation, defilement.* He must not let that happen. He would not.

The four riders spurred their horses and charged, their weapons raised. Ana let out a little whimper. Teo knew she understood that her life hung in the balance. He held her by both shoulders and looked into her eyes.

"Steady," he said. "I'll protect you, Anastasia. Trust me."

He took her hand and pulled her into a thicket where the horsemen couldn't attack all at once. "Get up in this tree! Stay there until I come get you!"

"Give me your bow and quiver. They're no use to you now."

As Teo handed them up, he heard the sound of horses charging through the underbrush behind him. He wheeled around, and then the fury descended.

The lead horse bore down on Teo. It was Rothgar, hissing like a lynx, his spear held low. Teo stood his ground as long as he dared, gripping his ax in his left hand and the sword of Armand in his right. Every sense came alive. His muscles tensed. At the last possible moment, he made his move. With the flicking motion he had practiced many times, though never in the face of such a deadly threat, Teo flung a metal ball at his enemy. The missile took Rothgar in the teeth with a loud crack. He cried out and dropped his spear, which allowed Teo to stay in the horse's path. Teo sidestepped just enough to slash the beast's shoulder as it went hurtling by, sending it crashing to the earth in a deluge of blood. The horse squealed, and Rothgar was thrown hard against a tree trunk where he lay still. *One down, three to go.*

Teo weaved through the trees, sensing another rider barreling at him from behind. He whirled with his ax to parry the blow of the attacker's sword. The enormous impact rang out in the forest. Teo's arm quivered, but his training didn't fail him. In a fluid motion, he spun the ax in his hand to catch the sword blade in its crook, yanking hard as the horse swept by. He expected the move to pull the sword from his assailant's hand, but the man had a firm grip on the hilt, so he came tumbling out of the saddle instead. He collided with Teo, and the two went sprawling into the briars. With thorns clawing at them, they lunged at each other, weapons extended, bellowing in rage. Teo's sword was the longer, and that made the difference. It pierced the man's ribs even as Teo felt the hot burn of a blade slicing across his forearm. Though the wound Teo received was bloody, the one he had just dealt was mortal.

Hooves pounding! Move!

Teo rolled aside as a pale gray horse flew by, its rider's spear barely missing. As the horse's great bulk thundered past, its hoof clipped Teo's shin, sending agony up his leg. He ignored the pain and dodged behind a tree as another rider's arrow smacked into the bark near his face.

Sprinting toward the enemy archer, who was fumbling to nock a second arrow, Teo flicked two balls at him in rapid succession. One missed, but the other hit the man in the knuckles. He grimaced and dropped his bow. Teo roared like a wild animal. With a look of fear, the man swept his weapon from its scabbard, and then Teo was on him with ax and sword.

Blades clashed as the two men struggled to survive. The horse shied and pranced, not liking the close combat and the smell of blood. The mounted attacker leaned from the saddle to make a thrust. Teo parried with his sword, and his ax countered with a crushing blow. He sank its edge deep into his enemy's skull, pulling the dead man headfirst from the horse's back. Grabbing the reins, Teo leaped into the saddle and kicked his heels just in time to avoid the *whiz* of an arrow.

Teo turned his mount to confront the last man, who rode the pale gray horse. Even at a distance, Teo discerned he was a superb fighter. The rider had been forced to circle a briar patch after his earlier charge. Now, as he rounded the briars, a confident smile spread across his face. He threw aside his bow, lowered his spear, and charged at Teo with a wild yell. Goading his own horse, Teo surged forward. The lust for battle had taken hold of him now.

As the galloping horses neared, Teo realized with dismay that his sword would be no match for his enemy's long spear. Its steel tip would run him through long before his own blade could be brought into action. Hooves and heartbeats pounded as the warhorses raced toward each other. Both warriors were shouting at the tops of their lungs. The spearhead glinted in the sun as the rider aimed at Teo's chest. The man wore a triumphant grin. Death was certain.

Now!

Teo stood erect in the stirrups. With all his strength, he hurled his ax at his assailant, then dove from the saddle as the two horses collided.

The force of Teo's impact against the ground stunned him, but he dared not hesitate. Gasping, he spun around. The two horses were rolling in the dirt, striving to regain their legs. Beside them, the spearman lay on his back, the ax embedded in his chest. The man tried to sit up, grunted, and fell back. Teo walked over to him, breathing hard, his bloodied sword extended. The outsider met his eyes with a rancorous glare. Death claimed him then, sealing his livid stare for all eternity. Teo yanked his ax from the man's sternum.

Anastasia!

Teo ran through the forest to the place he had left her. He looked into the tree, scanning the branches. She wasn't there.

Something leaped from the bushes with a ferocious growl. Teo pivoted in time to parry the thrust of a sword, though the unexpected attack knocked the blade from his hand. The force of the man's lunge threw Teo against the tree trunk. It was Rothgar, snarling through his shattered teeth, his dark beard glistening with blood. His fiendish expression was demented and subhuman.

Rothgar swung his sword in a vicious overhead arc, but Teo grabbed the haft of his ax and held it in two hands to block the attack, struggling to keep the deadly blade away. Rothgar did not relent. He was a big man and unbelievably strong. His jagged red teeth gnashed in Teo's face as he vented his murderous desire. Teo could feel his strength ebbing as he pushed against his enemy's sword blade with the ax handle.

Rothgar's free hand reached for a hunting knife at his belt. Horrified, Teo watched Rothgar grasp the knife and draw it back. There was nothing he could do. He needed both hands to fend off the sword. Teo's stomach muscles tensed as he prepared to receive the killing stab.

Suddenly a bloodstained arrowhead emerged from Rothgar's chest. The fierce press of his sword against Teo's ax diminished. His eyes rolled back into his head, and his knife slipped from his fingers. He gagged, went limp, and fell to the ground.

Teo raised his eyes from Rothgar's corpse. A few paces away stood Anastasia, beautiful and resolute. A bow was in her hand.

"You picked the wrong woman, Rothgar," she said.

Teo met Ana's eyes. They approached each other slowly, breathing heavily and shaking. She clasped him around the neck, and his arms encircled her waist. They stood like that for a long time in the forest, leaning on each other for strength and comfort.

"You know, Anastasia," Teo said at last, his hands resting on the small of her back, "this is the second time you've saved my life."

She drew back from the embrace to look up at Teo. "Let's hope there won't be need of a third."

◆   ◆   ◆

Ana pushed away the covers of her bedroll and adjusted the folded cloak that served as her pillow. The night was warmer than usual, but the copper leaves of the beech trees overhead told her it was certainly autumn.

Beyond the trees, brilliant pinpoints of light speckled the night sky. Chiveisian folklore said the stars were gods. Were they? Ana longed to know the answer, but who could tell her of such things? A stanza from her poem came to her mind: *I wait, alone, with longing heart / My soul begins to pine / For one who reigns o'er all to give / A prophecy divine!* Ana sighed and folded her hands across her stomach as she gazed into the mute cosmos.

After the battle, she had tended the cut on Teofil's arm with yarrow root for the bleeding and wild garlic to prevent infection. She had wanted to rest there, but the captain insisted on getting away quickly in case more searchers were in the vicinity. After gathering the horses, he put the injured one out of its misery, then fed the others oats from the outsiders' supplies. As for the hounds milling around without any masters to lead them, they could fend for themselves.

The excellent horses had confirmed Teofil's strategy of heading north on the ancient road. Using one as a packhorse and two as mounts, he decided to move out of the outsiders' lands once and for all. Secretly, Ana had been reluctant to go north. It seemed they kept moving away from Chiveis instead of closer, as if some invisible hand were propelling them in the wrong direction. But Teofil explained that a map in Rothgar's tent had indicated the presence of a bridge to the north at a spot marked as a "lost city." The captain preferred to sneak across the bridge rather than risk a difficult river crossing with three encumbered horses. Besides, an immediate crossover would have put them back in enemy territory. Teofil said it was better to press hard to the north, cross the river at the bridge, and make a wide circle around the outsiders' lands.

They had ridden until dusk, covering perhaps thirty leagues. After setting up camp in the beech grove, Ana cooked a stew of dried venison and leeks while Teofil cared for the horses. A skin of good ale had been recovered from the outsiders' belongings, and the captain was happy to wash down his meal with a drink. Ana didn't normally enjoy the taste of ale, but after the day's taxing events, she was willing to make an exception. Now she felt sleepy, and her head was a little light.

The campfire burned low. From her bedroll, Ana watched its embers fade, then brighten again as the night breezes chanced to blow over them. Teofil slept on the other side of the fire, his body turned away from her. A *remarkable man*, she thought as she stared at his back. Today he had confronted four mortal enemies and defeated them all. His strength shielded her; in fact, it had saved her life. He was a warrior, a man at home in the world of brave and heroic deeds.

"I will protect you, Anastasia," he had said. "Trust me."

Ana believed if she could trust anyone in the world to win a physical contest, it was the man who slept across from her. *But what of the other battles a man must face?* In those he was still unproven.

Ana's mind drifted from one thought to another as the warm evening and the rustling trees lulled her to sleep. She thought of her parents back in Chiveis—her wise father and her tender, joyful mother. How sad they must be, not knowing what had become of her! She longed for home—to feel their embrace, to tell them she was alive and well. Tears came to Ana's eyes, and her lower lip quivered.

Fearful thoughts invaded her mind. The faces of the evil men who had threatened her seemed to threaten her still. She thought of disgusting Rothgar, with his cruel streak, his offensive smell, his leering grin. She had killed him, yet revenge brought her no joy. She had only done what was needed. Even so, the sight of his dead body on the ground, with an arrow protruding from his chest, filled her with horror. Ana began to cry in earnest, the tears running down her cheeks, her shoulders trembling.

Teofil rolled over and sat up on one elbow. Ana didn't want to look at him, so she wiped her tears with her hands and sniffed.

"Can I do anything?" His tone was soft.

"N-no. I don't think so." Ana shuddered in the way that often happens after tears. "I just feel so—*oppressed*. There's been too much evil directed at me. I can't bear it all."

Teofil didn't answer right away. "You're right," he said finally. "There are many evildoers in the world. But, Anastasia, you aren't alone. You have a friend to bear the evil with you."

Ana turned her head then, looking directly at Teo. He had a gentle expression. "Thank you, Teofil," she said with genuine gratitude. "I'm glad for that because I'm feeling very lonely tonight."

"Do you want me to come over beside you? Sometimes the presence of another is a comfort."

Ana found herself longing to say yes, for she knew she would indeed be comforted by his nearness. Yet she was afraid to accept the invitation, though she couldn't quite say why. Perhaps it would be an acknowledgment of something she wasn't prepared to accept. Whatever the reason, she declined the offer. Teofil nodded and settled back into his bedroll. At last Ana fell asleep under the wheeling stars. No nightmares disturbed her dreams that night.

◆　◆　◆

The next morning they were on the road at dawn. Teo led the way, with Ana riding behind him as they passed through dense forests and ruined villages of the Ancients. Around noon, Ana noticed that the ruins had become more numerous.

"I think we're approaching a city," she remarked.

"The distance is about right to be reaching the lost city I saw on the map."

"Then let's find that bridge and get across, so we can go home."

As they came over a small rise, Teo reined in his horse so sharply that Ana's mount almost collided with it. "We'll find that bridge soon," he said. "But I think you may want to take a brief detour. Look."

Ana followed Teo's finger, and what she saw rising before her through the trees took her breath away. It was a building—a building whose size and grandeur were like nothing she had ever seen. The structure soared from the forest-encrusted city like an artificial mountain, impervious to the ravages of wind and rain and the many passing years. Its color was reddish brown, and it rose in multiple stories until finally a single spire ascended from its roof to unimaginable heights. The building was a work of spectacular beauty. It spoke to Ana's soul across the centuries in a language of the heart that transcended time and place.

Teo tilted his head. "What do you think it is?"

"It can only be one thing," Ana murmured. "A temple. The home of a mighty god."

"Let's check it out." Teo prodded his horse forward. In her excitement, Ana slipped ahead of him and wound her way down the rise toward the great edifice.

They were truly in a lost city now, one whose tenacious buildings had tried to resist nature's attempts to reclaim them. Nevertheless, the handiwork of man had lost that epic battle. Trees grew in the streets, shrubs sprouted from the roofs, vines draped the signs and poles. An eerie silence clung to the place, denying the reality of the bustle that must have occurred here long ago. Ana thought the buildings' empty windows stared at the city like great, sad eyes grieving for the loss of a life that once was. Yet one place remained alive: the magnificent temple had refused to succumb to a lonely death.

Teo caught up with Ana as she crossed a stream on a bridge with pointed towers. Apparently the temple sat on an island in the midst of the city. As they got closer, the surrounding buildings of crumbling plaster and black timbers obscured their view of the temple. But when they rounded a corner, Ana let out a gasp. They had arrived at the temple's base, and it was even more splendid than she could have imagined.

Though weathered, every surface was covered with intricate carvings. The stonework was as light and airy as lace. Human figures and heavenly beings vied for their places on the sandstone walls. High above her head, Ana marveled at the round, rose-like window that anchored the temple's main facade. Pointed arches and miniature spires soared everywhere, drawing the eye—and the soul—into the heavens.

Three magnificent doorways gave entrance to the temple, each recessed into portals decorated with statuary and reliefs. In the center portal, a queen with a timeworn crown held an infant at her shoulder. Ana longed to know who all these stern and saintly people were. Their mythic stories must have formed a grand saga. Sadly, she realized it was a story whose contours she could never know.

Teo nudged his horse next to Ana. She sat with her neck arched as she gazed upward, trying to comprehend the wondrous scene. Bringing her eyes back to earth, she looked at Teo. "What kind of god deserves worship like this?" she breathed.

"I don't know," Teo answered, dismounting. "Let's go inside and find out."

CHAPTER

7

The temple had been sealed for centuries, locking its treasures inside. When it was opened, what mysteries would be discovered? While Teo picketed the horses nearby, Ana stood at the temple's base and gazed up at its unfathomable heights. A lingering sense of trepidation disturbed her—not fear of mortal danger, but fear her world was about to change forever. *Perhaps that's a good thing*, she reasoned.

"Ready?" Teofil held up his ax.

"Not yet."

Ana knelt on the overgrown brick plaza before the temple's entrance. She lifted her eyes to the sky and held out her hands, palms upward, in the Chiveisian posture of prayer. "God of the Ancients! We beseech thee to do us no harm for entering thy holy place. We would learn of thy wisdom. Let it be so."

Teo shifted his feet and sighed—somewhat cynically, Ana thought.

"You aren't religious, Captain?"

"I do what's required. Or at least I did. I've recently become an atheist."

Ana was disappointed by Teo's nonchalant attitude. "Don't you want to know the god whose temple is so beautiful?" Her tone sounded more confrontational than she had intended.

"Actually, I'm just as anxious as you to get inside the building, but for different reasons. You seek personal devotion, Anastasia, and I find that very sweet." Teo's expression was honest. "But as for me, I want to know *about* religion. I've come to believe it's something a scholar should seek."

"So scholars are religious seekers?"

"Not normally. We're taught to be practical. But I've decided to seek religious knowledge."

"Why? Will it make you more virtuous?"

"It's not really about *my* virtue—I'm plenty virtuous already. The scholar doesn't need to seek wisdom for his own use, but for the good of his fellow man. If I can learn something about the philosophies of the Ancients, perhaps I can help the people of Chiveis. The outsiders aren't the only sinners in the world. We still have plenty in our kingdom too. If possible, I'd like to help them live an improved moral life."

"And what about you? Don't you need any spiritual wisdom? I mean for yourself, not just for your fellow man."

Teo seemed surprised by the question. He ran his hand through his dark hair, searching the distance for an answer. A cocky grin came to his face. He squeezed his right arm with his left hand. "Here's my religion," he said.

Ana's face fell. Different responses flitted through her mind, but she uttered none of them. Her mother had often said to her, "Ana, my love, a woman has to be willing to shake up a man's thinking. Sometimes men just don't see things the way they really are." Ana was tempted to grab this particular man by his jerkin and shake up his thinking, but her intuition told her that now wasn't the right time. He wasn't ready to hear. She lifted her eyes to Teofil's face—handsome, brassy, utterly sure of himself.

"Perhaps you could apply your religion to the door's lock," she said.

The captain was happy to oblige. The temple's middle door was made of bronze, but the adjacent ones were constructed of wood weakened by age. Even so, Teofil had to hack the lock several times with his ax. Shards of wood flew with each stroke until the latch finally loosened and the door could be pushed open, groaning on its ancient hinges. Teo stepped back from the entrance. "I'll give the spiritual seeker the honor of first entry," he said.

For a moment, Ana wondered if Teofil was mocking her, but a glance at his face told her he wasn't. Whatever else one might say about him, he wasn't an unkind man.

Ana peeked inside. A musty coolness blew from the temple's interior.

She slipped through the crack, and as she did, her breath caught, and her heart melted. She exhaled at the astonishing sight that met her eyes. "Oh, Teofil, come see! Come see this wonder and share it with me!"

The temple was a vast hall lined with two rows of columns, whose tops formed arches that supported the distant ceiling. The columns were like timeless oak trees carved from stone, still strong after so many years. Yet it wasn't the stonework that amazed Ana most—it was the windows. The iridescent glass was ablaze with color as the afternoon sun glowed through, splintering its light into a heavenly rainbow on earth. Many of the panes were broken, but that only heightened the surreal effect as dusty sunbeams pierced the windows and played upon the floor. Where the glass was intact, Ana was confronted by a panoply of mythic scenes whose meaning she knew not, but whose beauty she fully comprehended. In this place the sky met the earth; the sublime had descended to become physically manifest.

Teo came to Ana's side. "Impressive. The Ancients really knew how to build."

"They must have had a good reason to invest so much in a building like this. Do you think we can discover the meaning of this place?"

Teo put his hand on Ana's back and leaned close to her, pointing toward the far wall of the temple. "Look!" he said. "Do you see that cross? I know that emblem—it's a sacred sign of the Ancients! Let's go see if we can figure it out."

Teo hurried toward the rear of the building, but Ana trailed more slowly, not wanting to miss any aspect of the temple's beauty. She noted how the sun's rays interplayed with the shadows and how the brilliant hues of the windows spangled the floor with color. Everything was still and quiet in the cavernous space. In the awful hush, her footfalls seemed to echo off the floor like blasphemies.

At the far end of the hall, wide steps led to a raised platform. Ana joined Teo as he examined the gilded murals on the rear wall. The large colored window here was broken, and the ceiling had a few holes in it, so there was enough light to see the lofty paintings.

"Look up there," Teo said, pointing. "Notice the three rows of people wearing long robes. They have circles of light around their heads. That means they're holy men. And then, on the top row, there's the cross. I can't see any higher than that."

"What does the cross mean?"

Teo looked at Ana and shrugged. "I don't know yet. It's a matter for scholarly investigation."

"Maybe someday I'll understand," she said softly.

"Okay, now come over here. Look at these two lower paintings. See how they're set into niches, side by side? Obviously they're important. What do you see as their common theme?"

"Are you asking my opinion or teaching me yours, Professor?"

Teo chuckled. "Never be too proud to learn, Anastasia. I have some expertise in matters like this. Study the two pictures. What are they about?"

Ana examined the faded frescoes. Although they were situated above her head, they were low enough to be seen in detail. In the depiction on the left, two men stood on either side of a table marked with a six-pointed star. One man was primitively dressed in rough cloth, with his legs exposed, while the other man wore a rich, flowing garment. The first man held up a lamb, and the second offered a loaf in his outstretched arms. A heavenly hand reached down to accept both gifts.

Ana walked to the picture on the right. In this one, a bearded man stood against the backdrop of a jagged mountain. He rested one hand on the head of a boy, whose arms were bound behind his back. The man's other hand held an upraised knife, but a divine hand grasped the knife from above, preventing it from delivering the death blow. At the man's feet was a ram.

"Sacrificial offering," Ana murmured. "That's the common theme. The god of the Ancients was a god of sacrifice."

"Well done!" Teo laughed with teacher's delight in a student's learning.

"I see you're a man of brains as well as brawn, Captain. But what about in here?" Ana poked him in the chest.

"That's where I keep all my secrets," Teo answered with a rakish grin. "No one's allowed in there."

Ana glanced over Teo's shoulder at the fresco on the left. Something had caught her attention. "Teofil, do you see anything etched in that painting?"

He turned around to inspect it. "No. Why? What do you see?"

"There—on the man's sacrificial loaf."

Teo walked closer. "You're right. There is something. What do you suppose it is?"

"It's an eye. Someone has carved an eye on the bread."

Teo rubbed the stubble on his chin. "Hmm. Indeed. In our scholarly sources, we read of 'the eye' on numerous occasions. It's an important symbol in the lore of many historic sects. The eye's semiotic range can cover a wide array of referents. For example, it can signify *illumination*, which comes from an outside source. Or it can be decoded as *insight*, which might be—"

Ana interrupted Teo's learned discourse. "I think it just means 'look here.'"

Teo glanced at Ana with an annoyed expression. She bit her lip, gesturing with an upward nod of her head. "How about if you climb up and take a look?"

"In the name of academic research, I will." Teo went to the base of the wall and shimmied up a column, balancing uneasily on its capital next to the artwork.

"Don't break your neck in the name of academic research," Ana warned. Teo rolled his eyes and threw her a look of pretended disdain, then leaned close to the carving.

"Well, it certainly is an eye," Teo called down after a few moments. "But I don't see much else."

"Look around. There must be some hidden meaning to this."

"There's nothing."

"Perhaps, since the carving is on the man's offering, you should inspect the other one. See if there's anything on the lamb."

Teo leaned on one leg, counterbalancing his weight with his other leg extended behind him. He gripped an outcrop with one hand, his nose to the wall.

"See anything?"

"Yes, there's something here."

"Really?" Ana was excited. "What is it?"

Before Teo could answer, he lost his balance and began to wobble on his perch, his hands waving madly. Ana shrieked as Teo dropped from the column to the floor. He landed lightly on his feet, wearing a broad grin. Ana let out a sigh of relief. "Very funny! How would I get home if something happened to you?"

"Don't worry, I'll get you home eventually. But first we have to find the *trésor*."

"What's a *trésor*?"

"The word I found carved on the lamb. It was written very small. You'd have to climb up there to see it. You were right—the eye was a signal to look closer."

"What does it mean?"

"It's a word in the Fluid Tongue of the Ancients. In our language it means *treasure*."

"Treasure! Maybe there's treasure buried around here somewhere!"

"Perhaps, but where? This is a pretty big place."

Ana scanned the spacious hall. "If I were an Ancient, where would I bury my treasure?"

"There's no way we'll find it. The building is far too big. We'd still be searching for it next summer! I know you don't want that."

"Maybe there's another clue in the painting?"

"No, I examined it thoroughly. There's nothing more."

"Then where else might you look, Professor?"

Teo shrugged. Ana pointed over his shoulder at the fresco on the right. "You haven't looked at that one yet."

"Yeah, you're right. Not a bad idea."

Teo scaled a different column until he was balanced in front of the bearded man with the upraised knife. He inspected the painting for a long time. Finally he waved to Ana and pointed to the boy in the picture. "The other carvings were etched onto the sacrifices—the bread and the lamb. So I would expect to find something on the boy being sacrificed here. However, I've looked at it closely, and there's nothing."

"I don't think the boy is the sacrifice."

"What? Clearly he is. He's bound. The man's about to slit his neck."

"No, look again, Captain. The god is stopping him. See his hand from heaven? There's another sacrifice in the scene."

Teo was silent. Nodding his head, he squatted on the column's capital and studied the ram at the man's feet. Satisfied, he jumped to the floor. Ana approached him expectantly.

"What did you find?"

"I hope you don't mind heights," Teo said. "We need to get to the roof."

✦ ✦ ✦

Teo was breathing hard as he climbed one step after another. It had taken some time to locate the spiral staircase, but eventually he found the entrance on the temple's exterior. Now he regretted the weight of the rope looped over his shoulders, which he had retrieved from his gear because of his prior experience on a rickety staircase of the Ancients. Certainly there was nothing rickety about this one. It was made of solid stone, built to last the ages.

"I think we're getting close!" he yelled over his shoulder. Ana was several stories below him because she kept stopping at every window to admire the view, making gushy noises. Teo, on the other hand, wanted to press on to the goal.

He reached a balcony, thinking he had made it to the top. But more stairs awaited at the far end, so he kept plodding upward.

At last he reached a room that housed two giant wooden wheels. He leaned against the wall to catch his breath. Before long, Ana came trudging up the final steps. Her cheeks were flushed pink. The effect was rather nice.

"What—are those—big wheels?" she asked between breathy gasps.

"I'm not sure. They look like waterwheels at a mill."

Ana reflected for a moment, catching her wind. "Maybe the Ancients would grind grain for sacrifices on the rooftop?"

"Perhaps. Whatever it was, something big and heavy used to turn up here. Let's go outside."

The sun was lowering in the sky when Teo and Ana emerged onto the roof. They found themselves on a three-sectioned platform directly above the three great entrances on the ground below. One section was occupied by the temple's spire, which reached into the sky. The opposite section contained no spire, only a squat building that served as the exit of the spiral staircase they had just ascended. The middle section held the flat viewing deck where they now stood. The entire platform capped an ornate tower, so it was much higher than the copper roof of the great hall, which they could see below them. The lofty height afforded expansive views of the lost city, with its red rooftops peeking from the trees that had engulfed the buildings.

"How high do you think we are?" Ana asked.

"I counted 330 steps."

Teo and Ana walked to the edge of the roof. "Even if we don't find any treasure," she said, leaning on the railing, "just being up here is enough for me." She lifted her chin to the breeze with her eyes closed, inhaling deeply through her nose, letting the moment take her away.

Teo looked sideways at the woman standing next to him. The wind toyed with her honey-colored hair, and the afternoon sunshine gave it an amber tint. Ana's high cheekbones were still flushed, and her dark lashes seemed impossibly long as they brushed her cheeks. As for her lips—well, they were the kind of lips to make a man look twice. Teo knew Anastasia was savoring the temple's exquisite beauty, but to him, the real work of beauty was an arm's length away.

Cut it out, Teo, warned a voice in his head. *Keep your mind on the mission: return the girl to her parents.*

"Shall we search for the treasure?" he asked.

Ana awoke from her reverie. "Yes! What exactly did you see carved into that painting?"

"No doubt you've noticed this temple is lopsided?"

"You mean how there's a spire on only one side?"

"Right. Up here on this platform I'd expect twin spires. There should be one over there." Teo pointed to the southern section of the roof.

"But there's not," Ana agreed. "Just on the north. So what did the carving show?"

"It was simply a box with a point on it, like this." Teo stooped and arranged four twigs in a rectangle standing on its short side. On top of it—on the left side only—he laid two twigs to form a point.

"A diagram of the temple from the front," Ana said, kneeling beside Teo. "We're standing here on top. Anything else?"

"Yes. There was an X where the point rises from the box." He gestured at his twigs. "In other words, at the base of the spire, where it meets this roof!"

Ana looked at Teo with her eyebrows arched and her mouth open. She jumped up and ran to the spire, touching the stone with her hand. Teo joined her, and they wandered along its base, looking for anything unusual.

"Any luck?" Teo called.

"No, nothing. Wait! Look at this!"

Teo came and peered over Ana's shoulder as she knelt inside a niche in the spire. On the floor, markings had been carved into the flagstone. "A cross!" Teo exclaimed. "And letters!"

Ana turned her head and looked up at Teo. "What does it say?"

"It doesn't make sense to me. It says, 'J.D. MMXLV.'"

"I don't know what that means, but let's lift this stone!" Ana began to clear the dirt from its edge.

"Let me do it." Ana moved aside as Teo dug around the stone with his knife. Soon he was able to slip the blade underneath to pry it up.

"You found the treasure, Anastasia. You look."

Ana bent to the hole and squinted into the darkness. "I see something!" As she reached for it, Teo realized even his atheistic heart was beating more rapidly than usual. He told himself it was nothing more than the scholar's joy of discovery.

Ana lifted a strongbox from the hole. A broad smile lit her face, and she could barely contain her girlish enthusiasm. "What do you think it is?" she asked, clapping her hands together.

"Let's find out." Teo gave the lock a whack with his ax and lifted the lid. Inside, he found a package wrapped in cloth and string. Judging from the decay of the cloth, the package was very, very old.

"Open it!"

Teo unfolded the cloth to find a strange bag inside. It was clear like glass, yet flexible like fabric. Along one edge was a seal. He had never seen anything like it.

"I could think of a lot of uses for a bag like that," Ana remarked.

Teo broke the seal on the bag and removed a rectangular, paper-wrapped object. As he carefully opened the folded paper, Ana recognized what it was. "A book!"

The volume was bound in fine leather, its pages gilt along their edges. The first two-thirds of the book had survived the years well. The pages were in good condition despite the passage of time. However, the final third had gotten wet and moldy at some point, and the thin pages were destroyed.

As Teo flipped the book over, he heard Ana's sharp intake of breath when she saw what was on the cover. There was a cross and two words Teo had seen before: *Écriture Sacrée*. "Sacred Writing," he translated aloud. He felt a thrill rush though his body. "Do you realize what this is, Anastasia?"

"Yes! It's the holy book of the Ancients' high god!"

"It's the scholarly discovery of a lifetime! I'll be the envy of every professor in Lekovil!"

From Ana's crestfallen expression, Teo guessed she didn't care too much about groundbreaking scholarship. "What's that paper sticking out?" she asked.

Teo extracted a loose sheet from between the pages. It was written in the Fluid Tongue. Time had faded the ink so that all but the last few lines were illegible. He squinted at the faint handwriting and slowly translated for Ana:

> . . . the Word of Dieu cannot die. I have hidden this Book in the church as a treasure for you. Only if you are led by Dieu himself could you have found it. O finder, may the Eternal One bless you. I give you a precious gift—the Sacred Scripture. Know this: the truth will set you free.
>
> My name is Jacques Dalsace. Remember me! By the grace of Dieu, I have shared with you the gift of rebirth. Soli Deo Gloria. Amen.

Teo looked up from the paper. "That's all it says."

"Teofil, did you hear that? The letter gives us the god's name! It names the high god of the Ancients! He's called—how did you say it? Die . . . dei . . ."

"I think it would be pronounced 'Deu' in our speech."

"Deu." Ana practiced the sound. "Deu. I like it. I want to know more of him."

Teo slapped his forehead. "No—you can't!"

"What? Why not?"

Teo gripped Ana by the shoulders, and she seemed taken aback by his change in tone. Her desire to know more about Deu had jogged Teo's memory, reminding him of his conversation with the monk Lewth, who had been terrified at the prospect of being connected with this religion.

"I'm sorry. I didn't mean to startle you. But in all the excitement I forgot: this faith is prohibited in Chiveis! The Astrebrilian monks curse the god of the cross in their chants, but no one else can know about him. The High Priestess hates him. She forbids his name to become known."

"No, that can't be! I want to know everything about this god. I have to learn more!"

"Anastasia, listen to me. You *cannot* speak of this. Do you want the High Priestess coming after you?" Ana shuddered. "Then you have to keep this book a secret! Here's what I can do—I'll make you a private translation of it as soon as we get back. Well, actually, I might not get to that project right away because—" He paused, smiling ruefully and shaking his head.

"Because what?"

"Because I'm going to be in a little trouble with the Warlord when I go home. I'm not exactly supposed to be on this mission. It's what we might call *unauthorized*."

"Yet very much appreciated, Captain Teofil," Ana said. "Even more so now that I know it comes at a cost to you."

"To be honest, I never considered anything else. There was no question but that I'd come for you, Anastasia. The point is, the Warlord won't be pleased when I return. I imagine he's going to assign me to a nasty winter post as punishment. Probably some cold hut on the frontier, keeping watch on the passes until the spring thaw. So I won't be able to do any translation work right away. But when I get back to Lekovil, I promise to turn my attention to the book. Then you can have your words of spiritual comfort, and I can satisfy my scholar's curiosity."

"Okay, Teofil, I can live with that. I won't say a word to anyone about the Sacred Writing. But I have your promise: you'll eventually give me the holy words of Deu."

"Yes, yes, I promise. I'll give you what you want. Hail to the great Deu and all that." Teo waved his hands. Ana frowned at his inept joke.

From far below, the faint sound of a horse's nicker reached Teo's ears. A sinking feeling began to gather in his gut. *That's the sound a horse makes when it senses a threat.*

Teo crept to the edge of the roof and looked over. When he turned back toward Ana, his expression must have been grim, for the color drained from her face, and she rushed to his side.

"What is it? What did you see?" Ana's fear was palpable.

"Outsiders. They've found us again."

◆　◆　◆

Ana had started down the spiral staircase when she heard the echoes of rough voices reverberating up the steps. She turned toward Teo, and he motioned her back to the roof. Ramming the door shut with his shoulder, he braced it with a piece of steel railing that would take some work to dislodge.

"Now what?" Ana felt the butterflies flitting in her stomach as panic began to rise. "There's no other way down!"

"There is another way."

Ana scanned Teo's face, searching for the answer. When he pulled the coil of rope from his shoulder, her stomach jumped, and her butterflies turned into outright nausea.

"No! I can't do that. I'm terrified of heights!"

Teo came to her, putting his hands on her cheeks, forcing her to meet his eyes. "You *can* do it. I'll help you. It's the only way."

She trembled as she watched Teo tie the rope to the railing and drop it over the back of the tower platform. He turned to her, beckoning with his hand.

"I can't!"

"You must! There's no time!"

She approached the railing and peeked over. The rope's end dangled in the breeze, very far above the green copper roof of the temple's great hall.

"It's not long enough!"

"I know. I had to, uh, use some before."

"It's too far to drop!"

"We'll have to improvise. Climb onto my back, and hold on tight."

Ana backed away, waving her hands. Her breath was coming in shallow pants. Behind her, the sound of angry men rattling the door forced her decision. Leaping onto Teo's back, she clasped his chest in the tightest bear hug she could manage. She wrapped her legs around him and intertwined her feet.

"I trust you," she said, closing her eyes. And then they went over the wall.

The helpless feeling of swaying in midair on the thin rope made Ana feel like she was about to faint. Her forehead was sweating profusely, and not just from exertion. She opened an eye and peeked over her shoulder. *It's so far down! Help me!* Her heart pounded in her chest.

As they neared the end of the rope, the wind picked up, and a pendulum effect began to swing them back and forth in increasing arcs. Ana's stomach swam, and she felt she was about to vomit.

They lurched to an abrupt stop. Ana shrieked. Teofil had grabbed an indentation in the wall to arrest their swaying motion.

She heard men shouting from above. Something whizzed past her ear and clanged off the copper roof below. *They're shooting at us!*

"We're at the end of the rope! Jump!"

"It's too far! I can't!"

"You can make it!"

"I can't!" Another arrow flew past.

"Climb down my body and hang from my feet! Augh!" Teo grunted as blood spattered onto Ana's cheek.

"What is it?" she cried.

"Nothing! Climb down!"

Ana slid down Teo's torso, squeezing his legs in her arms. Finally she hung from his ankles, her arms extended. She saw empty space beneath her feet.

"Drop!"

With the loudest squeal she had ever uttered, she did.

Ana hit the copper roof to the left of its central ridge, tumbling down its pitched surface until she came to rest at a parapet along its eave. She rolled over to look up at Teo. She couldn't believe what she saw.

The captain had climbed hand over hand partway up the rope. Even at this distance, she noticed the blood glistening on his head. She watched, horrified, as he pulled his hunting knife from his boot and put it to the rope. *No! Not from there! It's too high!* He slit the rope. She gasped.

It must have been only a few seconds, but to Ana it seemed Teo fell through the air for an age. She saw his lean body plummeting down, down, down until he smashed into the roof on the far side of the central ridge and she could no longer see him.

Some of the outsiders had descended from the tower platform, and now they emerged on a much lower balcony not far from Ana's position on the roof of the great hall. With a yelp she leaped to her feet and ran along the eave. Arrows flew past her, but she ignored them and kept running until she reached the opposite end of the building. *Now what?*

A scrambling sound made her turn her head. Teofil slid down the roof's steep pitch and hobbled to her side. His thick hair was matted with blood.

"You're hurt!"

"Got grazed by an arrow and twisted my ankle. I'll shake it off. Come on! We're not out of this yet! Over the side!"

"Where?" Ana felt sick at the thought of more precarious dangling.

"See those arches? You're going to slide down that one!"

Like the wings of a bird, the arches flew from the temple's sides as they buttressed the weight of its stone ceiling. Teo gripped Ana's wrist and lowered her over the parapet, while her free hand and her feet sought traction on the crumbling wall. She slipped, dropped a short way, and smacked her rear end on a bumpy protuberance. Easing her body over it, she straddled the flying buttress. The bump was a rainspout shaped like a wild boar, and it gaped at her in mute disdain as she slid away from it on her belly. At the end of the smooth, downward arc, she scrambled onto a much lower green roof.

Teo slid down the buttress after Ana and joined her on the roof, which covered one of the side aisles of the temple. Like the central roof above, this one also had a parapet along its eave. But when Ana looked over it, she realized that while she was now lower than before, she was still very far from the ground.

"I hope you have another one of your plans, Captain."

He limped over to her and held up his remnant of rope. "Why do you think I climbed back up to cut this?" he asked.

Teo was about to tie it to the parapet for a final descent when an arrow pierced the air nearby. The outsiders were firing from a window in the spiral staircase. Teo shielded Ana's body with his and whisked her away from the roof's edge. Now they were out of the enemy's line of sight, but they were pressed against a window of the great hall with no way to get down.

"We can't go over the eave with the outsiders shooting at us," Ana said.

"No, but we can go inside!" Teo cocked his good leg.

"Wait! That artwork is probably a thousand years old! Surely you're not going to—"

Teo's boot burst through the window in a multicolored explosion of glass. Ana groaned as he kicked out the leaden framework in the stone opening. After he peered inside, he tied off the rope and pitched its end through the hole.

Ana looked doubtful. "That piece of rope isn't long enough to reach the ground from here."

"Not even close. But when you get inside, you can grab the chandelier chain and slide to the floor. You go first."

"Why me?"

"You'll see."

It wasn't easy, but Ana made it through the ruined window into the temple's dark interior. The rope came to an end, but she easily reached the chandelier chain that hung at the crest of a pointed arch, then slid down its length. After reaching the chandelier's iron rim, she dropped to the floor. Nothing had ever felt better than the strong, level surface of mother earth beneath her feet.

Teo clambered through the window and slid down the rope, then onto the chandelier chain. He looked up. "Uh-oh. Stand back." Ana stepped away.

Teo was still on the chain when it broke loose and sent him crashing to the floor. Ana ran to his side as he held his ankle, grimacing. She worked the joint with her hands to see if it was broken.

"I thought that chain might break under my weight," he said. "Good thing you're just a hard-working farm girl." Ana glanced up from his ankle with a smile, and he grinned back at her. "I'm fine. Let's get out of here."

In the waning evening light, Teo and Ana scurried toward their horses. Teo removed the Sacred Writing from underneath his jerkin and stowed it in the saddlebag on the packhorse.

Before he left the temple, he paused to prop a tree branch against the door to the spiral staircase, wedging it tight against an upturned stone. "I hope they brought their rations," he said, chuckling. "They're going to be inside for a while."

Back in the saddle, Teo and Ana meandered east through the abandoned streets. Soon they came to the riverfront, pausing under some trees to assess the situation.

A rusty steel bridge crossed the water—and what a strange bridge it was. Ana marveled at the two giant poles that supported the span at either end by means of cables fanning from their tops. The bridge was divided into a pair of narrow walkways with a wide gap between them. One of the walkways had sagged over time and had become impassable, but the other looked as if it could still be traversed. Although Ana thrilled at the idea of crossing the river and finally turning toward home, she was disheartened to see the outsiders' ship moored across the river, with warriors milling around on the near bank.

"Now what? They've set up their camp on this side to keep us from getting across."

"That's not our only problem. Look there, across the river, where that grass is. They've brought horses in the ship. Even if we make it across the bridge, they'll be able to track us on horseback. It's really the horses that put us in a bind."

They remained quiet for a moment, considering the matter. Ana looked over at Teo. "I think I know what you're going to say."

He smiled mischievously. "I have a plan," he said with a wink.

Hiding behind some buildings, they approached the outsiders' camp. Teo explained his plan, and Ana nodded in agreement. He handed her his bow and quiver.

"Ready?"

"Let's do it."

Kicking his heels, Teo leaped forward on his horse. Ana galloped behind him with their packhorse on a line. They charged into the outsiders' camp, rousing startled shouts and curses. As they stormed through the crowd of angry men, Teo leaned from the saddle and snatched a cask that sat on a crate next to several lanterns.

Ana hit the bridge first and raced across. At the far end, she turned in her saddle and watched Teo stop in the middle of the span. He smashed the cask with his ax and poured lantern oil across the width of the walkway. Lighting a Vulkain stick, he set the pool ablaze. Orange flames illuminated the dusk.

Teo reached the end of the span and sped past Ana with the words, "Hold the bridge!" He scattered the horses grazing on the riverbank as he dismounted and waded into the shallows. With a hard stroke from his ax, he severed the mooring rope on the ship, then shoved it into deeper water and disappeared over its gunwale.

Ana knew the make of knarrs like that one: they were clinker-built vessels whose strakes were sealed with tar or moss. The design let in a lot of water, requiring frequent bailing. It wouldn't be difficult to make a hole big enough to sink such a ship—and down to the bottom would go all the horse tack the outsiders had brought.

A furious warrior came charging from the flames on the bridge, batting his beard where it had caught fire. With a demonic scream, he sprinted down the walkway toward Ana's waiting horse, brandishing his sword. She waited for him to get close, then calmly put an arrow through his chest.

In the middle of the dark river, the ship was gurgling to its final resting place. Teo waded ashore and mounted his horse. He galloped to Ana as she put a second warrior on the ground with a well-placed shot.

"The outsiders might be decent horsemen," Teo said, water dripping from his hair, "but they won't catch us by riding bareback and holding onto the mane!" With a laugh, he took the packhorse's line from Ana and trotted toward the trees.

Ana turned her horse and caught up to the rangy man with the wide shoulders who sat so easy in the saddle. Side by side, they rode into the black forest that lay between them and their home.

✦ ✦ ✦

The next morning, Teo tightened his horse's girth and swung into the saddle. The air was crisp; he could see his breath. He and Ana had ridden well into the night before camping, and now he wanted to get an early start. Though he didn't expect to be followed, one could never be too cautious.

Ana spoke from the trail behind him as they rode along. "Teofil, I just want you to know, you were pretty amazing yesterday. At every turn, there was an obstacle. You overcame them all."

He grinned over his shoulder and pointed to his biceps. "See? My religion is worth something after all." A pine cone hit him in the back. He laughed.

At midday they came to a wider trail, one that might even be called a road. It led south, but there was no guarantee it would keep going that way. Teo noticed his horse's ears swivel. "Quick! Off the trail! Someone's coming!" They darted into a thicket.

A decrepit red wagon pulled by two old nags rolled into view. Its driver was a middle-aged tinker with a belly so round he could have set a stein on it—and probably did. Tools, cookware, and other odds and ends jingled from his wagon as he bumped along the road. The tinker was smoking a pungent weed in the pipe that jutted from his yellowed beard. Amused, Teo stepped his horse forward. "Hail, driver!"

The fellow jumped like a rabbit and grabbed a shortbow. His eyes scanned the undergrowth. "Lay back, ya hear? I'm armed! I'm dangerous!"

"And I'm friendly!" Teo rode into the open, holding the line to his packhorse. "Just a traveler who might wish to hire your services. You know your way around these woods?"

"Better than anyone."

"You know the green river to the south? Joined by a brown one, flowing north?"

"Aye."

"You lead us there, and this packhorse is yours."

The tinker's expression grew canny. "If you're gonna travel by river, fella, you need a boat. I got me an extra. I'll trade it for your ridin' horse."

Teo nodded and motioned for Ana to come out. When she emerged onto the road, the tinker's eyes widened. "That's quite a filly you got there. Nice figure." He looked Ana up and down. "Name's Dirk Bearbane."

"Bearbane?" Ana asked. "How'd you get that name?"

"Killed me a bear. No, three of 'em. With this here bow."

"It's too small for bear. And those are bird points."

Dirk sneered. "What's a woman know about such things?" He turned back to Teo.

"Listen, Dirk, you can be bear bane or bear bait for all we care. Just lead us to the river, and you'll be rewarded. Deal?"

"Alright then, it's a deal. But I'll have to hide my wagon in the woods. It won't roll on the trails we're gonna use." Dirk got down from his seat and began to unhitch his horses.

Once they set out, it didn't take Teo long to realize the man really did know the forest trails. He chose paths Teo would never have picked, yet they always headed in the right direction, and in good time. Without any wandering, they traveled at a pace that ate up the leagues.

That night they camped along a stream Dirk had insisted they visit, though it was slightly out of their way. "There's hot springs for the lady," he said, pointing downstream. "I'll fetch us some rabbits and get a stew going."

As Teo unsaddled the horses, Ana approached him. "Teofil, I'm suspicious of our guide. Can we trust him?"

Teo chuckled. "Not a bit. The guy's a greedy old codger. But don't worry, I know his type. He's no threat to me, and we need his expertise to find our way." To take Ana's mind off her worries, he reached into the saddlebag and tossed her a piece of soap. "Your mother packed it for you. Go enjoy it in the springs."

While Ana went downstream to a private place, Teo rubbed down the horses with bunches of grass. He had almost finished the third horse when he heard Ana scream. Running toward her, he met her in the forest barefoot, her boots in her hand. She was hastily dressed, and her hair was wet and uncombed.

"What is it?"

Ana looked sheepish. "Nothing, I guess. I felt exposed bathing in the springs. I thought I heard someone moving around in the bushes. Then a stick snapped."

Teo put his arm around Ana's shoulders. "It was probably just your imagination. Come back to camp. Dirk is out hunting. He'll return soon with his catch."

✦   ✦   ✦

Ana had to admit, despite her doubts, Dirk Bearbane made good on his word. In just four days he led the party to the green river. Two boats lay hidden among the reeds. Ana rejoiced in the knowledge that after a few days of paddling, she would be home.

"Well, Dirk, you've earned your pay," Teo said to their portly guide. "A horse for your services and a horse for the boat."

Dirk looked at Teo with a huckster's gleam in his eye. "Not so fast, friend! You still need me for one more thing! There's a little, er . . . *rapid* up ahead. Just a riffle, nothing more. You can usually run it in a quality boat like mine, save yourself the portage. But sometimes the water's too high. You'll need my help to scout it first. I'll hold you on a rope and let you choose your line before you run the rapid. In return, I get your third horse."

"You drive a hard bargain, Dirk Bearbane. On the other hand, what would I have done with that horse anyway?" Teo clapped the man on the back and began to unload his gear into the canoe. Ana gave him a hand. *I'll be glad to get rid of Dirk*, she thought. *He's creepy.*

After an hour of paddling, the current began to quicken. A chateau of the Ancients poked one of its turrets through the trees on the far bank.

Dirk pointed downstream to an old bridge, overgrown and dilapidated but still standing.

"We'll stop at the bridge. The lady can cross over and rest her dainty feet while the men do the heavy work. You can pick her up downstream of the rapid."

Though Ana didn't agree with Dirk's estimate of her abilities, she assented to the plan. The men dropped her off on the near shore so she could hike up the bluff to the bridge's entrance. It was a high span, and she looked forward to the view it would afford. Yet one thing troubled her: the closer she got to the bridge, the more it seemed the rapids were making far more noise than they should—for a riffle.

When Ana reached the top of the bluff and stepped onto the bridge, a cold knot of fear tightened in her belly. The whitewater was much more turbulent than Dirk had suggested. Shocked, she stared at the churning water below the bridge. *Those aren't rapids! It's an immense waterfall! How could someone who knows these woods be so mistaken about the danger?* With sudden clarity the truth dawned on her: Dirk was no harmless buffoon. He was a deadly threat who had been waiting like a snake for the right time to strike.

Ana ran onto the bridge. She spotted Teo in his canoe as he scouted the water ahead. Dirk stood on the shore, playing out a rope attached to the canoe's stern. Ana shouted a warning, but her voice was swallowed by the waterfall's roar. Teo turned to Dirk and signaled for an urgent retreat. At that moment, Dirk released the rope.

The current seized the canoe as Teo frantically tried to steer with his paddle. Caught in the violent flow, he gathered speed with every second. Seething plumes of water churned around two giant boulders that thrust up like fangs, sucking the boat into their greedy maw. Teo dived overboard, attacking the river with fierce strokes, a valiant figure fighting a losing battle. It was no use. As Ana watched, the unthinkable happened: Teo went over the edge.

NO! She covered her face in disbelief.

"Well, what d'ya know? Looks like your protector has had himself an accident! Guess it's just you an' me now."

Dirk began to advance along the bridge. His intent was obvious. Ana turned and ran.

The bridge led into a tunnel, but Ana veered off and sprinted toward the chateau, passing through a gatehouse into a cobblestone courtyard. She turned a corner and dodged through a doorway, hoping Dirk hadn't seen her. Her heart raced, and she tried not to pant. No footsteps sounded on the pavement outside. *Maybe I've lost him.* She withdrew the dagger from the neckline of her dress.

"Caught ya!" Dirk lunged through the door and seized Ana by the waist. She slashed his arm with the knife and broke free. He growled like an animal as she plunged through another door and down a stairway.

The steps were slippery with mist, and the sound of the waterfall had intensified. Ana stumbled down the stone trail, drawing close to the falls as she passed a series of viewing platforms. The river boiled with unbeliev-able power, pounding against the toothy boulders and kicking up spray like a rooster's tail. Grief overwhelmed her. Teofil couldn't have survived such a maelstrom of rock and thunder.

Ana tripped and fell to the floor of a grotto carved from the very cliff over which the cataract tumbled. The deafening crash of its water roared past an observation window, soaking her in its spray as she rolled over on the floor. Dirk stood there.

"You're mine now!" He descended onto her. Ana brought up her dagger in defense, but he grabbed it and pitched it into the frothy waters. Dirk's repulsive heaviness pinned her to the floor. She resisted him, but he only laughed at her. His nose nuzzled her hair, his hot breath was in her ear, his vile hands groped in forbidden places.

"No! No! No!" Ana thrashed, but Dirk was too strong. As she tried to lunge away, she knocked her head on the rough rock wall. The blow made her dizzy, and warm blood trickled into her eyes. Dirk greedily yanked at her clothes. Horrified, Ana realized her life would be forever changed this day.

And it was, but not in the way she thought.

She felt Dirk's body lift away from her, somehow rising into the air. Through bloody eyelashes, she watched his expression change from bestial lust to abject fear. A red haze clouded her vision. Dirk's terrified scream resounded in her ears as he floated upward, propelled by some unseen force. He paused in midair, then disappeared through the window into the deadly turbulence outside. Ana fell back on the stone floor, too weak to move. For a long time she lay still, exhausted.

At last she sat up, wiping the blood from her eyes. She made out the shape of a man's leg at the entrance to the grotto. Wet footprints up the trail led toward her from the riverbank. *Whose?* She willed her mind to focus. *Could it be . . . ?*

Yes!

Ana crawled to Teo. The right side of his face was smeared with blood, but he opened his eyes when she cradled his head in her lap.

"Oh, Teofil! You're badly hurt!"

He smiled weakly as he looked up at her. "Yeah," he murmured, "but I told you I'd always come." He passed out.

✦ ✦ ✦

Ana nursed Teo through feverish days and cold nights with healing herbs and her own soft touch. Sometimes he moaned in his delirium, and other times he lay deathly still. His body was bruised all over, and his head bore a deep gash. How he had found the strength to stagger up the trail and heave Dirk into the cataract, she didn't know. Something powerful must have motivated that superhuman effort. Ana stitched Teo's head wound with sinews and fed him with game she hunted herself. Though it wasn't easy, she portaged the remaining boat and its supplies around the falls.

On the tenth day, the fever broke. On the fourteenth day, Teo pronounced himself ready to travel. They floated downstream to the confluence with the Farm River, then turned south to paddle against its flow. After a week on the water, they reached the great bend and crossed into Chiveis.

The village of Edgeton came into view as the sun's rays were beginning to angle lower in the sky. Ana experienced a deep sense of peace. She was home. At last.

The frontier village lay quiet. With the growing season over, many of the farmers had left to spend the winter in more civilized lands. Yet Ana knew one family would still be there, waiting for her in steadfast hope. She smiled at the thought.

As Ana and Teo walked toward her home, the pedestrians and shop-keepers of Edgeton gasped and pointed. Ana approached her house and paused before the door with a lump in her throat. Collecting herself, she knocked.

Her father answered. When his eyes fell on the face of his only daughter, returned from the dead, they grew wide with shock, then joy—inexpressible joy.

"Ana! My Ana!" Stratetix sobbed uncontrollably and held her tight, stroking her hair. She hugged him as hard as she could, tears running down her face. The security of her father's embrace felt like her entire childhood wrapped into a single moment.

Ana's mother burst through the door with a euphoric cry of her own. "Oh, my love! How I've longed for this day!" She threw her arms around Ana and joined the weeping. The jubilant family huddled on the porch, pouring out their mutual love.

Ana motioned toward Teo. "Father, Mother, you must thank Teofil! His bravery is unrivaled in all the annals of Chiveis! We have so many stories to tell!"

Stratetix approached Teo and started to clasp his hand, then changed his mind and embraced him in a manly hug, pounding Teo's back with his palm.

"You're a man of incredible courage, Captain Teofil," he said through tears. "Come now, eat at my table, and stay the night as an honored guest in my home. I hold you in highest esteem!" When Ana heard her father's words, a strange sense of pride flooded her heart.

The foursome spent the evening as such an evening should be spent—with bold tales of mighty deeds, good food and drink, and much laughter. Stratetix and Helena kept touching their daughter as if to make sure she was real and not a dream.

Late that night, when the household had stilled, Ana heard a sound on the balcony outside her room. Dressed only in her night shift, she stepped into the moonlight. The wooden floor was cold against her bare feet. Teofil had come out from the spare bedchamber and stood at the railing, gazing north. Ana went to his side; it seemed right.

"You're a good man," she said quietly as they stared into the night sky. "You came to me with the sword of Armand at your side, like a hero of old."

"It was quite an adventure we had out there."

"I used to enjoy going into the wilds. Now I'm never going to leave Chiveis again."

Teo turned his head and looked at Ana. "Do you think our adventure is over?"

The question was strange to her, and she considered her answer. Finally she said, "I don't know. What do you think?"

"I think perhaps it has just begun."

Ana turned toward the man at her side. "I admire you so much, Teofil."

"You know, my friends just call me Teo."

She smiled. "My loved ones call me Ana."

"Ana," he said.

"Teo," she answered.

They looked at each other uncertainly. Teo moved forward, and Ana didn't shrink back, so he took her hands in his. Something profound passed between them then, though not a word was said.

PART TWO

COMMUNITY

8

Shaphan the Metalsmith tightened the hood of his cape against the biting wind. His eyes watered and his nose ran, making the olive-skinned young man wish he could afford more than the worn-out rabbit fur lining his hood. The vernal equinox was approaching, but it had been a cold winter, and it certainly didn't feel like springtime yet on the high mountainside in the swirling wet snow. "I ought to take the profits from this delivery and spend it on a decent cloak," Shaphan muttered into the wind. But of course he wouldn't do that; he would pay his tuition. Wiping his nose on the back of his mitten, Shaphan continued trudging up the trail.

A lonely chalet came into view ahead. Its owner obviously valued his privacy, for his home was nestled in a secluded forest outside the hamlet of Vingin. The chalet sat at the base of a steep incline whose blanket of snow was nearly the same color as the pale winter sky. In the bleached landscape, only the ribbon of smoke curling from the chimney proved the cold had not entirely suffocated the place. Shaphan focused his thoughts on the hot tea he hoped he'd be offered when he delivered the package.

For all its solitude, the home was a snug little cottage with good protection from the wind. A fenced yard surrounded a small barn, and Shaphan caught the sound of sheep bleating inside. Everything was tidy and well constructed. Though the location suggested the owner was reclusive, he was no deranged hermit living in a ramshackle hut. The chalet was in good repair, and its decorative touches implied its owner even had a sense of style.

A voice interrupted Shaphan's thoughts: "Hurry! Come in from the cold!" The inviting words startled him, not only because he hadn't seen their speaker open the door, but because the voice was female. Shaphan looked up to see a young woman beckoning him from the doorway. She smiled as he climbed onto the porch. Stepping across the threshold into the great room with its blazing hearth, Shaphan found himself immediately attracted to the woman who stood before him. Her hair was black, her eyes dark, her chin delicate. She had the slender figure of a woman still in her twenties. Though her manner wasn't seductive, Shaphan felt excited to be in her presence. He sensed she genuinely wanted him there.

"Uh, hello. I'm Shaphan." The metalsmith flipped his hood onto his shoulders and combed his fingers through his damp hair.

"Welcome, Shaphan. My name is Sucula. My husband will be home soon, but until then you can keep me company while you warm up and your cloak dries off." Without waiting for an answer, Sucula took Shaphan's cloak, which she shook out, then hung on a rack by the fire.

"I suppose you'll want to take a look at this." Shaphan handed Sucula a cloth-wrapped package. She took it from him and laid it on the mantel.

"Business can wait. Have something hot to drink first." Sucula pulled the stopper from a jug and poured mead into a pewter stein. Selecting a poker from the fireplace, she plunged its tip into the golden liquid, making a sizzling sound.

Shaphan accepted the stein from her and sipped the sweet drink. Its warmth trickled down his throat to his belly. He sighed deeply. "It's good. Thank you."

"It's an old recipe I learned from a witch-woman. The spices are unique. Who knows? Maybe I'm putting a spell on you."

Shaphan glanced up at his hostess, who stared at him with a hand on one hip. Her expression was coy. No doubt she was just being friendly—or was there something else behind her smile?

The sound of heavy boots on the porch broke the moment. The door swung open in a gust of cold air as the owner of the house stepped into the room and claimed it as his own. He was a tall, strong man with long red hair and a beard to match. He wore black woolen trousers and high boots made for the deep snow. The fur around his neck was wolverine, the very best. He crossed to Sucula's side and kissed her, then turned to Shaphan and extended his hand with a smile. "You must be the metalsmith!" he boomed. Shaphan found himself drawn to the handsome man with the winsome smile.

"You've guessed correctly, Master Valent," he said as he shook hands. "My name is Shaphan. I've brought your package."

"Excellent, Shaphan! Just call me Valent. This is my home, and you're here as an esteemed guest." He clasped Shaphan's hand longer than seemed socially acceptable, but Shaphan understood it to be a gesture of hospitality, so he waited until Valent finally let go.

Sucula went to the mantel and brought the package to her husband. "Shaphan just arrived a few minutes ago. I invited him to dry his cloak by the fire while we awaited your return."

Valent nodded and untied the string on the package. Unfolding the cloths, he removed an object and held it up to the light. It was a beautiful hunting knife in a scabbard inlaid with silver. The couple admired its craftsmanship, while Shaphan, a little embarrassed, lowered his eyes to take a sip from his stein.

Without warning, Valent yanked the blade from its sheath and pointed it at his guest. His eyes flashed, and he bared his teeth. Shaphan jerked back, dribbling mead down his chin. Valent belted out a laugh. "I'm just kidding, my boy!" He clapped the young metalsmith on the back.

"Oh! For a minute there I thought—"

"Nah, you have nothing to fear from me." Valent held the knife near a ceiling lantern as he examined it, gripping Shaphan by the back of the neck with his other hand and shaking him affectionately. "It's a fine piece of work, my boy, a fine piece!" Reaching into his belt pouch, Valent pulled out a large steel coin, plus another smaller one. "Such skilled work deserves a bonus!" He pressed the coins into Shaphan's palm.

Surprised at the generosity, Shaphan beamed at Valent. "Thank you, sir! But I can't take more than the agreed price."

"You can, and you will. I give it to you because you deserve it. Take it."

The praise made Shaphan even happier than the extra coin. He worked hard at his trade, and he always enjoyed acknowledgment of his efforts.

Sucula approached Shaphan with his dry cloak in her hands. "My husband must be very pleased with your workmanship. He isn't one to give compliments often."

Shaphan buttoned on his cloak and nodded to the lord of the house. "Master Valent, I'm honored to have been entrusted with a requisition of this magnitude. The blade of that knife is forged from the finest steel. It will not quickly go dull. May it serve you well and always find its mark." Turning to Sucula, he downed the last of his cup and thanked his hostess for her hospitality. She held the door for him as he stepped into the brisk wind.

Shaphan crossed the clearing outside the chalet and paused at the edge of the trees. Looking back over his shoulder at the house, he saw Valent and Sucula standing side by side on the porch. They lifted their hands to him, and he returned their farewell.

"Such fine people!" he marveled. He hunched into his cloak and turned his face to the trail. Though the weather continued to be blustery, Shaphan didn't mind, for he could still feel the satisfying warmth of Sucula's spicy mead.

◆　　◆　　◆

An overpowering stench hung in the air as the archpriest of the Elzebulian Order stepped from his carriage to the muddy ground. The two mares in the traces were entirely black, an appropriate color for a religious order that celebrated all things filthy.

The priest folded his arms and surveyed the hilltop monastery. A bald monk soiled with mud and who knew what else approached him and bowed low, awaiting his orders.

"I am here by the direct command of the High Priestess," the old priest announced to the monk. He snorted to clear his nose of the awful smell, then continued, "I am to determine if your work has been proceeding according to Her Holiness's satisfaction."

"All is in order, my lord," the monk replied. "You will be pleased with our progress."

"Show me everything! I am especially interested in the quality of your final product."

The monk in the stained garments led the archpriest to a series of foul-smelling mounds. As they walked, the priest noticed how clear the ground was of snow. The sun had been bright here, and it was sunshine he wanted more than anything else. The monastery's location on the Farm River had been chosen because it had longer, sunnier days than the mountain valleys. The flat hilltop with its southern exposure was one of the warmest spots in Chiveis. Although the last day of winter had not yet passed, the leader of the Elzebulian Order knew spring would come soon, followed by the hot days of summer. Then the sun would warm the mounds of feces and urine, doing the work of decomposition. He exulted at the thought of the sacred salt-stone it would make.

The pair stopped at a pile of oozing manure under a rough shed. The mound's protective tarp had been removed so men with pitchforks could turn the heap, while others with shovels threw straw, garbage, earth, and more dung into the mix. Another crew poured privy water onto the mound to keep it moist.

"This is one of the active ones," the monk said. "It isn't ripe yet."

The monk led the priest to another mound whose top was covered with a feathery white efflorescence.

"This one is ripe. Taste it, my lord."

The priest surveyed the workers, who awaited his next move. "We shall see if you men have pleased Holy Elzebul with your labors, or whether the god will be vengeful upon you." A hush fell on the small crowd. The priest licked his finger and inserted it into the black earth of the mound. Swiping his tongue with his finger, he was immediately struck by the strong taste of salt. After a long pause, he spit out a wad of dirty saliva.

"It is ready for harvest!" he declared. "Elzebul will do you no harm." A murmur of relief rippled through the onlookers.

Satisfied with his examination of the fecal mounds, the priest ordered his guide to lead him to the leaching factory. They entered a wooden hall whose odor, though notably different from the mounds, was no less offensive when it hit the nostrils. At the center of the room was a series of vats into which men poured barrels of water.

"The mound waste in the vat has decomposed for more than a year," the man said. "We're ready for the final extraction from this batch." He opened a stopper at the bottom of the vat, letting leach water run into a trough toward another vat, where men mixed it with wood ashes. Nearby, a large iron boiler sat over a blazing fire. A foreman ladled out some of the boiling water, dropping it onto an iron bar in his hand. The concoction sizzled and left a white powder behind. Nodding, he ordered the fire to be extinguished. Upon his signal, the workers tipped the boiler and poured the contents into a cooling tank.

The old priest surveyed the activities with growing excitement. He knew he was nearing the end of the manufacturing process, and he wanted to examine the final product.

"That one over there is cooled now, my lord." The monk pointed to a tank at the far end of the room. "Perhaps you would like to examine it?"

The priest plunged his arm into the tank and searched along the bottom. He could feel the small crystals that had separated from the cold, murky water. Pulling some from the tank, he dropped them in a basket and shook off the moisture. When they were dry, he carried a handful outside to examine in the sunshine. The crystals were translucent, almost colorless. He turned them over in his palm with the clawlike fingernail on his other hand. Satisfied with their appearance, he licked one of the little stones, savoring its salty taste.

"Yes," he murmured, "this is very good." He smiled as he clutched the crystals to his chest. "She will be most pleased."

For a moment, he let himself fantasize about the day he would deliver a barrel of the crystals to the High Priestess of Chiveis. He pictured her black lips smiling as she gazed at him from her throne. The thought of her praise washing over him gave him intense shivers of delight. Though he didn't know why the High Priestess liked the salt-stone so much, he enjoyed being the man who could please her by providing it.

"My lord?" The dirty monk interrupted his master's fantasy. "There is one more thing I wish you to know."

"What is it?" the priest snapped.

"We're running low on material for the mounds. It's time to start new ones, but we need more dung."

The archpriest turned toward the obsequious monk standing next to him. His smirk grew into a cackle as he considered the request. "Do not fear, servant of Holy Elzebul! Preparations for his great festival are underway as we speak. Filth you shall soon have, for the Wild Night approaches!"

A wicked expression crossed the monk's face at the mention of the Wild Night. "Of course you are right, my lord. And when that night comes, we at the monastery will be ready to receive the god's bounty!"

❖   ❖   ❖

Ana sat hunched over the table in her bedroom, her eyes straining to see the sewing needle in the dim light. She glanced out the window at the growing dusk, then rose from her seat to retrieve the lantern from the mantel above the fireplace. Lighting the lamp with a twig from the fire, she paused in front of the hearth to let its warmth envelop her body. Though it felt good, the urge to continue her task prompted her to return to the table. She resumed sewing the woolen lining of a bearskin cloak. A gust of wind rattled the little house in Edgeton.

I sure hope Teo appreciates all this hard work I'm doing for him, she thought. Immediately Ana regretted her selfishness. She reminded herself she was making the cloak as a labor of love, an expression of gratitude for a well-deserving man. She had been lost beyond all hope until, at great personal risk to himself, Teo had swept into the wilderness to find her and take her home. Ana would be forever grateful for his courage.

"What are you doing right now, Teo?" she asked aloud, preferring a one-sided conversation to the silence in the room. When Teo didn't answer, she gave a little laugh, imagining him in some "cold hut on the frontier," as he had put it, watching the passes in lonesome misery for the past several months. She hadn't seen Teo all winter. Now she wished she could be there to cheer him up and give him the cloak in person.

Someone knocked on the door.

"Come in!"

Stratetix entered the room carrying a pair of breeches with a ragged gash in the seat. "Your mother said you were sewing, so I brought this to be mended when you get a chance."

"I'll take care of it after I finish this stitch. Put it here on the table." Ana moved the bearskin aside. As she did, Stratetix bent to inspect it.

"You've been working awfully hard on this cloak. Now you're almost done." He fingered the soft hairs. "The fur has been well prepared. It's an excellent piece of craftsmanship."

"Thank you, Father. That means a lot, coming from you."

Stratetix spread out the cloak. "It's sized for a man," he remarked.

Ana didn't look up from her sewing, though a slight smile crept to her lips as she worked.

"A gift for your father?"

Ana peeked up at Stratetix from underneath her eyebrows. He was grinning at her with such a mischievous expression that the two of them burst into laughter.

As the laughter subsided, Ana laid the cloak aside and rose to hug her father, laying her head on his shoulder. "You deserve all I have to give," she told him with sincere affection.

"Perhaps. But so does the one for whom the gift is intended."

Ana nodded against Stratetix's shoulder. Then, realizing more fully what her father had just said, she separated herself so she could look at him. "What does that mean?"

"Captain Teofil is a noble man. He deserves a thank-you gift like this. That's all I meant."

"Are you sure?" Ana searched her father's face. "For a moment there, it seemed like you were trying to stir up something."

Stratetix smiled and held up his hands. "Would I do that, Little Sweet?" His use of Ana's childhood nickname always melted her heart. She knew it was intended to soften her defenses, but she resisted her father's wiles and kept her tone playfully firm.

"To this point in my life, you've let me sort things out for myself. But I know you like Teo a lot. You might start meddling."

"I won't meddle."

"There's nothing to meddle with," Ana insisted. "Teofil is a captain of the Royal Guard, a tournament champion, a respected scholar. He could have any woman in the realm. I'm just a farm girl from Edgeton."

Stratetix led Ana to the mirror. "There are many women in the Kingdom of Chiveis." He raised a finger to point at her reflection. "But look! There is the loveliest of them all, the one to whom he gave his garland."

Ana blushed. Fortunately Helena entered the room just then and changed the subject. "The soup is steaming in the bowls, and the cider is poured in the mugs," she announced. "Come and eat."

As the family sat down at the table, Ana's mind continued to dwell on Teo. Though she didn't intend it, her mood was pensive and detached.

"You've hardly touched your soup," Helena remarked. "Is something on your mind?"

"No." Ana stirred her bowl. "Well, maybe. Okay, yes."

"We were discussing Captain Teofil when you came in," Stratetix said. "Our daughter is sorting through her feelings."

Ana lifted her head and looked into her parents' eyes. The weight of her secrets had become too much. *It's time to explain my true feelings about Teo*, she realized.

"I know you probably think I'm just a girl with a silly crush—"

"We don't think that, Little Sweet."

Ana nodded appreciatively. "Good. Because there's much more to this than romance." She waved her hand. "I mean, it's not a romance at all! I don't know what it is. Just friendship, I guess. All I know is, Teo and I experienced things in the Beyond that will affect both our destinies. We made a discovery that will tie us together, though I'm not sure he fully understands that yet."

"What kind of discovery?" Helena's tone was gentle.

Ana took a deep breath. "A religious discovery. Something that got me thinking in new ways. I've been doing some hard evaluation of the gods of Chiveis."

Her parents glanced at each other. Helena nodded almost imperceptibly, and Stratetix chose his words with care. "Your mother and I are disturbed about how the gods abandoned you in the Beyond. We've come to believe the gods can't be trusted when it counts," he said in a low voice.

"That's what I've decided too."

"Keep these thoughts to yourself, my love," Helena warned.

Ana leaned forward on her elbows. "I've been keeping my discovery a secret since I got back, but I can't hold it in anymore! When I was in the Beyond with Teo, we found a book. Not just any book—a book of the Ancients! It describes their religion and their God. When Teo gets back from winter patrol, he's going to translate it for me. We intend to learn about this God together. I've seen his temple, and I know he's a God of great beauty!"

Helena slid her hand over Ana's. "I share your longings, but remember, these are very dangerous ideas. Freedom of religion in Chiveis is more a theory than a reality."

"We're leaving Edgeton soon to spend a few weeks near Aunt Rosetta at our chalet in Vingin," Stratetix said. "Vingin isn't far from Lekovil, so you might be able to see Captain Teofil there." He raised his index finger. "But as your father, I warn you to keep this secret to yourself. If you speak with the captain about this book you've found, you must share the knowledge with no one else. Do you understand?"

"Yes, Father." Ana bowed before his stern gaze. But when she glanced across the table at Helena, she was surprised to see her mother wearing a different expression. Helena's eyes were closed, and she had a satisfied smile on her lips.

"Mother? What is it?"

Helena's eyes popped open, bright and expectant. "I've been praying for this," she said.

◆　◆　◆

An onion, a bouillon cube, and a few scraps of dried beef were all that remained in the cupboard. It would have to do.

Teo gathered the last of his winter rations and chopped them into a pot on a cast-iron stove. "I wish I had some bread," he said woefully, but there was no one to hear his request. He scratched his scraggly beard and waited for the thin soup to simmer.

After dinner, Teo threw his last few sticks into the stove. When he'd arrived at the hut on the Great Pass in late autumn, he had been disappointed, though not surprised, to discover how meager was his allotment of food and fuel. The Warlord had been infuriated by Teo's escapade in the Beyond and ordered him to a hard tour of duty as punishment. Teo had spent many fireless nights huddled under his ragged blankets while winter storms howled outside. He could make it through one more night like that. In the morning, his relief would arrive.

Teo lay on his bed with his arms crossed, watching the flickering orange light inside the stove grow weaker. As the wind's icy fingers reached into the drafty hut to defeat the flame's warmth, Teo returned to the mental picture that had comforted him many times: the image of Anastasia sleeping peacefully under a down comforter in her room, a fire blazing in her hearth. *A few cold nights up here is a small price to pay for that*, he reminded himself.

The farmers of Edgeton would be burrowed in this time of year with no field work to do until warmer weather arrived. Perhaps this would be a good time to visit Ana. Teo considered the idea, analyzing his motives. The ostensible reason would be to give her a translation of the Sacred Writing of Deu, as he had promised. But was there a deeper reason? Teo's mind kept returning to their intimate moment on the balcony. He sensed something had changed between them that night under the full moon. *No*, he corrected himself, *it wasn't just that night. It was the whole adventure we shared.* The realization dawned on Teo that he and Ana had been deeply bonded by their experience in the Beyond. What exactly did that mean? Were they supposed to become lovers?

The orange light in the stove winked out as the last ember surrendered to the cold darkness on the Great Pass. Teo rolled over in bed and told himself to quit daydreaming like a girl. All these notions about balconies and secret bonds were too complex to figure out. *When the time is right to make your move, you'll know it. Until then, let things unfold at their own pace.* Satisfied with that conclusion, Teo closed his eyes to sleep, though the room was pitch-black already.

The next morning, Teo spotted the packhorses moving slowly up the Great Pass. He shouldered his rucksack and set off down the slope, passing the oncoming guardsman with a wave and a grunt.

Down in the Troll's Valley, the snow lay in patches on the ground. Though the vernal equinox was only a few days away, things hadn't started greening up in the valley yet. Even so, it was nice not to have deep snow underfoot.

Arriving at last at the Citadel, Teo was greeted with none of the acclaim he had received a few months earlier when he was a tournament competitor. Now, with his disheveled appearance and scruffy beard, no one recognized him as anyone but a soldier returning from field duty. He filed the appropriate papers at the Warlord's Bureau, then stopped at a bathhouse to clean up and get a shave and haircut.

As a barber scraped the whiskers from Teo's face, his thoughts turned to the academic work that lay before him. He had left the Sacred Writing of Deu in his rooms at the University last fall and had scarcely given it a thought since then. Now it was time to resume his studies. *Perhaps I should visit Ana and let her know.*

"Sir?" The barber paused his shaving.

"Huh? What?"

"I'm going to have to ask you to start thinking about something else. I can't shave you with that big grin on your face." Teo laughed at the attendant's jest and held his chin still until the shave was finished.

Cleanliness brought Teo a renewed sense of civility. He wandered the halls of the magnificent bathhouse at leisure, savoring the presence of people again. Vendors hawked dried fruits and baked goods from their carts. Teo was standing in a secluded window niche finishing a sweet roll when a woman addressed him from behind. "So," she sneered, "it's the great tournament champion!"

Teo turned around slowly, knowing from the familiar voice whom he would see. Yet when he saw her, he was unprepared for her manner of dress. The woman wore the gauzy attire of an Astrebrilian priestess. Though her black lips gave her a shocking appearance, there was no mistaking her red hair. It was Habiloho.

"Hello, Princess." Teo kept his tone cordial. "I didn't realize you had entered the Order of Astrebril."

"If you were as smart as you think you are, you'd see I'm still an acolyte. I haven't been initiated yet."

"I know. I can see you're not wearing the collar."

"Oh, forgive me," Habiloho replied, her voice dripping with sarcasm. "I guess I had reason to think your eyesight is *deficient*." She spat out the last word like poison, staring at Teo with steely eyes. Tension hung in the air.

Because Habiloho had broached the awkward subject of the tournament garland, Teo decided to be direct. "There's nothing wrong with my eyesight, Habiloho. I made my decision, and I stand by it even now."

Habiloho grabbed Teo's jerkin in her fists, thrusting her face into his. He had never seen such hatred in a woman's eyes. It smoldered like a malevolent fire.

"*It should have been me!*" she hissed through gritted teeth. "*I am the Flame of Chiveis!*"

"There's more to beauty than outward appearance," Teo said calmly. She slapped him.

Teo winced and turned his head back to Habiloho but said nothing.

"Watch yourself, Captain," she warned. "The power of the gods is great. You wouldn't want Astrebril to be angry with you." The princess spun around and stalked away, her hips swishing in the clingy gown.

Teo rubbed his cheek. "She'll hate me until the day she dies," he observed with a sigh.

❖   ❖   ❖

When Stratetix stopped his wagon in front of the tidy house on the outskirts of Vingin, Ana leaped to the ground and ran to the door. One of the main reasons her family often spent part of the winter at their tiny chalet in Vingin was to be close to Helena's sister, a widow who still lived in the house she had shared with her husband. Ana spotted her on the front steps. "Aunt Rosetta! I've missed you!" she cried as she embraced the plump middle-aged woman.

"Oh, child, we were so worried about you. Bless my soul, Ana, I can hardly believe it's you!"

"It's me alright! As good as ever, and ready for some of your pastries." Ana smiled at her aunt, who was wiping tears from the corners of her eyes.

Another figure appeared behind Rosetta. "Lina!" Ana threw her arms around her skinny cousin with the curly blonde hair.

"Ana, I'm *so* glad to see you! Vingin is so boring. Now that you're here, maybe we can cause some trouble." Ana laughed as the two girls went inside. Stratetix and Helena followed.

Rosetta offered her sister and brother-in-law hot tea and apple strudel drizzled with plenty of icing. Ana and Lina sat on the floor in front of the hearth, downing their pastries with gusto. The conversation began with small talk but inevitably turned to the account of Ana's abduction. Rosetta could hardly bear to hear the details, while Lina listened with rapt attention.

"I grieved for you, child, like my very own," Rosetta said to Ana. "When I heard you had come back safely, I couldn't believe it. Like a resurrection from the dead, it was. And now to see you here in person . . ." Tears came to her eyes again.

"We owe everything to the courage of one man," Stratetix said. "A valiant man who acted honorably." Helena nodded in agreement.

"I want to hear more about that part," Lina whispered to Ana with a sly smile.

The conversation moved to other matters, so the girls excused themselves. Upstairs, they chatted on the bed and giggled like long-lost sisters.

"Everyone says the captain is *so* good-looking." Lina had a touch of awe in her voice. "I've never actually seen him, except from a distance at the games."

"Yes, he's handsome," Ana acknowledged. "But it isn't his looks that draw you the most."

Lina's eyes were wide. "What is it, then?"

"His strength."

Lina squealed. "Are you lovers?"

"No!" Ana's reply was adamant.

"Well, what are you?"

"I don't know."

"You don't know? How can you not know?"

"We never, uh, defined it." Ana tilted her head. "Actually, I don't think there's anything to define."

"But you spent all that time riding through mysterious forests and camping together. Sleeping together," she added.

"Yes," Ana agreed. "*Sleeping*."

"When are you going to see him again?"

"I don't know. He's on winter patrol. I guess he'll come back to Lekovil at some point."

"Ana! Lekovil is down in the valley, a short walk from here. You have to go see him!"

"So I should just throw myself at him? Is that what you've learned about men in all your eighteen years of experience?"

"I'm not saying to throw yourself at him. But you have to, you know, put yourself in his path. It's what girls do."

"It's not what this girl does." Ana lifted her chin proudly.

"Then this girl might never get herself a husband! Ana, you have to take charge. Make it happen. Do what it takes."

"You don't know what you're talking about."

"No, *you* don't," Lina retorted. "You're not thinking straight. What day is coming soon? The great festival for Elzebul."

"Ugh. I hate that dirty god."

"Sh! Ana, don't say that so loudly!" Lina glanced out the window at the sky, then continued in a low voice, "Whatever you may think about the god, his festival is tomorrow. And who is required to attend his parade?"

"His priests?"

"Yes. And who else? At Lekovil?"

Ana thought about it. "Oh, right—the professors. I guess Teo will have to be there."

Lina intertwined her fingers against her cheek and fluttered her eyelids. "Oh, Teo," she mimicked in a breathy voice. "What a coincidence running into you here!" Ana laughed at her cousin's flirty strategies and toppled Lina off the bed.

"You're forgetting something," Ana said as Lina looked up at her from the floor in a mess of curls. "The festival of Elzebul ends with the Wild Night. There's no way my father is going to let me out of the house that night."

Lina's expression turned sneaky. "He doesn't have to know! We'll just go to the parade, bump into your lover, and be back before sunset."

Ana looked skeptical. "I doubt that would work, Lina," she said. "And I already told you—Teo is not my lover!"

◆   ◆   ◆

Maurice the Wise shook a bowl of potpourri to stir up its scent, trying to cover the foul stench that permeated the air. Several candles burned around his room at the University, but the stink outside was too strong to be masked.

"This is what passes for religion these days," Maurice complained. "The worship of filth! Elzebul was always Lord of the Flies, but in recent years they've started taking it too far."

Teo shrugged. "What can you do? The people love the wild abandon of this festival."

"Lack of self-control is unworthy of respect, Teo, my son."

"I know. We both know Elzebul is corrupt. For that matter, all the gods are."

Maurice raised his eyebrows. "It seems you've become quite the atheist." He handed his student a mug of juniper tea and waited for a reply.

"It's the only conclusion a logical person can make. Look at the evidence. Elzebul is about to be worshiped in a parade where people offer him the contents of their chamber pots. The chicken coops and stables of Chiveis have been ransacked just so the god can have what he cherishes most—excrement. How is that holy?"

Maurice nodded his agreement. "Alright, what about Pon?" he inquired. "Maybe he's good?"

"He values charcoal. What could be more mundane than that? As for the pleasures he offers in the forests—not so bad, I suppose. But the last time I tried that, look where I ended up." Teo grinned and jerked his thumb toward the north.

"Maybe Vulkain then?"

"His priests do some good with their matches. Their medicines and bleaches and food preservatives are useful to mankind. But if Vulkain is a good god, why are all the Vulkainians thugs? Why do they spray people with acid? Have you ever seen the burns those sprayers cause? It's ugly." Teo sipped hot tea as he sat on his master's couch.

"Continue the path of your investigation, wherever it may lead. Surely Astrebril the Beautiful is a good god."

"No, he's worst of all. He does harm to people, not good. His thunder at dawn is terrifying, and no one knows when it will come. No question, he's a powerful deity. I've seen the houses his thunder has visited. It's as if men with hammers have destroyed them to the last stone—yet it happens suddenly, with a boom and smoke. There's nothing like it on earth. Astrebril is a vindictive god to be feared."

Maurice stroked his chin. "So it's not that you don't believe in the gods. It's that you think they're unworthy of worship."

"Right. There certainly are powers out there, but they're not out to help *me*. They don't care for my well-being. That's why I rely on myself." Teo flexed his biceps and pointed. "Here's my god."

Maurice chuckled. "I believe that strong arm of yours can accomplish a great deal in this world, but not nearly as much as you think." He looked at the pendulum clock on his wall. "Come now, Teo. It's time to make our appearance at the ceremonies."

"I'm not going this year."

"Hmm. You'll be missed. The priests won't like it."

"Even so, I'm staying right here." Teo leaned back, crossed his arms behind his head, and put his feet up on the settee.

"Suit yourself, then. I'll make my perfunctory appearance and return as soon as I can. I only hope I don't vomit from the smell."

"It *is* bad. The Elzebulians have been demanding more excrement than usual from the people."

Maurice opened the door. "I'll be back before sunset," he said with an air of resignation.

"If not, I'm coming for you. You don't need to be out alone on the Wild Night."

❖   ❖   ❖

"There are a lot of people, Ana! Keep your eyes open." Lina dragged her cousin by the hand through the crowded streets of Lekovil. Collection barrels, into which people were emptying their chamber pots and stable waste, lined the sidewalks. Some men even used the barrels as latrines. The smell in the air was a noxious combination of dung, stale urine, and sour beer. Most of the revelers didn't seem to mind it, though. The beer had taken care of that.

"I knew I shouldn't have come," Ana protested.

"Then I'd be here alone, and you'd be worried sick."

"I know! That's exactly why I came." Ana huffed and shook her head.

"Well, now that you're here, you might as well enjoy yourself. Come on, let's find something to drink and watch the entertainment."

Lina ducked into a tavern and returned with two earthenware cups overflowing with foamy beer. She took a long swig from one of them, leaving a frothy mustache on her upper lip. Two handsome men in the crowd noticed it and toasted her raucously, so Lina threw them a wink. She handed the second cup to Ana, who began to sip from it, but someone jostled her and caused her to spill beer down the front of her gown. She sighed.

"Wait right here," she instructed Lina.

Inside the tavern, Ana asked to borrow the barkeep's towel. He obliged, and Ana cleaned her gown as much as possible.

"Buy you a drink?" A thin man with greasy hair slid over to Ana's side. Beads of sweat dotted his forehead. His breath was atrocious.

"I was just leaving." Ana turned to go.

The man grabbed her elbow. "Pretty girl like you won't drink with the likes of me, eh?"

Ana yanked her elbow from the man's grasp and walked away.

"You'd better be in by sundown, honey," the man warned. Ana's heart was beating rapidly as she left the tavern. She stepped out on the sidewalk and looked around.

Lina was gone.

Ana called her cousin's name and scanned the crowd but couldn't find Lina anywhere. A feeling of unease began to gnaw at her stomach. *Where could she be? I told her to stay put!*

A cheer went up as the leading edge of the parade rounded the corner. The onlookers surged to the street to watch the entertainers as they passed by on wagons. Strangers pressed close to Ana as she was swept into the crowd. The smell of body odor assaulted her nostrils and made her gag. A hand groped her from somewhere within the sea of bodies, but she squirmed away from the prying fingers.

The wagons neared the place where Ana was standing. Male and female dancers in skimpy outfits performed tawdry routines for the crowd's delight. Musicians played on harps and pipes, their music mingling with the coarse jesting from the onlookers. Beer was flowing freely now as the crowd's mood intensified. A man with two felt-wrapped mallets kept time on a large kettledrum, his fast rhythm mimicking a racing heartbeat.

Lina! Where are you? Ana didn't bother shouting anymore because she wouldn't be heard over the din. She despaired of finding her cousin in the tight-packed mass of revelers. A glance at the sky heightened Ana's sense of urgency: the sun was getting low. She had to act fast.

With renewed determination, Ana wriggled away from the street toward the storefronts, not bothering to be polite, but shoving the drunken revelers aside as she forced her way through the mob. At one point she stumbled into the arms of a man with an enormous belly. "Aha! Come to me, gorgeous!" he cried as he pressed his moist lips to her face. Ana pushed him aside and broke free from the crowd, taking shelter in a recessed doorway to catch her breath.

More wagons proceeded through the streets as the parade rolled along. The ones driven by the priests of Elzebul were drawn by black horses that seemed skittish in the pandemonium. Men began to lift the collection barrels to dump great quantities of excrement into the wagons' troughs as they passed. The fetid mixture splattered the crowd, but the mood was so lusty that no one paid attention to the filth on their clothes.

As Ana searched the throng, she finally spotted Lina, whose white-blonde curls identified her immediately. Down the street, two large men were escorting her into a seedy tavern. Ana ran to catch up, but when she tried the door, it had been locked. Desperate now, Ana circled around to an alley and found a door into the kitchen. She stepped around the kegs and crates on the floor until she could peek into the barroom. Her cousin sat at a table in the corner, hemmed in by the two men. The room was otherwise empty.

"Lina!" When Ana called her cousin's name, Lina looked up, but her expression wasn't that of a merrymaker having drinks with new friends. She had the fearful look of cornered prey. Lina started to rise, but one of the men placed a hand on her shoulder and forced her to sit. The two men turned in their seats to face Ana, and she recognized them as the pair who had toasted Lina earlier.

"We was just gettin' acquainted, all friendly like," said one. "How 'bout you join us?"

Ana kept her voice calm. "My cousin and I have other obligations. Come on, Lina, we should be going." She held out her hand to the terrified girl.

"Aw, now that ain't nice," said the other man, rising to approach Ana. He came too close, staring into her eyes. "I think you should sit down with us," he said.

From behind Ana, a level voice spoke. "The women would like to go."

All four faces turned toward the speaker. A dignified old man, wearing the blue robes of a senior professor at the University, had entered through the kitchen. His bald head was encircled with a diadem, and his manicured goatee was pure white. He was handsome for his age with a regal bearing. Ana had never seen him before.

The ruffian standing by Ana replied first. "Mind your own business, grandpa."

"My business is knowledge, my friend. And it is knowledge you lack."

The man sitting by Lina bolted from his chair and approached the professor, stopping a few paces away. "You sayin' we're dumb?" he demanded.

"I said you lack knowledge. But knowledge can be acquired."

"What knowledge?"

The professor faced the two men, who stood side by side with belligerent expressions. Ana beckoned to Lina, who rose from the corner table and joined her cousin. They clasped hands and began to ease away.

"Perhaps you lack knowledge of how to attain wealth." The professor held up a steel coin. He balanced the coin on his fist, snapped the fingers of his other hand, and displayed his palms. The coin had vanished! He made a throwing motion toward an adjacent table, which he then approached. Reaching into a bowl of nuts, he produced the steel coin again.

"See? There is much you don't know," the professor said with a smile.

214

The two men glanced at each other, then lunged toward the tables and began searching the bowls for coins. Ana and Lina used the opportunity to slip through the back door, followed by the professor. They ran, rounding a few corners in the alleys until Ana felt sure they couldn't be found. She turned toward the old man.

"We're in your debt, sir," she said, panting.

"I noticed your distress and followed you into the tavern. You shouldn't be on the streets right now, Anastasia."

"You know me?"

"Yes, by reputation. You are highly regarded by a friend of mine, but never mind that. My name is Maurice." He bowed to Ana, then turned to Lina and made her acquaintance as well.

"It's late! We have to be getting home," Ana said urgently.

"There's no time. You're in more danger than you know. The Wild Night has always been a festival of wanton license, but tonight the priests are taking things a step further. A decree is being made to the crowds even as we speak. The laws of Chiveis are being suspended from dusk until dawn. Crimes will be overlooked if the offender pays a sufficient tithe of excrement. Tonight will be a night of lawbreaking."

"That's horrible!" Lina exclaimed.

"You women must come to the University. You'll be safe there until morning. I'll show you a back way."

Maurice led Ana and Lina through a maze of alleys and side streets. Now that the decree had gone into effect, the sounds of revelry in Lekovil had been replaced by the sounds of anarchy. Glass was breaking, women were shouting, and buildings had been set on fire. At last the threesome arrived at the main street again. Hooligans were looting the stores and brawling in the filthy gutters. A short distance away, Ana spotted the University's gate.

"We'll have to make a run for it in the open," Maurice said.

Ana had just started to move when a hand yanked her back. She cried out, and Lina shrieked at the same moment. The two ruffians from the tavern had found them again.

"Goin' somewhere?" one asked. "We was just gettin' to know ya." He sneered at Ana and wrenched her arm to bring her face close to his.

"There weren't no more coins in them bowls, old-timer!" The second man knocked Maurice to the ground with a fist to the jaw. The professor struggled to rise, but the first man kicked him into a stone wall. Ana and Lina began to back into an alley as the two thugs advanced.

"Let them go."

The voice was firm and commanding. Ana recognized it at once. An immense wave of emotion overcame her—relief and something more.

The two men whirled. "You gonna make us?" one of them snarled.

"It won't be difficult."

The first man yanked a knife from his belt and lunged. Teo sidestepped the thrust and snapped the man's arm with a loud crack. The assailant screamed and clutched his arm, which dangled loosely at the elbow. The other man dropped his own knife and held up his hands. The pair scuttled out of the alley, darting past Maurice, who was dusting himself off and licking his bloody lip.

"Teo!" Ana ran to him and hugged his neck. "You came just in time!"

"I told you, I always will." He smiled warmly and looked into her eyes, his hands resting on her waist. "It's good to see you again, Ana."

Ana introduced her cousin, who gazed up at Teo in awe. "Hi," she managed to peep.

Teo returned the greeting, then went to check on Maurice, who waved off the attention and signaled that he would be fine. They returned to the women, and Teo explained that Maurice was his mentor. Ana sensed that the wise professor had been deeply disturbed by the night's events.

Maurice spread his arms and addressed the three young people. "My friends, tonight we've seen the face of madness. The filth of Elzebul has been exposed for what it is—not uplifting, not ennobling, not virtuous, but a worship that is detrimental to the human spirit." Maurice's face was angry. "How long?" he cried to the sky. "How long will the Kingdom of Chiveis bear the burden of such corrupt worship?"

Ana leaned close to Teo and whispered in his ear, "Teo, I think there's something you need to show your friend."

CHAPTER

9

Y ou're stalling, aren't you?" Teo grinned at Ana as she sat across
from him in the University's refectory. The room was nearly
empty. A bright morning sun shone through the windows, but
the normal breakfast crowd was absent. Lekovil had quite a hangover.

"Stalling from what?" Ana asked as she buttered her bread far too
meticulously.

"From going home. I don't blame you. I wouldn't want to face your
father right now. I'd be stalling too."

"I sent him a message as soon as I arrived here! He knows I'm safe."

"Safe, yes. But you sneaked away without his permission."

Ana looked glum. "I know. I hate it when I disappoint him." Her
shoulders slumped.

"He loves you. He'll be angry, but it will blow over. In the meantime,
feel free to stall. I'm enjoying breakfast, just the two of us."

"I'm *not* stalling," Ana insisted. "I always eat this slowly." She turned
her cheek and regarded Teo from the corners of her eyes, a playful smile
on her lips. "Like a lady."

Teo snorted. "Right! What about the time we ran out of meat for a few
days and then I finally took a doe? You made a sauce from some currants
you found. I remember how you wolfed down that meat, with sticky red
stuff all over your face!" He motioned toward Ana's mouth.

"I didn't wolf it down!" Ana protested in mock indignation. "I nibbled
it quickly."

Her description of the incident reduced Teo and Ana to a fit of boister-ous laughter. For a time they enjoyed the joke as they sat across from each other, not needing to say anything else because they both understood. At last they fell silent, and Teo sensed a more serious mood descending on the table.

"A lot happened out there in the Beyond," he remarked.

"And also when we got back."

"Good morning, you two!" Lina approached the table, all bouncy and cheerful and shiny in the sunlight. Teo rose to greet her and pulled up a chair. "I'm starved," she said, reaching for the bread and topping it with butter and jam.

The breakfast progressed at a leisurely pace, with Maurice making it a foursome a few minutes later. Teo felt there was more he wanted to say to Ana, but the moment had been lost.

The hour was late by the time Ana and Lina decided to head back to Vingin. Teo escorted the women to the University's gate. As they said good-bye, Ana leaned close to him.

"Remember, you made a promise to me."

Teo was startled. "I did?"

"To translate the book of Deu," she whispered.

"Oh, right. I'm planning to start that project right away. I finally have the time."

"Be sure and tell Master Maurice about it. I think he's a seeker too."

"I'll tell him today."

Teo paused, suddenly aware of the people coming and going at the gate. His thoughts were jumbled. *Should I say something about . . . us?* He decided to play it safe. "It was great to see you again, Ana. Please pass on my regards to your parents." He gave her a polite hug and patted her on the shoulder. Ana nodded and took her leave, though she seemed a little put out as she and Lina set off down the street.

When they were out of sight, Teo turned and made his way to his rooms. Retrieving a wooden chest from under his bed, he raised the lid and removed the leather-bound book, setting it carefully on his desk. He opened to the Table of Contents and read the headings there. They were divided into two groups, the Old Testament and the New Testament.

Unfortunately, the New Testament was lost to water damage. Perhaps no one would ever know how the book ended.

Glancing at the individual book titles, Teo realized he could translate a few of them, such as Beginning, Departure, Magistrates, First and Second Kings, First and Second Histories, and Maxims. However, many other titles he didn't recognize.

One particular heading caught his eye: Hymns. He turned to the first page and translated it slowly: "Happy is the man who does not walk according to the counsel of the wicked, who does not stop in the road of sinners, and who does not sit in the company of mockers, but who finds his delight in the law of the Eternal One and meditates on it day and night." *Ana will like this*, Teo thought. He resolved to give her Deu's poetic words as a special gift.

As Teo gingerly turned the pages and surveyed the entire book, a plan of action coalesced in his mind. Obviously he should translate the initial book called Beginning, as well as some of the hymns. But to ease into things and to get a feel for the Sacred Writing of Deu, he would also start translating the book called Ruth. Not only was it brief, it was a narrative, which made it easier to translate than the ones full of incomprehensible oracles. Furthermore, the main character was a woman. Teo thought Ana would like that. He decided to work on these texts when he had time from his other duties, sending them to Ana as he finished them.

Now only one problem remained. Teo realized he needed to secure the services of a copyist to transform his messy, marked-up notes into nice, clean scrolls. Not just anyone could do the job. It would have to be someone intelligent, academic, and willing to drop everything to work hard on the project. Most importantly, it would have to be someone who would do exactly as he was instructed, telling no one about the project. Teo scrawled a note on a piece of parchment, sealed it, and strolled to the University's main gate.

"How can I help you, Professor Teofil?" the gatekeeper asked.

"I have two tasks. First, I want you to send someone to locate Professor Maurice and ask him to come to my rooms right away. It's an important private matter."

"It will be done, sir. And the second task?"

"I want this sent out immediately."

"Where to?"

"Send it to my student, Shaphan the Metalsmith."

✦ ✦ ✦

A late-season snow was falling in Vingin as Teo and Maurice hiked up the path to a chalet on the outskirts of the village. It was dusk, and Teo was certain no one had noticed them pass by. Footprints in the snow told him some of the other guests Maurice had summoned to the chalet had already arrived.

Three weeks earlier, Teo had told Maurice about the Sacred Writing of the Ancients. With a wry smile, Maurice observed that it wasn't like Teo to keep secrets from him, though he understood that Teo's winter patrol had prevented them from having any scholarly discussions. Maurice wholeheartedly affirmed Teo's translation agenda. When Teo handed him the first chapter of the book of Beginning, Maurice had been astounded. He said the sentiments expressed in it were unlike anything in Chiveisian religion. Wisdom of this magnitude demanded further exploration, so Maurice had called a meeting of those he knew to be open to new ideas. "I suspect the fresh wind blowing in Chiveis is about to become a mighty gale," he had said.

The chalet's door opened as Teo and Maurice stepped onto the porch. Stratetix ushered them inside, then quickly closed the door behind them. "Greetings, Captain! You're always welcome in my home!" He grinned through his gray beard and shook Teo's hand, then turned toward the old professor. "And you must be Master Maurice. My daughter Anastasia holds you in high esteem."

"As I do her," Maurice answered.

"Your words are gracious. We look forward to hearing what you have to say. My chalet is small, but it is at your service."

"Thank you for allowing us to use it this evening. Its privacy will be to our advantage."

Stratetix introduced Maurice to Helena, and Teo was surprised when Maurice approached her and bowed, patting her hand in his palm. "You of all people will be pleased to hear my words tonight, Helena d'Armand," he said. Maurice was then introduced to Rosetta, and he also acknowledged Ana and Lina, who returned his greeting with a courteous nod.

A knock at the door signaled the arrival of another guest. As Stratetix let him in, a ripple of surprise circulated through the room, but Maurice intervened. "Don't be alarmed by this man's garb," he said to the startled group. "Though he wears the habit of the monks of Astrebril, this is my trusted friend Lewth. Rest assured, he shares our convictions—the convictions that prompted me to call this meeting."

More footsteps sounded on the porch. Teo turned from the window and announced, "My student Shaphan is here." He opened the door and shook hands with the handsome, olive-skinned youth, then said to the room, "Shaphan is a metalsmith by trade, and an excellent scribe as well. I know you'll appreciate his friendship if you ever need a knife sharpened or a document copied." The comment elicited polite laughter as Shaphan smiled and shuffled his feet. Introductions were made around the room for Shaphan's and Lewth's benefit, then everyone took a seat in chairs or on the floor. Only Maurice remained standing, his expression thoughtful and solemn.

The old professor stood tall in the center of the room, his hands folded into his sleeves as he waited for the stirring to cease. At last everyone quieted down. Candlelight flickered on the expectant faces huddled in a circle, and a hush of anticipation descended upon the group. The flames crackling in the hearth made the only sound. Maurice's demeanor became serious, matching the mood in the room. Taking a deep breath, he spoke.

"The nine of us gathered here this evening have come from many walks of life, many divergent paths, many differing experiences," he said. "Yet there is one thing that binds us, one thing we share in common: we have come to believe, each one of us, that the gods of Chiveis are not good."

At those words, some in the room sucked in their breath, while others shifted uncomfortably in their seats. Maurice waited until things had settled again, then resumed speaking.

"Now listen to me, friends. If the gods are evil, we are to be pitied; for all men seek to worship something, and nothing is more piteous than worshiping the unworthy. But don't despair—it isn't for pity's sake that I've called you to Stratetix's home tonight. Instead I offer you hope!"

Maurice removed a scroll from his sleeve and held it up. He beckoned to Ana, who rose and came to stand beside him. At Maurice's request, she described how she and Teo had entered the temple of the Ancients and discovered the Sacred Writing of Deu. When Ana finished her tale, she sat down amid whispers around the room.

From the corner, Lewth spoke up. "Master Maurice, don't keep us in suspense any longer! What does the book say about this god named Deu?"

"There is much to tell, so I will let the book speak for itself. Professor Teofil has translated it, and he will retain the originals in a safe place. The scroll you see here has been diligently copied by Shaphan. I will read it to you now." He cleared his throat. "The name of the first book is Beginning, and it opens with these words: 'In the beginning, Deu created heaven and earth.'"

Maurice proceeded to read the first chapter of the Sacred Writing while the assembly listened with rapt attention. No one said a word as his sonorous voice filled the room. When he finished, he set aside the scroll and asked, "What do we learn about Deu from these holy words?"

Ana was first to speak up. "He is the Creator. We were made by him, man and woman, in his image."

"In fact, everything is made by him," Shaphan added. "In heaven and on the earth."

"His power is indeed great if he has made all things," Stratetix said in amazement.

"Yes, he's powerful," Helena agreed, "but he uses his power to bless. The book says he made the earth *good*."

The comments came in rapid succession as the community of spiritual explorers attempted to make sense of the Sacred Writing. Teo could hear the excitement in their voices as they offered various interpretations. Everyone was animated and engaged, even young Lina, who suggested that Deu felt "clean" to her. Maurice beamed as he fielded questions and guided the conversation. As Teo watched the scene unfold, he purposely stayed out of the discussion. *I'm just the translator of this book, not a disciple of its god*, he reminded himself. *I rely only on myself.*

The candles had burned low and the hour was late when Maurice finally brought the meeting to an end with a word of warning and a promise. "My friends, tonight we've stepped across the threshold into a new era. There will be danger involved and perhaps sacrifice. We all know how the state cults frown on religious innovation. If the High Priestess hears about this, she'll do everything she can to stop it, even if it means circumventing the law. Yet I believe the age of Deu is dawning in our realm. The time will come to testify openly about him. We will recognize that moment when it arrives. Until then, let us long for the day when the Chiveisi will turn away from idols to Deu as their God."

"I will pray to be ready when that day comes!" Lewth exclaimed. Emphatic nods and murmurs of affirmation accompanied his bold statement.

With the meeting concluded, Stratetix thanked his guests for coming and showed them to the door. Since Lewth was facing a lonely hike up to the Temple of Astrebril, Maurice offered him hospitality at the University instead. Lewth nodded in appreciation. They stepped outside and started down the footpath toward Lekovil, along with Teo and Shaphan.

A few moments later, the sound of footsteps in the snow behind them caused Maurice to hold up his hand. "Someone's following us!"

"It's okay," Teo said. "It's Anastasia." He stepped away from the group to meet her along the trail.

It was dark, but the stars were out, and Teo could see Ana was carrying a bundle in her arms. "I—I have something for you, Teo," she said. Her voice held a note of shyness that took Teo by surprise.

"For me?"

She nodded and held up her bundle. "It's a cloak. I made it from the skin of the bear that we took." Ana draped it over Teo's shoulders, then reached to fasten it at his neck. She looked up at him with a tentative smile, her eyes bright in the starlight. "It was because of this bear that I met you," she said softly. "I'm glad I did."

As she said it, she dropped her eyes and stepped backward, but Teo recognized her gift as the vulnerable gesture it was. He moved toward Ana, standing so close to her it seemed the cloak had enveloped them both. He could feel her warmth against him. "Thank you," he whispered in her ear.

"I'll treasure it." They remained like that for a long moment, until finally they separated, and Teo rejoined the men as Ana returned to the house.

"That's a fine cloak, Professor Teofil!" Shaphan exclaimed. His voice was full of admiration as he stroked the bearskin garment.

"A symbolic gift from an excellent woman," Maurice added. "May it always remind you that you faced the wild beast with Anastasia at your side."

Teo gazed into the western sky and inhaled the night air. "Above me is more like it," he said, then turned abruptly to the three waiting men. "Come on, let's go home."

❖   ❖   ❖

The mountains of Chiveis often held surprises when it came to the weather, and today was no exception. The high terraces sometimes experienced temperature inversions in which warm sunshine bathed an elevated location like Vingin while a cold mist swathed Lekovil down on the valley floor. On this early spring morning, Ana dodged patches of snow as she hiked through a sunny meadow with a basket on her arm. The air was so clear and dry, she felt she could reach out and touch the towering peaks that sparkled all around in their frosted mantle of white.

Ana arrived at Teo's open-air theater on the peaceful hillside above Vingin. Finding a clear space on one of the risers, she removed a pillow from her basket and stretched out in the sun. The warmth felt good, so she hiked up her skirt and kicked off her boots to let the sun's rays shine on her legs and toes. They would probably be pink tomorrow, but Ana was enjoying the unexpected foretaste of summer too much to mind. Overhead, a black chough soared on the wind while the music of alpine songbirds floated to her ears from the nearby trees.

After a time, Ana removed two more items from her basket—a dried apple and the scroll Shaphan had just delivered to her home. The community had decided Stratetix would keep Shaphan's copies of the Sacred Writing at his chalet, while the originals would be retained at the University. Master Maurice had instructed the community to read Deu's book as often as possible, and Ana wanted to take advantage of this opportunity. Only a week ago, they had received the first chapter of Beginning, and now Shaphan had delivered chapter 2. Ana rejoiced at the prospect of spending some quiet time outdoors reading the sacred text.

I wonder if I should pray first? Ana had to admit she didn't know how. The prayers of Chiveisian religion were rote formulas, which seemed inappropriate for a good God like Deu. Ana recalled how she had prayed before entering the magnificent temple in the Beyond, with Teo watching skeptically as she asked the God of the Ancients for wisdom. *Perhaps that's all there is to it. Perhaps I should just speak to Deu and ask him to reveal himself.* Ana stood and tilted her head backward, closing her eyes and lifting her palms toward the sky. She remained like that for a long time as the sun's warmth caressed her skin, the breeze stirred her hair against her throat, and the smooth flagstones cooled her bare feet. In her heart she reached out to Deu—and he reached back.

"Mighty Deu," she prayed aloud, "I'm small; you are great. I don't know you at all. My people don't know you. Would you come to me today? Here I am, your handmaiden. Come now, you are invited. Come to me. Come to the Kingdom of Chiveis."

Ana opened her eyes. Absolute silence surrounded her. The sky was an empty blue dome. Yet Ana knew—she *believed*—that Deu had heard.

Reclining on the stone bench again, Ana took a bite of her apple and began reading chapter 2 of Beginning. The account continued the creation story begun in chapter 1 but went into more detail, describing the making of the first man. As she read, Ana felt she was being granted access to ancient and weighty mysteries. She was astonished at how the Eternal One had formed the man from the soil of the earth, giving him a special garden to inhabit and cultivate. Yet the man didn't have a "similar helper." Ana noticed this was the first thing in Deu's creation that was *not* good. All the animals were brought to the man, but none was considered suitable for him. Finally Deu took one of the man's ribs, from which he created woman. When the man saw her, he rejoiced, for he knew she was taken from his own body and thus belonged to him. The chapter closed with a beautiful description of marital union, an intimacy so close that a man and his wife became "a single flesh." Ana marveled that something

Chiveisian society had so perverted, Deu, in his original plan, had made so lovely. He was a different sort of God than any she had ever encountered.

At the end of the scroll, Ana found that Teo had appended one of the hymns of Deu. Though she knew it had been written long ago in the forgotten culture of an unknown people, the realization dawned on her that these holy words could speak to her today. Her heartbeat quickened as she read:

> Utter to the Eternal One a cry of joy, all you who inhabit the earth.
> Serve the Eternal One with joy; come with exhilaration into his presence!
> Know that Deu is the Eternal One.
> It is he who has made us, and we belong to him.
> We are his people, and the flock of his pasture.
> Enter his gates with praises, and his courtyards with songs!
> Celebrate him! Bless his name!
> For the Eternal One is good;
> his kindness always endures,
> and his fidelity, from generation to generation.

Ana sat up on the stone riser and set aside the scroll. Powerful emotions resonated inside her, quivering there like a vibrant chord playing on her heartstring, a feeling too profound for words. Tears welled up, and Ana refused to stop them. At first they merely wet her eyes, but then they became abundant, until they rolled down her cheeks in streams. For the first time in her life, she realized she had never worshiped the one who most deserved it. Deu towered above the heavens—the Eternal One, whose mighty hand had raised the snowcapped summits to their heights in aeons past. Ana intentionally went into herself, crossing her arms over her chest and bowing her head. Even so, she felt conspicuous. Humbled by her puny pretenses at glory, she collapsed on the ground and knelt before the stone seat with her fingers interlocked in front of her lips. Her shoulders began to shake, and for a long time she wept in the lonely theater, squeezing out tears of contrition for her secret sins and regret for repenting so late. But soon, mingled with her sorrow, the tears of rejoicing came flowing down. *How sad!* she mourned. *How sad to have lived twenty-four years without knowing you! But oh, Deu, how joyous, how joyous to begin a new life this very day!*

It was love that finally dried Ana's tears. The warm breath of divine passion washed over her, banishing her sadness and replacing it with grace. Her soul sang a new song out of its ineffable fullness: *How great you are, my Savior God!* She opened herself then, and the Eternal One came to her, all-radiant in the perfection of his power and love and purity. Ana felt her heart overflowing with a secure and confident joy. She knew Deu was real. She knew he was good. And she knew he was her God.

✦   ✦   ✦

Valent dropped the bundle of ermine pelts onto the counter at the furrier's shop in Lekovil.

"Nice work, Valent," the clerk said. "You're the best trapper on our payroll." He handed over a pouch of coins.

"I think you may be right," Valent answered with a grin, tying the pouch to his waist. He winked at the clerk and exited.

Across the street, a tavern beckoned, and Valent decided he could afford a good ale. He entered the dim room, furnished with walnut tables and chairs, and found a seat near the door. Raising a finger to the barmaid, he called out, "Your best!" She brought him a stein and set it on the table with a saucy flounce of her hips.

In the corner, some University students were engaged in a heated discussion, indulging themselves in cheap beer and even cheaper logic. One of them was Shaphan, the young man who had made the excellent knife hanging from Valent's belt. The fur trapper chuckled to himself and approached their table.

"Shaphan, I see you make keen arguments in addition to keen knives!" The students ceased their arguing and gazed up at the red-haired stranger.

"Master Valent, how nice to see you!" Shaphan seemed genuinely pleased.

"May I join you?" Valent turned to the barmaid and signaled for her to bring a round of the good ale, then seated himself at the table.

"We were just discussing the problem of evil," Shaphan said. "Where does it come from, and what is its nature?"

"Shaphan has the crazy idea that we're all cursed because of it," one of the students said.

Valent took a long draft from his stein and swallowed the ale thoughtfully. "He's right, if you understand what evil really is."

The students looked skeptical, but the barmaid arrived with the new round of drinks, so they waited until she left before resuming their debate.

"What do you know about such matters?" another student demanded.

"What I know isn't available to you. You have to earn my favor."

The student rolled his eyes. "How do I do that?"

"Some gratitude for that mug in your hand would be a good start."

"That's right," Shaphan admonished. "Master Valent bought you drinks. The least you can do is hear him out!"

Valent smiled and leaned back. "Shaphan is indeed courteous. But the fact of the matter is, I can't add anything to you men right now."

"Why not?"

"You can only add to what is empty. He who would receive must first divest."

The students scoffed at this remark and dismissed Valent with a wave of their hands. "Thanks for the ale," one of them said. "You're generous, but that's not the same thing as being wise." They moved to the back room, leaving Shaphan alone with Valent. An awkward silence lingered between them.

"I think you're wise, Master Valent," Shaphan offered.

"I think you're wise to believe me wise."

"You're a spiritual seeker, aren't you?"

Valent nodded. "And a finder."

Shaphan lowered his head and glanced around the room. He leaned close to Valent and asked in a whisper, "Do you want to know about some new wisdom coming to Chiveis?"

"All wisdom is my domain."

"I have access to a secret book. A book of the Ancients."

Valent's ears perked up when he heard these words. In his youth he had led a group of religious dissidents seeking a more personal experience of the divine than the state cults could provide. Eventually the group had disbanded, but Valent always remembered the thrill of exploring radical ideas and the exhilaration of being revered as an authority. He looked across the table at the innocent young man with the naive smile and the puppy-dog eyes.

"Tell me more, Shaphan," he said.

✦   ✦   ✦

Teo set down his quill and rubbed his forehead between his fingers. Translating the Fluid Tongue of the Ancients was no easy task.

There was a knock at the door.

"Yes?"

"Professor Teofil, you have a visitor waiting at the gate."

Teo sighed. "Alright. Let him in. I'll meet him at the waterfall."

"It's a woman, sir. I'll admit her."

A *woman?* Teo considered the possibilities. He decided to hope for one of two outcomes—that it would be Ana, or it wouldn't be Habiloho.

What if it is Ana? Teo knew he had been beating around the bush with her for too long. The guys at the local barracks of the First Regiment had been ribbing him about his lack of progress. *Maybe it's time I made this beautiful woman my lover.* He chided himself for being so slow and resolved to turn on the charm. It had never failed him before.

When Teo arrived in the University's courtyard, he knew right away he'd gotten the outcome he wanted. Though the woman standing by the waterfall had her back to him, Teo had ridden too many trails staring at that long, honey-colored hair not to recognize it at once.

"Hello, Ana."

She was wearing a green velvet dress with an embroidered neckline. Purple amethysts hung from her ears, and she wore a delicate silver bracelet around her wrist. Her heart-shaped mouth broke into a smile when she turned to greet him. She was absolutely stunning.

"Teo! I hope I'm not interrupting your work! It's just that—well, I wanted to tell you something."

He gave her a rakish grin. "I think I've been wanting to tell you the same thing."

Ana reacted with a funny look, but he dismissed it. "You go first," he said. "I'm listening."

She took Teo's hand and pulled him down until they were seated on the low wall that encircled the waterfall's plunge pool. It was a sunny day, and a rainbow arced through the mist. *A good setting*, Teo thought.

"I've come to realize something," Ana said, her tone earnest. "Something so important, it has consumed my soul. Changed the whole course of my life, in fact."

Teo nodded in an understanding way. "Go on."

"I've pledged my heart—my life—"

"I know. Just go ahead and say it." Teo beamed as he took her delicate hand in his.

Ana inhaled deeply and looked Teo in the eyes. "I've given my life to Deu!" she said triumphantly.

Huh?

Teo jumped up from the plunge pool and turned away, his hands on his hips. *She's given her life to Deu? What is she talking about?* Quickly, he tried to collect his thoughts.

"What do you think of that?" Ana's voice was uncertain. "Do you feel the same way about him?"

Teo turned back toward Ana, forcing himself to be as polite as possible. "Well, uh . . ." He kicked a pebble with his toe and scratched his head. *What should I say?* "I . . . I've certainly enjoyed my study of the ancient book," he said at last.

"But what about Deu himself? He has shown me his goodness. Don't you sense it too?"

"I guess . . . I guess I would have to say no. Mine is more of an academic interest."

"Academic? Aren't you moved by what you read about him?"

"Moved intellectually, yes."

Ana stood up and approached Teo, her lovely face crestfallen.

This isn't going like you had hoped, he thought. *Maybe you can salvage it.*

"Ana, listen. I think it's great that you've found religion. I really do. It's just not something I need."

"I think we all need the one true God." There was deep hurt in Ana's voice.

"That's not all a woman needs," Teo said, stepping closer to Ana.

"Teo, what are you doing? I'm trying to talk about Deu."

"I don't care about Deu!" Teo burst out in frustration. "I care about you!" He started to take Ana in his arms but immediately recognized it was the wrong move and recoiled. At the same moment, Ana pushed him away. Thrown off balance, Teo slipped on a patch of moss and fell against the low wall of the plunge pool. Before he could catch himself, he toppled backward into the freezing water.

Horrified, Ana stared at him with her mouth open as he sputtered in the pool.

"I'm . . . I'm sorry I came," she stammered, then ran from the courtyard.

❖ ❖ ❖

Lewth was eating a meager meal of bread and water in his hovel at the High Priestess's temple—his only food for the day—when someone rapped on his door. He poked his head outside and peered at the visitor from deep within his cowl.

"The abbot summons you," the messenger said without further explanation.

Lewth's heart lurched. *My secret meetings with the house community must have been discovered!* Torture was probable, and because he was a monk sworn to the High Priestess, she had the power to execute him. He prayed as he strapped on his sandals and hurried outside. *May Deu be with me!*

In the chapter house, the abbot of the Fraternal Order of Astrebril was seated on his throne, accompanied by some government officials from the royal palace. Lewth swallowed and slowly approached the throne, whispering another prayer for divine aid.

"Brother Lewth, greet me."

Lewth fell to his knees and kissed the ring on the abbot's extended hand. His lips trembled as he did so, but he hoped the abbot wouldn't notice.

"You may rise," the abbot said. "I have sad news to report today, my son. One of our own, Brother Tumas, has passed on to Astrebril's halls. Did you know Brother Tumas, by chance?" The abbot arched his eyebrows.

"Reverend Father, I knew him only by reputation."

"And what was his reputation?"

"That he was a learned man, adept in many forms of knowledge, both natural and divine."

"Brother Lewth, take pride in the fact that such is also your reputation."

"I take pride in it, Reverend Father, as you command."

The abbot smiled benevolently as he gazed down at Lewth from on high. The whiskers of his chin were waxed to a sharp point, making him resemble Astrebril himself. Lewth shuddered at the thought.

"Do you know what task occupied Brother Tumas during the years preceding his demise?" the abbot asked.

"I do not. I only knew him from his scholarly writings on flora and fauna."

"He was a teacher. Several years ago, our blessed and glorious King Piair"—the abbot paused to receive nods of acknowledgment from the royal officials standing beside him—"requested a learned monk of Astrebril to tutor the crown prince."

Suddenly Lewth understood. Though he felt some relief that he wouldn't be sent to the rack, he also experienced a new sense of unease. He feared an immense set of complications was about to invade his life.

"Reverend Father, how may I be of service in this matter?"

"You are to become the next tutor of Crown Prince Piair II." There was no equivocation in the abbot's voice. It was a direct command.

Lewth didn't respond right away, for his mind was racing. He no longer believed the theology of the Order of Astrebril, so how could he teach it to the prince? Of course, most of their discussions would dwell on scientific matters, not religious ones. Even so, the question of religion was bound to come up. What then? Would he be courageous enough to say something about Deu to the heir apparent? Lewth's pulse quickened as he considered the incredible opportunities his new role would offer. *Could this be how Deu will come to the people of Chiveis?*

"I await your response!" The abbot's tone was sharp with impatience. Lewth snapped out of his reverie.

"It is an honor I willingly accept."

Deu, give me strength!

❖   ❖   ❖

The house community had already arrived at Stratetix's chalet in Vingin by the time Maurice got there—everyone except Shaphan and his two guests.

Helena took Maurice's cloak and hung it up as he turned to address the expectant group. "Our brother Shaphan will be here shortly," Maurice announced. "He has invited two visitors to attend our meeting. Their names are Valent and Sucula, a husband and wife who wish to learn of Deu."

From the murmuring and fidgeting in the room, Maurice could see the community was uncomfortable with the announcement. They all knew how much trouble would come to them if the religious authorities got word of their gathering. Although no laws forbade spiritual exploration, the High Priestess and her clergy had a reputation for harassment.

"Master Maurice, I'm not sure that's wise," Stratetix said. "We can't go speaking about Deu to everyone we encounter."

"I understand your concerns, Stratetix, and I share them in part. I confess, when Shaphan proposed the idea of inviting guests, I too was skeptical. But Shaphan insisted his friends were genuine seekers of divine truth. As I thought about the matter, I realized that if Deu is the All-Creator, then he's a God for all of Chiveis, not just for us. We must consider how we can bring the people of this kingdom to him, even if it involves risk. Perhaps Shaphan has begun that process already."

"Here he comes now," Helena said as she looked out the window. "With his guests." She opened the door.

Valent entered first, followed by Sucula, then Shaphan. Valent was a handsome man, around forty years old, with a well-trimmed beard and a powerful physique. His clothes were outdoorsy but impeccably kept. Maurice discerned right away he was a capable and charismatic individual. Valent's petite wife, Sucula, was much younger than he, perhaps in her late twenties. She was unquestionably beautiful, with raven hair and full red lips. Though she didn't have the commanding presence her husband possessed, she was by no means shy; she carried herself with confidence as she entered a room full of strangers.

"Welcome to our gathering, friends," Maurice said. He introduced himself, then everyone else. Valent and Sucula greeted each member of the community, shaking hands with them before taking their seats next to Shaphan. Helena distributed mugs of hot cider to her guests.

Maurice stood. "May the blessings of Deu be on each of you," he said. "As we begin our gathering this evening, Anastasia has something she'd like to propose." He held out his hand toward Ana.

Ana rose from her seat. "We're just starting to learn about Deu. He's a good and loving God who made the entire world. And I think he must also enjoy music if his book contains—I forget—how many hymns? Do you remember, Teofil?"

Teo glanced up from the loose thread he was picking on his sleeve. "Sorry, what did you say?"

"How many hymns are in the Sacred Writing?"

"Oh. A hundred and fifty."

"Right, a hundred and fifty. That's a lot of songs, and they must be important to Deu's worship. I thought perhaps we could sing one of them?" Receiving several nods of affirmation, she continued, "I took the liberty of setting one to music. I'll teach it to you, and we can sing it whenever we gather. I have my harp."

"A worthy idea, Anastasia," said Stratetix. "Teach it to us."

"The hymn is called 'Utter to the Eternal One a Cry of Joy.' It goes like this." Ana plucked a prelude on her harp, then began to sing. Her crystal voice mingled with the harp's resonant notes to create a sweet melody in the chalet. She increased her volume and let the music carry her away as a spirit of holiness entered the room. With the final words, *His kindness always endures, and his fidelity, from generation to generation,* she lowered the harp and looked up.

"That was beautiful, Ana," Lina breathed.

"I think we should all sing it," Maurice said.

Ana recited the lyrics to the group, indicating the proper tune as she went along. Soon everyone seemed to have it, so on Ana's cue, they began to sing. The addition of male voices created a pleasing harmony as the community worshiped their newfound God. Maurice smiled as he surveyed his flock. Most of them were singing with enthusiasm, though he did notice Teo's contributions appeared halfhearted. Maurice resolved to speak to his student about it later.

After the hymn was sung, Maurice motioned toward Lewth, who announced his new appointment as tutor to the crown prince. The assembly seemed to grasp the potential significance of this turn of events.

"I'm terrified," Lewth admitted, "so I ask for your prayers. Pray that I might be resolute when the time comes."

"Deu has put you in a strategic place," Maurice said with conviction. "Let us be praying for our brother Lewth, and also for the heart of Crown Prince Piair."

Maurice reached into his sleeve and produced a scroll. "It's time for the reading. Professor Teofil has worked hard to translate this for us, and Shaphan has copied it for our use. We thank them both for their efforts. I hold here the third chapter of the book of Beginning. It has some difficult things to tell us. Listen now to the words of Deu."

By the flickering light of a candle, Maurice began to read as the community listened intently. He described how the serpent, a crafty beast, tempted the woman named Eve to eat from a magical tree whose fruit Deu had forbidden. She also gave some fruit to her husband, Adam, who ate it as well.

"Notice that Deu is displeased," Maurice said. He described how Deu came to the garden and found the man and woman hiding their nakedness. Deu inquired about the magical tree, and Adam confessed he had eaten of it, blaming his wife for the sin. Deu then confronted Eve, and she blamed the serpent. In response, Deu instituted three grievous curses. The serpent was condemned to go about on its belly and to be hated by mankind. The woman would have increased pain in childbirth. In addition, her desires would be directed toward her husband, but he would dominate her. Finally, the man's labors would be made difficult. Deu declared the ground itself accursed, requiring much toil to make it productive.

Maurice paused his reading and glanced around the silent room. Every eye was focused on him; several mouths were agape. Maurice concluded the narrative by describing how Deu banished the man and woman from the garden forever, placing a flaming angel at its gate to prevent reentry. Adam and Eve were prevented from attaining eternal life.

"Deu was angry at this disobedience of his law," Lewth observed. "His penalties are severe."

"Indeed. And what else do you discern from this reading, my friends?" Maurice asked.

"I see damage to relationships," Helena said, her voice tinged with sadness. "The man and his wife were together in their nakedness, with no shame between them. But after they transgressed, they felt compelled to hide. Their oneness was lost. Did you notice how Adam's protective instinct became corrupted? When he was confronted with his sin, he tried to divert Deu's anger toward Eve! The Sacred Writing teaches that a wife's desire will be for her husband, but sadly, he will dominate her."

"It's true," Stratetix agreed. "Men are stronger than women. Our constant temptation is to mistreat our wives instead of loving them."

Helena took her husband's hand and stroked it gently.

"Let us consider what we have learned here," Maurice said. "This chapter reveals something new about the All-Creator. He is a God who will not tolerate sin and punishes it when it occurs."

Valent stood and began to pace, his brow furrowed. At length he turned to the assembly and spoke. "I know I'm just a guest tonight," he said. "But may I offer something?"

Maurice nodded. "Of course."

Valent heaved a sigh. "I'm not sure we're on the right path here. I think we're reading these holy words at face value without accessing the secret knowledge they contain."

"What are you trying to say, Valent?" Lewth asked.

"Might we be reading these words too simply? I think there's something hidden within them."

"Like what?"

"Well, to begin, let's not jump to the conclusion that Deu is an angry God or that he's worried about our sins. Is it worthy of the All-Creator to be concerned with our day-to-day morality? I don't think so. Wouldn't he focus on more important things? I suggest we read the text symbolically to uncover its arcane meaning."

"Master Valent has a good point," Shaphan said. "Deu is too lofty to care about the minor sins we commit." Lina nodded in agreement.

"Thank you for that affirmation, Shaphan." Valent wandered the room, looking each person in the eye. "I think what we find in the book of Beginning is a symbolic account of how to attain knowledge. What is sin? I don't think it's a moral failing. It's our lack of divine enlightenment! Think about it. The real hero of the story is the serpent, for he's the one who offers access to the Tree of Knowledge. Adam stands for the common man, the man who dares to take hold of knowledge but then turns away from it as if it's something shameful. He hides because he fears the nakedness of possessing elite wisdom. Don't you see? The reason Deu is displeased isn't because Adam broke some arbitrary law. It's because after Adam had tasted knowledge, he shrank back from using it to the fullest! Therefore, Deu banished him from the garden of further enlightenment."

"So you're saying we're supposed to finish what Adam started," Rosetta said. "To reach out and take hold of forbidden knowledge." She looked around the room. "That makes sense to me."

"Me too," Lina said meekly.

Ana rose from her seat. "It makes no sense at all," she said firmly, "and I'll tell you why."

"Go ahead, Anastasia." Maurice motioned for Valent to sit.

"First of all, why are we making this so complex when it doesn't need to be? The narrative should be understood plainly, not according to secret symbols. It's obvious: Deu was angry at the sin. He says, 'Because you did such and such, here is the curse I'm implementing.' Second, we cannot doubt that Deu takes sin seriously. In fact, I believe he requires blood sacrifice in exchange for it. Remember when Adam and Eve were cast out

237

of the garden? God clothed them with animal skins. Notice that their sin required the death of an animal."

Sucula spoke up for the first time. "I don't think that point is emphasized in the text, Anastasia."

"I agree it's not entirely clear," Ana countered. "But let me tell you something I discovered about Deu in his temple." The community fell silent as Ana described the two murals she had seen on the temple's rear wall in which several men were depicted offering sacrifices, and a heavenly hand reached down to accept them. "I believe Deu is a God who hates sin and requires sacrifice," she concluded.

"That's a powerful idea," Helena said.

"Nevertheless, I think it's incorrect." Sucula stared at Ana. "The way my husband explained it offers us hope—hope that we might one day achieve inner enlightenment. But if Anastasia is right, there is no hope, just the endless repetition of bloody sacrifices."

Ana held her ground. "Didn't you hear what Deu said to the woman? He told her she would be in conflict with the serpent. The serpent would bite the woman's descendant on the heel, but the descendant would crush the serpent's head! See? There *is* hope in this passage."

Sucula folded her hands in her lap. "Maybe you're right," she said demurely. "I'm just a visitor here. What do I know?"

The community sat back and took a collective breath. "We will consider this important matter and discuss it another time," Maurice said. His words signaled that the evening was concluded, so everyone finished their cider and rose to find their cloaks.

Outside in the bright moonlight, the group began to disperse. The temperature had dipped below freezing, and the wind had picked up. Maurice tightened his hood and started down the trail toward Lekovil, accompanied by Lewth, Teo, and Shaphan.

"Professor Teofil! Could you wait a moment?" Sucula approached the four men in the snow, her breath coming in little white puffs that swirled around her head.

"Yes? What is it?"

"Uh, I just wanted to say how much I appreciate your translation work. I know you spent a lot of time doing it, and I'm sure it's not easy. So I'm . . . I'm grateful to you." She put her hand on Teo's arm.

"It's a labor I enjoy," he said. "But thanks. You're kind to mention it."

A gust of wind blasted down the mountainside, staggering Sucula under its force. "That wind is so bitter!" she exclaimed.

"Your cloak is too thin, Sucula. Where's Valent?"

"Oh, right, Valent . . ." She fiddled with a lock of her hair. "He, uh, he had to go up to his cabin on the trapline tonight. *Again.*" There was a note of exasperation in her voice.

"Where do you live?"

She explained where her home was. "I think I can make it. Really. I'll be okay."

"That's a long walk. You'll freeze. The wind saps your warmth."

Sucula snapped her head toward Teo, her eyes wide. "Hey, I have an idea! Perhaps you could accompany me. To make sure I get home safely?"

Maurice cleared his throat. "Teo, my son, it's getting late. The University's gate will soon be locked for the night. Wisdom would dictate you come with us. Sucula knows her way home."

Teo sighed. He unbuttoned his bearskin cloak and wrapped it around Sucula's shoulders, fastening it securely at her neck. "That should keep you warm until you get home," he said.

She leaned forward and said something in Teo's ear, causing him to nod at her uncertainly.

"Good night, Sucula," Maurice said. "May Deu go with you." He waited as she turned toward her house, while his own group started down the other path toward Lekovil. Lewth led the way, followed by Shaphan, then Teo, who hunched his shoulders and crossed his arms over his chest in the biting wind. Maurice remained in one place as he watched each person leave.

"Sometimes, Teo, you're *too* noble," he said under his breath.

Maurice turned and looked back at the chalet one last time. A slim figure stood at the window. Suddenly the curtains were drawn shut with a jerk.

The old professor shook his head and moved to catch up to his companions.

CHAPTER

10

Dawn was Astrebril's time. He had chosen it, sanctified it, and claimed it as his own, for it symbolized his triumph over apparent defeat. Long ago, in the age of the Ancients' great war, he had almost been forgotten. His mighty power was curtailed, forcing him to manipulate events behind the scenes. Few worshiped him openly. But now in Chiveis, Astrebril had once again achieved the rank of supreme deity. Like the sun waxing in the morning sky, his glorious reign would nevermore be broken. Or at least, such were the teachings Princess Habiloho had learned during her training as an acolyte.

Habiloho stared at the flame of a single candle whose flickering glow cast eerie shadows on the idol niches of the chapel at the High Priestess's temple. Though she was supposed to be meditating before the altar, Habiloho was too weary to focus. Her strict fast the day before and her sleepless vigil through the night had left her in a state of exhaustion. Outside the window, a gray light had begun to grow in the east. Habiloho had been told to expect a momentous event when the dawn finally came, though she had no idea what it would be. She awaited that magic hour with trepidation and desire.

The chapel door creaked open, though no one had touched it.

"Who's there?" Habiloho rose from her kneeling position at the altar, tiptoed to the door, and peeked out. The hallway was empty. She sighed and slumped against the door frame.

"Come!" said a voice behind her. Habiloho shrieked and spun around.

THE SWORD

The High Priestess of Chiveis stood beside the altar, her white face stark against the gloom. Habiloho trembled as the priestess approached. A smoky, herbal aroma emanated from her body.

"You must learn to access the revelations of Astrebril, young acolyte," the High Priestess intoned. "Come with me."

Habiloho followed the High Priestess behind a tapestry on the wall. It led through a secret portal to a spiral staircase. The two worshippers ascended the stairs, rising higher and higher as the tower reached toward Astrebril's face. Habiloho's thighs burned with the exertion of so many steps. Just when she thought she would have to stop and take a rest, they reached an oaken door. Habiloho panted against the wall as the High Priestess turned a key in the lock.

"Enter the sacred chamber," said the High Priestess. She did not seem at all winded by the climb.

The circular room had four windows and a table with some implements on it, yet its most prominent feature was the great pit at its center. Smoke rose from it, exiting through a hole in the roof. Chains attached to a windlass hung from the ceiling. Habiloho could feel her heart thumping in her chest.

"If you are to be a priestess of Astrebril, you must learn how to contact the heavenly spirits," the High Priestess said. "Do exactly as you are told and you will survive, though the experience will terrify you, as it should."

Two blond effeminates entered the room. One took Habiloho's shoes and set them aside. The other handed her a goblet of red wine. He instructed her to drink it while he gathered the chains from the ceiling and brought them near. At the ends of the chains were manacles, which the eunuchs fastened to Habiloho's wrists when she finished drinking.

"In time you will learn to hold yourself in place of your own volition," the High Priestess said. "Until then we must bind you."

Habiloho realized she was about to be lowered into the pit. Her knees buckled as she was overcome by a wave of terror. "I . . . I can't do this!" she pled.

"You must." The High Priestess pushed her into the pit, and the nightmare began.

Habiloho dangled by her wrists, raw fear clawing at her gut. The manacles gouged her skin as they supported her entire weight. A tiny orange light danced far below in the abyss. She gasped and coughed as the sickly sweet smoke engulfed her, cloying her nostrils, fogging her brain. The sensation of vastness beneath her toes made Habiloho want to scream, but she choked back her cries of terror lest she call forth the wrath of some underworld spirit. Lights and colors swirled around her. Sometimes they congealed into leering faces; other times they flitted about like pestering imps. Habiloho kicked her legs wildly as she struggled against the shapeless beings.

An angel with yellow eyes, sharp fangs, and great wings spread out like a dragon materialized out of the darkness. He extended his clawed hand, and Habiloho found herself willing to receive him. As she did, a more serene feeling came to her—a thrilling, frightening, exhilarating pleasure. She lost awareness of the world above. Time slid by uncontrolled. Finally, in the dreamlike state of her trance, she could feel herself being hauled up and loosened from her manacles.

The princess was led to a table. She leaned on it with both hands as her head swam. From what seemed to be a great distance, the High Priestess spoke in sluggish, distorted words. "The god will not give unless he first receives." She drew a razor across Habiloho's arm. A delicious, burning pain radiated from the crimson trail left by the steel edge. It made Habiloho feel alive.

"Take the quill and write," the High Priestess commanded.

Habiloho took a deep breath and tried to focus her thoughts. Finding a quill in her hand, she set it to a piece of parchment. Her hand seemed to move of its own accord as she scrawled some words with the ink of her own blood.

"Read it."

Habiloho squinted. The words were indistinct.

"Read it!" the High Priestess insisted.

"I think it says . . ." Habiloho bent to the page and tried to discern what was written there. "He who comes . . . with the sword . . ." She blinked and shook her head, trying to clear her blurry vision.

"FINISH!"

". . . is—is in your midst."

The High Priestess snarled and whirled from the table. As she strode past the eunuch standing on the edge of the pit, she shoved him hard in the back, and he tumbled into its infinite depths with a terrified, fading scream. Grabbing the other man by the throat, she thrust her face into his and shouted, "Issue a summons at once! I want the archpriest of Vulkain brought to me right away! His men are needed for an urgent task!" The frightened eunuch nodded at the furious priestess. "Now!" She threw him by the neck, and he stumbled out the door.

Habiloho dropped to the floor and closed her eyes. It was all she could do.

✦   ✦   ✦

Teo had been translating all morning when a knock on his door interrupted him.

"I'm not in!" he shouted.

"Is that any way to treat a friend?"

Teo jumped from his chair and opened the door to Maurice. "I'm sorry! I didn't realize it was you."

"No offense taken. I understand what it is to be absorbed in scholarship. In fact, that's why I've come. You've been so focused on your work, you haven't had time for conversation."

Teo smiled ruefully. "You're right. That's what I like about you, Master. You always watch out for me."

The old professor smiled and clasped Teo on the shoulder. "Put away your things and come to my rooms. I'll have tea ready."

Teo hid the Sacred Writing and his translator's notes under his bed, then stepped outside, locking the door behind him. The morning was brisk. Even though it was the fifth month and the buds were on the trees, a chill lingered in the air as Teo walked down the colonnade to Maurice's rooms. Hot tea would be a welcome treat, and he could use the break from his studies.

Teo took his usual place on the settee, while Maurice sat in his upholstered leather chair. They drank their juniper tea in silence, the wall clock making the only sound in the cozy room.

"What are you thinking about?" Maurice asked at length.

Teo chuckled. "To be honest, I was thinking about you."

"My charm, wit, and good looks?" Maurice had a twinkle in his eyes.

"Of course," Teo answered, returning the mischievous expression. "How could I ever forget it?" The men shared the laughter of close friends.

After a few moments, Teo looked at Maurice more seriously. "Actually, I was remembering when I first met you," he said.

"Ah, yes. You were just a boy. Cocky and insecure at the same time."

"Now I'm just cocky."

"I won't argue with that."

"Do you remember how we met? I had just been sent here from the orphanage."

"I remember it well. You could hardly walk because the wardens had caned you for some offense. You were hobbling around like a sailor after a long horse ride!" Teo jumped to his feet and mimicked the bowlegged gait as Maurice laughed at his antics.

Teo returned to his seat and sipped his tea, looking out the window. "The wardens always told me I was wicked. Every single day I had to tell myself I wasn't." Teo lowered his eyes and gazed at the floor. "You were the first person who ever treated me like I was worth something."

Maurice set his cup on his saucer. "Teo, my heart loved you right away. Not only because of your great potential in life, though I could see that well enough. It was something more—something I can't explain. You were the son I never had."

"Why didn't you have a family, Master?"

Maurice explored the depths of his teacup. "There was a time I thought I might," he said, rising to refill his cup from the pot. "But never mind that. Ancient history isn't the subject for today." He poured more tea into Teo's cup, then handed him a little pitcher of cream. "I want to talk about religion."

"It seems to be your favorite subject these days." Teo poured the cream. "The house community is thriving under your care."

"I think so, too. However, I'm worried about one of its members."

"Which one?"

"You."

Teo glanced at Maurice. "Me? How come?"

"You seem, if I may say so, rather *uninvolved* at times, like you're going through the motions. Your head is in it, but not your heart."

"As always, you have me figured out. That's exactly how I feel. And it's intentional, I might add."

"Why?"

"Because I don't need gods and religion in my life. Everything is going fine as it is."

"Everything? Including all your relationships?"

Teo sighed. "Well, now that you mention it, things are a little rocky with Ana."

"Tell me about it."

"We had a disagreement a few weeks ago, and now things are strained between us."

"Hmm. Not to add to your troubles, but you should probably know that Anastasia saw you talking with Sucula after the last meeting. That will increase the strain."

Teo waved his hand. "Nah, I doubt it. She won't care about that."

"I think she will. Men care about actions. Women care about the meaning *behind* the actions. When you gave Sucula the cloak, you gave away the symbol of Anastasia's affection for you. To another woman."

Teo puffed out his cheeks and expelled a long breath. "I don't think I'm cut out for romance," he said. "When it comes to fighting with swords and axes, I can do it. Finding a trail, hunting game, coming up with a plan—that I know how to do. But all this stuff with Ana and her religion is too confusing. Maybe I should just forget about her!"

Maurice frowned. "Could you do that?"

"No," Teo admitted. He brightened a little. "One time when we were out in the Beyond, we were sitting around the campfire, and I was looking at Ana. She's so gorgeous, you know, and the soft firelight was on her face, and I just . . . I just couldn't take my eyes off her! Her cheeks, her mouth, the shape of her neck—she's flawless, like a priceless jewel! She didn't see me because she was looking away, so I kept staring at her. I couldn't help it. And I thought to myself, 'By the gods, she is *so* beautiful!' I was completely captivated. I knew right then—" He paused.

"What did you know?"

"I'm not sure how to say it. I guess I knew that our lives had become permanently intertwined."

"I think you're right, Teo. So what should you do?"

"I need a new plan. My old ways don't seem to work on Ana." He thought it over as he sipped his tea. "Maybe I should try to be more religious. I could be more talkative in the meetings, do good deeds, write holy poems and everything. She would like that, and then in no time I'd be back in her favor. What do you think?"

"I think there's a flaw in your plan."

Teo was surprised. "What is it?"

"The problem is, that's *Teo's* plan, not Deu's plan."

"I don't understand."

"Deu is the All-Creator. He's not a God to be manipulated by rituals and good deeds and token offerings. He makes the plans; your place is to heed them."

Teo rose from the settee and set down his cup. He rebelled at Maurice's implication, though out of respect for his mentor he didn't want to show it. "I can't accept that," he said at last. "I've tried fearing the gods before, and it didn't work out. Now I chart my own course in life. If Deu wants to join me, he's welcome to. If his religion helps me patch up things with Ana, great. If not, so be it. But I don't want any deity telling me what to do." He folded his arms across his chest. The clock ticked on the wall.

For a long time, Maurice rubbed his shaved head in his palm, until at last he looked up at his student. "Teo, I think you have to let Deu be the God he is, not the god you want him to be."

It wasn't the answer Teo was seeking. "Master Maurice," he said, "I admire your faith." He politely excused himself and returned to his study.

✦   ✦   ✦

"Blessings on you this evening," Maurice said to the community assembled in Stratetix's chalet. "It has been a fortnight since we last gathered, and it is good to be with you once more in the presence of Deu. Let us begin with the hymn that has become our own, 'Utter to the Eternal One a Cry of Joy.' Anastasia, would you please lead us?" He motioned toward her, and she retrieved her harp.

"Sing it to Deu alone," Ana said as she played a prelude. "Enter his gates with praises, and his courtyards with songs."

As the harp's notes and the harmonious voices ascended to heaven, Maurice stole a sidelong glance at Teo. He was singing, but his heart still wasn't in it. Maurice regretted their sharp words earlier that day, though he wouldn't have changed anything he'd said. *Soften him, O Deu*, he prayed.

After the hymn, Maurice inquired about the welfare of the community. He asked that any needs be mentioned aloud, so they could be brought before Deu.

Lewth raised his hand. "May I speak first? I continue to seek courage for my appointment as tutor to the prince. I begin my new role in two weeks." Everyone offered words of encouragement.

"Chiveis will come to Deu someday," Maurice predicted. "Who else has a need?"

Rosetta lifted her hand hesitantly. "I'm sorry to mention it," she said, "but my mare will be foaling soon. I'm sure Deu doesn't care about such small matters. It's just that, well, I've always wanted Lina to have her own horse, and—oh, never mind."

"Do not doubt that Deu cares about such things, sister," Maurice advised. "He is the All-Creator. I believe he cares about the daily needs of a widow and her daughter."

Rosetta nodded at Maurice, the gratitude clearly etched on her face.

"I have something," Lina said. She kept her eyes on her lap. "I need wisdom about . . . um, a friend . . . and . . . what I should do. Uh, that's all."

Maurice smiled warmly. "Such matters of the heart are important to a young lady. Yes, indeed, we will ask Deu's blessing on this relationship of yours." Lina giggled, while next to her, Shaphan blushed.

"Everyone get down! NOW!"

Teo's sharp command was obeyed instantly. Valent alone remained standing while the rest of the group scrambled to the floor. He joined Teo at the window. "What is it? What did you hear?"

"Armed riders. Several of them. There's no good reason for them to be around here at night."

Valent put his back to the wall and lifted the curtain's edge with a finger. "Vulkainians!" Frightened moans arose from the room. Teo drew his sword, and Valent pulled out his knife.

Stratetix rose from his crouch and put his hand on Teo's arm. "No, not that way. Now's not the time. Quick! Everyone into the root cellar!"

Stratetix ran into the back room, which served as the kitchen. He lifted a trapdoor and helped everyone except his family members descend into the cramped space. Closing the trapdoor, he covered it with a rug. The cellar went dark.

A fist hammered on the front door. "Open up immediately, in the name of the High Priestess!"

In the musty cellar, Maurice whispered to the frightened group, "Silence, everyone. Just pray."

Above, Stratetix set the stage. "Ana, get upstairs! You're reading quietly in your room. Don't come down. Helena, you're cooking back here. I'll get the door."

The front door squeaked open. The footsteps of several men pounded on the floorboards as they barged into the chalet.

"What do you think you're doing?" Stratetix protested. "We've done nothing wrong!"

"That's what we're here to find out," said a rough voice.

"Who are you?"

"Vulkain's militia. The High Priestess has received a vision that heresies have sprung up in Chiveis. We're supposed to be looking for anything suspicious."

"I'm no heretic. What do you want with me?"

"We're keeping an eye out for secret meetings. We heard singing coming from this direction."

"So what? My wife and I enjoy music. We were singing. You should try it."

"Can you explain all those tracks leading to your door?"

"Friends stopping by throughout the day. Is there a law against that?"

"There might be soon."

"That's outrageous!"

Boots stomped across the floor. Stratetix made a choking sound.

"Maybe you don't understand who's in charge here!" said the rough voice. Stratetix gave no reply.

"I think he needs a dose of medicine, Sarge!" another voice said. "Give him a squirt of acid!" Cruel laughter filled the house.

In the darkness, Rosetta whimpered, and Maurice clasped her hand tightly. Teo stirred and loosened his sword in its scabbard.

"See that candlestick?" the leader asked. There was a long pause. "Look at that! If my spray can do that to metal, what do you think it will do to your skin?"

Helena's calm voice broke in. "My husband is no criminal. Please release him. We will give you the information you seek, and you can be on your way."

"You hear that, men? The pretty wife wants us out of here! Search the place, and let's get going." The militiamen scattered throughout the house. A man entered the kitchen.

"Whatcha cooking, honey?"

"Pastry," Helena said.

The man walked around the kitchen, his boots thumping on the trapdoor. His foot caught, and he stumbled, landing on the floor with a thud. A corner of the rug flopped over, causing light to stream between the planks of the trapdoor. "Hey!" the man cried. "Why don't you keep your rug flat so a man don't trip?"

We are your people, the flock of your pasture, Maurice prayed silently. *Deu, protect us!*

"I'm so sorry," Helena said. "Here, take this pastry to make it up to you." The man stood up, and Helena folded down the rug's corner with her foot. The cellar became dark again.

Another man entered the kitchen. "What's up there?"

"Two bedrooms," Stratetix said. "My daughter is in one of them, reading."

"Inspect it," the leader ordered. Men ascended the staircase, their weapons and spurs jingling.

After a pause, a voice yelled from upstairs. "There's no one up here but a girl, Sarge!"

"She's good-looking!" called another voice. "Maybe she needs to go back to the station for questioning!"

Teo rose to his feet, but Maurice tugged on his jerkin. "No," he whispered.

"Quit foolin' around, you two!" the leader said. "Let's go." The footsteps moved toward the front room.

"I can't say I'm sorry to see you leave." Stratetix's tone was defiant.

"I'm filing a report on you, just in case."

In the root cellar, Lina sneezed loudly.

"What was that?" the leader demanded.

Light footsteps hurried down the stairs into the kitchen. "Oh!" Ana exclaimed as she entered the front room. "You men have stirred up so much dust, it's deplorable!"

"Be glad that's all we did, sweetheart." The door slammed shut.

Silence.

After what seemed like forever, Helena entered the kitchen and knelt on the floor. "Stay down there. I'll put out the lights as if we're going to bed."

Lina started to cry softly. "That was so awful," she said in a tremulous voice.

"It's okay, Lina," Shaphan whispered. "We were never in danger. Teofil was here." In the dark, Teo snorted.

Eventually the rug was moved aside. "I think it's safe to come out now." Helena lifted the trapdoor and handed a candlestick to Maurice so those in the cellar could see. One by one, they climbed up the ladder into the darkened kitchen.

"We need to talk about this," Maurice said. "Let's stay in this room and sit on the floor. If they come back, we can hide again."

The community huddled in a circle around the candlestick, its meager light offering scant comfort after the perilous events of the evening. It was the only illumination in the house.

"First of all, we must give thanks to Deu." Maurice offered a heartfelt prayer of thanksgiving accompanied by several murmurs of agreement.

After the prayer, Maurice addressed his traumatized flock. "Stratetix, I commend you. You did nothing rash, but neither did you back down."

Stratetix rubbed his neck. "The guy choked me hard. Then I thought for sure they were going to hit me with their sprayers. Look at what that stuff can do!" He gestured toward the candlestick, whose metal surface was badly corroded where the acid had touched it.

Maurice nodded. "It's an evil weapon they wield. Praise Deu for your deliverance." He turned to the women of the house. "Helena and Anastasia, I commend you as well. Your level heads and quick thinking were admirable tonight." Mother and daughter gripped each other's hands and exchanged understanding glances.

"So where does all this leave us?" Lewth asked. "Should we disband?"

"No!" Valent rose to his feet. "We shouldn't disband. Not by any means!"

"Take a seat, friend," Maurice advised.

Valent sighed but obeyed. "Listen to me! Tonight is an example of *exactly* what we should expect. I was trying to tell you this before. This religion of ours is secretive by its very nature. It's intended only for the chosen few. I'm talking about elite wisdom. Special enlightenment! Obviously that's not for everyone, but only for those who make themselves worthy in Deu's eyes."

"I agree with my husband," Sucula said. "We should continue to meet, though with greater caution. Tonight we've seen how the institutional religion will persecute us. Nevertheless, we must continue to seek the inner meaning of the book. Deu came to us because he saw our great potential. We mustn't shrink back from his arcane knowledge or fail to master his esoteric wisdom—like Adam, who was afraid to be naked!"

"Arcane knowledge? Esoteric wisdom?" Ana was incredulous. "Where do you find those things in the Sacred Writing?"

"Such knowledge lies hidden within." Sucula smiled mysteriously.

"No, it doesn't. The knowledge of Deu is plain to see. His goodness is for everyone."

"Well, Anastasia, you've just witnessed what would happen if Deu were revealed openly. Are you suggesting we do that?"

"Of course not! At least, not in a foolish way. We must be wise about how we speak. Even so, we must always be looking for ways to bring Deu to Chiveis. I long for that! I can even imagine a day when I could preach his name in the streets, and my people would turn away from their idols."

"Ana, don't get ahead of yourself," Stratetix warned. "If you did that, it would be at great cost."

"Perhaps it would." Ana lifted her chin.

Helena put her arm around her daughter and pulled Ana close. "Let's take a cautious approach, my love."

Valent leaped up again. "Okay, everyone. Anastasia has made her case. I've made mine. Let's decide the issue right now! Who's with me?"

Before anyone could answer, Stratetix bolted to his feet as well. "Listen here, Valent! I've had about enough from you. This is my house, and you're a guest in it. Master Maurice is the leader of this community, not you. I will not allow you to come in and take over!"

For a long time, Valent and Stratetix glared at each other. Maurice broke the tension. "My friends, it has been an arduous night. I think we should all depart now and come back together when we've had a chance to reflect."

Valent's expression softened. "I'm sorry, everyone. I guess my passions sometimes carry me away. Stratetix, I intended no offense to you. Please excuse me." Valent looked down and offered his hand to Sucula, who rose to stand at his side. "We should leave here tonight in small groups, so as not to call attention to ourselves. My bride and I will leave first. Deu be with you all."

Maurice watched the red-haired trapper and his wife exit the chalet. He closed his eyes and shook his head. *I asked for a new wind to blow in Chiveis*, he thought. *But am I truly ready for its power to be unleashed?*

❖ ❖ ❖

Valent slammed the door of his chalet and threw his cloak on the floor. "Who does Stratetix think he is, trying to tell me what to do? I deserve more respect than this!"

"He's nobody!" Sucula declared.

Valent spun and faced his wife, his arms spread, palms up. "Don't these people see I'm smarter than him?" He arched his eyebrows.

253

"I can see it, but they can't. They appreciate Stratetix for his steadiness."

"You're right. Stratetix is an obstacle." Valent stroked his beard as he paced the room.

"What are we going to do about it?"

Valent looked at Sucula with a cunning expression. "Have you ever seen a pack of wolves hunting?"

"Wolves are your domain, not mine."

"I've seen them hunting the red deer. They don't attack the whole herd. They choose the one they want and separate it. That's what we need to do—divide. The old professor I can handle. I can edge him out eventually. But Stratetix is strong. He needs to be dealt with if I'm to assume my rightful place as the head of this religion."

"How? We can't do anything that would put our lives at risk. And we don't want to destroy the community, just expel Stratetix."

"I'll think of something. We'll get him out! And Helena and Anastasia will go with him."

"Good riddance," Sucula said with disdain.

"I'm thirsty. Get me some mead while I think." Valent tumbled into an overstuffed chair by the hearth. Sucula retrieved the jug, poured a stein, and warmed it with a poker. Valent took it from her and gulped it eagerly.

"Killing him would be the best way," he mused. "But I don't want a blood trail leading back to me."

"There are men who would do it for hire."

"Too risky. They might betray me if pressed. We need something more clean."

Sucula stirred the coals in the fireplace with the poker. Suddenly she whirled, the hem of her black gown fanning out as she turned. She had a look of triumph on her face. "I have it!" she exclaimed. "The answer is staring us in the face!"

"Go on," Valent said from his chair.

"Let's use the events of tonight to our advantage! The High Priestess is on edge. She's like a cornered badger who will lash out at any threat. If she becomes certain Stratetix is undermining her religion, she'll go after him for sure."

Valent threw back his head and laughed. "That's it! And with Stratetix out, Maurice won't have any allies. Everyone will be running scared. They'll be looking for a strong, steady hand." He thought about it some more as he drank his mead. "Yeah. This could work. I'll promise to keep them hidden. No more of this public preaching Anastasia keeps talking about. We'll be a secret cult for the chosen few. If I can get my hands on the Sacred Writing, I know I can take things in that direction. I just have to break Stratetix. Then I can take over."

"How will you do it?"

"The Vulkainians already suspect him. An anonymous tip is all that's needed to get him arrested."

"Or worse, the High Priestess might call down Astrebril's Curse." Sucula shuddered as she spoke of it.

Valent gazed into space, lost in his thoughts. Sucula came to him and sat on the armrest, stroking his red hair. "So, my husband," she said softly, "you liked my idea?"

Valent brushed her hand away. "Stop. I'm trying to make plans."

"It's time for bed. Can't we plan in the morning?"

Valent shot his wife an exasperated look. "The morning? By morning I'll have slipped a message to the Vulkainians! I just need to figure out how to do it." He rose and began to button on his cloak.

"Where are you going?"

"The tavern. A man does his best thinking over a good ale. Don't wait up." He opened the door and stepped into the cold night.

✦　✦　✦

Rosetta's mare had been showing signs of labor all day. As darkness fell, she hung a lantern in the barn and sat down to wait. Her thoughts turned to the request she had expressed to the house community two nights earlier. Master Maurice had been certain Deu would care about something as mundane as a horse giving birth. The idea that a god would care about such things was deeply comforting to Rosetta.

The barn door opened, and Lina entered. "How's she doing?"

"I think the foaling will begin very soon, and then you'll know whether you have a colt or a filly."

"I hope it's a colt."

"Do you think Deu already knows?"

Lina looked uncertain. "I guess so. Master Maurice says everything belongs to Deu. Even horses."

"What do you think of Valent's ideas about Deu?"

"Well, I can't imagine ever siding against Ana, if it comes down to that." Lina bit her lip. "But I have to admit, I'm drawn to Valent. He's very persuasive. Shaphan thinks highly of him."

Rosetta glanced at her daughter. "And you think highly of Shaphan, don't you?" Lina's bashful smile was all the answer Rosetta needed.

The mare whinnied, and Rosetta went to the stall to investigate. "It's begun! Lina, come help me and meet your little horse!"

Lina complied, but the foaling didn't go as planned. As the night wore on, the mare struggled to deliver. Sweat beaded on Rosetta's forehead as she tried to help the distressed horse. It lay on its side in the straw, exhausted from the effort.

"The foal is breach! It can't come out!" Rosetta was desperate. "Lina, go get your uncle! He'll know what to do!" The blonde girl ran from the barn.

Rosetta pounded her fist on the stall. *Deu, why are you doing this to me? What purpose could you have in taking this foal from a widow's daughter?*

❖   ❖   ❖

Ana awoke with a start. *What was that strange noise?* She listened, but the night was still. Outside her window, a full moon shone in the sky. No wind blew. Dawn was still an hour away.

Earlier that night, Lina had arrived with urgent news about the mare. Ana's parents rushed to help, leaving Ana alone in the chalet. Normally she wouldn't have minded, but this night had an eerie feel she didn't like. *It's strange,* she thought. *I felt safer sleeping in the wilderness with Teo by my side than here in my own house.* She burrowed under her comforter, but it didn't provide any comfort.

As she lay in bed, Ana's thoughts drifted to Teo. "What am I going to do about him?" she whispered to the dark. They had hardly spoken since the incident at the waterfall pool, though that had been several weeks ago. Teo wasn't actually being rude to her. In fact, he wasn't even avoiding her. He was just *there*. While she was moving ahead, he was standing still.

Ana had asked her mother about it. Helena advised, "Take your time; don't throw yourself at him. Just give him space and wait." Stratetix's counsel was the opposite: "Don't be foolish, Little Sweet! Go kiss and make up right away. He'll make a fine husband for some lucky girl, and I'd like it to be you!" Ana had scolded her father for that comment, but secretly she wondered if he might be right.

"I should talk to Master Maurice about it," Ana decided. "He knows Teo better than anyone. And he's very wise."

There's that sound again!

Ana held her breath and listened but heard nothing more. It had sounded like digging, like a spade scraping against a stone. The noise seemed to come from the rear of the house at its base, but her window didn't face that direction, so she wouldn't be able to see from her room. Ana threw aside her covers and went downstairs, her bare feet padding on the wooden steps. She pulled on some boots and stepped onto the front porch in her night shift. The door creaked shut behind her. Everything looked normal in the pale moonlight.

Should I take a peek around back? Ana resolved to be brave. She crept along the side of the house, feeling ridiculous in boots and a short chemise. At the corner, she took a deep breath and poked her head around. The chalet's eaves and the overhanging trees shrouded the rear wall in darkness. Though she couldn't see much, Ana saw nothing to give her alarm.

It was probably just an animal rooting around. The night air was cold against her skin. She shivered and hurried inside.

In her bedroom, Ana dressed quickly and combed through her hair. It would be dawn soon, and by now she was too awake to go back to bed. She wanted to greet the new day in the presence of Deu, and she knew the perfect place to do it. Not far from the house, a rock ledge provided a lovely view of the mountains to the west. Although she couldn't see the eastern horizon from there, she enjoyed watching the morning alpenglow paint the snowcapped peaks across the valley. The ledge had become her favorite refuge when she needed to be alone.

Ana entered her parents' room and knelt in front of the chest at the foot of the bed. She had always loved this chest because of its clever secret compartment. As a girl, she used to hide her childish treasures inside, never imagining that one day she would have something of real value to keep in it. She slid open a panel and removed the leather satchel in which Stratetix kept the scrolls Shaphan had copied.

Show me which one you want me to read this morning, she prayed as she carried the satchel downstairs. With a warm cloak around her shoulders, Ana stepped outside into the half-light and hiked up the rise toward her secret place.

Seated on the rocks, Ana watched the first hint of color touch the highest peak to the southwest. Far below, in the Maiden's Valley, Ana could see the milky white waterfall tumbling into the pool where she had argued with Teo. She inhaled deeply and put that unpleasant thought from her mind. With her eyes closed, she prayed aloud. "O Deu, here I am, your handmaiden. I await you like I await the new day."

In the trees, the birds began to sing their morning songs. The tinkling of cowbells wafted up from the valley. Soon it became light enough to read. Ana reached for the satchel with the scrolls in it.

KABOOM!

The ear-splitting concussion rammed Ana so hard, she tumbled from the rocks like a rag doll. Never had she heard anything like it, the thunder of the sky assailing her on earth! Ana's ears pounded, and her heart seemed to jump out of her chest. She couldn't speak, she couldn't think—all she could do was cower on the ground. Violent echoes reverberated around her. An enemy rang bells inside her head. The sky itself turned cruel, raining down clods of earth and chunks of wood. A piece of debris clubbed Ana on the head, making the world spin out of control. She put her hand to the ache, and her fingers came away moist and red, but in her stupor she couldn't comprehend what it meant. White smoke billowed around her, rank with the stench of Astrebril. It choked and smothered her. She stumbled. Dizziness engulfed her. *Deu! Help me!*

✦　✦　✦

The distant boom roused Teo from a dead sleep to an instant state of readiness. He sprang from his bed and grabbed his knife in a single motion, lowering the blade only when he realized he wasn't in imminent danger.

What was THAT?

Immediately he knew. Astrebril's Curse.

Teo pulled on his breeches and buckled his sword around his waist. As he tucked his ax into his belt, more explosions shattered the sky. He ran to the balcony. Above the saddleback ridge between Pon's and Elzebul's Heights, colorful fires thundered in the morning twilight. Red, gold, and green sparks blasted in every direction, showering the mountains with flame. Teo didn't know what was going on, but he intended to find out.

He had just inserted his key to lock his door when Shaphan called to him from the University's courtyard. "Professor Teofil! Come look! There's smoke coming from Vingin!"

Teo's blood turned cold. *Astrebril's Curse at Vingin? That might mean . . .*

He ran to where Shaphan was standing and looked up toward the mountain terrace, gauging the smoke's location. *No!* He started to run, but Shaphan grabbed his arm.

"Wait! I'm coming with you! I want to check on Lina!"

Teo yanked his elbow from Shaphan's hand. "I don't have time to wait for you!" he yelled as he sprinted to the stable. An Elzebulian priest was leading a saddled horse, but Teo shoved him aside, mounted, and galloped out of the University's gate.

On the trail to Vingin, Teo passed many terrified villagers evacuating their homes. He ignored them as he sped past. The closer he got to Ana's house, the tighter the knot in his stomach grew. He tried to tell himself that the smoke wasn't rising from her home, but it was becoming increasingly hard to deny. Desperation took hold of him. He kicked his heels into his horse's flanks, urging it to greater speed.

At the chalet, Teo reined in and leaped from the saddle before the horse stopped moving. The building was a smoldering ruin, a complete devastation. Nothing remained but a pile of charred debris. Teo circled the house, calling Ana's name, looking for signs of life, but in his heart he knew no one could have survived such an intense fire. Amid the rubble, he noticed something purple and shiny. He picked it up. It was one of Ana's amethyst earrings. Teo fell to his knees and gripped his head in his hands. He couldn't believe what he was seeing.

"Teo! You came to me!"

"Ana!" Teo ran to her as she stumbled out of the woods. Blood caked the side of her face and matted her hair. "Are you hurt? Ana! Are you hurt?" He supported her in his arms.

"I think I'm okay. Just scared. What happened?"

"The evil of Astrebril. The High Priestess has cursed your home. Where are your parents?"

"They weren't at home. Oh, praise Deu! They were at Aunt Rosetta's!"

"Let's get you there and figure out what to do next." He helped Ana into the saddle and swung up behind her.

As they started up the trail, Ana reclined against Teo's chest. "Here we go again," she said over her shoulder. Teo shook his head and marveled at the woman's grit.

Stratetix and Helena burst from Rosetta's chalet when they arrived. Both were covered in soot.

"Ana! For the second time, you've come back to us from the dead!" Stratetix threw his arms around his daughter and embraced her with his eyes closed.

Helena's voice quivered with anguish. "We searched for you, but nothing was left! When we couldn't find you, we feared the worst!" Although her face was joyful, tears had left their trails on her blackened cheeks.

"I ran into the village for help," Ana said. "I called for men to come with buckets, but they looked at me as if I were accursed."

Stratetix held his daughter's shoulders in his two hands and gazed into her face. "The fire consumed everything! How are you alive?"

"Deu led me outside! He preserved me—and also this!" Ana lifted the leather satchel containing the scrolls.

"Deu is good." Helena joined her husband in hugging Ana.

"Stratetix?" Teo reluctantly interrupted the family's rejoicing. "We need to get you and Helena out of sight. Then we need a plan. Let's go inside."

As they entered the chalet, Rosetta gasped. "Child, you're hurt!"

"Something hit me. It bled a lot, but I think it looks worse than it really is."

"Come here and let me wash that blood off you!" Rosetta moistened a rag and made Ana sit on a low stool so she could dab at her head. Lina sat down beside Ana.

"How's the foal?" Ana whispered.

"He died. It was a colt."

"I'm sorry." Ana patted Lina's arm.

Stratetix raised his palm. "Sh! Listen! Someone's coming!"

Teo crossed to the window and peered out. "It's okay. It's Shaphan." He opened the door and let the young man slip inside. Lina greeted him in an awkward embrace.

"Listen up, everyone," Teo said. "Here's what we're going to do. The High Priestess has obviously gotten wind of our meetings, or at least she suspects Stratetix of heresy. Stratetix, did you or Helena enter Vingin today? Has anyone seen you alive?"

"No. We only ran to the chalet, looked for Ana, then returned here. We saw no one. The curse kept them away."

"Good. That's to our advantage. Ana, what about you? I think you said you've been seen?"

"Yes, I went into town."

"Okay, then. You're now playing the role of the grieving orphan. You'll have to act as if your parents are dead."

"What are we supposed to do?" Stratetix asked. "Helena and I can't live in hiding forever."

"Not forever, but for now that's exactly what you're going to do. We need to see how the situation plays itself out. You two have to disappear for the time being."

"Where?" Helena asked.

"I know a place. A hunting cabin on a lake at the back of the Maiden's Valley. No one uses it anymore because most of the ibex are gone now. It's a real wilderness up there. You should be safe until I can sort things out. Let's get some things packed."

"Anything you find in the house is yours to have," Rosetta said. "Take what you need."

When the supplies were ready, Teo loaded them on his horse. He also packed heavy rucksacks for Stratetix and himself and a lighter one for Helena.

Shaphan tapped Teo on the arm. "Professor Teofil, I could carry a load, too. I could accompany you on the mission."

"No, this is something I need to do alone. You stay here and take care of things."

"What things?"

"I don't know. Whatever you think needs doing."

"Sure," Shaphan said, dropping his chin.

Teo turned to Stratetix and Helena. "Here, wear these cloaks. I'm taking you by the back trails, but if we run into any herders or dairymen up there, just put up your hood and don't speak to them."

"Teo, what should I do with this?" Ana held up the satchel containing the scrolls of Deu.

"Take it to my teaching theater and hide it in the cottage. No one will bother it there. The key is under the flat rock by the nearest tree." He looked at Stratetix and Helena. "Ready?"

Tearful hugs were exchanged as the family said their good-byes. Teo watched Ana as she embraced her parents. So many things in her life were uncertain. He wished he could think of something to say to her, but the day was wearing on, and they needed to get going if they were to make it to the cabin before dark. "It's time to leave," he said. "Let's move out."

"Could we pray together before you go?" Ana asked.

"There's really no time for that," Teo answered.

She accepted it. "Deu be with you all."

Rosetta, Lina, Shaphan, and Ana waved from the porch as Teo and the two fugitives left the chalet with their packhorse. Ana bolted from the porch and caught up to them, putting her hand on Teo's arm.

"Take care of them, Teo," she said earnestly. "And take care of yourself."

"Ana, I—"

She remained silent, her eyes wide, waiting.

"—will take care of your parents," he finished.

Ana nodded and lifted her hand as they walked away.

The trail entered the forest. An eerie wind, abnormally hot, had begun to stir through the trees as the travelers left Vingin behind.

"What's the name of this place you're taking us to?" Stratetix asked.

"It's called Obirhorn Lake," Teo called over his shoulder. "It's a little lake way up in the mountains. Very remote."

"When you get back, I want you to check on Ana. She's all we have, you know."

"We're trusting you to protect our daughter while we're gone," Helena added. "She means everything to us. We need you to keep her safe from harm."

Teo nodded. "Don't worry. I always will."

When the trio arrived in the evening, Obirhorn Lake lay quiet, its turquoise depths shimmering against a background of dark green. Teo was tired, and he knew Helena and Stratetix must be exhausted from the trip. The hot foehn wind had continued to blow all day, fatiguing the travelers and making them jittery. They had journeyed far from Vingin, descending to the floor of the Maiden's Valley, then climbing into the wild hinterlands at its head. Two hours earlier, they had left the trees behind and emerged into alpine meadows. Still they continued to ascend until finally they attained the upper reaches of the valley, where scrubby tundra and gray stone predominated in place of grassy pastures. The great peaks of Chiveis, normally viewed from the villages as a pleasant backdrop, now towered over the travelers like an enclosing fortress. The valley was a dead end, and they had arrived at its limit—the natural rear wall of the safe little world behind the Citadel's ramparts. Atop the summits, the crumbled glaciers created a barrier no man could pass. Teo didn't know what lay on the other side of that bluish white ice. He only knew it was the Beyond.

Helena slumped against Stratetix as he supported her. "We made it," she sighed.

"What are you cooking us for dinner tonight?" he asked with a grin. She smiled wearily and thumped his chest with her palm.

The hunting cabin was unlocked, and Teo went inside first, opening a window to let in light and fresh air. Two cots lined the walls, and a potbellied stove sat in the corner, its supply of firewood adequate for late springtime. A few stools, a small wooden table, and an archery cabinet rounded out the furnishings.

Helena entered the cabin and set down her rucksack, taking stock of the place. "It's not home, but it'll do," she said with an air of resignation. She unfurled a bedroll and flopped onto the bed.

Stratetix came to Helena and removed her boots. "Take your rest, love. I'll make something to eat."

"Both of you can rest." Teo rummaged in his pack and pulled out two wheels of cheese and a flask of white wine from the vineyards along the Tooner Sea. "I'll get a fire going and make us something filling."

The three travelers shared a meal of bread dipped in melted cheese. After supper, the conversation gradually settled into a pleasant silence. The fire crackled in the stove with reassuring warmth. Helena yawned on her cot.

"Would you say the prayers tonight, my husband?" she asked. Stratetix nodded and gazed heavenward, his palms up. He invoked Deu's protection and guidance for Ana, Teo, the house community, his wife, and himself. Although Stratetix wasn't an eloquent man, his prayers were wise and heartfelt. Helena was asleep before he even said, "So be it."

Teo wrapped himself in a blanket on the floor, thinking about Stratetix's prayers. *What must it be like to be a religious man like that?* he wondered.

The next morning, Teo rose early. He opened the archery cabinet and removed the lone excuse for a bow. It was misshapen, and the string was brittle. The arrows weren't much better, but they would have to do.

"Going hunting?" Stratetix asked from his bed. Helena was still asleep.

"With this bow, I'm probably just going shooting."

Stratetix laughed. "If you can hit a falling apple, Captain, you can hit anything."

"We'll see. Don't expect me back right away."

"You know where to find us."

The air was warm when Teo left the cabin. A wall of puffy clouds loomed over the summits at the rear of the hanging valley, and white patches still dotted the tundra despite the work of the snow-eating wind.

Teo squatted and looked at his reflection in the still waters of Obirhorn Lake. His face was tanned by the sun, with a strong square jaw and clear eyes. Many women had called him handsome; some had even called him more than that. What had Sucula whispered in his ear when he had given her the cloak? "A sexy man like you would keep me warm." It was a strange joke for a married woman to make. He tossed a pebble into the lake and stood up.

As Teo ascended through the tundra onto the rocky escarpments at the base of the summits, his eyes searched for the movements of a cliff-dwelling ibex, but his mind searched for a solution to yesterday's events. Stratetix had been cursed by a powerful god. When Astrebril was invoked by the High Priestess, he visited his wrath on the patriarchs of Chiveisian families by destroying their homes at dawn. Though Ana was in no immediate danger of further reprisals, Stratetix might be cursed again if the High Priestess learned he was still alive. Teo couldn't think of a way to reintegrate the family into Chiveisian society. Perhaps they could simply return to distant Edgeton and keep a low profile. He was unsure what the next steps should be.

Teo climbed the moraine beneath a glacier, knowing any ibex would still be on the highest crags at this time of day. The wild goats only descended in the evenings to graze. As he squatted behind a boulder and scanned the rocks above, he couldn't escape the mental image of Stratetix's destroyed chalet. Teo recalled the anguish he had experienced when he had seen those smoking ruins. The fear that Ana was inside when the divine curse fell had been more than he could bear. Teo was prepared to endure many hardships in life, but not the thought of Ana suffering or even dying. After all the adventures they had shared together, after all the dangers they had faced side by side in the Beyond, how could she then be killed in her own bed? Teo shook his head, trying to clear such a horrific thought from his mind. As he squatted next to the boulder, he felt a renewed sense of relief that Ana had chosen to go outside at dawn. Was it mere coincidence? Teo knew Ana didn't think so. She attributed it to the inner promptings of Deu. Teo looked toward the sky. *Does Deu really get involved in our lives like that?*

"Are you there, Deu?" he said to the silent mountains. "Everyone seems to think so, but if you want me to follow you, you're going to have to give me a sign." Teo considered how he might put Deu to the test.

Far above and to the right, something moved. Teo focused his eyes on the area, trying to pick out an animal shape among the jumbled rocks. *There!* It was an ibex, its long, backward-curving horns signaling it was a lone male. Though its meat wouldn't be as flavorful as a female's, Stratetix and Helena would appreciate any fresh game during their stay at the remote cabin.

"This is it, Deu. If you want me to follow you, prove it by helping me bring in that ibex." Teo arose from his crouch and began to edge his way upward, keeping an eye on his quarry.

The ibex sensed danger and began to ascend. Teo followed. By the time he thought he could attempt a shot, he had attained the highest elevation he had ever reached. Obirhorn Lake sat like a tiny aquamarine jewel far below, and the view to the northern horizon was incredible. Teo gauged the distance to the ibex as he drew his bow. It would be a tough shot. When the powerful gusts of wind calmed momentarily, he let an arrow fly. The wild goat flinched and leaped onto the glacier above. Teo cursed and jumped from rock to rock in pursuit.

Wet snow began to spit from the cloud wall that always towered above the peaks when the foehn was blowing in the valleys. The rocks became slippery, but Teo kept climbing toward the glacier. At the edge of the ice, he paused. He had never stepped onto a glacier. Chiveisians didn't venture this high in the mountains, for the summits were regarded as useless waste-lands of rock and ice with dangers lurking everywhere. Crevasses often lay underneath a thin crust of snow, ready to condemn the unsuspecting traveler to a frigid death. It was even rumored that demon spirits and white trolls roamed the glacial summits. Although Teo didn't believe those old wives' tales, he had no desire to put his life at risk. At the same time, he had wounded the ibex and wanted to bring it in. He put his foot on the ice. It seemed firm enough, so he began to ascend into a different world.

The ibex had left tracks, and as Teo followed them, he soon spotted a red stain on the snow. *It can't be far ahead now*, he thought as he trudged higher, but the tracks continued into the mists ahead. The snow began to fall harder. Teo stopped and assessed the situation, realizing he was in a dangerous position. He had ventured far onto the glacier. The swirling snow and frozen landscape had disoriented him. Which way was north? He looked back at his tracks in the snow, his only sure landmarks. How long before they would be covered? Bagging a stringy wild goat wasn't worth his life. Ahead, a mountain peak rose from the center of the glacier. Teo decided to go that far and no farther.

As he neared the peak's base, where it thrust from the ice, Teo spotted the ibex again. Lifting his bow, he took a shot but missed. The ibex struggled onto the rocks. As Teo circled around to the left of the peak, he watched his quarry climb the side of the mountain. Suddenly his eyes caught something else—the outline of a building constructed by human hands! *A building up here?* It couldn't have been made by anyone from Chiveis. Only the Ancients possessed the means to erect a structure like that in such a remote and desolate place. He started forward to investigate.

Beneath his feet, the snow gave way to empty space. Teo dived backward, clawing at the snow as he tried to arrest his fall, but there was nothing to hold onto, and he plunged into the hole. Immediately he lurched to a stop, wedged into a tight place at his waist with a yawning void on either side. The fall had caused Teo to spill his arrows and drop his bow. The sound of them clattering off the walls as they tumbled down the crevasse continued for a very long time.

Teo remained motionless as he tried to calm his rising panic. *Get ahold of yourself, Teo, or you're lost!* He closed his eyes and slowed his breathing. Finally he dared to look up. The crevasse's rim was within reach. If he could get purchase on the ice wall, he might be able to climb out. Teo lifted his leg and withdrew his knife from his boot, careful to make no sudden movements that might dislodge him from the narrow place in the ice. One mistake here would guarantee a slow, dark death.

Teo carved a series of notches in the ice from waist level to as high as his hands could reach. With his blade between his teeth, he used the upper handholds to lift himself so he could poke his foot into a lower notch, and in this way he scaled the wall until his head was above the rim. As he was about to climb out, one of the footholds crumbled under his weight, and he slipped down again. Teo threw his arms forward, digging into the snow while his feet dangled over emptiness. His strength began to wane as he struggled and kicked. At last he managed to find enough traction to scramble out of the crevasse and collapse on the snow. The knife had cut his tongue, and he spat out blood as he lay panting on the glacier.

When he had regained his breath, Teo lifted his head. The ibex stood on a boulder beside the stone hut of the Ancients, watching the drama unfold. It shook its head, waggling its tufted beard and brandishing its curved horns like two giant sabers. Then, with aloof dignity, the ibex moved into the rocks and disappeared.

Teo stood up and brushed the snow from his clothes. He retraced his steps, not deviating to the right or left of his tracks. The falling snow had completely covered the indentations by the time he reached the glacier's edge. Teo was glad to be alive as he stepped onto solid rock. He resolved never to take such risks again.

At the hunting cottage on Obirhorn Lake, Stratetix was outside chopping firewood. The sun was shining, and the weather here was much warmer. It hardly seemed possible Teo had just come so close to an icy death.

"No luck hunting?" Stratetix asked.

"Deu failed me," Teo replied. He saddled the horse, and with a warning to Stratetix to stay out of sight, he started down the valley toward Lekovil.

✦　✦　✦

Ana could feel the cold stares as she walked the streets of Vingin toward the market. The frightened populace had trickled back to the village after the smoke of Astrebril's Curse cleared. Of course, everyone knew whose home the god had destroyed. The farmer's daughter from Edgeton was now an orphan, but it wasn't compassion Ana sensed from the people. It was fear, and even hostility.

She entered the open-air market, a basket under her arm, and began perusing the stalls. Teo had taken virtually all the food from Rosetta's home, so Ana intended to replenish her aunt's larder. The thought of Teo made her wonder how her parents were doing at the distant cabin. Had they arrived safely? Were they discouraged or frightened? Ana decided to visit Teo at the first opportunity to get a report on their condition.

A shriveled peasant woman hawked dried fruit from a corner stall. Summer was on its way, so fresh fruits and berries would be available soon, but until then Ana would have to rely on the dried variety. The priests of Vulkain used their sacred yellow stone to preserve fruit over the long Chiveisian winters.

"How much for the pears?" Ana asked.

The wrinkled old woman glared at Ana from underneath her head scarf. "They're not for sale."

"What do you mean? They're right here, displayed in your stall."

"What can I say? I'm a god-fearing woman. They're not for sale." The woman shooed Ana away with the backs of her hands. "Go on then. Move along."

Ana didn't fare much better at any of the other stalls. She managed to get some hard bread and inferior cheeses at less than fair prices. It was the best she could do. Many of the merchants wouldn't even talk to her, treating her as if she carried some horrible disease that might infect them if they so much as said hello. Ana returned to her aunt's house and set the basket on the table. Rosetta was churning butter.

"How was your shopping?" she asked, working the churn.

"Miserable. No one would deal fairly with me. Some wouldn't even deal with me at all."

"In their eyes you're accursed."

"I'm still a human being. You'd think they would have pity on a poor orphan."

"I know what you mean, but try to see it from their perspective. If the god is angry at your family, any sign of friendship might make him angry at them, too. They're afraid."

"True religion shouldn't make you afraid."

Rosetta didn't answer, but she paused from her churning to put the stale bread and cheeses in the larder. She pulled the stopper from a jug and poured cider into a wooden cup, setting it before Ana on the kitchen table. "I'm beginning to wonder what the purpose of religion is altogether."

"What do you mean?"

"Well, it's just that . . ." Rosetta chose her words carefully. "I guess I thought Deu's religion would bring me more happiness than it has. You know—his blessings. A better life. Good things."

"Hasn't Deu brought you a peace you've never had before?"

"Yes, I suppose you're right. But sometimes I wonder if it's worth the cost. My sister and brother-in-law are in exile. Their house is destroyed. My niece is treated like cow dung on a trail. What's next? Will my house go up in flames too?"

Ana sipped her cider without replying. She wasn't sure how to answer such heartfelt, searching questions. Rosetta took a seat across the table. Tears welled in her eyes, and she sniffled as she wiped them away. Ana took her aunt's hands in her own.

"It's hard," Ana said.

"What are we supposed to do, child? You seem to trust Deu so much! Tell me—what's a doubter like me supposed to do?" She implored Ana with tearful eyes.

Ana sighed. "I think we're supposed to believe, Aunt Rosetta. Believe that Deu is good, even when circumstances seem to say otherwise. Remember, we can't see everything he sees. He has purposes we may not understand. All we can do is keep walking ahead, saying to Deu in our hearts, 'I believe you're good. Please take care of me!'"

Rosetta stared at Ana, nodding. "You have uncommon wisdom for such a young woman."

Ana didn't feel wise—she felt vulnerable. Everything she counted on for security had been yanked away. Her parents. The house community. Even Teo. *Especially Teo*, she admitted to herself.

"Do you mind if I find a quiet place to read?" she asked her aunt. "I'm hungry for Deu's words."

"Run along, child. I'll go to the market and see what I can find."

Ana collected a few things and put them in her rucksack along with the satchel of Shaphan's scrolls. She closed the door behind her and set out for Teo's theater, intending to read for a while, then hide the Sacred Writing there as he had instructed.

The key was where Teo had said it would be, under a flat rock by the tree nearest to his cottage. She unlocked the door and entered, taking a seat at his desk. The hot winds were too gusty for outdoor reading, but the cottage was pleasantly cool inside. Morning sunlight streamed in the windows as Ana unrolled a scroll she had not yet seen. It was a collection of holy poetry.

As Ana read from the book of Hymns, one poem in particular caught her attention. Its words seemed to have been written just for her at that very moment:

> *The Eternal One is my shepherd. I will lack for nothing.*
> *He makes me repose in green pastures.*
> *He leads me near peaceful waters.*
> *He restores my soul.*
> *He guides me on the footpaths of justice because of his Name.*

Ana looked out the window and lifted her hands to the sunshine. She could easily imagine herself as a helpless lamb who needed a strong protector. That was exactly how she felt. "Lead me, holy shepherd," she whispered. Turning her eyes back to the page, she noticed a shift in the language of the hymn. It became more personal as the composer, David, now spoke directly to Deu:

> *When I walk in the valley of death's shadow,*
> *I won't fear any evil, because you are with me.*
> *Your crook and your staff reassure me.*
> *You set a table for me in front of my enemies,*
> *You anoint my head with oil,*
> *And my cup overflows.*
> *Yes! Goodness and grace will go with me all the days of my life,*
> *And I will live in the Eternal One's house until the end of my days.*

Ana had just finished reading the hymn when she heard footsteps on the gravel outside.

"Anastasia? Are you in there?" It was a man's voice. She quickly hid the scrolls among the others lying on Teo's desk.

"Who is it?" she called.

"It's Valent. I was passing by and noticed you. May I come in?" He barged into the cottage before Ana could answer, closing the door behind him. "I am so sorry for your loss," he said in a kindly and sympathetic tone. "Stratetix was a good man, and your mother was a real beauty."

"They're in Deu's hands now," Ana replied, unsure if she was supposed to play the role of orphan with Valent. Though she didn't want to lie to him, something told her to hold back the full truth.

"The community's future is uncertain," Valent said, stepping closer to Ana. "I assume you'll be returning to Edgeton to grieve?"

"It remains to be seen what I will do."

"I'm sure Deu will show you what's best. In fact, I'll mention it to Sucula. She's something of an oracle, you know. Perhaps we can determine Deu's will by means of a vision."

"Or through the Sacred Writing." Ana put her hand on the leather bag but immediately regretted it.

"Is that it?" Valent's face lit up with interest. "Let me take a look at it."

Ana rose from the desk and held the satchel to her breast. "I'm not sure I should, Valent."

Valent's eyes flared. "Why not? I'm a member of the community too! Maurice said we should read the Sacred Writing."

"Yes, but that was when my father was available to oversee who had the scrolls. He's gone now, and Master Maurice may have different plans."

"Give me the bag, Anastasia. I want it." Valent lunged at her, but she dodged around the desk and backed into a corner, clutching the bag.

Valent glared at Ana. "Are you going to make me take it from you?"

Ana held his gaze. "Yes. You'll only have it from me by force. And then the community will hear of it."

Valent's expression softened into a smile. "Well, aren't you a feisty little girl?" he teased. "Have it your way then. I didn't mean to offend you. I only wanted to learn more of Holy Deu. I'll leave you to your reading." He bowed and backed out the door. Ana's heart pounded.

As she watched him leave the theater, Ana questioned her actions. *Didn't Valent have a right to read the scrolls?* Perhaps. Yet her instincts had warned her otherwise, and she was glad she had followed them. Ana considered what to do with the scrolls. She couldn't leave them in the cottage, for it was no longer a secret hiding place. She'd have to take them to the University. *Teo will take good care of the Sacred Writing*, she thought.

✦ ✦ ✦

Valent arrived home angry, but he knew he needed to set those feelings aside for the moment. Shaphan and Lina had been invited for lunch, and it wouldn't do to appear irritable or out of sorts. He washed his face, smoothed his hair, and put on his best smile.

At the appointed time, Valent opened the door to his chalet and welcomed Shaphan and Lina inside. "Sucula, bring some mead for our guests! It's hot and windy outside, and their throats must be parched!" He shook Shaphan's hand as he entered, then kissed Lina on the cheek. Everyone took a seat around the kitchen table as Sucula set down a tray with four steins and a bowl of salted pine nuts.

"Thanks for inviting us to your house, Master Valent," Shaphan said as he reached for a stein.

"Please, Shaphan! It's just Valent between friends!" The young man nodded and broke into a smile.

"Lina, your hair is so lovely," Sucula said, extending her hand to bounce the blonde curls. "How do you get it so wavy?"

"It just does that naturally," Lina answered with a shrug.

"Well, now," Valent boomed, "it seems you two have developed quite a friendship over the past few weeks—or maybe it's something more?" He tilted his chin and raised his eyebrows, a knowing grin on his face. Shaphan and Lina blushed and gazed into their mugs.

"Ah, yes, young love! I remember those days when I was young and in love!" Valent leaned back in his chair and clasped his hands behind his head.

"Did Sucula take your breath away?" Lina asked, her eyes shining.

"Oh, this was long before Sucula. I'm talking about when I was young. I had quite a few fillies in my stable back then. Too many to count, in fact." He punched Shaphan in the shoulder. "Know what I mean?"

Sucula intervened. "Now, Valent, we didn't ask our guests here to talk about romance. We should discuss the future of the house community."

"Indeed." Valent leaned forward, resting his elbows on the table as he regarded Shaphan intently. "I see a real future for you, young man. You have leadership skills, that's for sure." Lina slipped her hand over Shaphan's as it lay on the table.

"Thank you, Valent," he said. "I like to think so, but sometimes I doubt myself. I'm not sure how to lead. I need someone to show me the way."

"Exactly!" Valent held up his index finger. "That's precisely what I had in mind! With the loss of our beloved brother Stratetix, Maurice isn't going to be able to hold things together. He's old, you know. Somebody stronger is going to have to fill the leadership void in the community. With Deu's help, I'm willing to do it, and I'd like to rely on you for assistance. Can I count on you, Shaphan?"

Before the metalsmith could answer, Lina broke in. "Shaphan is the kind of man you can count on, sir." She gripped his hand in hers, and the pair exchanged affectionate glances.

"Good! I was hoping for that. Despite the horrendous events of yesterday, I continue to be optimistic about the future of the community. The only problem I foresee is that I don't have access to the Sacred Writing. It's hard to lead when I can't consult the holy text directly and have to rely on translations."

"Can you read the Fluid Tongue of the Ancients?" Shaphan asked in astonishment.

A mysterious smile crept across Valent's face. "Do you think I was a trapper my whole life? Before your friend Teofil was even born, I was a young student at the University, reciting my lessons. 'Je suis, tu es, il est.' The monks had great expectations for me, but I grew bored, so I gave it up for the outdoor life." Valent became thoughtful, gazing out the window with a wistful expression, his finger tapping against his chin. "I sure wish I could see the Sacred Writing for myself. Of course, that's probably impossible."

"Yeah," Shaphan agreed. "Professor Teofil keeps it under his bed, locked in his room. But who knows? Maybe he'd loan it to you?"

"Not likely. I doubt he'd let his prized possession out of sight for my sake." Valent turned toward Shaphan and leaned close. "But what if you— his favorite student—asked to borrow it?"

Shaphan's face fell. "I'm not his favorite student. He doesn't seem to have time for that kind of thing."

"Hmm. I don't know why he's shunning you, Shaphan. You deserve better. You're a talented young man. I can see you have promise."

"You think so?" Shaphan lifted his eyes, and Valent grinned at him.

"I sure do. Why don't you see what you can do about the book, okay?" Valent turned toward his wife. "Now, Sucula, how about some lunch for our guests?"

Sucula arose and brought a steaming tureen of lentil soup to the table. After the hearty meal, she set out a plate of little cakes dripping with honey. Valent kept the conversation light during the pleasant lunch until at last he stood and offered an apology. "I'd like to stay and enjoy your company," he said, "but unfortunately I have business I must attend to."

Sucula looked surprised. "Business?"

"Surely you didn't forget I'm headed to the Citadel this afternoon!"

"Oh, right. The Citadel."

Sensing the visit had come to an end, Shaphan and Lina took their leave, thanking the married couple profusely for their hospitality. They exited the chalet and headed down the trail to Vingin, holding hands.

"Remember when we used to hold hands like that?" Sucula asked as she watched them go.

"I need you to pack my rucksack," Valent said. "Be sure to include my best clothes. It's contract negotiation time with the Furriers' Guild, and I want to make a good impression."

"I'll pack for you right away, my love. Will you be gone long?"

Valent frowned at his wife. "Several nights, unless everything goes perfectly and I can break away early. Of course, that never happens."

Sucula sighed. "I'll think of you every moment until you get back," she said sweetly.

✦   ✦   ✦

The sun slipped behind the mountains as Teo rode down the Maiden's Valley toward Lekovil. The fields of the small farms on the valley floor had been tilled recently and were ready to receive the spring rye. Teo liked nothing better than a dark rye bread slathered with butter, but with no food on his stomach since yesterday, he could eat boot leather tonight and be satisfied.

The winds had been gusting all day, creating an unpleasant warmth that numbed the brain and brought lethargy to the body. The unnaturally dry air made far-off locations loom closer than usual. Teo felt he could almost look inside the windows of distant Vingin, which normally appeared as a brown patch of chalets up on the grassy terrace.

At the University's gate, Teo dismounted and handed the horse's reins to a stable boy. He desperately wanted a bath, though a meal sounded good too. Teo couldn't decide which he would enjoy more. *Maybe I could eat a meal in the bath?* He approached the gatekeeper, preoccupied with his dilemma.

"Greetings, Professor Teofil."

"I need my key." Teo held out his hand. The cut on his tongue made his mouth hurt as he spoke.

"You didn't leave your key with me, sir."

Teo's head snapped around. "What do you mean I didn't leave my key! Where else would I have left it? It's here somewhere."

"I'll look for it. Just a moment." The gatekeeper shuffled through his log as Teo drummed his fingers on the desk. "No, sir. There's no entry since you last picked it up."

"Let me see."

The man pushed the log across the desk. Teo scanned it, but it contained no record that his key had been left at the gate. A glance at the empty cubbyhole on the wall confirmed it wasn't there.

"You must have forgotten to record it. Check the wall for misplaced keys. Mine is 4N."

"I know, sir. I'll check." The man inspected every key in the cubbyholes. "It's not here. Could you have kept it in your rucksack?"

Teo dropped to his knee and began rummaging around, but a sinking feeling was beginning to gather in his stomach. The heavy iron key wasn't in the pack. *When did I last leave here?* He tried to recall the circumstances of his departure, but his brain was scrambled by his exhausting day. Suddenly it hit him: *Astrebril's Curse!* In all the confusion of that terrible morning, he had left his key in the lock! Teo leaped to his feet and ran to his room. The keyhole was empty. When he tried the knob, it turned. He swore and threw open the door.

Everything was in its proper place. The parchments on Teo's desk lay undisturbed, his good bow was still in the cabinet, and the sack of coins he kept in his dresser had not been removed. He breathed a sigh of relief. Whoever had found the key wasn't out for a quick snatch-and-run. Still, Teo needed to check one more thing.

He climbed the stairs to the upper room, which served as his bedroom. The bedcovers were rumpled and unmade, just as he had left them when the explosion had awakened him at dawn. Teo held his breath as he slipped the wooden chest from under his bed and raised the lid.

No! It can't be!

The box was empty. The Sacred Writing of Deu was gone. An overwhelming dread settled onto Teo's shoulders. He ran downstairs, hoping he had left the book sitting out, yet all the while knowing he always put it away when he was finished translating. Frantically, he searched the little room again and again but found nothing. A few messy translator's notes lay scattered about, but there was no sign of the ancient book. He returned to the chest upstairs and reopened the lid, as if somehow the Sacred Writing would have found its way back inside. Bare wood stared back at Teo, mocking him.

No! No! He held his head in his hands. *What have I done?*

Teo collapsed on his bed, physically and emotionally spent. Without the book, the house community would come to ruin. And it was his fault.

❖　❖　❖

"I'm here to see Professor Teofil." Ana folded her hands on the gatekeeper's counter. The satchel of Shaphan's scrolls was in the rucksack at her feet.

"You're in luck. He just arrived a little while ago."

"If you could send someone to let him know I'm here—"

"That won't be necessary. He authorized you the other day. Go ahead. It's number four on the right."

"Thanks." Ana hoisted her rucksack to her shoulder and entered the

University's courtyard. The sound of the waterfall in the dusk reminded her of summer rain falling on the Farm River.

"Excuse me, miss?" Ana turned toward the gatekeeper at his desk. "You should know, the professor isn't in the best of moods. I hope you're not thinking of dunking him again." The gatekeeper was trying to disguise his warning as a joke, but nothing about it made Ana feel amused.

Teo's door was closed when Ana arrived, though the lamps were lit. She hesitated, then knocked firmly.

No answer.

Ana knocked again. "Teo? Are you there?"

"Who is it?"

"It's Ana."

The door opened and Teo stood there, disheveled and worn. "You're the last person I wanted to see right now," he said. "But come in."

Ana sensed something serious had happened. "What's wrong? Are my parents okay?"

"They're fine. They're at the cabin with everything they need for now."

Ana sighed in relief. But as she looked into Teo's face, she found an expression there she had never seen before. He was pensive, avoiding her gaze. Ana gently patted his shoulder. "You look upset, Teo. What's wrong?"

Teo spun away from the touch of her hand and swept all the parchments off his desk. He pounded his fist on the desk, barking, "Everything!" Ana was stunned by the outburst. Teo shut his eyes and rubbed his temples with his fingers.

Silent, Ana waited.

Teo slumped into the chair behind his desk, holding his forehead in his hand. The clock ticked on the wall. Finally he raised his eyes and looked at Ana. "I've lost the Sacred Writing," he said quietly. "I left my key sticking out of the lock. Now the book is gone."

Ana inhaled sharply, her eyes wide. "How will we know the words of Deu?"

"I'm aware of that problem!" Teo burst from his seat and slapped his palm against the wall.

Gathering her strength, Ana approached Teo as he stood with his back toward her. "Teo, I—"

Before she could continue, he whirled around with a look of determination. "I'll find the thief and make him pay!" he vowed. "That book didn't walk out of here on its own. Someone took it, and I'm going to find out who!" He snatched his sword belt from a peg and began to buckle it on.

Ana spoke in a soft voice. "Teo, your sword isn't what's needed now. Deu is the All-Creator. He can help us find the book. We should look to him."

"Right now, Deu could use a good sword in his service, and I aim to provide it!"

Ana frowned as Teo pulled his belt tight. He thrust his knife into his boot sheath and picked up his ax as well. As he started out the door, Ana crossed to a couch and sat down.

"Are you coming?" he called from the doorway.

Ana looked at him and asked, "Where are you taking me?"

The question seemed to throw Teo off, and he regarded Ana in bewilderment. "To recover the Sacred Writing, of course."

"The Sacred Writing isn't what I care about most."

Now Teo seemed even more confused. "What are you talking about? You love every word of that book!"

"I do. But it's not my greatest concern."

"Well, then what is?"

"Teo! Don't you know I care more about *you* than that book? Deu can find another way to give us his words. I trust him for that! Right now, I'm more worried about what I see coming from inside of you!"

Teo threw his hands in the air. "The problem isn't me, it's the *thief*! Some evildoer took the book that *I* found in the Beyond! It's mine, and I'm going to make him pay!"

"Yes, the thief was wrong. But rushing around blindly won't solve our problem. We need to stop and think before we take action."

Teo gritted his teeth and groaned, cupping his hands like claws in front of his face.

Ana began to feel desperate. "Please, Teo! Don't act like this. I need you to be strong for me!"

"What's *that* supposed to mean, Ana? I don't even understand what you're asking! I thought you wanted the book back, and that's what I'm trying to achieve!"

"I do want the book back! But more than that, I want *you* back! We've hardly spoken since the day by the pool. I can't go on like this, with you holding yourself apart. The house community needs you! Shaphan needs you! *I* need you!"

Teo's expression was incredulous. He hunched his shoulders and held out his palms. "What exactly is it you don't have from me? I brought you to safety after Astrebril's Curse! Then I took your parents all the way to Obirhorn Lake! I admit, I messed up by losing the Sacred Writing, but I can fix that!"

Ana rose from the couch, her heart beating rapidly as she prayed for wisdom. She approached Teo and stood close to him, tilting her head back so she could look into his eyes. Slowly she lifted her hands and placed them on the cheeks of the tall man who stood before her.

"Teo, I want you to know I'm *for* you and always will be. I admire you for the amazing things you can accomplish—for all you've already done on my behalf! I owe you my life many times over." Ana bowed her head and calmed her emotions, then looked up again into Teo's gray eyes and continued, "What I'm asking is for you to be the man I know you can be. You've protected me from many physical dangers. Your strength has been a shield to me. Now give me another kind of strength. Help me trust Deu! I'm hurting right now in so many ways, and you could come alongside me, but you refuse! In your stubbornness you're unwilling to let Deu be your strength. Why won't you bend your knee and depend on him?"

At Ana's last words, Teo's expression became hard. He backed away from her, removing his face from her hands. "I'm sorry, Ana," he said sternly. "But that's not who I am. I'm not a submissive man, and you can't ask me to be." He stepped outside into the courtyard, leaving Ana alone in the room.

For a long time, perhaps an hour or more, Ana sat on Teo's couch and prayed. Finally, with a heavy heart, she stood and left Teo's room. After reporting the stolen key to the gatekeeper, she wound her way up the trail to Vingin. Although she hoped a nighttime hike would clear her mind, she couldn't shake the sense of foreboding that had settled upon her. At her aunt's chalet, a single candle burned on the mantel, though Rosetta had already gone to bed. Ana went upstairs to the bedroom she was sharing with Lina and began to undress.

She had hung her clothes on a peg and brushed her hair for bed when the front door creaked open. The door closed again, and footsteps sounded on the stairs. As soon as Lina entered the room, Ana could tell something was wrong. She had been crying and couldn't lift her gaze from the floor.

"Lina? What's the matter? Did something happen?" Lina nodded, tears springing to her eyes as she sat on the edge of the bed. Ana sat down beside her and brushed a lock of blonde hair from her forehead. "You can tell me. What is it?"

Lina hung her head. "I'll tell you, Ana. But it's going to hurt."

"Go on," Ana said, suddenly afraid.

"It's Teo. We saw him a little while ago, Shaphan and me. We saw him come out of a tavern in Vingin. He didn't see us. He . . ." Lina paused, her lower lip quivering as tears rolled down her cheeks.

Ana held her breath, unsure what to say or think.

Lina took a deep, shivery breath, then reached for Ana's hand and held it. "He was with someone. We followed them secretly. It was Sucula. They went inside her house."

Ana bolted up from the bed and stared at Lina. "That doesn't mean anything!" she cried. "He was probably making plans with Valent!"

Lina's face was ashen as she sat on the bed. "No, Ana. Valent is away on a business trip. We peeked in. They were alone. And then . . . and then—"

"What? Tell me! What happened?"

"They went in the bedroom and shut the door."

Ana's body went limp, her chin falling upon her chest, her arms hanging loosely at her sides. She began to weep in anger and humiliation and despair. Her breath came in ragged shudders, and her eyes burned with the hot tears of a broken heart. Lina stood up and hugged her cousin tightly, but nothing could soothe the pain that stabbed so deep into Ana's soul.

◆   ◆   ◆

"The water's ready, Teofil!" Sucula poured a kettle of boiling water into a wooden bathtub behind a dressing screen in her bedroom.

"Thanks. I don't think I've ever wanted anything more than this bath." Teo exchanged places with Sucula behind the screen.

"You might be surprised at what you want," she said as she sat down on the bed.

Teo hung his clothes over the screen and stepped into the steaming water. In some distant part of his mind, he understood he was playing a game, all the while knowing where things were headed. But as quickly as the thought came to him, he dismissed it and resumed the charade.

"I really appreciate this, Sucula. Just let me soak for a while and clean up, and I'll be on my way."

"Take your time. I like having you here, which is more than I can say for my husband."

"Where is he again?"

"He's in the Citadel. Took a bag of money with him. He won't be back for several days."

Teo reclined in the bathtub, feeling the hot water soak into his muscles. He reached for the soap.

"You know, Teofil, I was thinking about what you were saying at the tavern about your fight with Anastasia. I think I see what's going on here."

Teo lathered his hair. "Yeah? What is it?"

"It's a typical woman's trick. She wants to control you—to make you into something you're not. I don't think that's right. In my opinion, you're fine just like you are."

"Thanks. I needed to hear that right now. Ow!" Soap stung Teo's eyes. "Do you have a towel?"

Sucula stepped into the main room and returned with a towel and another kettle. She came around the screen and handed Teo the towel.

Dipping her finger into the tub, she said, "Let me warm that up for you. Sit back." Teo complied, and she trickled hot water into the bath.

"It's a good thing I'm not easily embarrassed," he said.

"Believe me, you've got nothing to be embarrassed about." Sucula returned to her seat on the bed.

Teo soaked in the tub for a long time, growing warm and sleepy as he chatted with Sucula. Finally he gathered the will to stand up and get dressed. He had pulled on his breeches and was reaching for his linen shirt when Sucula appeared again. She slipped her arms around Teo's body.

"Stay the night," she said.

The game was over. It was real life now.

Competing thoughts swirled through Teo's mind. *You know you want to, so why not?* For a moment he returned Sucula's embrace and pulled her close. Then another thought flashed into his brain: *No! Don't do this to Ana!*

Teo swallowed. "I can't," he said, pushing the dark-haired woman away. "I won't."

Sucula dragged Teo to the bed. "Just rest here then! I've washed the sheets—can you smell the roses? I know you're tired. Nothing has to happen. I just don't want to be alone tonight."

Teo allowed himself to be pulled onto the feather mattress. The weight of fatigue was heavy upon him. *There's nothing wrong with taking a little nap*, he told himself. Sucula lay beside Teo, tracing her fingernail up and down his forearm. Sleep took him.

All the lamps were out when Teo awoke. The night had the feel of a very late hour. Through the window, moonlight filled the room with a pale glow. Sucula breathed quietly at Teo's side. He sat up in bed, causing her to stir and roll over. "Are you awake?" she asked sleepily.

"I should go now," he said. But he didn't move.

"Don't go. I want you."

Desire rose within Teo, but a voice began to shout inside his head, forcing him to consider the ramifications of what was about to happen. *What about all those quiet nights with Ana in the Beyond? All those dangers you faced together? All those experiences only the two of you can understand?*

Will you throw it all away for a night with a sad and lonely woman with whom you've shared nothing?

Teo stood up and grabbed his shirt, buttoning it on. "I'm leaving, Sucula."

The bedroom door flew open, slamming into the wall with a bang as the shape of a large man filled the doorway. "Surprised to see me?" Valent snarled. His massive knife glinted in the moonlight.

"Wait! I can explain!" Sucula leaped from the bed and moved toward Valent. The look in his eyes was demonic.

"No!" Teo pulled Sucula's arm, trying to keep her away from her enraged husband. The movement threw her off balance. At the same moment, Valent lunged and shoved her hard. Sucula careened across the room and smashed her head against a wooden chest with a sickening thud.

Teeth bared, knife held low, Valent charged. Teo deflected Valent's wrist with his forearm, then wrapped his arm under Valent's elbow to hyperextend the joint. A firm slap against the flat of the blade sent the knife clattering across the floor. Valent threw his knee into Teo's stomach, knocking the wind from him, then followed with a fist to the jaw. Teo's head spun as he stumbled into the dressing screen, toppling it with a crash. Before he could rise, Valent dived on top of him, pinning him to the floor. Hard blows rained down as Teo tried to ward them off with his arms. Valent's face bore an inhuman expression of murderous rage.

Teo felt strong fingers curl around his throat. He clawed at the hands as they sought to throttle the life from him, but he couldn't break free. The room began to spin, and he gasped for breath. Though he struggled against the deadly grip, his punches to Valent's ribs grew weaker. Darkness clouded his vision. He turned his head to the side, his lungs crying for air.

Sucula sat by the chest in a daze. Blood glistened on the side of her face. She held Valent's knife in her hand. Deliberately, she set it down and slid it across the floor.

Teo's hand curled around the hilt. With all his remaining strength, he thrust it deep into Valent's chest. The man roared and released his choking grip. Teo shoved him off, retaining his hold on the knife as Valent tumbled away. Blood cascaded from the wound, coating the floor in a glossy black sheen. Valent lay still.

"Teofil! Help me!" Sucula sprawled on the floor, pressing her hand to her temple. Blood dripped from the corner of the wooden chest behind her. Teo crawled to her side.

"It hurts. It's pounding. Ohh . . ." She began to cry softly. Teo tried to comfort her, but her headache intensified as time went on. She moaned and writhed and mumbled as the pain increased. Twice she vomited with violent retching.

As the sun began to rise, Sucula grew sleepy. She motioned for Teo to come close. He leaned over her, and she put her hand on his shoulder.

"Shaphan," she whispered.

"It's Teofil. I'm here with you, Sucula."

"Shaphan," she repeated. Her limp finger pointed over her shoulder. "He brought it. To Valent. In the chest—"

Sucula's eyes lost focus and fixed into a blank stare. Her respiration became shallow and irregular. For a long time, she lay perfectly still, unconscious and gasping. Then, as Teo stroked her cheek, her breathing ceased.

Teo stood up and staggered backward, smearing bloody footprints across the floor. He was numb. Nothing seemed real. Valent's corpse lay in one corner of the room and Sucula's in another, her lifeless finger still pointing over her shoulder at the bloodstained chest.

Why had she spoken about the chest? Teo knelt and lifted the lid. As he looked inside, he inhaled sharply, and his eyes widened. There, wrapped in cloth and bound with string, lay the Sacred Writing of Deu. Teo snatched the book and ran like a madman from the house of death.

CHAPTER

12

At dawn Ana arose, washed her face, and tied back her hair with a ribbon. She put on her gown as well as some makeup as an extra touch. She didn't intend to go around moping but would hold her head high and conduct herself with dignity. She had a job to do.

At Teo's teaching theater, she entered the cottage and pulled a blank parchment from a drawer. Dipping a quill into the inkwell, she began to write:

Dear Teo,

She wrinkled the parchment and threw it in a corner. Taking another sheet, she began again:

Teofil, your late-night adventures have come to my ears. You are free to pursue the lifestyle you please, but as for me, I no longer wish

Ana lifted her quill and stared at the page, stunned by all it implied. *I no longer wish what?* Whatever she wrote, it wouldn't be true. Despite everything that had happened, she still *wished.* A tear ran down her cheek and fell to the parchment, making the black ink run.

The sound of a horse outside interrupted Ana's thoughts. *Who could be coming here so early?* Peeking out the window, she felt a rush of relief. It was Maurice.

Ana met him at the doorway. "Good morning, Master Maurice. You're up early."

"As are you, dear one," he replied, smiling down from the back of his horse. "But I have the excuse of being an old man. What's yours?"

When Ana didn't answer right away, Maurice took a second look at her. He dismounted and approached with a look of concern. "I know you've been through a lot of distress lately, Anastasia. It's natural to be upset. I do believe your parents are safe for the time being."

"It's not that. It's—oh, I just don't know what to do." She held her head in her hands.

"Would you like to tell me about it?"

Ana nodded, so Maurice led her to one of the risers in the theater. He listened quietly as she recounted the story of the loss of the Sacred Writing, her argument with Teo, and his subsequent actions. Though she had vowed not to cry today, the tears came anyway.

"I woke up this morning intending to leave a farewell note," Ana concluded, wiping her eyes. "But I couldn't go through with it."

"Of course you couldn't. You're bound to him."

Ana looked at Maurice with a quizzical expression. "I am?"

"The final outcome is unclear, but yes, you're bound by the experiences you've shared. And that isn't a bond easily broken—by either of you. So don't fail to hope, dear one."

"What should I do?"

Maurice reached into his voluminous sleeve and withdrew a scroll. "I came here today to add this to the collection of scriptures. It's fresh from Shaphan's quill." Ana felt the thrill she always experienced when she received new words from Deu.

"I've been keeping the scrolls with me," she said, "because when I tried to hide them here, Valent discovered me. Perhaps I could give them to you for safekeeping?"

"Yes, I'll hold them. From what you've told me, they're all we have of the Sacred Writing for now." He took the satchel from Ana and stowed it in his rucksack.

"So you think we can recover the original?"

"Deu will provide a way to hear from him."

"I know."

Maurice unrolled the new scroll. "I have an assignment for you, Anastasia. I hold here the story of a young woman—at least, that's one way to see it. Her name was Ruth, and she lived in the land of Deu called Juda. I want you to read it and tell me what you think." He rose and left Ana alone with Deu and his words.

Though the narrative was short, it captivated Ana from the beginning. Ruth was a young widow who faithfully followed her widowed mother-in-law, Naomé, to a country called Juda. There the two women encountered poverty and an uncertain future. At harvesttime, Ruth found herself in the fields of a good man named Bohaz. To protect the vulnerable Ruth from assault by wicked men, Bohaz allowed her to glean in his fields. Impressed by this gesture of goodwill, Naomé devised a plan. She instructed Ruth to approach Bohaz at night on the threshing floor and uncover his feet, then lie down beside him. When Bohaz awoke and discovered a woman next to him, she made a strange request: "Spread your wing over your servant, for you have the right of redemption." Bohaz didn't take advantage of Ruth but arranged with the town elders to marry her. Blessed beyond all her expectations, she went on to give birth to a son, which greatly pleased the widowed Naomé. The baby was the great-grandfather of David. *I wonder if it's the same David whose name appears on Deu's hymns?* Ana rolled up the scroll and waved for Maurice to rejoin her.

"From the smile on your face, I see you enjoyed Ruth's tale," he said.

"It's lovely, and moving, and very worthy of Deu."

"Ruth was a lot like you."

"Yes! I felt a connection. She faced danger and hardship, but Deu came to her."

Maurice regarded Ana with a twinkle in his eye. "You know, I believe there are many ways to encounter this story. Could you read it again through a different character's eyes?"

Ana considered the suggestion. "Naomé?"

"Perhaps. But I was thinking of another."

Ana thought some more. "Well, Bohaz is the other main character."

Maurice's face lit up. His eyes crinkled at the corners, and his goatee framed his white teeth as he smiled. "That's a good idea, Anastasia. Try rereading it through Bohaz's eyes." He left her alone again.

Ana studied the scroll uncertainly. Maurice's request was somewhat strange. "Deu, show me your thoughts," she whispered as she began reading. Unlike the first time, Bohaz now leaped off the page, striding into the narrative as a noble protector, an initiative taker, a gentle defender. Surely he was a man of Deu, a man whose life was infused with the grace of the Eternal One. From his intimate knowledge of the one true God, Bohaz displayed loyal love to all under his care. His kindness culminated when he took a widowed foreigner to himself, spreading his wing over her to make her secure. Tears came to Ana's eyes again, but they were tears of a different sort than the ones she had shed earlier. Her spirit was deeply touched by a feeling she couldn't explain.

Maurice sat down beside her and put his arm around her shoulders. "Did Deu give you wisdom?" he asked gently.

"Yes, Master Maurice. I see Bohaz was a good man. The kind of man I wish—" Ana faltered, for she knew if she expressed the wish aloud, it would become real.

"What made Bohaz such a good man?"

"He was a man of Deu."

"And how did Deu call forth his goodness?"

Ana looked at Maurice's wise face, the implications of the story becoming clear to her. "Through Ruth," she answered. "Ruth was righteous and earned Bohaz's respect. He called her a virtuous woman. He said, 'All that you've done has been reported to me. May the Eternal One reward you for it.' And then he acted out of his admiration for her."

"Do you recall what he said next? How did he describe Deu?"

Ana found the place in the scroll and read, "Deu of Israël, under whose wing you came to find refuge."

"Aha!" Maurice smiled broadly. "Do you see? The wing is an important link! Ruth finds refuge under the wing of Deu by coming under the wing of Bohaz. In this way, Bohaz becomes the means of divine grace for her. At first he wasn't intending to do it, but Ruth went to him in holiness and demanded it from him. See how Bohaz became more of a man because of Ruth? She called him to his true identity and received his care, and Bohaz rejoiced to be the protector he was meant to be. This is Deu's way for men and women, I think."

Ana sighed deeply and smoothed her skirt. Anger and hope mingled in her heart, confusing her about the way forward. "I know what you're telling me, Master Maurice, and I want to believe it's possible. But nothing that happened yesterday gives me reason to expect it! I asked Teo to lead me to Deu, and instead, he . . . he . . ." Ana stopped, unable to give voice to the hurtful deed. She scrunched her eyes and clenched her fists as she felt the fresh wounds of betrayal torn open again.

Maurice sat motionless, waiting for her.

"I can't do this," Ana said through gritted teeth.

"Can't forgive him?"

"He doesn't deserve it! I'm so furious at Teo! When I think of him with that woman—" Ana shrieked in frustration and threw her hands in the air. "I don't ever want to see him again!"

She knew it wasn't true. *Oh, Deu, will you help me? I need you!*

Maurice stroked his beard. Ana turned to him, and he met her gaze. The creases around his blue eyes softened as he looked at her with a depth of tenderness she had only experienced from her father. "Tell me what I should do," she said.

"I know you're suffering, dear one. I understand, believe me. But you mustn't fail to hope. You must walk the path laid before you. Teofil is on the edge of a knife. If you turn against him now, he may turn against himself, to his own destruction. But if you turn toward him—" Maurice hesitated.

"If I turn toward him . . . what?" Ana wanted to hear what would happen.

"It's much to ask, I know. You're angry. You would rather give up. But if you can turn toward Teofil and put yourself under his wing, then you could be like Ruth, who called forth the spirit of Deu from the man Bohaz. There is no guarantee Teofil will rise to the challenge, and therein lies the risk. Yet he certainly won't do it unless someone demands it of him. Only you can play this role in Teofil's life, because it's you to whom he is bound."

Ana's emotions swirled inside her for a long time. Fear warred against hope, and wrath against grace. Memories of bitter betrayal attacked her soul, while the hot winds assaulted her body, beguiling her, denying a way out. Finally the breeze shifted, and a coolness touched her face. Ana lifted her chin. "I choose to forgive," she said.

Maurice regarded her with an appraising eye. "You choose well, Anastasia. It will be a matter for much thought over the coming days. I'm sure your pain is still fresh. It has only been two nights. Give it some time in prayer."

"Actually it hasn't even been two nights. This all happened last night."

Maurice jumped from the stone bench and stared at Ana, his face aghast. "Last night? I thought it was two! Deu be merciful!"

Ana put her hand to her chest and recoiled, disturbed by Maurice's sudden reaction. "What is it? What's the matter?"

"I was in the Citadel last night! It was late. I encountered Valent in the street, and . . ." Maurice slapped his forehead and gazed at the sky.

Ana held her breath. The tension was unbearable.

Maurice looked into Ana's eyes. His expression was grim. "Valent concluded his business earlier than expected. He was returning home last night!"

✦   ✦   ✦

The fork in the trail didn't present a difficult choice for Teo. The one path led into Vingin, which meant contact with human beings. The other trail slabbed up the side of a ridge to a remote meadow. The last thing Teo wanted was to encounter anyone else. Besides, the hard uphill hike would feel like penance, and he certainly wanted to punish himself for his crimes.

Murderer!

The awful events of the night pressed on Teo like a roof beam strapped to his shoulders. The memory of the knife sliding easily into Valent's chest troubled him unlike any of his battles with the outsiders. The fight with Valent wasn't the noble art of war but a dirty struggle for survival. Valent was a Chiveisian . . . a member of the house community . . . a friend! Now he was a corpse, and his death was the direct result of Teo's choices.

Though the memories of Valent's death were horrific, Sucula's pale face haunted Teo even more. He couldn't shake the image of her crying as she writhed on the floor. When she had approached Teo at the tavern the previous evening, so flirty and carefree and pretty in her black gown, who could have guessed that before the sun's next rising she would lie dead in her own bedroom with a crushed skull?

You did this, Teo! You killed her! Murderer! The voices kept accusing him as he hiked swiftly up the trail.

He reached the crest of the ridge, having passed no one but a dairy-man coming down from the alp. The ridge formed a wall above Vingin, separating the village from the precinct of the High Priestess's temple on the other side. Teo had circled around the end of this ridge when he visited Lewth several months ago, but now he had climbed directly up its side to stand on top. The crest was open, providing an all-encompassing view of the mountainous heart of Chiveis. To the south lay the jagged snowy peaks that receded one after the other into the Beyond. The biggest and most foreboding of them were the three summits of Vulkain, Pon, and Elzebul, which towered nearby and mocked Teo's puny insignificance.

He stumbled through the open meadows to the highest point of the ridge, then fell to his knees in the grass. At the edge of Vulkain's north face stood the temple of the great High Priestess. An intervening peak obscured Teo's view of the temple except for the white tower that projected into the sky. He recalled the bad smell that lingered there, the dank mist, the aura of secrecy and power. The High Priestess only had to utter a single incantation from her unholy spire, and the dawn god would rain down fire and thunder on a man's home. That was true dominion.

An object was in Teo's hands, and he stared at it without processing what it was. Gradually he realized it was the Sacred Writing of Deu. *What am I supposed to do with this now?* The wind stirred its cloth wrapping.

An idea occurred to him, and he glanced toward the temple of Astrebril. What if he were to surrender the book to the High Priestess? Surely that would be a meritorious action! Although Teo had little regard for Astrebril, he knew he needed a heavy dose of divine power to blot out his bloodguilt. What could be a more worthy penance than to hand over the book to the High Priestess? It would certainly earn the god's favor. With this deed, perhaps the great scales of justice would be returned to balance.

Of course, to do so would utterly betray the house community. Yet did that matter anymore? Teo was a murderer, and more or less an adulterer as well. The community would no longer want his translations of the holy book. *I'm the only one who can read it, and now I'm unworthy to touch it!* The Sacred Writing had become useless to those who loved it most. Deu wouldn't come to Chiveis after all. Teo had murdered him too.

Scrambling to his feet, Teo walked to a trail junction. A rough path led down the far side of the ridge to the temple precincts. No shepherds or cow herders would dare to use it, but it was navigable enough, and Teo could reach the High Priestess's temple in a couple of hours. He clutched the book under his arm and paused on the edge of the abyss.

One step, and you're committed. If you do this, you'll never speak to Ana again.

Indecision tore at Teo's soul. Part of him wanted to take the radical step that would earn divine favor, yet an invisible hand seemed to hold him back. His legs felt like lead weights. He couldn't go forward, but he couldn't remain still either, so he tottered on the brink of madness. *Curse it all! So what if I never speak to Ana again? Stratetix won't let me near his daughter anyway! He'll chase me out of his sight! For that matter, so will Ana! Once she discovers what's happened, she'll revile me and walk away.* Teo gripped his forehead in despair as the full weight of his choices descended upon him. The unthinkable was happening. His bond with Ana—forged by so much adversity, strengthened by so much intimacy—was about to be severed forever.

A black chough landed on the trail. It cocked its head and blinked its beady eyes. Teo watched as it opened its yellow bill and uttered its distinctive call. "Alright, I'm coming," Teo said as he started down the trail toward the temple of Astrebril.

From behind him, a voice cried out, "Wait!"

✦ ✦ ✦

As Maurice reined up in front of Valent's chalet, Ana leaped from the saddle and ran to the house. The front door hung open. Everything was still.

"Valent? Sucula?" Maurice shouted the names, but no one answered.

Ana noticed something on the porch. Bending to examine it, she sucked in her breath when she realized it was a bloody footprint. The tread was from the boot of a Royal Guard. She backed away and leaned against Maurice.

"I'll go inside," he said. "You might want to wait here."

"No, I'll come too. I need to know."

The living room looked normal. Two half-drunk cups of mead sat on a table, and a few embers smoldered in the fireplace. A peg on the wall held the bearskin cloak Ana had given Teo. The sight of it caused anger and hurt to flare in her heart. "Deu, give me strength," she whispered.

Maurice knelt before another bloody footprint outside the bedroom. Ana came to his side. "It's Teo's," she said. "I've seen it many times."

Maurice straightened and put his hand on Ana's shoulder. "The bedroom will contain a scene you won't quickly forget. Are you sure you wish to look?"

Ana considered it. Though she wanted to know what had happened, she decided she didn't need to sear her mind with violent images. Shaking her head, she asked, "Would you be willing to bear that burden for me?"

"Of course."

Maurice turned toward the bedroom, but Ana pulled his sleeve. "Let me pray for you first." Quietly she invoked Deu's protection over Maurice's eyes as well as her own heart.

When she had finished, Maurice entered the room and returned a few moments later. The smell of vomit was on his clothes. His face was pale, but he was composed. "Valent and Sucula are both dead," he reported. "There was a fight. Valent died of a wound to the chest from his own knife. Sucula struck her head on a wooden box and died from the blow. Teofil's footprints are in the room."

Ana hung her head. "I feel sorry for them. They were kind people, though misguided. Evil is rising, and they were caught in its snare."

"Yes. I feel powerful forces stirring against us. The traditional gods do not want to see Deu come to Chiveis. But it was you, Anastasia, who taught us to hope for the serpent's defeat. We must cling to that promise."

"What's next, Master Maurice?"

"I'll bury the bodies. You must find Teofil and say to him whatever words Deu gives you. The main thing is to pursue him—to reach out your hand to him in spite of his failure."

"It's hard," Ana admitted as she stared at the bloody footprint. "I'm so angry at him."

"As you should be. He has sinned grievously."

Ana glanced up. "And yet?"

"And yet you remain loyal. That is Deu's character, made real through you."

Ana nodded as Maurice escorted her outside the accursed chalet. As she was about to step into the saddle, she noticed the little barn across the yard. Quickly she entered and returned with a bundle in a burlap sack. She tied it to the saddle, mounted, and turned toward the wise professor.

"Go in peace, daughter," he said.

"Pray that I would have it." She goaded the horse down the path.

Although Ana found no more bloody footprints, she had hunted enough game to be able to follow Teo's trail. She arrived at an intersection and scanned the ground, looking for his tracks. Just then a mountain dairyman came hiking around a bend in the trail.

Ana waved to him. "Greetings, sir! I'm trying to find my friend. Have you passed anyone on the way?"

"Aye! A guardsman rushed past me less than an hour ago. Didn't even bother to give me a grützi!"

"Deu be with you!" Ana cried. The dairyman threw her a funny look as she galloped up the trail.

After a long uphill ride with several steep switchbacks, she topped out on the ridgecrest, and a wide vista opened before her. The warm wind stirred her hair, and bells tinkled as cows grazed in the meadow. The bright blue sky was spangled with puffy clouds. To the south, the sawtooth summits of Chiveis gleamed in the sun. A man stood on the far side of the ridge, looking down. Ana dismounted and began to walk toward him. He did not see her.

Halfway there, she stopped.

Ana could feel her heart beating rapidly. *What am I doing? Perhaps it isn't my place? What if he gets angry? What if he rejects me?* She felt the urge to run to her horse before she was noticed and then flee down the trail.

With her eyes closed, she staggered backward, terrified by the cruciality of the moment. A panicky feeling took hold of her—the same dizzy sensation she felt whenever she looked down from a height. The raw fear in her gut reminded her of that day on the roof of the ancient temple when Teo had asked her to go over the wall. *No! I can't do this! Help me, Deu!*

Teo started to walk down the trail.

"Wait!" she cried.

He spun, and Ana ran to him.

✦   ✦   ✦

Teo watched Ana run across the meadow, her hair streaming behind her in a golden cascade. Often when she appeared unexpectedly, Teo's heart would skip a beat, but not today. Shame held his heart in a vise grip. He bowed his head and refused to look at the most beautiful woman in Chiveis.

She stopped a few paces away. Silence hung between them. *Don't speak. You have nothing to say.*

"Teo—"

He kept his eyes on the ground.

"Teo, I've come to you."

"How did you find me?" he asked bitterly. "You wouldn't be here if you knew all that had happened."

"I do know, yet here I am."

Hope flooded Teo's soul. He raised his eyes for the first time and looked at Ana. She was radiant—more like an angel than a human being. The sunlight was in her hair, her blue-green eyes were bright, her face glowed with overpowering beauty. Beyond this, a divine radiance now shone from Ana, as if she were lit from within by a heavenly flame.

She stepped closer, reaching out a hand to touch him.

"Stop!" Teo barked. Shame at his own foulness welled up. He was untouchable, unworthy, undeserving.

"I didn't come all this way to be kept apart from you," she said softly. "I won't have that anymore. I want you with me again."

"No, you don't! You don't know the whole story! There's more to it than the lost book!" He held up the Sacred Writing.

"You found it! Praise Deu! How did you get it back?"

"I got it from—" He grimaced. "It doesn't matter. Just leave me alone." The burning disgrace was too much for Teo. He covered his face with his hand and turned away. The hot wind blew across the meadow as he fought to keep tears from coming to his eyes. He hoped Ana would go, but at the same time it was the last thing in the world he wanted.

A hand touched him. He flinched.

"I know you went to Sucula," Ana said. "I know she's dead, and also Valent. But I'm still here, Teo, and I always will be, no matter what."

How can she say that? It's impossible!

Teo faced Ana and sank to his knees. She stood over him, and he grasped her by the waist, burying his face in her dress. He couldn't hold back his tears any longer. "I'm sorry!" he sobbed. "Ana, I've hurt you, and I'm so sorry!" He said it over and over as she stroked his hair.

"I won't deny it or pretend otherwise. It's true. You—" Ana's voice caught for a moment, but she gathered herself and continued. "You hurt me more than Rothgar or Dirk ever did."

The pain in her words was obvious. Teo felt it deeply, acknowledged it, and owned it.

"Forgive me," he said.

"I forgive you, Teofil."

He looked up at her. She was smiling at him. *What grace is in this woman!* "I'll make it up to you," he promised.

"It doesn't work like that. My forgiveness is already granted. There's nothing more between us."

"Just like that? It's over?"

"No, there's one more thing. Remember the paintings we saw in the temple of the Ancients? There was a man with a boy and a ram. Deu is a God of sacrifice."

"I know. I was reading ahead, and I found that story in the book of Beginning, the twenty-second chapter. The man's name was Abraham. Deu commanded him to sacrifice his only son, but in the end he didn't let

300

Abraham go through with it. Deu provided a ram instead. 'On the mountain of the Eternal One it will be provided.' That's what the book said."

"See? When you confess your sins, sacrifice is Deu's provision to remove them."

Teo nodded, though he felt unsure. "I don't know how to confess. Will you help me?"

"Yes. Wait here." Ana walked to her horse and returned with a sack in her hand. She knelt in the grass across from Teo. Opening the sack, she removed something white—a new lamb, its legs bound. It bleated as Ana laid it on the ground and held it down.

"Give me your sword," she said, "the sword of my grandfather Armand."

"Wait—I'm not sure we should do this. We don't know what to do. We don't have a priest."

"I'll be your priest. Deu is a God who abhors sin and requires sacrifice. Until we know how to do it properly, we'll offer this to him in faith."

Teo drew his sword and handed the hilt to Ana. She sacrificed the lamb, its lifeblood bleeding out beneath the blue sky of Chiveis. Teo swallowed, awed and humbled by the sight.

"Should I say some words?" he asked.

"Deu has given us the right words already, I think. Do you remember translating the hymn of David when he went in to Bath-Schéba?"

"Vaguely. Was it the one with the hyssop plant?"

"Yes. I've set it to music. Just make the words your own."

As Teo knelt in the meadow, Ana stood over him and began to sing. The tune was a mournful dirge, brimming with sorrow and regret.

O Deu!
Have pity on me in your goodness.
According to your great mercy,
erase my transgressions!
Wash me completely from my iniquity,
and purify me from my sin.
For I recognize my transgressions,
and my sin is constantly before me.
I have sinned against you alone,

and have done what is evil in your eyes,
so that you will be just in your sentence,
and without reproach in your judgment.
See! I have been born in sin,
and in transgression my mother has conceived me.
But you wish that truth might be deep in my heart.
Therefore make wisdom penetrate inside me.
Purify me with hyssop, and I will be pure.
Wash me, and I will be whiter than snow!

Ana's sweet voice conveyed a mystical quality, as if she had opened a portal to another world. With gladness, Teo let each verse wash over him. As Ana's voice swelled to the hymn's climax, a more hopeful sound replaced her earlier dirge. Her holy song became like a balm to Teo, accomplishing in his soul the very things of which she sang:

O Deu! Create in me a pure heart!
Renew in me a well-disposed spirit!
Cast me not from your face,
nor remove your holy spirit from me!
Give me back the joy of your salvation,
and sustain in me a spirit that wills the good!

The final stanza of the hymn spoke about the sacrifices Deu desires—not meaningless offerings, but a broken heart. Only then could animal sacrifices delight him. Teo gazed at the lifeless lamb. "I'll never again deny I'm a sinner," he whispered.

As the song's final notes echoed away on the peaks, Teo stood up, dumbstruck by what had just occurred. Ana faced him a short distance away. They remained like that for a long time, each staring at the other, delighting in the holy aura that had descended upon them.

Ana finally broke the spell. "Let's go home," she said with a smile.

Teo nodded, but as Ana turned to go, he hesitated. "Hold on. Before we go, there's one more thing. I, uh . . ." Ana waited for him to collect his thoughts. "I want to tell you something about Sucula."

Ana waved her hands and shook her head. "No, Teo, don't."

"I need to tell you! I want you to know!"

"Please, no! I don't need to hear it."

"You do!" Teo approached Ana and grabbed her two hands in his. His voice became urgent. "I want you to know, I was tempted at her house, but I didn't go through with it! Nothing happened! The truth is, I couldn't because . . ." She looked up at him with her long-lashed eyes. "Because of you," he finished.

"Me?"

"Yes, you! I'm not exactly sure what that means. All I know is, I couldn't betray you. Not after all we've been through."

She smiled mischievously. "Well, you know, I have saved your life two times."

Teo returned the smile. "Actually, it's three times now." Ana cocked her head and thought about what Teo'd said but didn't reply.

They walked to the horse. Ana mounted while Teo put the Sacred Writing in the saddlebag. He gathered the reins to lead the horse down the trail.

"Ride with me," she invited.

Teo climbed into the saddle in front of her. He felt Ana's arms slip around his chest.

"It's nice to have you back, Captain," she whispered in his ear.

◆　　◆　　◆

Maurice threw a final scoop of soil onto the grave, then planted the shovel in the ground to rest against it with two hands. The exertion had winded him, so he stood for a while and caught his breath, wiping the sweat from his forehead. It had taken him all morning to scrub the floors, prepare the bodies, and dig the grave. He buried Valent and Sucula behind the house, wrapped in linen sheets, their arms folded across their chests. A flat stone incised with a cross served as a marker. He didn't know what the symbol meant, but he knew it was important to Deu.

Maurice shook his head at the tragic events, pained that Teo was involved. He would have to find out exactly what had happened and deal with the authorities if necessary. Perhaps it was a case of self-defense against an enraged husband. That wouldn't be considered murder in the magistrates' eyes. In the eyes of Deu, however, Teo was guilty. Maurice resolved to have a long conversation with Teo about the spiritual implications of his actions.

The aroma of wood smoke reached Maurice's nostrils. *Smoke? That's strange,* he thought. *This house is far from anyone else's. The gusty wind must be carrying smells farther than usual.*

He walked across the yard to the barn. Valent and Sucula had no near relatives, so their property would revert to the government for auction. Since it might take a few days for some bureaucrat to visit, Maurice made sure the ewes had enough water in the trough and adequate fodder. Satisfied that everything was in order, he locked up the chalet, then began walking toward Vingin. The satchel of Shaphan's scrolls was in his rucksack, and so was Teo's bearskin cloak, which Maurice had removed from the house.

When the town bell started to ring, Maurice knew something was wrong. Every Chiveisian village had a shrine to Astrebril on the main square. The architecture was always the same. Like the High Priestess's temple, the shrines consisted of a central building topped by a spire whose bell signaled holy days and festivals. Maurice knew no religious celebrations were scheduled for the day, so the ringing of the bell could only mean an emergency.

As he rounded a bend in the trail, he caught sight of gray smoke billowing toward the sky. Instantly he knew what had happened. The foehn winds had a dehydrating effect, causing plants to droop and laundry to dry quickly on the line. They also parched the wooden roofs and haylofts of Chiveis, making them vulnerable to errant sparks. Obviously something in Vingin had caught fire, and now the town was in danger. Maurice hurried down the trail to see how he might help.

By the time he reached Vingin, a serious blaze had developed. Flames had destroyed an inn and some nearby shops, and the villagers were scrambling to put out the many smaller fires that had spread to other roofs. Their efforts were disorganized. Men scurried back and forth with buckets, lacking coordination. Maurice ran to the fountain on the town square and stood on its rim.

"Over here, men!" he cried. "Form a line! That's it!" The townspeople obeyed Maurice's commands as he arranged a bucket brigade. He ordered ladders to be thrown against certain buildings that could create a buffer around the conflagration. "Wet the roofs! Soak them well! Extinguish every spark!"

For a time Maurice thought his plan might be working, but as the day wore on, the relentless fire began to get the upper hand. One by one the buildings of Vingin ignited as the winds roared down the valley and carried sparks over the buffer. The townspeople couldn't hold back the orange flames that spread from house to house. In the confusion, looters began to pillage the burning shops while mothers ran through the streets, clutching their wailing babies. Everyone was shouting in terror and despair.

Standing on the fountain in the town square, Maurice watched the situation become increasingly dire. Smoke clogged his lungs, and the waves of intense heat felt like a smith's furnace, almost too much for a man to endure. He wiped the stinging sweat from his eyes and looked around. A fiery wall was closing in on the heroic bucket brigade, threatening to surround them and cut off escape. If the people didn't get out now, they would be consumed along with everything else. Vingin had become a blazing death trap. The town was lost.

"It's no use, men! The fire has overtaken us! Leave now, before it's too late!" Some dropped their buckets and ran, but others held their ground. Maurice was still urging the men to flee when a eunuch priest of Astrebril and four Vulkainians galloped into the square.

"Attention, everyone!" the priest yelled. "You will not abandon your posts! Your duty lies here! Follow me!" He drew some of the remaining men toward the shrine of Astrebril.

The shrine was constructed of stone, though its roof was made of wood. Thanks to the efforts of the Astrebrilian monks who had concentrated their firefighting efforts at one spot, the main building hadn't ignited. Nevertheless, Maurice could see it was only a matter of time. A wall of flame encircled the structure, and some of its outbuildings were already ablaze. Any effort to protect the shrine would only result in further loss of life. The building stood in the middle of an inferno; it couldn't be saved.

Shouting from the back of his horse, the priest ordered the men to send their buckets toward the shrine. "Astrebril commands you to stay! He'll curse you if you leave! Faster! Keep them coming!"

"No! Stop, men!" Maurice waved his hands vigorously. "The shrine is lost! Get out of the village now, before the forest catches fire too!"

A Vulkainian pointed his acid spray gun at Maurice. "Who are you?" he demanded.

"The only one speaking reason right now!"

The Astrebrilian priest rode up to Maurice and eyed him from the saddle. "Grab a bucket, professor. You're no longer in charge."

"If these men stay here, they'll die."

"The lives of peasants do not concern me. If they must be expended to save the shrine of the god, so be it."

Maurice regarded the priest with a cold stare. The man's cheeks were streaked with soot, and the flames flickered across his face, putting an evil glint in his eyes. Behind him, the men of the realm toiled in the deadly heat, hauling buckets in a futile attempt to save a doomed building. It wasn't water they were pouring on the fire. It was their own souls.

Maurice straightened his shoulders and stood tall on the rim of the fountain. A sense of peace settled onto him, the serene and confident knowledge that now was the time for action. With utter clarity, he realized he stood at a turning point in the history of Chiveis. Deu had appointed him for this very hour. Maurice could feel divine power coursing through his veins. He raised his arms, drawing the crowd to himself. Then, opening his mouth, he began to speak.

"Men of Vingin and all who dwell in Chiveis, let this be known to you, and give ear to my words! A new God has been discovered in our realm—not one to be feared, but one to be loved! His name is Deu, and he alone is God. The gods of Chiveis are false idols. Don't waste your lives for them! Deu would have you live!"

The Astrebrilian priest's ruddy face took on an impossible shade of red. He clenched his fists and bared his teeth; for a moment he looked like he would explode. "Seize that man!" he screamed.

The Vulkainians advanced toward Maurice, but he turned and leaped onto the fountain's upper basin, standing ankle deep in the water. The Vulkainian sergeant pointed his spray gun at him. "Get down from there, or I'll melt your face," he snarled.

Maurice was staring at the four militiamen circled below him, wondering how he was going to get out of the situation, when the priest of Astrebril said something unexpected: "Lower your weapons, men. Let the professor speak."

The surprising statement made Maurice glance up, and he saw the reason for the abrupt change. Teo was there on horseback, his sword at the priest's throat. Anastasia was behind him in the saddle. Maurice smiled to himself. *Deu, give us courage!*

A crowd had gathered, and Maurice addressed them boldly. "People of Chiveis, today I bear witness that the one true God has come to our land! Deu is the Creator of all we see! Long ago he was worshiped by the Ancients! Now the words of his holy book have come to us as well!" He gestured toward the rucksack lying at the base of the fountain. Ana slid from the horse's back and darted to it. Removing a scroll, she raised it above her head. The crowd pressed close to see.

A crash on the far side of the town square sent a cloud of ash and sparks billowing into the sky. The roof of Astrebril's shrine had finally caught fire, and now it had collapsed. Every street leading away from the square except one was blocked by flames and burning debris. Maurice clambered down from the fountain and began to move toward the remaining escape route.

"Follow me!" he cried. "We'll shelter at the hay barn by the southern brook! Bring your families, and hang on to your buckets—we'll need them!"

While Teo kept the Vulkainians at bay, Maurice and Ana fled the burning village with a horde of desperate townspeople. Portions of the surrounding forest had now caught fire, and the flames were spreading from tree to tree. Ana supported Maurice as they fought their way through the choking smoke and swirling ash.

As the barn came into view, Teo galloped up to his friends and dismounted to walk alongside. Though Maurice was exhausted, he found the strength for a friendly gibe. "Well, you certainly waited until the last minute to show up back there!" He smiled, gripping Teo's shoulder affectionately. "But thanks for getting me out of danger."

Teo glanced at Maurice with a grim expression. "I think the danger has just begun."

✦　✦　✦

The fire raged around the barn through the afternoon and into the evening. A new bucket brigade was formed, and for many hours the villagers transported water from the nearby brook to the barn's thatched roof. Even the children helped the firefighting effort by stamping out the little blazes that arose wherever sparks fell. The area near the barn was a patchwork of singed grass.

From the rooftop, Teo examined the damp thatch, scanning for places that could use more water or pouring buckets onto the bright orange embers that floated into the straw. His body ached with fatigue, and the hard work made him thirsty. He took a swig from the bucket and splashed water on his face. Down below, Ana stood knee deep in the brook with her skirt bound around her thighs, filling bucket after bucket.

Vingin was a charred ruin, and much of the surrounding forest was still ablaze. Teo looked at the slope where Valent and Sucula's house lay. Fire had engulfed the area, and he knew nothing would remain there except a few blackened tree trunks and perhaps the chalet's chimney. Teo took comfort in knowing that with all the deaths this day had seen, the authorities wouldn't have time to investigate a crime of passion and self-defense. The memory of Valent and Sucula would simply perish like everything else in the fire's path. A pang of guilt stabbed his heart, but he reminded himself of Ana's priestly sacrifice. *Deu must be a gracious God if he can forgive a murderer like me*, he thought.

As night approached, rain began to fall in heavy drops. Wisps of steam rose over the sizzling landscape, emitting a smoky, wet smell. The soot-blackened villagers staggered into the barn. A few had brought food, and Teo was gratified to see them pass it around, sharing it like brothers and sisters united by tragedy. Maurice climbed onto a tool chest and offered a prayer of thanksgiving to Deu. The people murmured among themselves at the idea of a new God. Some of the men approached Maurice afterward, and Teo watched his animated mentor talk with them and read passages from the holy scrolls.

When the meal was finished, the exhausted villagers fell asleep wherever they collapsed in the hay. A few babies cried against their mothers' bosoms, but soon they became quiet, and the barn grew still.

A woman's slim body slipped into Teo's arms, leaning against him for support. "I can hardly stand up," Ana whispered.

He hugged her tightly and stroked her back with his palm, then took her by the hand. "Come with me. If you can find a little more strength, I know a good place to sleep." He led her to the hayloft ladder and sent her up first, following close behind. The hay was thick in the loft, and they found a place in the corner to lie down. Ana moved close to Teo, cradling her head on his shoulder. In all their nights in the Beyond, they had never actually slept as close as they were now. A certain distance had seemed appropriate then, but tonight it was more fitting that they should draw comfort from one another in this way. Teo felt Ana was where she was supposed to be. Her breathing became regular as she lay next to him, and very soon so did his.

◆　　◆　　◆

"The old man said *what?*" The High Priestess grabbed the Astrebrilian priest by the robe and yanked his soot-streaked face to hers.

The priest blanched. "Uh, Your Eminence, he said the 'one true God' had come to Chiveis, the Creator worshipped by the Ancients. 'Deu,' the man called him. We're supposed to love him. A holy book has been found. And it wasn't just the old professor saying it. A guardsman of the Fifth Regiment was helping him. There was also a beautiful peasant woman with them. That's all I know."

"Nothing else?"

"I've told you all I can remember."

"Then listen to me." The High Priestess drilled the eunuch priest with her stare and poked him in the chest. "If you *ever* mention this again, your life will be forfeit. Am I understood?"

"Yes," he peeped.

She released him. "Now get out." The priest nodded and scuttled off.

Grinding her teeth, the High Priestess turned toward Princess Habiloho. "It seems we have a problem."

"I heard the man. A superstition of the Ancients has resurfaced in the realm." Habiloho waved her hand. "I'm sure we can stamp it out. Vingin is destroyed. The people are scared. They fear Astrebril's continued wrath. Perhaps another town will burn while the hot winds blow."

The High Priestess stalked to her window and looked into the darkness. Earlier that day her servants had secretly lit fires in Vingin. There was nothing like the capricious act of an angry god to make the people afraid. All afternoon she had watched the smoke billowing from behind the ridge where the village lay burning. Now the orange glow in the sky had been extinguished by the rain.

"The flames consumed what Astrebril wished and then died out," she said. The High Priestess turned around and faced Habiloho. "Unfortunately, this superstition of the Ancients won't die out the same way. It's tenacious and must be suppressed with all our means."

"The people have lots of superstitions and cults. What's so bad about this one?"

"The god of the Ancients is my mortal foe," the High Priestess answered. "He claims to be the only god. He won't let Astrebril have any glory. I curse his very name." She spat on the floor. *Crush him, Astrebril my lord!*

Habiloho gulped. "He sounds very wicked."

"He is." The High Priestess put her arm around Habiloho's shoulders in a conspiratorial way. "You must acquaint yourself with the Enemy if you're to assume your place at my side. After you're initiated tomorrow, I'll give you his book to read. You must learn his ways so you can know exactly how to combat him."

"We'll never let him return to Chiveis," Habiloho vowed.

"Never!"

"What about the professor? He's out there spreading heresies. I know who he is. His name is Maurice the Wise. He's Captain Teofil's mentor."

"Yes, I know. It doesn't surprise me those two are involved in all this. And no doubt the third accomplice is that girl the captain plucked from the Beyond. She's proving quite difficult to eliminate."

"I don't know what Teofil sees in her," Habiloho muttered.

The High Priestess licked her lips and chuckled as she looked at the princess. "Rest assured, my young acolyte. You're about to get more revenge than you can possibly know what to do with."

"It's about time." Habiloho's voice was bitter.

"I've ordered a squad of Vulkainian militiamen to arrest those three. We'll see if their newfound faith can withstand my favorite kind of dissuasion—*pain.*"

Habiloho glanced up. "Torture? Why?"

"To break them. If you can't seduce them to your side, you have to force them into submission. One way or the other, the people must see them deny what they have embraced, or the heresy will keep spreading. The name of Deu is out in the open now. These three troublemakers will publicly recant their faith in him or else."

"Or else what?"

"Or else I'll put them to death."

Habiloho recoiled. "They're not your clergy—they're citizens of the realm! Can you get away with that?"

The High Priestess approached the red-haired princess and stared at her, relishing the girl's full, black lips and darkly painted eyes. She was beautiful, and would be a useful assistant. The High Priestess sneered. "Watch me," she said.

◆　　◆　　◆

"Out of my way!" The harsh voice woke Ana from her sleep. *Where am I?* She blinked her eyes, trying to get her bearings. Bright morning sunlight shone through the wall slats. *The fire. The barn. The hayloft.* She sat up. Teo was peering over the edge to the floor below, his sword in his hand. She crawled to his side.

A high-ranking priest of Astrebril and a squad of fifteen Vulkainian militiamen were terrorizing the frightened crowd. One of the villagers accidentally obstructed a Vulkainian, who punished him with a squirt of oily liquid from a spray gun. The victim clutched his forearm and yelped.

The priest seized Maurice by the wrist. "Maurice the Wise, you are hereby placed under arrest for heresy to be remanded to Her Eminence the High Priestess!"

In the hayloft, Teo started to move toward the ladder, but Ana grabbed his jerkin. "No, wait!" she whispered. "You can't fight that many! They'll end up taking you, too!"

"I have to help Maurice!"

"The best way to help him is to stay free. They have the upper hand right now. Wait for the right time, like you did with me at the outsiders' hall!"

The Vulkainians grabbed some of the villagers, shaking them by the garments and waving spray guns in their faces. "Where are the others?" they demanded. The terrified peasants pointed with trembling fingers to the loft, and the Vulkainians followed with their eyes. Teo and Ana ducked into the hay, but it was too late. The men shouted and ran to the base of the ladder.

Ana glanced at Teo. He winked at her, then scrambled to his feet. Kicking the top of the ladder where it was nailed to the loft, he broke it loose and sent it flying backward amid curses from the men already on its rungs. At the back of the loft, he threw open the external door. A rope dangled from a block-and-tackle system intended for hoisting hay. Teo reached for it, but the rope hung beyond his grasp. He leaned toward Ana with a grin. "You trust me, right?"

She covered her face with her hands and shook her head. "Oh, no, not again."

"Climb on my back! Quick!" He turned around. Ana snatched the saddlebag containing the Sacred Writing, then leaped onto Teo's broad back, wrapping her legs around his waist and holding him around the neck.

A man's voice shouted behind her. The ladder had been repositioned against the loft, and a Vulkainian's head now poked over the top. "Halt where you are!" he ordered.

Ana closed her eyes and took a deep breath. Teo jumped into space.

They fell until a force jerked Ana so hard she nearly lost her grip on the saddlebag. She squealed as they dangled in midair.

"Almost missed it," Teo said as he slid down the rope, slowing their descent with his boots. They hit the ground running as the Vulkainians shouted from the hayloft door. Teo lobbed the end of the rope into a tree so it would hang out of reach of the men in the loft.

The militiamen's horses waited nearby with only one man guarding them. When the soldier saw Teo running toward him, he lifted his acid weapon. A ball from the end of Teo's ax took him in the stomach, and the man doubled over. Teo thrust him aside as he and Ana ran to the horses. They each mounted and kicked their heels hard, sending the animals surg-ing forward. A squirt of acid stung Teo on the thigh. The horse whinnied and ran even faster.

They took the same trail Teo had used to reach Obirhorn Lake but didn't go that far. Instead they turned off and meandered through the uninhabited forest until they were certain they had lost the Vulkainians, who were inexperienced woodsmen. Not far above, a waterfall plunged over the lip of a hanging valley.

"Your parents are up there," Teo remarked. "But we shouldn't approach them right now."

Ana sighed. "My parents are in exile. Valent and Sucula are dead. My aunt is wavering, and so are Lina and Shaphan. Master Maurice is under arrest, and here we are, fleeing from the authorities."

"Yeah. I guess the days of our secret community are over."

Ana sat straight in the saddle and turned her head toward Teo, buoyed by a sense of peace. "I'm finished with secrets," she said. "It's time to take a stand. It's time for Deu to come to Chiveis."

PART THREE

SOVEREIGNTY

CHAPTER

13

Princess Habiloho sat in a cushioned window seat, carefully painting her toenails in the sunshine. The view from her high window in the royal palace overlooked the Citadel and the great wall that spanned the cleft in the mountains. Spread out below the wall lay Entrelac, with a sea on either side like twin jewels. On this day, however, Habiloho wasn't paying attention to scenery. She was focused on her pinky toe.

From behind her, rough fingers dug into her ribs. She yelped at the tickle and painted a black swath across the top of her foot. *Who would DARE?* Male laughter filled the room as Habiloho spun toward her tormentor. It was the only person in Chiveis who could get away with such a thing—Piair II, heir to the realm and pest-in-chief.

"Look what you made me do!" Habiloho hurled the bottle of nail polish at her eighteen-year-old brother. He caught it in midair and whipped it back toward her. It sailed past her head and out the window to the street below. Habiloho stared at him in exasperation, her mouth agape.

Piair approached the angry princess and grabbed her ankle. With the sleeve of his expensive tunic, he wiped the polish from Habiloho's foot. "Good as new," he said.

"What do you want, Piair?"

"Nothing really. Just a friendly visit with my sister. I came to tell you the news. Did you hear Vingin burned to the ground yesterday?"

Habiloho curled her lip and tossed her hair. "It wasn't much of a town."

"It was to the people who lived there." Piair changed the subject. "Why are you getting all fixed up?"

"In case you forgot, I'm to be made a priestess of Astrebril today, a slave in his holy service."

It was Piair's turn to be exasperated. "I don't understand why you'd want to do that! I know you used to follow Pon, but I always thought it had more to do with his forest orgies than any real devotion on your part. Now you're taking the collar of Astrebril! That's a whole different matter."

Habiloho glared at her brother, then rose from her seat and gestured out the window. "See that? All those lands, those people? That's why I want to join the order. When I met the High Priestess, she awakened something in me, a hunger I never knew I had."

Piair glanced sideways at Habiloho, skeptical. "A hunger for what?"

"For power. Power over all I see."

Piair snorted, shrugging his shoulders and throwing his palms in the air. "Power? You have all the power you need! You have Father wrapped around your finger, and your beauty gives you power over men. Politics and seduction—those are the two most powerful forces on earth!"

"You're wrong."

"Not often."

Habiloho faced the prince, her chin out. She poked him in the chest. "This time you are, sweet brother."

He stared at her without answering.

"The most powerful force on earth isn't politics, nor seduction." She smiled coyly. "Though I'm very good at both."

Piair rolled his eyes. "What is it then?"

"It's *religion*. It lets you manipulate people's fear of death or their desires for things they can't control. Religion will bend them to your will like nothing else. Once you have them good and afraid, there's nothing they won't do for you. That's absolute power."

"And what do you plan to do with your absolute power?"

Habiloho turned toward the window and uttered a single, bitter word: "Revenge."

Piair chuckled. "You're still mad about your Royal Guard boyfriend, aren't you?"

The accusation infuriated Habiloho, and she whipped around to face Piair with genuine rage welling up inside. "What if I am?" she snarled.

"That girl from Edgeton was stunning! She was a perfectly valid choice for the garland. Let it go, Habiloho."

"I'll let it go—when I've tasted revenge. And Astrebril will help me get it."

Piair shook his head. "Religion is supposed to make you noble and virtuous. I don't think you're headed that way, sis."

Habiloho didn't answer. Instead she stalked across the room, retrieved another bottle of black nail polish from a dressing table, and returned to her window seat. Coldly ignoring her brother, she began to paint her toes again. "Close the door on the way out," she said.

◆　◆　◆

The High Priestess slapped Maurice. Hard. He licked his lip but said nothing.

"Maurice the Wise! I should've known you'd try to introduce heresy to Chiveis! Your impious curiosity is well-known to my servants at the University." The High Priestess paced around Maurice as he sat bound to a chair in the middle of the room. Two Vulkainian guards stood by the doorway.

"It is the role of the scholar to explore new ideas for the good of mankind," Maurice replied.

The High Priestess lifted a black-nailed finger to her brow and slid a wisp of long dark hair behind her ear. She approached Maurice and bent toward him, staring into his face. He was a distinguished man with a shaven head and clear eyes. Red blood stained his white goatee. The High Priestess gripped his chin and pulled his face close. "It is for *me* to decide what is best for mankind," she hissed.

With a wave of her hand, she summoned one of the Vulkainians to her side. He was a thick-chested man with a dull expression and the face of a pig. The High Priestess ignored him and addressed Maurice. "Since you're so keen to share new ideas with the people of Chiveis, perhaps you could enlighten me as well. What is your message, preacher?"

"I preach the one true God, the God of Israël, whose name is Deu. The Sacred Writing declares he is the Creator of all things. He's loving and good. He alone is God. The gods of Chiveis are evil."

The High Priestess felt a nameless fear claw at her soul. *How had the old sage found the scriptures of Christianity, that dead religion of the Ancients? It had been excised from all the records. Had something been missed?* She covered her alarm with a melodious laugh. "Tell me more, preacher," she said. "Perhaps I shall convert to your Deu."

"I'm certain Deu does not suffer mockers lightly."

The High Priestess scowled and motioned with her fingers toward the Vulkainian guard beside her. He cocked his meaty arm and smashed Maurice in the ribs, the sound of fist on flesh making a delicious smack in her ears. The old man's chair tumbled backward with a crash, and he writhed in the ropes, groaning and rasping. The High Priestess spat on the floor. "That's what I think of Deu," she said.

The Vulkainian set the chair upright again. Maurice's head hung low, and he breathed with difficulty through gritted teeth. The High Priestess stood across from him, her hands on her hips. "It's time to make a decision, Professor. Deny your beliefs or face the consequences."

Maurice raised his eyes. "I will not . . . deny." He had to take several shallow breaths before he could continue. "It's not . . . too late. You can still . . . turn to him!"

His words told the High Priestess everything she needed to know. *So the old man is fully committed to Christianity? Fine. If he won't recant, then he will die.* Sneering, she asked, "Why should I turn to the impotent god of the cross?"

"Deu . . . is strong."

The High Priestess threw back her head and laughed. "Fool! You think he's powerful? I've read his book. I know all about this weak deity of yours. He's called *Dieu* in the Fluid Tongue, or *Deus* in the Old Words. He's the Father of the Son, who was killed on a cross in shameful defeat." She paused, narrowing her eyes as she noticed Maurice's uncertain expression. "You don't know about that, do you?"

"I know his symbol." Maurice winced. "Not its meaning."

"And how did you come upon this knowledge?"

Maurice remained silent.

The High Priestess flicked her fingers again, and the Vulkainian administered another devastating body blow. The old man couldn't take many more of those hits and survive. Though some of the civil magistrates might want to launch an investigation if he died, she'd take that risk. The High Priestess had powerful allies at the courthouse. She looked down at Maurice as he lay on the floor, bound to the chair, his chest quivering as he gasped for air.

"Do whatever it takes to make him recant," she said to the guard, who broke into a malicious grin. "Hold nothing back." She spun away and stormed out.

In her study, the High Priestess summoned a scribe. "Take dictation from me and draft a proclamation. It shall be read throughout Chiveis immediately." With a parchment clipped to a wooden board and a quill in his hand, the scribe seated himself on a stool.

The High Priestess gazed out the window of her spire. Though it was springtime, the air was cool. The sky overhead was deep blue, a color precious to Astrebril. Only crimson pleased him more.

Sipping a glass of wine, the High Priestess considered the turn of events. Christianism had been rediscovered and the name of Deu proclaimed to a few peasants. However, there was still time to eradicate the heresy before it spread. With her free hand she fondled the slave collar at her neck as it if were a talisman, a soothing and clarifying habit of hers. Astrebril's inner voice began to speak to her soul, driving home one essential point: *The people of Chiveis must never turn to Christianism!*

"I'm ready to begin," she said to the scribe. He put his quill to the parchment. "O people of our great realm! The Curse of Astrebril has visited us. He has destroyed our fair village of Vingin. Other towns will certainly suffer the same fate unless you repent. Astrebril's thunderous fires will appear again in the sky, proving his fierce wrath toward us. When you see them, you will know for certain he is angry at the preaching of a false god of the Ancients called Deu. Pay no attention to this foul deity! If you do, the Curse of Astrebril will surely descend upon you. There is but one escape from his terrible fires: I alone, your beloved High Priestess, will propitiate the anger of the Beautiful One. Only by my intervention can you be saved!"

She paused. "Read it back to me." The scribe obliged. Satisfied with her eloquence, she nodded and waved him away with the back of her hand. He bowed to her and scurried from the room.

◆　　◆　　◆

"I have a plan." Teo rose from where he was squatting beside a stream and looked at Ana, his hand resting on his sword's hilt. She regarded him with strong emotions. Admiration was certainly one of them—the captain was very capable in moments like this. He was also headstrong and brash, which made her feel uncertain. *Could he ever change?*

"You always seem to have something up your sleeve," she said. "What is it this time?"

Teo walked over to Ana, excitement written all over his face. She could practically see the wheels turning in his head. "I'm going to steal a monk's habit and sneak into the High Priestess's temple, pretending I'm doing research. When I'm finished, instead of leaving, I'll go around back. I know a secret way in. I'm certain I can find where Maurice is being kept."

Ana held up her hands, palms out. "First of all, what do you mean, *I*? Surely you don't intend to leave me behind?"

Teo frowned. "Ana, be reasonable! It's not safe for you."

"It's not safe for you either!" She looked into his face. A lock of his dark hair dangled over his forehead. "I'm part of these events too, Teo. You know I can hold my own up there, even fight if necessary. Besides—" She lowered her eyes. "You're not the only one who loves Maurice."

Teo sighed. He started to argue, but when his stern expression softened, Ana knew he had understood her concern for Maurice. Teo's protests were feeble. "You can't go. There are no female monks of Astrebril, only priestesses. You'll have no disguise."

"I can go as your household servant—one of those women who do chores for the monks."

"That's not all they do for them."

Ana tucked her chin and arched an eyebrow at Teo. "Don't get any ideas."

He laughed, and the two of them mounted their horses, heading for Lekovil by the back trails. Arriving at the University, Teo was pleased to discover his lock had been changed, and the gatekeeper was holding a new key for him. Teo entered the room and hid the Sacred Writing under the floorboards, then packed some writing instruments and glass jars in his rucksack. He didn't think he would need his ax, so he hung it on the wall. On the way out, Ana made sure he locked the door and put the key in his pack.

Out in the courtyard, Teo and Ana wandered toward the waterfall. Nobody paid them much attention; they had been seen together before. Teo led Ana to a ladder that had been laid against the cliff over which the waterfall plunged. The outer wall of the University abutted the cliff in two places, forming a semicircle around the waterfall's pool. Rooms for the professors and clerics lined the interior of the wall.

"What's up there?" Ana pointed at the ladder.

"A natural fissure in the cliff. It runs behind the waterfall. In the time of the Ancients, there was a hillock here, and they would ascend it to reach the fissure. The Chiveisi excavated the hillock and created the plunge pool. But the crack is still there, of course. People sometimes climb the ladder to see the falls up close."

"And how does this help us rescue Maurice?"

"I said we need a disguise, right? I'm going to do some breaking and entering."

Teo grabbed the ladder, then ascended halfway to the top. Ana shaded her eyes and watched him climb. Suddenly she realized what he was about to do: he had reversed his stance on the rungs and was preparing to jump from the ladder to the roof of the buildings that abutted the cliff! She scanned the courtyard nervously. Few people were in it, and no one seemed to be looking their way. When she turned back to Teo, he was gone.

She waited for what seemed like an eternity, but he didn't return. Ana went to the low wall that ringed the plunge pool, taking a seat in the cool mists. Droplets sprinkled the pool's surface. Teo was nowhere to be seen.

A rough hand grabbed Ana's shoulder. She jumped and let out a cry when she saw a hooded monk. "I have some chores for you, wench!" he said from deep within his cowl. The monk laughed in a very familiar way.

Ana exhaled in relief and leaned close to the monk of Astrebril. "Careful," she warned. "I might get the notion to short-sheet your bed." Teo removed his hood and handed Ana the drab shoes, dress, and head scarf of a servant girl.

After changing into her disguise, Ana rode beside Teo toward the charred remains of Vingin. They turned onto the path that led to the precincts of the High Priestess's temple. Although they saw a few people along the way, everyone was too preoccupied with salvaging what they could from the fire to notice the Astrebrilian monk and his handmaiden.

Just before they rounded the ridge that would bring the temple into view, Teo dismounted and asked Ana to do the same. He scooped some dirt into his hands and held it toward her. "You don't look much like a servant. Rub this on your face."

Ana wrinkled her nose. "Do I have to?"

"Yup. You're too pretty to pass as a common housemaid."

Ana heaved a sigh, but she dutifully smeared the dirt on her cheeks, chin, and forehead. "How do I look now?"

Teo shrugged. "Still gorgeous, just dirtier."

The statement made Ana smile. "You've never told me I'm pretty," she teased.

Teo threw her a look of pretended indignation. "What are you talking about? I declared it in front of forty thousand people."

Ana bit her lip and cocked her head. She had to admit he was right.

A mist was gathering as Teo and Ana approached the intimidating spire of the Temple of Astrebril. The three great summits of Chiveis were lost in the clouds. Ana peered at them with a sense of awe. "People say Astrebril has another temple up there on the ridgeline," she said.

"It's not a temple. It's just a rocky knob that sometimes glints in the sun."

At the gatehouse, a surly Astrebrilian monk stopped them. Ana hunched into her scarf, her eyes downcast, while Teo dismounted and stepped forward.

"Your business?" the guard demanded.

"I've come from Lekovil. I have some research to do in the archives. I might have to collect some plant specimens too." Teo opened his rucksack to display his parchments, quills, and jars.

"What's the woman for?"

"Errands. Sharpening quills. Fetching books. Hey"—Teo slapped the man on the chest with the back of his hand—"listen, I've got orders from the provost to do this research! You gonna let me in or what?"

The intimidation approach seemed to work. The man sneered, but he backed down and opened the gate for Teo and Ana, telling them where to go. They hurried toward the archives before anyone else could question them.

The Temple of Astrebril consisted of a central grandiose building crowned by the immense spire that soared into the sky like a granite spike. Many tiny hovels for the resident monks dotted the grassy slope in front of the main building. Level ground was virtually nonexistent. The whole place was surrounded by an outer wall, while high interior walls separated certain parts of the temple complex from view.

"Spooky, huh?" Teo whispered.

"Evil."

The archives were located in the main building. Teo and Ana entered through a side door and moved to some isolated shelves at the rear of the stacks.

"Now what?" Ana asked in a low voice.

"We can't get into the rest of the temple from here. So we'll just wait, to lead them to believe we're researching. Then we'll leave and sneak around back. I know how to get in."

"And after that?"

Teo held open a slit he had cut in his monk's habit at the hip. The sword of Armand was there. "After that, I unleash my wrath!"

The tone of Teo's voice and his prideful demeanor grated on Ana. She knew if Maurice would be rescued today, it would be because Deu helped them, not because of skillful swordplay. She considered saying that to Teo but decided against it. Now was not the time.

Teo was scanning the bookshelves. "While we're waiting here," he said, "I might as well see what they have in their holdings." He walked to the Ancient Languages section and pulled a book from the shelves. His eyes lit up. Ana came over to see what it was. The book was titled *A Complete Lexicon of the Speech of the Ancients Known as FRANSAIS, Commonly Referred to as the Fluid Tongue.*

Teo glanced up. "This is a fantastic reference work! Look at this! The word for 'god' in the Fluid Tongue, *dieu*, is defined as the one true God."

"That's how Jacques Dalsace used the word in the letter he left with the Sacred Writing—as a proper name. In our speech it's 'Deu.'"

"Right! But none of our lexicons at Lekovil ever render *dieu* like that. They define it only as a generic god. Obviously the word meant something more in the Fluid Tongue. The Ancients used it to name God himself. This dictionary should be in the University archives. I'm keeping it."

Ana tsked. "The clergy are always trying to keep us from the truth," she said bitterly. "They don't want us to know the Creator."

Teo looked at Ana and nodded. "The people of Chiveis need to hear about Deu."

"I guarantee you, they're about to find out." Ana could feel a fire rising within her soul.

"Well, we're going to need Master Maurice's wisdom for that. I think it's time to move. Let's slip around back and see if we can find him." Teo put the lexicon in his rucksack and led Ana from the archives.

◆　◆　◆

It was a secret room for a secret deed. Candelabras lined the wall, illuminating the central aisle with their flickering glow. As for the shadowy corners of the room, who knew what might be lurking there? It might be human, or it might be something else.

At the far end of the center aisle stood a single structure. A cage. Its bars were made of iron. Its door hung open, hungry.

Princess Habiloho could feel the wine starting to take effect. It had been spiked with a drug that made the room grow fuzzy and her mind grow dim. The effect was surreal.

The congregation consisted of men and women dressed in the gauzy robes of the Order of Astrebril. They sat with their eyes closed, chanting, though not in unison. Each was at a different point in the liturgy, so the hubbub of their voices made an indecipherable sound that filled the room with speech but not meaning. The otherworldly noise was very holy. *Right? Isn't this how religion is supposed to feel?*

The great oaken door, the only entrance to the room, slammed shut behind Habiloho. There was no going back now. The chanters quieted as an expectant hush settled upon them.

A very old woman rose from the front row. Her back was a misshapen hump, and one of her eyes was clouded. The other eye stared into the distance, seeing nothing, or perhaps seeing things that couldn't be described. She had a parchment in one hand and a knife in the other.

The hag shuffled down the center aisle in a trance. All the clerics watched her walk. The light of the candelabras danced on her wrinkled face.

"I greet you from the world below!" she croaked. "I am among the spirits, even as we speak."

Should I say something? "Hail, wise one!" Habiloho cried. The congregation murmured its approval.

"Your hand," the hag demanded.

My hand?

"Your hand!" The hag's movement was fast for someone so old. With a quick grab and a flick of the knife, she drew blood from the princess's palm. It trickled over Habiloho's black fingernails. The cut burned, though it wasn't deep.

The hag held up the parchment and read in her froggy voice, "Freely do I bind myself to thee! Freely do I become thy slave! My soul I give to thee forever, O Beautiful One! Here in the presence of all, I do swear an oath in my blood to Astrebril, my lord!"

The hag proffered the contract. *I'm supposed to sign it.* Habiloho's bloody finger smeared a single letter on the page: *H.*

The deed was done. A lusty cheer erupted from the room, though Habiloho didn't feel like celebrating. Events seemed to be racing out of control, events that couldn't be changed. She felt tears well up, but she suppressed them and told herself to continue with the plan.

The High Priestess materialized from the shadows. Her face was painted white, and her diaphonous gown billowed behind her like the wings of a dragon. The serpentine scepter she carried glinted in the candlelight. "Your soul is Astrebril's forever," she intoned. "Let us now proceed to the Ritual of Enslavement, that you may enter his holy order."

Habiloho was led to the cage. She stopped at the door. Her desire for revenge against Teo had driven her to this day, but now that it was here, the sacrifice seemed to require more than her soul could offer. The crowd leaned forward in excitement and began to chant again. This time they uttered the same word over and over: *Astrebril! Astrebril! Astrebril!* The name bounced off the walls and filled the room with tension. Habiloho entered the cage.

The High Priestess turned her around so she was facing away from the crowd. "Hold on here," the priestess instructed. "Do not release." Habiloho gripped the iron bars tightly, her wrists trembling. She knew something terrible was about to happen.

Astrebril! Astrebril! Astrebril!

SMACK!

The unexpected pain exploded across Habiloho's back. She cried out as the whipping switch made contact, slicing a line of fire along her shoulder blades. It took all her willpower not to let go of the bars, not to turn around. Again the switch fell, and again. Habiloho's eyes watered. The pain was intense.

How many will there be?

She gasped with each blow. There were six in all, and then they stopped.

"Six more," said the High Priestess.

No!

The next six blows came from a bundle of switches instead of just one. Habiloho's pain was continuous, excruciating, unbearable. Finally the beating stopped.

"Six more," the High Priestess demanded. "No mercy."

Please! No! Someone help me!

The last six came from a leather whip. By the end of it, Habiloho knew she would have blood on her gown, perhaps even permanent scars. Her knees sagged.

"All kneel," said the High Priestess. Habiloho fell to the floor of the cage, still facing away from the crowd, her bloody hand sliding down the iron bar. She heard the congregation move into a kneeling position as well.

A black cloth fell from the wall above. There, protruding from the shadows, was Astrebril himself, spreading his bat wings to the ceiling. The idol's serpentine body coiled up from the floor, and his wicked head hung over the cage. Astrebril's bearded face grinned as he surveyed his newest slave.

"FEAR HIM!" At the High Priestess's words, a fountain of flame and sparks shot from Astrebril's mouth onto the caged princess. Habiloho shrieked, and even the congregation made fearful noises. Pungent smoke filled the room, the stench of the Beautiful One.

Two men grabbed Habiloho's shoulders, one holding her right side, the other her left. She could not move or turn around.

Something cold touched her neck. Metallic. It encircled her throat, too tight, constricting, yet not enough to choke. A hammer rang against a pin at the nape of her neck. The men turned Habiloho to face the congregation.

"Behold Astrebril's eternal slave!" The High Priestess raised her scepter. Through the smoke, the priestesses and eunuchs cheered Habiloho from their kneeling position.

Astrebril's eternal slave? Oh god . . . what have I done?

✦   ✦   ✦

The glacier dangled from the cloudy summits into the lesser mists below, ending not in pristine, blue-white splendor like its upper reaches but in a dirty crumbling of ice and rock and gray soil. Meltwater ran down a gully, above which loomed the rear wall of the High Priestess's temple.

"This is the place Lewth showed me." Teo scanned the wall, looking for a crack in its stony face.

Ana shivered. "I don't like it here. It has a bad smell."

Teo and Ana had exited through the temple gatehouse with a mumbled excuse about picking plant specimens, using the same ruse Lewth had employed months earlier. Now they left their horses picketed in the grass and looked for an opening in the wall.

"Is this it?" Ana peeked into a narrow crack. "I think I see a mill."

She stepped aside as Teo approached. "Good. That's it." He thrust his head into the crack, glanced around, and wriggled through. Ana's slender form slipped inside much more easily.

The place appeared deserted. High walls hid it from the rest of the temple. The largest structure was a gristmill for grinding grain, an odd thing to find so far from any arable fields. Its large external wheel could be turned by horses. Wagons stood outside other smaller buildings.

"Do you think Master Maurice is being kept in the spire?" Ana glanced at its foreboding height. "We need to find a way in."

"It looks the like millhouse is connected to the rest of the temple. Let's see if it is."

They crossed the open space to the stone building, seeing no one, yet feeling exposed as they ran. Inside, wooden shafts and gears were connected to the horse wheel outside. The gears turned two massive millstones, each as tall as Ana. The stones were set into a shallow depression coated with a residue of black powder. It emitted a sharp aroma.

"That's not flour," Ana remarked.

Teo glanced around the strange room. It was cluttered with barrels and sacks. He pointed to a flame emblem stamped on the side of a barrel. "Look at this—Vulkain's symbol."

Ana lifted the lid. "And this is his brimstone!" The barrel contained the yellow rock that the Vulkainian priests wore around their necks as an amulet. "I wonder what it's doing in a temple of Astrebril?"

Teo knelt beside a pile of sacks, each marked with the laughing-goat symbol of Pon. One of the sacks was ripped, and he pulled something black from it. "Charcoal! Pon's followers make it in the deep forest along the Tooner Sea."

"And then they go to their filthy parties." Ana scrunched her face and shuddered.

"Let's not bring up that touchy subject."

"Right."

Teo considered the two substances in the room—the brimstone of Vulkain and the charcoal of Pon. *What about Elzebul?* He crossed to a table lined with mortars and pestles. Each bowl was marked with Elzebul's symbol of a housefly. Teo stirred the white crystals and feathery powder in one of the mortars. "Look at this stuff. I wonder what it is?"

Ana bent to inspect it. "I know what it is." She moistened her finger and touched the white powder, lifting it toward her lips.

Teo seized her wrist. "Stop! It might be poisonous!"

Ana craned her neck and licked her extended finger. Teo released her wrist, rolling his eyes to the ceiling and throwing his hands into the air with an exasperated sigh.

"Don't worry," Ana soothed, "it's not poisonous. It's salt stone. It grows naturally on the walls of stables and henhouses—anywhere there's manure." She smiled. "Remember, I'm a farm girl. I know about these things. If you put this salt on your garden, it really makes the vegetables grow."

"Oh, I suppose the High Priestess is into gardening, and she doesn't want anyone to know." Teo's tone was playfully sarcastic.

Ana shrugged, wearing a mischievous expression. "You're the brilliant professor. Shouldn't you have realized the salt stone isn't for gardening? It's for mixing with brimstone and charcoal. Grind them all together and they make that smelly black powder. See?" She pointed to the residue beneath the giant millstones. Some of it hadn't been well mixed and was still visible as a yellow or white powder.

Teo moved toward a staircase at the back of the room, a little bit miffed that Ana had figured out the mystery first. "I suppose you're right, but what's the powder for? When Lewth showed me this place, he thought it was very important to the High Priestess."

"That I don't know," Ana admitted. "Let's keep an eye out for more clues as we go along."

Teo began to climb the stairs. "I'm going to check that door up there," he said. "It looks like it might lead to the rest of the temple. Maurice is probably being held in the main building."

At the top of the stairs, Teo put his ear to the door. He listened for a moment but heard nothing. Slowly he opened it, wincing as it squeaked on its hinges. He peeked through. No one was there.

"This way, Ana!" He beckoned with his hand. "It connects."

Ana joined Teo in a bare room. A second door made of the same sturdy oak was recessed into the opposite wall. The room's third door was much larger, obviously designed for wagon traffic. It was closed and chained with an imposing iron padlock. The only object in the room was a covered wagon to which two lanterns were affixed on poles. Teo lifted a flap of the canvas tarp on the wagon's arched framework, trying to see what was inside.

Male voices sounded from outside the room. Horses' hooves clip-clopped on the flagstone floor.

"Someone's coming!" Ana whispered.

"Quick! Back to the mill!" Teo started for the door but pulled up short. It had swung shut behind them. He tried the knob. "It's locked!"

Keys jangled in the latch on the other door. There was nowhere to run. Teo reached into his monk's habit for his sword.

"No! In here!" Ana slipped inside the covered wagon, and Teo followed, pulling down the tarp just as three men leading a pair of horses entered the room.

"You get 'em hitched," a man said. "I'll get the lanterns going. It's gonna be a long, dark ride."

Teo and Ana sat perfectly still, afraid even to breathe. The wagon was filled with many leather backpacks. A pungent smell, the same as in the mill, hung in the air.

Soon the team was hitched to the wagon, and Teo could see the glow of the lanterns through the holes in the tarp. One of the men rattled the iron chain. The large double door swung open, blowing a stale mustiness into the room. The air that came in was noticeably cooler. With a snap of the reins, the driver directed the wagon forward into a dark tunnel. The double doors squealed shut, and then the only light was from the two lanterns.

On the far side of the door, a man's muffled voice called, "I'll be here when you get back!"

"He'd better be," said one of the drivers to the other. The wagon rolled up a gradual incline into the heart of the mountain.

Ever so carefully, Ana shifted her position so she could whisper into Teo's ear. "Now what?"

Teo cupped his hand and buried his nose in Ana's soft hair. "Can't get out of the tunnel. Locked in. Guard below. Have to wait."

The wagon traveled uphill for what seemed like hours, though Teo couldn't be sure in the darkness. Twice the wagon stopped at places where windows had been carved from the tunnel to the outside world, admitting natural light and fresh air. The drivers didn't linger there, only tending the horses a bit before moving on. Time slowed. In fact, time became irrelevant. There was only the darkness, the stale air, the plodding hooves, and the upward climb. Always upward.

Finally the wagon stopped.

Teo heard one of the drivers dismount and open a door, allowing the wagon to proceed. The man locked the door behind him, then returned to the wagon and said in a jittery voice, "Let's unload this thing and get back down. I hate it up here."

"I gotta get some air, boss. Can we open the outer door for a minute and take a breather?"

"Good idea."

The two men walked with one of the lanterns down a passageway. When they opened the door at the far end, Teo felt a welcome breeze waft down the hall.

"Now's our chance," Teo said. "If they're going to unload, we need to get out."

Teo and Ana jumped from the wagon and hid behind a pile of rubble. Soon the two men returned. They opened the rear flaps of the wagon and set all the backpacks on the floor. Climbing into the drivers' seat, they urged the horses into a different passageway, which apparently circled back to the main tunnel.

"What time will Her Eminence arrive, boss?"

"She'll get here well before dawn tomorrow. If we hurry, we won't have to pass her on our way down."

"Gods! That's a scary thought," said the first man as the yellow glow of the lanterns began to recede.

"Teo!" Ana whispered urgently. "They're taking the lamps!"

"I know. We'll follow at a distance, just inside the circle of light. When we get the chance, we'll jump into the wagon. Let's go!"

Teo rose from his hiding place, trying to pick his way forward in the gloom. Ana was right behind him.

A door slammed shut ahead, and the tunnel plunged into the utter darkness of the blind. Ana cried out and threw her arms around Teo's chest, holding him fiercely from behind.

"Uh-oh," he said. "That wasn't in my plan."

✦ ✦ ✦

Rosetta's chalet, unscathed by the fire except in a few small places, sat proudly among the burned trees. The hand of Deu had shielded it from the worst flames. To achieve this purpose, Deu had used the heroic firefighting efforts of Shaphan the Metalsmith. Lina sighed dreamily. *Thank you, Deu, for Shaphan!*

He was shirtless, up a ladder on the side of the chalet, repairing a few boards that had briefly caught fire. Lina called to him, "Do you want a drink?" She held up a jar of ale. Shaphan nodded and descended. His body was sweaty which made his muscles glisten in the late evening sun. She was embarrassed to realize she noticed it, though she didn't look away.

Shaphan sat with Lina in the grass. "It's good ale," he said.

Lina stared at the house. "Deu was gracious to us. Almost everybody lost their homes, but ours was spared. Deu used you to do it."

Shaphan nodded, though his face fell. Lina noticed. "Is something wrong?" Shaphan didn't answer. "Tell me," she urged.

"It's Valent." Shaphan stared into the distance. "I think he's led us astray in our understanding of Deu."

"I know. I think so too. I've been afraid to say it." Lina stroked his hand.

Shaphan grimaced. "You know, I guess I got caught up in Valent's idea that Deu was a big secret for special people—the insiders—like we could all sit around in secrecy and be the only ones to enjoy his favor."

"Well, Deu did spare our house, but no one else's. Maybe he does favor his followers."

"Of course he does! I definitely believe his protection was on your mother's house. How many prayers did we shout to him when the flames were raging and the sparks were flying yesterday? 'Help us, Deu, help us!' We said it over and over—and he heard us! Don't you see, Lina? He blesses his followers, and that's why people need to hear about him. It saddens me to think of all the people in Vingin who didn't know to call on Deu. They were roaming around like sheep without a shepherd. Could they call on Astrebril? He's worthless! Chiveis needs the one true God. I'm going to tell Valent he's mistaken. I want to stand with Anastasia. Deu is good and merciful and strong. He should be proclaimed in the open."

"I agree with you. Let's do that."

"We will, at the right time." Shaphan fiddled with a blade of grass. "But Lina—there's something else."

"What is it?"

"I've done something horrible—a sin." He shook his head and stared at the ground. "It has to be fixed before we can move ahead."

Lina was nervous. "You can tell me." She bit her lip.

Under the blackened trees, Shaphan confessed his crime. Using a key Teo had left in his lock at the University, Shaphan had stolen the Sacred Writing and given it to Valent. Lina's mouth gaped. She couldn't believe what she had just heard. Shaphan's action was a serious betrayal of trust.

"Why would you do such a thing?" she asked.

"I took the key to keep it safe. But then, when we had lunch with Valent, he made me feel so good. He gave me his attention in a way Professor Teofil didn't. I liked it." Shaphan hung his head. "Do you hate me?"

"I love you, Shaphan."

"How can you? I'm a traitor."

Lina scooted over and put her arms around Shaphan's sweaty shoulders. "I'm with you," she declared. "No matter what. You need to confess this sin to Deu, then go make it right with Teofil."

Shaphan met Lina's eyes. "You really love me, don't you?"

"I do."

"I love you too, Lina. Thanks for sticking by me."

✦ ✦ ✦

The tunnel was dark, black as night, blacker than night. Ana couldn't see a thing.

"I'm scared, Teo. We can't navigate the tunnel in this darkness." Ana clung to him, her heart pounding.

"Hang on." Teo fumbled for something inside his monk's robe, then a Vulkain stick flared and lit the cavern, chasing away the blackness, though only for an arm's length. "Let's look in the backpacks for lanterns or something." Before the match could burn down, they dashed to the pile on the floor.

The match winked out. Teo lit another.

They quickly opened the backpacks. Most contained strange melon-sized balls, perched on little stands and wrapped in parchment. Strings protruded from each ball. Ana had no idea what they were.

Again the match went out, and all was dark.

The third match gave them time to open the remaining backpacks. *Yes!* One of them contained candles and matches instead of balls. Teo lit a candle with the fourth match, and Ana's comfort level surged as the steady flame blossomed to life.

"I'm going to check the doors. Want to come with me?" Teo stood up with the candle.

"No, I want to sit here in the pitch-black dark all alone."

Teo chuckled. "Come on then. Grab another candle, and hold on to my robe. If a gust puts the flame out, we won't be separated." He lit Ana's candle with his, and they moved cautiously to the doors through which the wagon had passed. Both were firmly locked.

A panicky sensation rose within Ana at the thought of being trapped in the dark cave. She steadied herself against Teo and found his nearness reassuring. She put her hand to her head. "I feel so queasy in here! It's like I can't get enough air to breathe!"

"We're very high, Ana. Higher in the mountains than either of us has ever been. The air gets thin up high. You just have to take things slower." Teo slipped his arm around her waist and pulled her close to himself, looking her in the eye. He traced a knuckle along her cheek. "Don't worry, okay? I'm going to get you out of this."

"I know."

Teo led Ana down the short hallway to the door the men had opened to the outside. It, too, was locked, though Ana could feel cold drafts seeping through. Faint sunlight shone through the cracks, but the hour was late. Soon even this meager light would be gone.

Teo kicked the door; it didn't budge. "I guess we'll have to wait for the High Priestess to arrive. The driver said she was coming up here. Something big is happening with those balls, but I don't know what it is."

Ana sighed. "Alright. I suggest we find a hidden place to sleep, and in the morning when she comes, we'll get past the doors and sneak down the tunnel with a couple of candles."

"Agreed. But first I want to look at those balls again. I'm curious."

"The scholar's ever-present malady."

"Or virtue." Teo grinned, and they returned to the room with the backpacks piled on the floor.

Holding his candle aloft, Teo inspected one of the spherical devices. It was rigid, yet seemed breakable. The ball nestled on top of a round stand, into which a long string ran. The whole thing was wrapped in parchment. Ana stood over him, squinting at the strange contrivance. "Break it open," she said.

He pounded it on the floor. Black powder spilled out in a little pile. "It's the powder from the mill," Teo observed.

"What is it?"

"I wish I knew. We'll find out in the morning, I suppose."

"What's that book?"

"Book?"

"There, in the front pocket." Ana pointed at it.

Teo snatched it from the backpack and examined it in the candlelight. It was a Chiveisian printing, not Ancient. *The Secret Lore of Astrebril.* He flipped the pages.

337

"It's a formula! Seventy-five percent salt stone, 15 percent charcoal, 10 percent brimstone. There are instructions for grinding and milling it. And listen to this: 'How to Ignite Astrebril's Powder.'"

"It ignites?"

"Yes, if you put a flame to it. Look at the diagram. The strings carry the fire."

"Light some of the powder. Maybe it shines like a lantern."

"Back up, and I will." Teo extended a match toward the little pile and dropped it. Bright flame shot up in a tremendous flash, filling the cavern with smoke. Ana coughed and waved her hand in front of her face.

Teo was jubilant. "Did you see that, Ana? That's the secret! Astrebril's Curse isn't fire from the sky at all! It's just a flammable powder made of three simple ingredients!"

Ana clapped her hand to her forehead, her mind racing. "If that tiny pile flares up like that, think of the explosion a couple of kegs would cause! That must have been how my house was destroyed! In fact" —she paused as full understanding dawned on her—"that explains the digging I heard under our foundation!"

"Do you realize what this means?" Teo was pacing around with his candle. "This discovery will change everything! With this knowledge, we can undercut the High Priestess's power. Once the Chiveisi find out Astrebril's dreaded curse is just a human concoction, they'll have no reason to fear her religion!"

Ana came to Teo's side, gripping his sleeve in her fist. "And then the people will be open to a new God! Teo, I can see it all coming together. Deu is answering our prayers! He's coming to Chiveis, and the people are being prepared to receive him!"

Teo smiled at her. "You did it, Ana! You believed, and you made it happen!"

"Not just me, it was both of us—and Maurice and the house community. We all took the right actions. We persevered through trials; we proved ourselves. Now we're seeing the rewards! We opened the door for Deu and let him in!"

Teo leaned toward Ana and hugged her, holding the candle away from her back. "I'm so happy for you," he said.

"Thanks for being excited about this, Teo. It means a lot to me that you're not acting aloof anymore."

He smiled and patted her on the shoulder. "Things have taken a good turn, but we're not out of this yet. We still have to spring Maurice out of here. Then we can let everyone know what the High Priestess is up to. They'll abandon her in droves once they find out! But we can't do any of that until tomorrow, so we'd better get some rest before Her Eminence shows up."

Ana nodded. "Yeah, I'm really tired. I'll find us a spot to sleep."

Teo closed the backpacks and stuffed the secret book in his own rucksack while Ana found a nook shielded by a pile of boulders. The ground was hard, but they were tired, and they quickly fell into a fitful sleep.

❖   ❖   ❖

The blond eunuch dismounted from the carriage and pranced to the locked door, turning a key and swinging it open for his queen. Her coach rolled into the little room at the top of the world.

The High Priestess stepped down and surveyed the backpacks on the floor. Lifting a flap, she examined the contents. All was as it should be.

"Open the door to Astrebril's sky!"

Two eunuchs scurried down the hall while others hoisted backpacks to their shoulders and followed close behind. The High Priestess strode down the passageway in full ceremonial regalia, wrapped in an ermine cape. It was always an august occasion when Astrebril's fires were lit.

The exterior door stood open. Dawn had not yet come to Chiveis, but the sky had lost some of its deep blackness. Far above the mountains, the morning star shone brightly. The High Priestess stepped onto the glacier in the bitter predawn cold.

14

All was quiet. The High Priestess and her entourage had exited the room, taking most of the backpacks with them. Teo rose from the hiding place behind the rocks where he and Ana had spent the night. He began to sneak down the hallway to the outside door.

"Where are you going? The tunnel's this way!" Ana gestured with her candle.

"I know, but—"

Ana tsked. "Curiosity again?" She arched her eyebrows.

"No! Well, maybe just a little bit. But it's more than that. We need to understand what the High Priestess is doing out there if we're going to defeat her." He rummaged in one of the wagons that had followed the High Priestess's carriage until his hand closed on a fleece-lined cloak left by one of the priests. "Here. Put this on. I don't want my housemaid to get goose bumps."

Ana donned the cloak and buttoned it. "Just a quick peek, and then we go, okay?"

"Of course."

They walked to the end of the passage but were unprepared for what they found when they opened the door and stepped outside. Though they had seen glaciers before, the one that stretched before them now made the glaciers of Chiveis look like ice chips in a summer drink. It was a frozen river many leagues wide, snaking off into the distant mountains of the Beyond. Great stripes of crushed rock streaked its entire length.

Ana exhaled slowly. "Unbelievable," she whispered. "It's enormous."
Teo nodded.

The sun was starting to brighten the eastern sky, though it hadn't yet broken over the jagged horizon. Teo drew the brisk air into his lungs, feeling slightly dizzy at such a high altitude. On his left, fresh tracks led up a snowy slope. Steps had been carved into it, and ropes were strung through poles as handrails. Where the slope ended, a rocky knob thrust up from the snow. Teo moved forward to get a better view. Something on top of the knob caught his eye. He looked more closely, trying to make it out in the twilight. He gasped as he realized what he was seeing.

"Ana, look!"

She swiveled her head in the direction he was pointing. Her jaw dropped, her mouth making a perfect circle. "There *is* a temple up here!"

A building sat on the knob. Though Teo couldn't believe his eyes, nonetheless there it stood—a large building topped with a silver dome. Apparently there was no limit to what the Ancients could achieve.

"Let's investigate it," he said.

"Let's get down before we're seen!"

"We'll just go up the slope a ways. It's still dim—we won't be noticed. If we see anyone, we'll clear out right away."

Ana shook her head reluctantly but followed Teo up the steps in the ice. At the top of the slope, they realized the climbing would become more difficult for anyone trying to reach the building on the knob. Rope ladders had been affixed to the rock in the steepest places.

"I guess that explains why they put everything in backpacks," Teo said.

"The High Priestess must be pretty agile to have climbed up there."

Whoomph!

A bright light flashed from the silver dome, leaving a puff of smoke in its wake. Teo and Ana looked at each other. There was no wind. The top of the world was completely still.

Then it happened.

An incredible concussion shattered the heavens, reverberating off every summit, echoing through all Chiveis. The sound seemed to physically assault Teo and Ana as they hunched on the slope beneath the rocky knob. Colored sparks trickled from the dark blue sky.

Ana held her hands over her ears. "What was that?"

"They're shooting those powder balls into the air!"

"It's so loud!"

Teo stared at the silver building. *Whoomph!* Another fire streak shot from the dome accompanied by smoke and a shrill whistle. Seconds later, another deafening explosion threw red-hot coals across the sky.

"I see what's happening!" Teo said. "The first explosion propels the ball. When it's high enough, more powder explodes. It's loud, it's spectacular, but it's just salt stone, brimstone, and charcoal! What a charade!"

Another flash. Another tremendous boom.

Ana's eyes were wide. "I can't believe they ignited that infernal powder under my house! I could have been asleep in my bed. I should have been!"

"We have Deu to thank that you weren't."

Ana caught Teo's eye, holding his gaze. She said nothing, but a faint smile seemed to play at the corners of her lips.

Teo broke the moment. "Let's get out of here. I've seen what I need to. With this evidence, we can blow Astrebril right off his evil throne." He gestured down the snow slope. "Watch your step there in your little handmaiden shoes."

Ana curtsied. "As you please, master." Teo laughed and helped Ana down the slippery steps.

Back in the tunnel, they opened one of the remaining backpacks and grabbed some extra candles and matches. "I think we should move quickly," Teo said. "We have enough of a lead to beat them to the bottom, but we'll hurry just in case."

"No arguments here."

They set out at a fast pace. The gradual slope made for an easy descent, and the candles illuminated just enough space to show Teo and Ana where they were going. Infinite blackness stretched before and behind them. Only their footfalls on the tunnel floor broke the stillness.

After a long, silent walk, Ana spoke up. "It's getting brighter ahead."

"It's the windows to the outside. Let's take a look."

The windows overlooked an expansive glacier much like the one Teo and Ana had viewed above. They returned to the main tunnel and reached the lower windows after more walking. Again they turned down the side passage to investigate. In ancient times the panes must have been filled with glass, but now they were empty. Teo took off his rucksack and dug into a pocket, handing Ana his last piece of beef jerky. She accepted it gratefully, along with some water from a flask.

When he finally approached the window and looked out, he did a double take. Unlike the barren view from the higher set of windows, the view here revealed several Chiveisian villages nestled in the valley below. A sheer drop-off plunged away beneath him. Teo craned his neck upward. The cliff soared straight into the clouds.

"Ana, can you tell where we are?"

"I don't have my bearings. I've been inside a mountain since yesterday, you know."

"That's the Troll's Valley down there. That means this cliff we're in—"

Ana surveyed the landscape. "If that's the Troll's Valley, then we—"

"We're standing inside Vulkain's north face!"

"Whoa."

"Yeah."

Ana let out a long sigh. "I'm so tired, Teo. I wish I were a bird. I'd hop off this cliff and fly away to my cozy nest and leave all these dangers behind."

Teo glanced sideways at Ana as she looked out at her beloved Chiveis. Beautiful, sweet Ana. He sensed she had just said something important, something that had spontaneously welled up as she struggled against burdens too large for her. He didn't pity her; she was far too strong for that. Yet he knew she was only human, a woman with desires and dreams and longings that may or may not come true. For some reason, it moved Teo to think of it, and he felt compelled to offer comfort. He slipped his arm around her shoulders. "I'll fly with you, little bird," he said.

"Seize the intruders!"

Ana shrieked. Teo whirled, drawing his sword awkwardly from under his monk's habit. Four eunuchs with curved short swords faced him, advancing slowly. Behind them, the commander sat on horseback, holding a bright torch. He bore a wicked grin.

Teo pulled Ana close. He understood right away: only one of them was going to escape.

"Put down your weapon!" the commander ordered.

"Come and get it!"

Teo handed his rucksack to Ana, speaking quietly to her. "Follow me when I move. Ready? One . . . two . . . three . . . Go!"

He charged to the right side of the passageway, swinging his sword in an arc and forcing the eunuchs to dodge left. The move cleared a lane into which Ana could run. Barreling directly at the mounted commander, Teo launched himself with his fists extended. The impact against the commander's body hurled him from the saddle. Knowing the four attackers were right behind him, Teo spun just in time to parry a stabbing blade. Two more joined the attack, seeking to encircle him. He forced them back into the side passageway.

"Grab the torch, Ana! Into the saddle!"

She snatched the firebrand from the ground and jumped onto the horse's back. "Come on!" she screamed.

Teo danced from one attacker to the other, staying out of their range, neither advancing nor retreating, but simply holding them at the mouth of the corridor to the window. They couldn't get past him. It was a stalemate.

"Let's go!" Ana was desperate.

Teo knew it was impossible. The men had their own horses in the main tunnel. Unless he held the attackers in place, they'd give chase, catch up, make the arrest. He would have to remain behind so Ana could get away.

"Ana, you have to do this yourself! Listen to me! Maurice hid the scrolls in a toolbox in the barn. Get them, and go hide with your parents!" Teo lunged at a eunuch who had gotten too close.

"I won't leave you!"

"I'll catch up! Run!"

"No!"

"I love you, Ana." Teo smacked the horse's rump as hard as he could with the flat of his blade.

✦　　✦　　✦

Rosetta, Lina, and Lewth sat on the edges of their seats in the chalet as Ana recounted her story. She told them everything—the discovery of the secret powder factory, the ride up the tunnel in the wagon, the sky explosions, and the attack by the High Priestess's servants.

"I galloped down the tunnel by torchlight, praying to Deu the whole way that the door would be open at the bottom!"

"Was it?" Lina could hardly stand the tension.

"No. I had to bluff my way through as a poor servant girl who had been dragged up the tunnel by a cruel monk trying to scare me. The guard got a laugh out of it, but he let me into the mill to resume my duties. I went through the outer wall and came straight here. Of course, I left the other horse up there for Teo. He's probably . . . ." She paused. "He must be, um, you know . . . ."

The little group fell silent and wouldn't meet her eyes. Ana told herself to be brave, but dread gripped her soul. She rose from her chair and went to the window, her hand upon the glass. *Come to me, Teo! Come to me like you said you always will!*

Through the forest, a horse approached the chalet. Ana sucked in her breath as a joyous surge of relief swept over her. The rider emerged from the charred trees. *No.* It was Shaphan, returning from the barn with the satchel of scrolls Ana had sent him to fetch. Her face fell as the weight of anxiety settled onto her shoulders again. In her heart she knew: if Teo was free, he would have arrived by now.

Shaphan entered the chalet. "I found them." He held up the satchel.

Ana collapsed onto a chair, tears rimming her eyes. "Read me something, Shaphan. I need Deu's words now more than I ever have."

"Yes," Lewth agreed. "Read us something, quickly! Our sister is in pain. We're all afraid."

Shaphan dug into the bag. "How about the twenty-third hymn? It seems fitting: 'When I walk in the valley of death's shadow, I won't fear any evil, because you are with me.'"

Lewth nodded. "A good choice."

Shaphan began to read the hymn in a steady voice. As he did, Ana felt a sense of peace return. Though she was still afraid, the holy words of the Sacred Writing reminded her that Deu was on her side. When Shaphan read the final words, "I will live in the Eternal One's house until the end of my days," Ana closed her eyes. *Oh, Deu! Will it turn out like that for me? Will there be a happy ending to all this?* She prayed there would be.

Setting aside the scroll, Shaphan lifted his hands toward the ceiling. "Let's unite our hearts as one," he said. Everyone held out their palms and looked upward. Shaphan prayed fervently for Deu to protect Maurice and Teo from evil, then interceded for each member of the house community by name.

"Thank you, Shaphan," Ana said when he was finished. "You've helped us remember that everything is in Deu's hands." She handed him Teo's rucksack. "Would you keep this for me? It contains some important books Teofil wants. Guard it well, and give it to him when"—she gathered her strength—"when you see him again."

"I'll do it, Anastasia." He took the rucksack from her and gave her a reassuring squeeze on the shoulder. Then, looking to the group, he said, "Much has happened in the past few days. Let's take a moment to celebrate how Deu has been faithful to us amid all our recent trials."

The remaining members of the house community took turns sharing their stories. Rosetta told of the great fire, with Lina adding the details of Shaphan's efforts to save the chalet. Lewth described his preparations for his new role as Prince Piair's tutor, which he would begin in a few days. He also reported that Valent and Sucula were on the official presumed-dead list at Vingin, since they hadn't been seen and their chalet had been consumed by the fire. A sadness descended on the group at the news. Ana considered speaking up to clarify the matter but decided against it. She realized some things, even if true, didn't need to be repeated. When it was her turn to report, she briefly recapped her trip to the temple and the discovery of Astrebril's secret fire. Rather than bringing relief and confidence to the group, the story seemed to frighten everyone.

"Child, I think it's time you found refuge someplace else," Rosetta said. "The High Priestess might come after you! I'm going to pack you some food. Shaphan can get you to the hiding place where your parents are." The rest of the community stared at Ana and nodded in agreement.

Ana straightened in her chair. With sudden clarity, she realized she was at one of those junctures in life where her choices would have profound consequences. Resolve steeled her heart. "Listen, everyone. I've been trying to deny it, but it's time for me to admit that Teo has been arrested. Otherwise he would be here. If Teo and Maurice are in the High Priestess's hands, I am *not* going to run away and leave them. I refuse to hide anymore. It's time somebody stood up to that witch."

"Don't be foolish, child!"

"Ana, what are you saying?" Lina's tone was urgent. "You can't take on the High Priestess!"

"Perhaps not directly. But we can't let her do whatever she wants! Chiveis is a civilized land. On what legal grounds is she detaining Teo and Maurice? I'm a citizen of the realm. I have recourse to the law courts. I could . . . I could lodge a protest with the magistrates!" The idea had just popped into her head, but as she thought about it, it made a lot of sense.

Shaphan didn't think so. "The magistrates are afraid of the High Priestess," he warned. "They do her will."

"Even so, there's no actual law against adopting alternative religions. Maybe I can sway the crowd at the courts. It might put pressure on the magistrates to do the right thing."

Lewth's expression was grave. "The real power in this kingdom lies with the religious authorities, not the people or the courts. Your course of action is too risky, Anastasia."

Ana didn't reply. Instead she bent to the satchel of Shaphan's scrolls and found the one she wanted. Untying its red string, she unrolled it and read, "The Eternal One is my light and my salvation. Whom shall I fear? The Eternal One is the support of my life. Whom shall I dread?" She lowered the scroll and gazed at the faces surrounding her.

"Ana, please don't do this!" Lina looked terrified. Rosetta began to cry.

I am your light and your salvation. Do not be afraid. The voice that spoke to Ana wasn't audible, yet it was real. It flooded her with assurance and conviction. It was time she took a bold stand. How could she doubt it? Deu was her salvation. He would spread his wing over her.

"I've made up my mind," she said firmly. "I'm going to the Citadel."

Lina and Rosetta were distraught, and Lewth covered his forehead with his hand. Shaphan signaled for attention. "Since Deu has called our sister to do this," he said, "let's pray for her."

✦　✦　✦

The chains on Teo's wrists pinched his flesh unmercifully. He glanced around for something he could use to pick the lock. Nothing. He tried pulling the chains out of the wall, but they were fixed tight. *What good would it do anyway?* The only window in the cell was too high to reach.

Had Ana escaped? Teo had heard nothing to indicate she'd been arrested. He desperately hoped she wasn't chained up in the dungeon somewhere, alone and afraid.

It was hard to tell how many hours had elapsed since his capture. After Ana galloped away in the secret tunnel, more eunuchs arrived, surrounding Teo until they wrestled him to the ground. They took his sword, his knife, his belt, even his leather jerkin and linen shirt. The air in the cell was cold on his exposed skin.

Out in the hall, Teo heard footsteps approach. A key rattled in the lock. The door creaked open, and the High Priestess entered the cell. Teo stared at her. White face. Pitch-black hair. Painted lips and eyes. Voluptuous body. And always, that commanding presence, her mysterious aura of power.

Don't let her fool you, Teo.

"I've done nothing wrong. Release me." Teo's tone was matter-of-fact.

The High Priestess stood a few paces away, sizing him up with her hands clasped behind her back. She smiled. *Why is she smiling like that?*

"Such a handsome man," she remarked. "The Kingdom of Chiveis needs men like you, Captain Teofil, men the people can look up to." She slid closer to him, and Teo caught the aroma of black powder. "The people need heroes to admire, men who will demonstrate our cherished virtues.

Obedience. Patriotism. Loyalty. *Piety*." As she uttered the last word, her eyes narrowed.

"I am loyal to the realm."

"Are you, Captain?" The High Priestess stared into his face. "Then what is *this*?" Her tone became savage as she whipped her hands from behind her back. Teo heard the metallic sound of a blade being drawn from its sheath. The High Priestess laid the tip of Teo's sword against his chest. Slowly she increased the pressure, twisting as she pressed. He remained still.

"The sword of Armand. A famous blade! The king shouldn't have given it to you. Such a mighty weapon in the hands of one so—*rebellious*."

Teo clenched his jaw as he felt the sword's tip flick across his chest. Warm blood trickled down his belly.

"You think you're so clever, don't you, Captain Teofil? Perhaps you think you can use this sword to destroy me, hmm?" She held up the blade, its tip glistening red in the shaft of light from the window.

"The only thing I intend to destroy is the power of evil."

Scowling, the High Priestess went to the door of the cell and spoke to the men outside. She turned back to Teo, her eyes aflame with malice. "I think you need a lesson in the true power of evil."

A Vulkainian guard heaved a shirtless old man onto the floor. In the silence, the man groaned as he rolled over. It was Maurice, bloody and bruised.

He was dying.

"The stubborn fool wouldn't agree to deny Deu in front of the people. Consider whether you wish to end up like him." The High Priestess exited the cell and slammed the door shut behind her.

"Master Maurice!" Teo struggled against the chains that pinned him to the wall. "It's Teo! I'm here with you!"

"Teo . . . my son." His voice was weak.

"Deu, help him!" Teo was in anguish, but there was nothing he could do.

"My breath . . . is failing. I'm going to Deu."

"Don't say that! Crawl to me so I can reach you!"

"Teo . . . listen!" Maurice spoke with such gravity that Teo knew it was time to hear his master's words. Maurice panted for several moments, his breath coming in ragged gasps. "Deu will come . . . to Chiveis. I was the breeze . . . before the storm. It's enough. I'm . . . at peace."

Teo wanted to rush to Maurice's side, to comfort him, to heal him, to make things right again. He strained forward, but the unyielding chains held him back. "Deu, you can't let this happen, not like this!" Teo clenched his fists and thrashed in his bonds, desperate to stop what was happening before his eyes. "No!" he cried. "You can't take him from me!"

Maurice's eyes opened, and he lifted his head. Teo met his gaze in the dim cell. They communed with their eyes, master and disciple sharing their final moments together.

"Understand, Teo!" Maurice's voice grew strong. "I gladly lay down my life to stand for Deu! It isn't for us to fight against his will. His ways are good. He can be trusted. Always yield to his plan. When he calls you down a path, *walk it.*"

Maurice laid his head on the stone floor. His respiration was erratic now.

Deu! No!

"I love you . . . Teo . . . my son." Maurice exhaled a long, steady breath, and then his broken body lay still.

❖   ❖   ❖

The courthouse at the Citadel bustled with lawyers, merchants, bureaucrats, and magistrates, all conducting the necessary business of the realm. Ana felt conspicuously small in the presence of such important officials. She had arrived the previous afternoon and requested an appointment. The clerk gave her a time the following day, and she spent the night at a nearby inn. Now she waited for her opportunity to speak.

Sitting in a quiet anteroom, Ana took a moment to collect her thoughts. A quiet confidence had calmed her nervousness. Her peace was more than she could understand. It seemed to guard her heart from fear.

Ana's mind went to Teo. Where was he now? She could only assume he was alive and imprisoned; the alternative was too much to contemplate. And what of poor Maurice? Was he suffering? Or did he have Deu's comforting presence? Ana reminded herself to be strong for the sake of these two noble men.

Outside the window of the anteroom, the citizens of the realm passed back and forth. Ana noticed one lawyer in particular, a younger man obviously just starting his career at the bar. He greeted his pretty wife and scooped up their laughing toddler in his arms. The wife carried a lunch basket, and she kissed her husband with a warm smile as the threesome headed outside.

A shadow darkened Ana's thoughts. *Why?* she asked herself. *Why must I walk this road?* The mental stress of what she was about to do in the courtroom became too much for her, and she fled from it into the comfort of fantasy. She imagined a rose-covered cottage. It was near Edgeton, though not too close. The kitchen was an inviting place, and Ana was making dinner. Delicious aromas permeated the room. Footsteps sounded on the porch, and then a man filled the doorframe. He was tall, dark-haired, wide in the shoulders, narrow at the waist. Glad to see her, he showed it with a passionate kiss. After the meal, there was a quiet evening in the candlelight. Down pillows . . . a thick duvet . . . warm bodies . . . romance . . .

Why not that road? That I could handle! You ask so much of me, Deu! Too much!

The clerk poked his head in the door. "The magistrates are ready for you, miss."

Ana rose from the bench in the anteroom and took a deep breath, her heart pounding. Holy words came to her mind—from where, she didn't know, but she let them come and whispered them aloud to Deu: "I am your servant; let it be done to me according to your will."

The courtroom was a spacious stone hall lit by skylights. Five elderly magistrates in black robes and white wigs sat behind an imposing wooden table. On the floor, the citizenry vied for the best seats. Law was entertainment in Chiveis. Everyone loved a good courtroom drama.

Ana was introduced by the clerk, and she stepped to the podium in front of the magistrates. She wore a light blue gown borrowed from Lina, and her hair was done up around her head in a fashionable style. Makeup and polished-stone jewelry completed her attire. It was an important occasion requiring a dignified appearance. Strangely, her heart wasn't racing anymore.

The crowd was unsettled, but Ana waited until they grew silent. The chief magistrate, who sat in the center of the five and held a gavel, regarded her with a penetrating stare. "What is your business with us, Anastasia of Edgeton?"

Ana's voice rang out in the packed courtroom. "Esteemed magistrates of the realm, and good people of Chiveis, I am here to protest the illegal actions of the High Priestess!"

The crowd burst into an uproar. "*Order! Order!*" The judge pounded his gavel on the table until the crowd quieted.

"Those are incautious and inflammatory words, young lady," said a magistrate on the end of the row. "By what actions has our esteemed High Priestess violated the law?"

"She has illegally detained two of my friends—Maurice the Wise, a senior professor at the University, and Captain Teofil, tournament champion and soldier of the Fifth Regiment!"

Again the crowd broke into a buzz, but the tone was different this time. The people were intrigued by Ana's accusation.

The chief magistrate looked skeptical. "What was the basis of the arrests?"

Now the time had come. It was the moment Ana had been waiting for. "Your Honors, my friends were arrested because they understand that the gods of Chiveis are wicked and false—"

Tumult. The crowd didn't like it at all. "Shame! Shame!" someone cried. Others booed and hissed. Their hostility was palpable.

"—wicked and false," Ana repeated. "There is only one God—" Somebody threw an apple at Ana, forcing her to duck. "One God, named Deu, who is coming to Chiveis this day—" Her words faltered, drowned by the commotion.

"Blasphemy!" The word hung in the air like a poisonous fog. Though the shouted accusation was anonymous, it represented the general opinion. Others joined the chant: "Blasphemy! Blasphemy! Blasphemy!" Feet began to stomp the floor, making the whole building shake.

"*Order! Order in my courtroom!*" The chief magistrate pounded his gavel, but that only added to the din.

Ana wasn't sure what to do next. *Deu, I will follow you, come what may!*

The magistrate looked to his left and snapped his fingers. "Bailiff! Take this woman into custody!"

✦　　✦　　✦

Four heavyset Vulkainian militiamen entered Teo's cell, waking him from a doze in the afternoon sun. He had barely slept during the night on the cold floor, unable to stretch out because of his chains and tormented by grief at the loss of his master. Around noon, he had received some stale bread and a jar of brackish water. Maurice's body was then removed, and at last Teo had fallen into a fitful sleep.

Two of the Vulkainians held drawn swords. The third reached out and clenched Teo's throat in his fist, while the fourth unfastened his chains from the wall. Teo briefly considered making a move, but with no weapon and with his throat in the grip of a muscular man, he knew it would be futile to try. They bound his hands behind his back and led him from the cell.

The High Priestess awaited him in a windowless room with a high ceiling. A rope dangled from a pulley, and torches lined the walls. To one side of the room, a red-haired priestess stood watching. Teo looked at her more closely in the flickering light. It was the Flame of Chiveis.

"We've come a long way, Habiloho."

She nodded. "And now it has come to this."

"Is it what you hoped for?"

Habiloho fingered the collar at her neck but didn't answer.

Teo was shoved forward by the guards. The High Priestess approached him, her gauzy gown swishing as she walked. She wasn't arrayed in her formal regalia, and without it, she seemed more normal. More earthly. Like a real human being. She came very close. Teo could feel her breath on his cheek. The fabric of her garment touched the bare skin of his chest, and it wasn't an unpleasant sensation.

"I'm giving you one last chance," she whispered into his ear, "because

I like you, Teofil. You're an incredible warrior. We could be quite a team, you and I. If you're willing to cooperate, I'm willing to show you my . . . *favor*."

Teo was taken aback by the woman's unexpected nearness. His heartbeat quickened. *Why?* It wasn't fear, he decided. Was it lust? *Yes, a little.* The High Priestess exuded a beguiling sensuality as she swayed against him. Teo reminded himself this was the person who had murdered Maurice. His twinge of desire flashed into anger.

"Favor? You should've shown your favor to the wisest man in the realm! What will happen to his body? He deserves an honorable burial."

The High Priestess licked her lips. "Well, Captain, I think everything depends on you now. Your choices in the next few minutes will determine many things. A proper burial is still possible for the professor. And that isn't all—I offer you much more. Freedom. My recommendation to the Royal Guard. Promotion. Who knows—I might even summon you to my personal chambers. To advise me, hmm?" The High Priestess smiled slyly. "You can have a good life, Captain, as long as you remain in my favor."

"And what is the price of your favor?"

"It's simple. You've gotten yourself entangled in an extinct superstition. I can understand that. A heroic man like you would obviously seek dangerous and radical ideas. Insurrection is exhilarating, I know. But you see, Captain, it isn't good for the people. I need you to set a better example."

"Meaning?"

The High Priestess took a step back, her nostrils flaring. "You will publicly recant your superstition, curse the name of Deu, and never speak of him again!"

Teo's pulse quickened. Time slowed, and his mind staggered at the significance of the moment facing him. A million scenarios flashed through his brain at once—some filled with honor, prestige, and acclaim, others with pain and suffering. Yet one overpowering fact cut through the cluttered images: he belonged to Deu.

Yes. To Deu.

He, Teofil, belonged to Deu.

Like Maurice, like Ana, he, too, was a follower of Deu, the forgiving All-Creator. Teo gathered his courage.

"Never. I will never forsake Deu. How could I blaspheme the one who saved me?"

The High Priestess's face turned darker than a demon's. She spat on Teo, and he felt the saliva dribble down his cheek. "You will regret that decision, Captain Teofil." She snapped her fingers. "Guards!"

The Vulkainians grabbed Teo by the shoulders, forcing him toward the rope that dangled in the middle of the room. They bound his wrists, still fastened behind his back, to the rope.

Strength, Teo. Don't give in.

Teo tried to steel himself for the approaching pain, but when it came, it was beyond anything he could have imagined.

The rope went taut. Teo's arms were wrenched up behind him. His feet lifted from the floor, and he hung in the air. The agony was overwhelming. His shoulders were contorted in a monstrous way, their sockets threatening to burst. He groaned through clenched teeth. Excruciating pain ravaged his body. He could scarcely breathe.

"Where's your Deu now?" the High Priestess sneered.

Teo's head swam. *Make it stop! The pain! Make it stop!*

"Drop him!"

Through the haze of torture, Teo felt relief at the prospect of being let down. He longed to take the pressure off his inverted arms.

He dropped. But instead of touching the ground, the Vulkainian stopped him short with a jerk of the rope. The sudden wrenching of Teo's arms took the pain to new heights. He cried out.

The High Priestess signaled with her fingers, and two Vulkainians came forward. One was carrying a heavy stone ball. The other man fastened it to Teo's ankles, and then he was hauled up again. The additional weight was more than he could bear. He panted, sweat pouring from his face and running down his body in streams. The room grew dim. Lights flashed in his brain. His arms were on fire.

A messenger arrived and spoke to the High Priestess. She nodded. "Let the captain think on his sins for a while," she commanded as she exited the room. The guards followed her.

Teo dangled from the rope, alone. His head hung low. "Deu . . . help me." His whisper was barely audible.

"You still call on Deu?"

Teo was confused. *Who? What? Who said—*

"It's Habiloho."

He could see her feet as he swayed. "My friend," he gasped. "I'm sorry."

"Sorry?"

"For what . . . you've become." Each word took great effort to utter.

"What have I become?"

"Slave. A slave."

Her voice was tremulous. "Do you hate me, Teofil?"

"Forgive. I forgive you." He moaned at the unrelenting agony.

"Well, I can't forgive myself! There's no way back for me!"

"Deu. He forgives. Always."

"Impossible!"

"Come . . . to him . . . Habiloho."

A bead of sweat rolled down Teo's nose and dropped to the floor. Then he saw another droplet fall—though not from him—to the stones between Habiloho's feet. Without a word, the princess ran from the room, leaving Teo in his torment.

❖   ❖   ❖

A eunuch knocked on the door of the study, but the visitor he ushered in wasn't the person the High Priestess had been expecting. Instead of the girl from Edgeton, recently arrested for seditious statements at the court-house, it was Princess Habiloho.

The High Priestess rose from her desk and welcomed her disciple with a kiss. "How does it feel?" she asked.

Habiloho's expression was uncertain.

"How does it feel to taste revenge?"

"Oh! It's—it's very satisfying."

"Relish it. It's one of life's greatest pleasures." The High Priestess turned toward her desk. "So what brings you to my rooms?"

"Uh, the captain, actually. Our prisoner."

The High Priestess scowled. "He will deny the Enemy before this is finished."

"That's what I've come to talk to you about. I've had some thoughts about how we might achieve our purposes."

The High Priestess poured herself a goblet of wine. "Go on."

"I'm not sure we can break the captain through torture. He's incredibly strong. Even if we were to succeed, what would we have accomplished? He's in our grasp now—no danger to us anymore. But what about the rest of Chiveis? The seeds of heresy are flying on the wind as we speak."

The High Priestess drained her goblet and hurled it into the fireplace. Shards of broken glass ricocheted onto the floor. "The people of Chiveis will never embrace Christianism! I swear it by Astrebril!"

The room fell silent. Rage simmered in the High Priestess's soul.

Habiloho finally broke the silence. "I know Captain Teofil very well. He's stubborn. Pain won't work on him."

"It works on everyone eventually."

"Even so, what of the people? Christianism may already be spreading among them like wildfire."

The High Priestess stalked toward Habiloho. Though the princess flinched, she held her ground. *Impressive*, the High Priestess thought. *I've seen generals wilt under less intimidation.* Staring into Habiloho's eyes, she asked, "Do you have a better idea? Or can you only offer criticism?"

Habiloho straightened her shoulders. "What we need is a way to discredit the captain in front of the people. We have to show them Christianism is false, weak, a religion unworthy of a great kingdom like Chiveis."

The High Priestess tilted her head and rested her hands on her hips as she considered Habiloho's words. "Now you're speaking like a servant of Astrebril. What do you suggest?"

"First, we should end Teofil's torment. We need him at his strongest for what I have in mind."

"It can be done. Not yet though. What else?"

"As you commanded me, I've been reading the book of the Enemy. I came across something that might work for us. We could use the Enemy's own methods against him, and so prove the superior power of Astrebril once and for all."

The High Priestess walked to her desk and removed a leather-bound book from a drawer. She laid it on the desktop. "Show me."

Habiloho approached the desk and turned the pages with her lovely fingers. Her hair shimmered red and gold in the sunlight as she searched for the text. *No wonder the people desire this pretty little thing*, the High Priestess mused. *That desire could prove useful.*

"Here it is." Habiloho pushed the book across the desk. "The First Book of Kings, eighteenth chapter. It's a confrontation between the prophets of the god Baal and the Enemy's prophet, Élie. A great duel was proposed. Two bulls would be sacrificed, and the one on which heavenly flames fell would be the victor. In the story, the Enemy won. But what if he were to face Astrebril himself? We know *his* power is greatest of all! Surely the Beautiful One would win the duel, and then all the people would reject the heresy of Christianism forever."

The High Priestess turned the idea over in her mind, toying with her iron collar. "It's true our problem isn't the captain himself—it's the spread of his ideas. Maurice the Wise has been eliminated, but he was never popular among the people like Captain Teofil. The last thing we want is to make a tournament champion a martyr. But if we could turn the people against the captain . . . shame him publicly . . . reveal the totems of his religion as impotent . . ."

"It wouldn't be difficult at all! We're servants of Astrebril! We know he's the strongest god. Once the people see that, they'll never want to follow the Enemy."

A messenger knocked and entered the room. "The prisoner from the courthouse has arrived," he announced.

"Bring her to me." The High Priestess turned toward Habiloho, smiling benignly. "You've done well today, faithful servant. Your mind is full of holy ideas. Go now with my blessing."

Habiloho turned to leave, then paused and looked back. "What will happen to Teof—I mean, our prisoner? Will he be returned to his cell right away?"

"Soon. Why do you ask?"

"Oh . . . uh, no reason. I thought I might, you know, relish my revenge. Gloat over him in his cell."

"Of course. Revenge is sweet. You may go."

Habiloho bowed and left the room. The High Priestess watched her leave. *The girl is wavering,* she thought. *Something will have to be done about that.*

❖   ❖   ❖

Ana was afraid. She was at the temple of the High Priestess again, this time as a prisoner. *How will it all play out?* She had no idea.

A blond priest walked ahead of her in a loose shift and sandals. Another eunuch followed behind. They came to a door. Before they could knock, it swung open, and the High Priestess stood there.

"Leave us." The men fled. "Come in, little one."

Ana entered the High Priestess's study. A desk sat in the middle of the room, illuminated by a beam of afternoon sunlight. A book lay open on the desk. Ana turned to face the High Priestess. "Where are Maurice and Teofil?"

"I will do the talking here, Anastasia of Edgeton." The High Priestess circled around Ana, watching her from the corners of her eyes. "The last time we were together, you rudely refused my hospitality. When the outsiders grabbed you, I assumed you were lost forever."

"Teofil came for me."

"Your hero, hmm? Well, the captain certainly is strong." She looked at Ana, an eyebrow raised. "Would you like to see him?"

Ana's heart jumped, and she knew her face lit up more than she intended. "Of course I want to see him," she said.

The High Priestess snickered, then scooped up the book from the desk and beckoned Ana toward a door at the rear of the study. It led down a narrow spiral staircase to another door. The High Priestess eased it open. Torches glowed in the dim room. "There's your hero."

No! Teo! No!

Ana ran to him. He hung from the ceiling, his arms cruelly wrenched behind his back. A heavy stone weight around his ankles strained his bulging shoulders. His body glistened with the sweat of his torment. Pain twisted his face into a grimace she scarcely recognized.

"Teo, it's me! I'm here!"

His only response was an incoherent sound.

Ana whirled on the High Priestess. "Let him down, you monster!" Ana charged at her, but a Vulkainian stepped from the shadows and intervened. Ana thrashed in his arms. "Let me go! Let him down now!" Teo's suffering was more than she could bear.

The High Priestess released a winch on the wall. Teo fell in a heap, the stone weight cracking loudly against the dungeon floor. Ana tore herself from the Vulkainian's grasp and went to Teo's side.

"I'm here with you, Teo!" His arms hung limp, as if disconnected from his body. His shoulder muscles were in spasm. He groaned. Ana stroked his sweaty forehead. "Can you hear me? It's Ana!"

He opened his eyes to a squint. Awareness of his surroundings seemed to return. "Ana?" he whispered.

"Yes, I'm here!"

He struggled to gain an upright position, but without the use of his arms, he couldn't manage it. "Have they hurt you, Ana?"

"No, I'm fine! Never mind me! Oh, it's so horrible!" Tears spilled down her cheeks at the immensity of the agony Teo had endured. *And yet he asks about me* . . .

"Very touching. Now get up!" The High Priestess's tone was scornful. The Vulkainian hauled Ana to her feet. "We have business to conduct."

"I don't do business with the enemies of Deu," Teo said from the floor.

"Deu is nothing, the impotent god of a dead religion. But if you think otherwise, I'm offering you the chance to prove it. Your choices are simple: comply with my offer or face public execution. I can charge you both with sedition, and not one of the magistrates will cross me. You would be wise to accept my proposal."

"What's your proposal?" Ana demanded.

The High Priestess held up the leather-bound book. "Professor Maurice believed a new book had come to Chiveis. What he didn't know is, the book isn't so new. I've had it for years—this so-called Sacred Writing of yours."

Ana inhaled sharply. *The Sacred Writing of Deu—a complete version, translated into Chiveisian speech!*

"My offer is this: the eighteenth chapter of the First Book of Kings describes a confrontation between your god and another. Two bulls were sacrificed, but fire from heaven fell on only one, and in this way Deu's prophet Élie defeated the prophets of Baal. An unlikely little fable, but one with an interesting premise! I propose a similar duel in which we each sacrifice to our gods. You both must remain in prison here until the summer solstice. On that day, all of Chiveis will be summoned to the coliseum. Two great altars will be erected. You may have all your tokens of power, and I will use mine. Each of us will call on our gods as we see fit. The one whose sacrifice catches fire will be the winner. But I warn you, Astrebril is the supreme god. His power is far greater than some tribal deity of the Ancients."

With great effort, Teo struggled to a sitting position. Ana helped him gain his feet. He was shaking, but he stood tall. "Deu is the Creator of everything," he said. "We don't fear you, nor your god."

The High Priestess's lips curled into a haughty sneer. "Perhaps you should." She snapped her fingers at the Vulkainians. "Take them to the cell," she ordered, then faced Teo and Ana. "You may take some time to discuss my proposal. I will come soon for your answer."

The High Priestess handed the Sacred Writing to a eunuch, instructing him to read the marked portion. The stone weight was cut away from Teo's ankle. Four Vulkainians led Teo and Ana to a bare cell with a high window and chains hanging from the wall. The eunuch read the story of Élie and the prophets of Baal aloud, then everyone left the room.

Ana retrieved an earthenware jar from a corner and knelt beside Teo as he sat on the floor, his hands resting loosely in his lap. She put the jar to his lips, and he accepted it gratefully. After taking a long drink, he closed his eyes and leaned his head against the wall.

"Ana, I have some sad news. Maurice has been taken into the arms of Deu. The High Priestess had him beaten to death. He died here in this cell with me."

"Oh! Oh!" Ana covered her face with her hands, overcome by the terrible swirl of events. "Not Maurice! Oh! It's too much." She wept softly.

"Don't despair. There was a death, but also a birth. The firmness of Maurice's resolve . . . his absolute trust in Deu . . . his final admonitions to me . . ." Teo broke off. Ana looked at him as she knelt at his side. The expression on his face was different than any she had ever seen. His whole demeanor had changed, and even the darkness in the cell couldn't hide it. "What is it?" she asked.

"I'm on Deu's path now. I always will be."

The revelation made Ana smile. "I knew you'd come to believe."

"I couldn't have without your example."

Ana turned around and sat next to Teo against the wall. She caressed his hand. He intertwined his fingers with hers. They sat like that for a while, exchanging no words, since words would have been less eloquent than the intimacy they shared in silence.

At last Ana sensed their time beginning to wane, so she addressed the matter at hand. "What should we do about the High Priestess? Should we accept her offer?"

"Definitely. We've been praying for Deu to come to Chiveis. Now we're going to see it happen in the most dramatic way possible."

"That's what I was thinking, too. These events are a perfect answer to our prayers! Soon everyone will know who has true power in the world."

"The imprisonment between now and the solstice won't be easy," Teo warned. "It's five weeks away."

"I can do it with Deu's help. Perhaps they'll let me stay in this cell with you."

Teo chuckled and shook his head. "I've never met a woman like you, Ana." He squeezed her hand in his. "But I'm glad I did."

Approaching footsteps sounded outside the cell. When the High Priestess opened the door, Teo and Ana stood side by side. She stared at them with her arms folded across her chest, two Vulkainians flanking her. "Well? Have you made your decision? Do you agree to my proposal?"

"We agree," Ana said.

"On one condition," Teo added. Ana looked sharply at him.

"You're in no position to bargain, Captain."

"On the contrary, you're in no position to refuse. You proposed the duel. Unless the condition is met, I won't participate."

363

The High Priestess eyed him warily. "What do you want?"

"Anastasia will not remain here. I alone will stay as surety for both of us."

"Teo, no! I want to stand with you!"

The High Priestess shook her head and laughed. "I accept your condition, Captain Teofil. The deal is done. But be warned, my spies will be watching her. If she so much as breathes a word about Deu to anyone, the deal is off, and I'll string you up for good this time." She motioned toward the Vulkainians on her way out the door. "Guards, escort the girl to the gatehouse."

Ana turned to Teo, holding his face in her hands. "Why?"

"It's better this way. Trust me. The dungeon is no place for you."

Ana didn't know what to say. She only knew she didn't want to leave Teo behind.

"Let's go, woman!" one of the Vulkainians barked.

"Take this," Ana whispered urgently. Without letting the guards see her, she slipped a slender scroll tied with a red ribbon from her bosom. "I hid it near my heart for courage. You need it more than I do now! I'll drop it on the ground behind you."

The guards were impatient. "Get the wench and let's go!"

Ana threw her arms around Teo's body. She dropped the scroll just as a Vulkainian grabbed her elbow and hauled her toward the door.

Teo stood in the middle of the cell, his head held high, like a statue carved from a piece of granite. "Be strong, Ana! Five weeks! I'll see you in the coliseum in five weeks!"

"I love you, Teo!"

The door slammed shut.

The Eternal One is my light and my salvation. Whom shall I fear? Ana knew Teo would need all the words of Deu's twenty-seventh hymn in his lonely cell at the Temple of Astrebril.

CHAPTER

15

Stratetix sat in a flower-strewn meadow, looking north toward the Maiden's Valley. He imagined the journey through the Citadel's wall at the valley's mouth, then into Entrelac. There he could pick up a boat to cross the Tooner Sea, then follow the Farm River down to Edgeton. *Home!* He missed it badly. He missed his chalet at the center of town; he missed the fields whose dark soil he knew so well; he missed the public house where he would gather with his friends for an ale. Most of all, he missed his daughter. Stratetix's enforced solitude at Obirhorn Lake was about to drive him crazy.

Helena came to him from the cabin, carrying a small basket. She was the one bright spot in all their weeks of exile.

"Let me guess—cheese and dried beef?" Stratetix's tone was more sarcastic than he intended.

Helena smiled as she sat down next to her husband. "Cheese and dried *mutton*. I like to change things around." She held up a bottle. "And for even more variety, this water is from the southern side of the lake!"

Stratetix glanced at Helena's face. He wanted to continue in his self-pity, but she was looking at him with such a sparkle in her eye that he was forced to laugh. Her sweet spirit broke through his bitterness, and he rolled her flat on her back in the grass, resting above her on his forearm. "You're a good woman," he said. "Much more than I deserve."

"Every man should feel that way about his wife." She kissed him as if to make sure he always would.

Under the warm sun, the married couple shared a lunch of cheese, dried mutton, and south-shore water from Obirhorn Lake. No summer Stratetix could remember had ever started this way. No planning, no plowing, no planting—just he and his wife with nothing to do but talk to each other. In that regard, it had been nice. But he was growing restless.

"I miss Ana," he said.

"Me too." Helena reclined in the meadow, watching the puffy clouds float by. White mountain-star flowers surrounded her head like a halo. "She's in good hands, though. My sister will take care of her."

"I wish Lewth would come with another report. He said everyone's talking about the big duel. All of Chiveis is buzzing about it. I'd like to hear the latest news."

"What is it now—a week away?"

"Eight days! Eight days until everything changes. Then we won't be outcasts anymore."

"I wish I could be there to see it." Helena smiled at the thought. "I'd like to be able to tell my grandchildren I was there when the realm bent the knee to Deu. The people are going to be surprised when they see his power!"

Stratetix gazed at Helena, so confident and serene as she lay there under the sun, her blonde hair splashed out in the grass. A spirit of fear descended on him. "What if Deu doesn't win? What if he really is weaker than Astrebril?"

Helena sat up on one elbow. "Are you having doubts, my love?"

"Maybe. It's just that so much is riding on this duel! Can we really believe the Sacred Writing is true? Can we expect Deu to be victorious over so strong a god as Astrebril?"

"Of course! Don't you see how he's brought all these events together? First he brought us the book through Captain Teofil and Ana. Then he formed a community of his followers. And then he used Maurice's testimony at Vingin to prepare the way—"

"At the cost of his life."

"Yes, I know. It was a high cost indeed." Helena sighed as a mournful expression darkened her face, but she gathered herself and continued, "When you look at the big picture, you can see how it all fits into a greater plan. That's what we have to keep our eyes on, Stratetix, the greater plan. Deu will come to Chiveis in glory as he proves his awesome might. And he's going to use our daughter to do it."

Stratetix nodded. "Ana has the strongest faith of us all."

"And the most courage."

"I wish Lewth would come back and tell me how she's doing. I miss my Little Sweet so much!"

"Lewth is busy with his new duties at the palace. He'll come when he can. Until then, there's nothing we can do."

"Yes, there is."

Helena met her husband's eyes, waiting for him to speak.

"We can pray." And there on the grass, they did.

❖ ❖ ❖

"Your Highness? Are you listening to me?"

"Huh? Oh, yes. Of course."

Lewth smiled at his student. "What did I just say?"

"Uh, you were talking about the history of Chiveis. Jonluc Beaumont gave our kingdom its original name."

"And that name was?"

Prince Piair II tapped his chin. He stared out the window. Finally he grinned. "You know what? A fly happened to buzz by my ear just as you said it. So I missed what you said. Could you repeat it?"

Lewth narrowed his eyes. "Hmm. That's funny, I didn't see any fly."

"He was really small." Piair fluttered his fingers past his ear. "Just buzzed right by."

Lewth knew they were both playing a game. It was the kind of game one had to play as the teacher of a teenaged crown prince. He shot Piair a displeased frown. "La Nouvelle Suisse."

"La Nouvelle Suisse!" Piair raised his forefinger in triumph. "I thought that's what you said!"

"That was the name Beaumont gave our kingdom, though it didn't catch on among the peasants already living in these mountains. They kept calling it Chiveis until finally that became its true name. *La Nouvelle*

Suisse was relegated to the history books as a piece of historical trivia to bore a young prince."

Piair smiled ruefully. "I'm sorry, Brother Lewth. I'm just a little distracted today."

"Something on your mind?" Lewth closed the history book he was holding and pulled up a chair next to the prince.

"Oh, not really." He shrugged. "Well, maybe there is. I've been thinking a lot lately about religion."

Religion? Lewth's heart began to race. "That's not your normal train of thought, Your Highness. Usually it's hunting, tournaments, and politics."

"And girls. Don't forget the girls."

Lewth rolled his eyes. "How could I forget that?"

"Exactly! But here's the thing, Brother Lewth. This duel has gotten me thinking. Maybe the gods really do matter—I mean, matter to *me*. I've always thought they offered nice rituals for the people to follow. But now that Habiloho has found religion, it seems like she has something I don't. I wonder if I ought to pay more attention to the gods and stuff like that. You're a monk of Astrebril. You must know what I'm talking about. What are your views about the gods?"

Lewth swallowed and studied his feet. He decided to answer with a question of his own. "Why do you want to know about the gods?"

Piair thought about it. "Not for the same reason as Habiloho. She wants to use the gods to get revenge. I don't care about that. But I would like divine power in my life. I need a god on my side, a really strong one."

"What for?"

"Well, you know, I'm going to rule Chiveis someday. I want to be a good king, like Father has been. I want the people to love me as much as they love him. It's a big job being king! A god of my own would be a great help."

"Chiveis has a supreme god and the triad and many others. Is something wrong with them?" Lewth hoped he was steering the conversation in the right direction.

"I suppose I could choose one of them. They're each powerful in their own spheres. But I need power in many different areas. What I really need is a god who rules over everything."

Lewth saw his chance. "You know," he said cautiously, "I think that's what the Ancients claimed about their god, Deu. He's the one who's going to be tested in the duel."

Piair scoffed. "Habiloho says he's weak. She says we're going to see how powerless he is on the day of the duel."

"What if she's wrong? What if he wins the duel?"

The idea seemed to startle Piair. "Do you really think that could happen? Astrebril is the god of the dawn. You've seen his firebursts in the sky, his thunder, his curse on the houses of men! How could any god be stronger than that?"

"Let's just imagine Deu wins—what would you do?"

Piair puffed his cheeks and blew out a breath. "I guess I'd be inclined to follow him. Do you know anything about Deu? Is he willing to share his power with mortals? I don't know anything except his name."

Lewth stood up and went to the window. *How much should I say? If word gets out that I'm a follower of Deu, I could lose everything!* He turned toward the prince, who watched him with a bewildered expression. "You don't have to decide your religious destiny right away, do you?" Lewth asked.

"I suppose not."

"Then let's see what happens at the duel. You can make your decision then."

✦ ✦ ✦

As the sun came up, Teo knelt at the window and met its light, just as he'd done each day for the past five weeks. He communed with the true God of the dawn—not Astrebril, but Deu, the one to whom all things belonged.

Teo untied the red string on the scroll Ana had given him. The parchment was ragged from heavy use. Each morning Teo had made it his habit to pray to Deu and meditate on a brief portion of Hymn 27. Today he focused on the last three verses:

> *Do not deliver me to the good pleasure of my enemies;*
> *For false witnesses rise against me, and those who breathe only violence.*

Oh! What if I weren't certain to see the Eternal One's goodness in the
  land of the living?
Hope in the Eternal One!
Fortify yourself, and strengthen your heart!
Hope in the Eternal One!

Teo watched the sun's rays illumine the Kingdom of Chiveis. The words he had just read seemed fitting for a day like this—the day of the duel. Courage would be needed, and faith.

Over the past five weeks, Teo had rested and recovered his strength in the Temple of Astrebril. He had been moved from the dungeon to a better room, with a cot and a stool and a window looking out over the realm. Teo's ravaged arms and shoulders improved over time, until finally he was able to exercise a few hours each day. Even the food wasn't bad. Apparently the High Priestess didn't want him looking weak in front of the crowd at the coliseum. She intended to defeat him at full strength. *O Deu*, Teo prayed, *do not deliver me to the good pleasure of my enemy!*

Though Teo had been confident he could overcome the physical challenges of incarceration, he hadn't been as certain about the mental aspects. During the first few weeks, his greatest torment was his profound grief at the death of Maurice. The gnawing pain of loss and anger was severe. But to his surprise, the imprisonment began to have a purifying effect on Teo's soul. The lonely cell gradually became his teacher. Teo had learned more about Deu in the past five weeks than in all his days of translating. Hymn 27 taught him well. Each word seemed to contain a fountain of truth and insight. But even beyond this, a mysterious spirit of holiness had taken up residence in the room. Teo could sense the unmistakable presence of Deu at his side during his solitary confinement. Now that the day of the great duel had arrived, he looked forward to seeing how the All-Creator would defeat the liar god.

Keys jangled in the lock, then a servant entered carrying a ewer and bowl. Teo cleaned up with a piece of soap and shaved himself with a straight-edged razor. The servant left a bundle on the cot. When Teo opened it, he found a brand-new uniform of the Royal Guard's Fifth Regiment. He donned the familiar woolen breeches, linen shirt, and leather jerkin, then laced up his boots and tucked the scroll of Deu in his pocket. Now he was ready.

Four Vulkainians came for him, armed with their sprayers, though the men kept the weapons tucked into their holsters. Teo wondered if the guards would bind his hands, but they didn't.

"This way," the sergeant said. None of the other men spoke.

Teo was led to a horse, which he rode under armed escort down to the Troll's Valley. There he was transferred to a carriage, its curtains drawn over the windows. A decanter of wine sat on the floor. Teo reached for a drink but thought better of it and decided to live with his thirst.

After a long ride on the forest road, the sound of the carriage's wheels changed. Teo realized he had arrived at the paved streets of the Citadel. He could hear people laughing and talking as they swarmed toward the gate in the great wall. Peeking out the window into the plaza, he caught a glimpse of the monumental statue of Jonluc Beaumont. *Was it only last autumn that I rode through here on my way to the tournament?* It seemed like many years ago; so much had happened since then. Teo winked at the statue of Chiveis's glorious founder. The man who had brought Astrebril to the realm could never have envisioned the events that would transpire today!

The carriage passed through the Citadel's main gate and crossed the causeway over the moat. However, instead of following the central thoroughfare into Entrelac, the driver turned onto a side road that skirted the town and avoided the crowds. Teo noticed several catapults had been rolled into place along the way, though the route wasn't along the kingdom's defensive lines. He shrugged and dismissed the thought.

At last the coliseum's imposing bulk came into view through the carriage window. The crowds were starting to converge on it now that the appointed time for the duel was less than an hour away. Teo's heartbeat quickened, and he couldn't stop tapping his fingers on his thighs. He knew his jittery sensation was partly caused by the heightened tension accompanying the big event, but he also realized he was excited to see Ana again. It had been five weeks since she had been torn from his side in the prison cell. He wondered how she had fared since that day. Certainly she would know the High Priestess's spies were watching her, so she wouldn't have risked a visit to Obirhorn Lake. Teo hoped Rosetta and Lina had been able to comfort Ana during the long weeks of waiting.

Teo's mind went back to that day in the cell when Ana had been led away. He had been relieved to see her go. The last thing he wanted was for her to remain imprisoned in the harsh dungeon. Teo pictured Ana's face as the Vulkainian guards dragged her out the door. Those blue-green eyes of hers had been wide with anguish and sorrow. *And anything else?* She had met his eyes at the last moment, crying, "I love you!" as the door slammed shut. Teo considered those words. Ana had never expressed any romantic interest in him, so he doubted she meant that kind of love. At the same time, he understood that she possessed a tender affection for him. Their many adventures had bonded them in ways he couldn't fully comprehend. Teo had no words to express what Ana meant to him, or he to her. *A close friend? A sister? Yes—an innocent and familial kind of love.* He decided that must be right.

The carriage came to a halt. One of the guards opened the door. Teo stepped into the brilliant sunshine and was led down a staircase into the belly of the coliseum.

◆　◆　◆

As Ana waited beneath the coliseum, a squad of Vulkainians barged into the room, leading another man. She craned her neck to see who it was. *Teo!* He looked strong and self-assured in his guardsman's uniform. Her confidence surged.

"Wait here until you receive further instructions," the sergeant ordered gruffly. The Vulkainians left the room, closing the door behind them.

Ana ran to Teo and embraced him. "Teo! How are you? Have you recovered? I prayed for you every day!" She looked him up and down. He seemed to have fared well in the dungeon. His uniform was clean, and he carried himself with his usual poise.

"I'm okay," he said, holding her by the waist. "They didn't torture me any more. What about you? Are you alright?"

"Aunt Rosetta took good care of me. But it was so hard to wait! I couldn't stand the thought of you in prison all this time. And I miss my parents so much! And also . . . Maurice." Her lower lip trembled, and she squeezed her eyes shut, covering her mouth with her palm. Ana felt Teo's comforting hand on the back of her head.

"I know, Ana. This is all so hard. But listen to me." She looked up into Teo's gray eyes. "We can't despair. It isn't time for mourning right now. It's time to make good on Maurice's testimony. Today Deu comes to Chiveis!"

At those words, Ana's heart leaped in her chest. Though she couldn't pinpoint the feeling, she experienced a deep sense of reassurance and joy. Teo—the same tall, handsome man she had come to admire so much over the past year—smiled down at her. Yet behind his smile, she sensed something different in him.

"You've changed," she said.

"I've been changed."

Ana didn't have a ready reply, so she just stood there, beaming at Teo. He caught the moment, laughing as he returned her gaze.

Abruptly the door to the room opened, and the archpriest of Vulkain marched in with his retinue. His sour demeanor sucked all the joy from the room. "I've come to inform you of the rules," he said. "The duel will begin shortly."

"We're ready for it." Teo's tone was defiant.

The archpriest haughtily smoothed the folds of his bleached robe. A large piece of brimstone dangled from his neck in a golden medallion. "You're ready, are you?" A sneer contorted his face. "There are tournaments you can win, Captain Teofil, and those you cannot."

Teo remained silent.

"Here, then, are the rules. Two large altars made of dry wood have been erected on the floor above us. Each party will be allowed to use its chosen talismans—whatever you deem useful for winning your god's favor. You may also address the crowd as you see fit. Your words will be proclaimed to the people by heralds in their midst. One bull will be sacrificed on each altar. Each party will touch its bull with a piece of burning wood. The sacrifice that blazes into mighty flame is the victor. Her Eminence will go first. She will say her incantations and call upon the power of Astrebril.

Then you may take your turn, in the futile hope that your god can kindle a fire." The Vulkainian guards guffawed.

Teo approached the archpriest and stared him in the eye. "Our God kindled the fire of the sun! Deu is the All-Creator. Everything in the world belongs to him. You'll soon see his power!"

Ana went to the corner of the room and retrieved the Sacred Writing of Deu from her rucksack. She held up the ancient book. "We choose this for our so-called talisman. These are the words of our God."

"So be it. And you are also to have this." The archpriest beckoned toward one of his retainers. A Vulkainian stepped forward and unfolded a cloth-wrapped bundle. The sword of Armand gleamed in the torchlight. Teo grasped it by the scabbard and took it to himself.

"Her Eminence will destroy you at your strongest," the archpriest said scornfully. "Your trinkets won't be enough."

"The living God is more than enough."

"We shall see." The archpriest spun toward the door, followed by his men. "You will be summoned in a moment," he said over his shoulder as he exited.

Ana came to Teo's side, tilting her head and looking up at him. "You were bold," she said.

"'If an army encamps against me, my heart will not fear. If war is raised against me, I will be confident in spite of it.'"

"That's Deu's hymn!"

Teo grinned. "Yeah. It kind of sticks with you when it's all you have to read for five weeks."

Ana took Teo's hands in hers. "Pray for us," she said.

"I'm just learning, you know. I'm not eloquent."

"Deu won't mind. I don't mind."

Teo nodded. He lifted his eyes to the ceiling and offered a heartfelt petition for Deu's power to descend in their moment of need. As he prayed through the words of Hymn 27, Ana felt Deu's presence come to her. "Yes, come to Chiveis," she whispered. *Come today!*

Teo and Ana had just finished praying when a messenger arrived for them. They followed him down a hallway to a trapdoor hanging from the low ceiling. The trapdoor formed a ramp to the level above. Sunlight streamed through the opening, and the roar of the crowd reverberated in the tight passageway. Teo and Ana ascended the ramp and emerged onto the arena floor. The trapdoor slammed shut behind them. Ana squinted against the glare. Two altars had been erected in the middle of the sandy oval, and between them sat the royal throne. The crowd's mood was more raucous than Ana would have predicted. The people were hungry to be entertained by spectacles.

Trumpets sounded from a gateway, announcing the arrival of King Piair. He rode up on his stallion and gazed down from the saddle with a benign expression. The king's gray beard was well manicured, and he wore a richly embroidered robe. Teo and Ana bowed to him.

"Lift your head, warrior! And you, daughter of the realm, raise your eyes! You have the chance to prove yourselves today! If your god is worthy, he will let us know."

"He is worthy, Your Majesty," Ana said.

King Piair turned his horse and looked up at the crowd. Heralds with megaphones were stationed a short distance away, while others stood along the aisles of the coliseum's seats. The king raised his scepter, and the crowd held its breath in expectation.

"People of Chiveis, I greet you! Today two gods will clash—Astrebril and Deu!" The heralds relayed the words, and the crowd cheered. The mention of Astrebril's name brought more cheering than Deu's. *Not for long*, Ana thought.

"My son, Piair the Second, is wise," the king continued. "He has given his father good counsel. Chiveis should serve the strongest god! Today I make this solemn vow: I pledge to serve the god who wins. My people, do you agree?" He raised his arms, and the people shouted their assent.

A large trapdoor in the arena floor fell open with a thud, creating a ramp to the rooms below. The eunuch priests of Astrebril led up a pair of bulls by rings in their noses. King Piair reared on his horse and raised his fist in the air. "To Chiveis!" he cried. The crowd went wild. He dismounted and assumed his place on the royal throne.

Another gate opened at the far end of the coliseum. The High Priestess entered, driving a chariot drawn by a shaggy bison. Her golden robe glinted in the sunlight, and she stood straight and tall, holding the reins like an immovable statue. Ana sensed the awe that fell upon the crowd at the impressive sight.

The High Priestess stopped at one of the wooden altars. She beckoned a priest with a haughty wave of her hand. He led one of the bulls up a ramp on the side of the altar. Two other eunuchs followed him, one carrying a sledgehammer, the other a knife. Standing on top of the altar, the muscular priest with the hammer brought it around in a wide arc.

Crack!

The glossy black bull fell to its knees, stunned by the blow to its skull. Swiftly the priest with the knife grabbed the bull's nostrils and yanked its head back to expose its throat. The knife sliced deep. A crimson cascade gushed onto the wood of the altar. Ana winced at the sight.

The High Priestess mounted the altar as her priests scurried away like cockroaches in the presence of the sun. She stood over the slain bull, victorious and triumphant. Bending down, she cupped red blood in her palms and lifted it high. Her head was thrown back, and her long black hair dangled over her shoulders. Reverent murmurs swept through the watching audience. Ana shook her head. *Deu, open their eyes! Let them see!*

Suddenly, on the rim of the coliseum, a bright light flashed. Something had caught the sun's glare and was reflecting it into the crowd. Ana stared at it, trying to make out what it was. A man was there, directing the beam. It flitted across the seats, and wherever it touched, the people recoiled.

"Teo, what is it?"

He stood beside her with his arm around her shoulders. "It's the Mirror of Astrebril."

"The one the Ancients left in the temple on the summit? I never believed it actually existed."

"I didn't either. But then, I never believed the temple existed until I went there."

"Everybody's afraid of it. See how they avoid the light?"

Teo swatted his hand in the air. "It's all just a charade! The High Priestess is putting on a big show. She's playing the people for fools!"

"We know that, but they don't. They need to hear the truth."

"They will."

The light beam slid across the arena floor and came to rest on the altar. The High Priestess stood still, holding her bloody hands to the sky. The mirror illuminated her in its brilliant ray like a golden goddess from another world.

Quietly all the heralds began to chant, "Astrebril! Astrebril! Astrebril!"

The crowd caught the emotion and joined in. "Astrebril! Astrebril! Astrebril!"

A flaming wand was brought to the High Priestess. She descended halfway down the altar and took it from the eunuch. Turning toward the great bull, she tossed the fire onto the wood and hurried to the arena floor. The bull's carcass gleamed in the reflected sunbeam.

The wand burned low. It sputtered. Something flared up, and then— *whoosh!* A mighty blaze burst from the altar in a cloud of white smoke. The crowd gasped in collective amazement. Flames licked the altar, and the bull was engulfed in fire.

"It's the powder!" Ana cried. "It's trickery!" Teo pounded his fist in his palm.

Throughout the coliseum, people began pointing to the sky, trying to catch something falling from above. Others were reaching under their seats. A few small objects dropped into the sand near Ana. She picked one up—a steel coin. "Teo, look! Money!"

He frowned. "Astrebril has no power! This is bribery! There are catapults outside throwing coins!"

"But the people love it—look at them!" They were scrambling everywhere, fighting for the god's riches.

The High Priestess strode to the center of the arena and raised her scepter heavenward. The light from the Mirror of Astrebril followed her every move. "Servants of the Beautiful One!" she boomed. The heralds echoed her words across the stands, and the people grew still.

"Today you have seen power! Today you have seen glory! Today you have received bounty! Do you need any god but Astrebril?" The crowd didn't reply. Again the High Priestess asked her question. "What do you say?" she demanded. "Do you want Deu or Astrebril?"

The chanting burst from the crowd again, but this time it wasn't prompted by the heralds. It welled up from the people spontaneously: "Astrebril! Astrebril! Astrebril!"

The High Priestess stood in her sunbeam and raised her hands for silence. "The followers of Deu will come forward now. They claim to have mighty weapons. They claim their god has power. Let them do their best! If their god can make flame, serve him. But I warn you, Astrebril is not pleased. He curses the name of Deu. His wrath is great. People of Chiveis, serve only Astrebril or *be judged!*" The mood of the crowd reached a fever pitch when they heard these terrible words.

"Ana, we have to pray against this." Teo huddled with her on the arena floor and said a quick prayer to Deu. Ana gripped his sleeve and murmured her assent to Teo's urgent words.

Now the remaining bull was led to the second altar. The man with the sledgehammer followed it, but the priest with the knife did not. A figure emerged from the rooms below the coliseum, wearing the gown and collar of a priestess of Astrebril. In her hand she held a sacrificial knife. Her hair was flame-red. The crowd roared its approval.

Habiloho ascended the altar. Adoration rained down on her from the stands, and she stood still, receiving its overwhelming force. Ana could feel the crowd's fickle love striving to possess the beautiful woman. It wasn't tender affection they felt for her—it was selfish and ravenous desire.

"She's frightened," Teo said.

Ana looked more closely. He was right. The princess wasn't enjoying the moment as Ana would have expected. Habiloho's face was laden with apprehension.

The hammer fell with a heavy thud, and the bull bellowed its dying breath as its knees buckled. Habiloho straddled the beast and grabbed the ring in its nose. Her hand trembled. The knife fell from her grasp. The eunuch with the sledgehammer snatched it and slit the bull's throat. A satisfied groan gushed from the crowd.

Teo and Ana exchanged glances. *It was time.*

Teo took the Sacred Writing from Ana and walked to the middle of the arena floor. King Piair watched him from his elevated throne, though the High Priestess was nowhere to be seen. Deliberately, Teo turned the pages of the ancient book, then raised his eyes to the crowd and spoke. "Citizens of Chiveis, I greet you in the name of Deu!"

A few jeers came from the stands, but most of the audience remained quiet, waiting to hear what Teo had to say. He adopted the staccato way of speaking that allowed the heralds to repeat his words. "I come with the Book of the one true God!" he cried. "Hear the word of Deu: 'The Eternal One is great, and very worthy of praise! He is fearsome beyond all the gods. For the gods of the peoples are idols, but the Eternal One made the heavens!'" Holding the Sacred Writing in his hand, Teo lifted his other palm toward the crowd. "Today, my people, I come with truth! Listen to me! You need to know—the magic of Astrebril is deception and tricks!" More jeers accompanied this assertion, but Teo went on undaunted. "His fire isn't from heaven. I've seen it myself! It's a human device, an earthly powder! Not divine!"

The people showed their disapproval with boos and hisses. "Blasphemy!" someone shouted, and others joined the accusation. Though Teo tried to explain more about the powder, the shouting crowd drowned him out. Ana bowed her head; she had seen this before.

Teo returned to Ana's side, handing her the Sacred Writing. He shook his head in disgust. "Reasoning with them won't work. They don't *want* to hear the truth. They're only swayed by dramatic displays of power."

"Deu is powerful! Let's give him the chance to reveal himself." Ana removed a burning stick from a brazier. "We've been waiting for this day, Teo. Go now! Go in Deu's strength." She leaned forward and kissed him on the cheek. Teo took the stick from her and turned toward the altar.

Habiloho and the priests stood at the altar's base. As Teo began to ascend the ramp, he paused to speak with the princess. His action didn't anger Ana or make her jealous. She could see he was speaking about Deu. Teo's demeanor toward Habiloho was warm and caring. His words obviously made an impact. The princess closed her eyes and nodded silently.

Climbing to the top of the altar, Teo stood over the bull, holding the piece of kindling. With his other hand, he drew his sword from its scabbard and lifted it high, brandishing it over his head in the sunshine. "Behold the sword of Armand! This sword has fought many battles! It is a strong and noble weapon! A symbol of strength!"

Teo, what are you doing? Ana cringed at his words, but the crowd seemed to like it.

"People of Chiveis, you have seen me win victories on this field. I have fought our enemies with this sword. But today I tell you the truth! It isn't by the sword that Chiveis lives! It is Deu who gives the victory!" Teo emphatically shoved the sword into his scabbard to make his point. Jeers and catcalls erupted from the crowd, but Teo ignored them. He dropped the burning stick next to the sacrificed bull.

Nothing happened.

Oh, Deu, let it catch! Make a flame blaze up! Ana's heart was pounding in her chest as she stared at the altar.

The crowd had fallen silent. Everyone waited in hushed expectation.

Next to the flickering piece of kindling, a shower of sparks shot up. It caught Teo's eye, and he crouched to inspect it. The tiny blaze disappeared under the wood. Suddenly Teo sprang to his feet. He met Ana's eyes with a look of sheer horror. She sucked in her breath. Something was terribly wrong.

"*Run!*" Teo leaped off the altar and hit the ground at full speed. "*Get below!*" He grabbed Habiloho by the arm, dragging her toward the trapdoor despite her protests. Ana dashed in the same direction, not understanding the situation but trusting Teo's instincts. At the opening to the rooms below, she turned around. Habiloho had wrenched herself from Teo's grasp and was angrily refusing to follow him. Teo looked at her, then at Ana. Anguish was written all over his face.

Teo sprinted toward Ana. He tackled her, and they slid down the inclined trapdoor, their bodies intertwined. They lurched to a halt at the bottom. Teo was on top of her.

And then the world exploded.

❖   ❖   ❖

In the stands, Lina shrieked as a fireball shattered the altar. The ear-splitting concussion echoed around the coliseum—a sound so loud, it clubbed the crowd into submission. Smoke billowed to the sky from the arena floor, while flaming debris rained upon the terrified masses. Everyone was wailing. They had never seen Astrebril's Curse up close.

"Where's Ana? Shaphan, where's Ana?" Lina was panicked. She clutched Shaphan's arm.

"I think she got down in time, but look at the king!" The corpse of King Piair lay sprawled in the dust, his arms and legs splayed out at unnatural angles. The overturned throne was a burning wreck.

"It's terrible! Ana, where are you?" Fear clawed at Lina's heart. Her ears were ringing, and the acrid smoke stung her nose. Everything around her was in tumult. Some people were fleeing the coliseum, while others were staring at the carnage in horrified fascination.

A man in the aisle pointed to the arena, his mouth agape. "Look! The Flame of Chiveis is dead!"

"It's Deu's fault!" screamed another. "Astrebril is angry!"

Shaphan leaned toward Lina and whispered in her ear, "We should leave—now."

"There he is—the blasphemer!" The man in the aisle bared his teeth. "Let's kill him!"

Lina saw Teo, far below in the haze, come up the ramp from the underground rooms. He knelt beside Habiloho's motionless form. Men in the stands began pointing and shouting. "He's desecrating her body!" one of them yelled. Across the coliseum, groups of men began moving down the aisles.

Teo scooped Habiloho into his arms and carried her down the ramp formed by the open trapdoor. An angry mob had gathered at the railings that separated the stands from the arena floor. One man jumped the rail and began to run across the oval. Emboldened by his action, the rest of the mob followed. From below, the trapdoor quickly lifted into place. It had just closed when the pursuers reached it. They stamped on it in frustration.

"Shaphan, I'm scared! It wasn't supposed to happen like this!"

"Don't give up hope, Lina. Come on, let's get out of here." He took her by the hand and moved toward the aisle.

"Where are we going?"

Shaphan turned to Lina and pulled her near, speaking so no one else could hear. "We need to find Teofil and Anastasia so we can make a new plan."

"How will we find them?"

"I know my master. I know where he'll go." Shaphan interlocked his fingers with Lina's. "Now hang onto me, and stay close!"

As Shaphan moved toward the exit, Lina allowed herself to be pulled through the agitated crowd. Nothing was going as it should. The foul god Astrebril was winning. The injustice made Lina sick. *Deu!* she prayed bitterly. *Where are you?*

◆　◆　◆

The world was a red haze. Then she succumbed to darkness.

Lights flashed. Voices. A man. Dark again.

She opened her eyes. The room was spinning. Someone called her name. A face came into focus. *Teofil?*

"Habiloho, wake up!"

Everything hurt. She couldn't breathe. "T-Teof . . ." It was more of a groan than a word.

"Habiloho! Can you hear me?"

Teo was there, looking down at her. She loved that face. She always had. "Teofil . . . I need you . . ."

"I'm right here! We're going to get you to a doctor!"

"No! I'm slipping . . . I'm losing . . ." She gasped for breath. There were hot things in her body, things that shouldn't be there.

Habiloho looked up from where she lay on the stone floor. Teo knelt over her, and beside him was that beautiful girl from Edgeton. She had a kind expression on her face. A lovely woman. They should have been friends. *Now it's too late . . .*

Blood choked her throat. Gagging, she rolled on her side and spit it out. Pain ripped through her body. Habiloho knew it was the end.

"Help me! This collar!" She clawed at her neck.

"You want it off?"

Habiloho nodded weakly.

Teo grabbed a rock and rapped on the pin at the back of Habiloho's neck. The iron collar fell away. Anastasia hurled it into the corner, where it clanged off the wall.

Habiloho felt she could breathe again. Things seemed more peaceful now. The world had grown small. It felt good to lie there and rest. "Teofil," she whispered, "tell me about Deu before I go."

"He's good. He's loving. He cares for you."

She knew he was right. "Will he take me? Even me?"

Ana stroked Habiloho's hand. "Yes, Your Highness. Deu is merciful to all who repent."

"I repent. I've seen evil. I choose Deu."

Teo had tears in his eyes. "My friend, I'm sorry."

Habiloho smiled. *I always knew he was the right kind of man. The brave captain with the noble heart. I wasn't worthy of him.* A sense of regret overwhelmed her. She decided the future of Chiveis would be very different from the past. "Can you . . . write?"

"Write what?"

"A message . . . to my brother." She swallowed and closed her eyes, feeling her strength ebbing away. "Hurry, Teofil."

Ana held up the Sacred Writing. "You could write on the letter of Jacques Dalsace," she suggested. Removing it from the book, she flipped it over and handed it to Teo, along with a piece of charred wood.

"Go ahead, Habiloho. I'm ready."

Habiloho opened her eyes and stared into Teo's face. She knew whatever words she uttered next would be her last, so she wanted to make them count. "My dear Piair, I love you. Astrebril is wicked. I choose Deu. Bring him to Chiveis!" She touched her hand to her forehead, feeling warm stickiness there. With a shaky forefinger, she traced her mark on the message. *H.*

"Good-bye, Teofil."

His handsome face receded. A warm light engulfed the princess, and then she heard the gentlest of voices welcome her home.

❖   ❖   ❖

"There! I see them!" Shaphan pointed to the trees below.

"Where? Where?" Lina scanned the forest from her vantage point just above the tree line.

"They're back in the woods again."

"I missed them!"

"Of course you did. Professor Teofil is a master woodsman. He knows how to move without being seen. Even when we know where they're going, we still can't find them."

"Did you see Ana? Was she okay?"

"Seemed to be."

Shaphan stretched and enjoyed the feel of the late afternoon sun on his shoulders. He had stopped at a place he knew Teo would have to pass to reach Obirhorn Lake. The Ancients had constructed a couple of buildings at the site, but now only the foundation stones and some debris remained. While they waited, Lina poked around to see what she might find.

"Look at this, Shaphan." He turned around. Lina held up a sign, its ancient lettering still legible. "Can you read it?"

He took it from her and studied the white letters. "It says, 'Berghotel.' I'm not sure what that means."

From out of nowhere, a voice spoke. "You have a lot of nerve coming here." Shaphan's heart skipped a beat, and Lina let out a startled cry.

Teofil stood watching them with an impassive look on his face. Behind him, Ana emerged from the trees, leading two horses.

Shaphan swallowed the lump in his throat. He deduced from the unfriendly greeting that his professor must know about the theft of the Sacred Writing.

"Professor Teofil, I have something to confess to you." Shaphan approached slowly, his eyes downcast.

"So it would seem. Sucula told me what you did. You have no idea what course of events your treachery unleashed. You stabbed me in the back, Shaphan. You betrayed me."

Shaphan's face burned. "I see that now. There's nothing I can do but ask your forgiveness. I wanted your approval, and when I didn't get it, I tried to get it from Valent. I was wrong."

An awkward silence hung in the air. The moment was poised on the edge of a knife.

Teo closed the distance to Shaphan. *Is he going to hit me?* Shaphan braced himself.

"A wise woman once taught me the meaning of forgiveness when I needed it. Now I forgive you, Shaphan. And I ask you to forgive me for not being the mentor you deserved."

Shaphan's eyes brimmed with tears as he looked up at Teo. He thrust out his hand. Teo clasped it and pulled him into a manly hug, slapping him on the back several times. The slaps were hard enough to hurt, but Shaphan didn't mind.

Lina rushed to embrace her cousin. "Oh, Ana! When that altar exploded, I thought you were dead!"

"No, not yet. Deu spread his wing over me."

The two women joined Teo while Shaphan went to his horse, then returned with a pair of rucksacks, one of them Teo's own. "Look what I brought! I figured you'd need some stuff if you're going to hide at Obirhorn Lake for a while."

Teo chuckled. "So you knew where to find me. Am I that predictable?"

"Not to the average citizen. But I knew where you'd take Anastasia."

"Fortunately I know how to hide my trail in the woods. The citizens are out for blood. It was all we could do to get here without being lynched. The High Priestess has them running scared. Deu lost a major battle today."

Ana intertwined her arm with Teo's. "Deu may have lost the battle, but not the war. Don't lose heart."

He glanced at her and nodded thoughtfully.

Shaphan dug through Teo's rucksack. "Look here! You have your ax, good arrowheads, new bowstrings. Your bow is over by the horse. Plenty of food here too. Dried meat, cheese, waybread. And look what else!" He removed a fur garment from the pack. Ana gasped.

"My bearskin cloak!" Teo's eyes widened. "How did you get that?"

Shaphan smiled proudly. "Maurice hid the scrolls in the barn where you took refuge during the fire. When I went to fetch them, I opened his rucksack, and the cloak was there."

"It was hanging in Valent's house," Ana said. "I saw it when I was with Maurice. He must have picked it up after I left."

Teo scratched the back of his head and kicked a pebble with his toe. "I won't let it out of my sight again," he vowed.

"Good idea," Ana agreed.

Teo put his hand on Shaphan's shoulder. "You've done well. You analyzed the need and planned wisely. I'm grateful."

Shaphan felt his cheeks redden. "Thank you, Professor Teofil."

"Enough with the fancy titles. We share the faith of Deu. Just call me by my name."

Shaphan nodded.

"What now?" Lina asked.

Teo met Shaphan's eyes. "Anastasia and I have made a public profession of Deu. We have to hide. I want you to take care of Lina and Rosetta while we're away. Stay out of sight—keep a low profile. Can you do that?"

"I can."

"You must tend to more than their physical needs. You'll have to give them the strength of your spirit."

"I've seen him doing that already," Ana said.

"Good. You're the man for the job, Shaphan. Hold the fort until I return."

"I will, in Deu's strength."

The four friends mounted their horses and circled them in front of the ancient Berghotel, where they spent a few moments in prayer. When the prayers were finished, they moved off in opposite directions.

Lina sniffed and wiped her eyes. "I'll pray for you, Ana!"

"And I'll pray for you. I love you! See you soon!"

◆　◆　◆

The shepherd's elderly wife had been having digestive troubles, and according to her, there was only one solution—an extract made from the white mountain-star flowers of Chiveis. She nagged her husband until finally he pulled on his boots, took up his staff, and headed to the high meadows to see what he could find.

He knew the flowers sometimes grew near Obirhorn Lake. It had been years since he'd trekked all the way up there, back in those wild lands at the head of the Maiden's Valley. After an afternoon of searching, his pouch was full of mountain stars. The old lady would be pleased.

Movement on the trail below caught his eye. He hadn't seen anyone all day, so it seemed strange for two riders to be approaching in the waning light. There was no reason for them to be in these hinterlands unless they were going to the hunter's cabin to try their luck with an ibex in the morning. If so, they'd be young guardsmen—probably drinking too much, and perhaps willing to make sport of a gimpy old man. *Better to avoid them.* He crept off the trail to hide and let the visitors pass by.

As the horses approached, the shepherd was surprised to discover that one of the riders was a woman, and not just any woman. This one was a real beauty—the kind he used to chase but could only dream of now. The other rider was a guardsman with thick, dark hair who sat tall in the saddle. He seemed familiar. Suddenly the old man recognized him: he was that fellow who competed in tournaments who shot an arrow through a falling apple last year. *Wasn't that a trick!*

The riders passed in silence on their way to the lake. When they disappeared around the bend, the shepherd resumed his journey toward the village in the valley. His throat was parched. Perhaps he'd stop for a drink. He'd have an interesting tale for the other gaffers at the alehouse tonight.

CHAPTER

16

"Y our Majesty, the High Priestess is here." The doorkeeper awaited his instructions from the new king, Piair II.

"Send her in."

Piair stood beside an open casket in his private rooms at the palace. Habiloho looked so beautiful as she rested there. Her bloody gown had been exchanged for a white robe, and her hair had been washed and combed. Nevertheless, Piair was bitter, for he knew her peacefulness was an illusion. His sister's death had been violent. The doctors had said they removed numerous metal shards from her body. The same was true for Piair's father, but somehow the offense seemed greater in Habiloho's case. She was so pure and delicate. Now she was gone.

The High Priestess swept into the room, her aura of sensual power permeating its every corner. Several eunuchs stepped lightly behind her, ready to do her bidding. "I offer you my condolences, King Piair," she said. "Your father was a noble lord, and your sister is a holy sacrifice to Astrebril."

"Thank you for those words, Priestess. There will be time enough for grieving in the days ahead. Right now anger burns in my heart."

"As it should. It burns in Astrebril's heart as well. We have sinned by mentioning the name of a foreign god in Chiveis. For that, we were punished."

Piair grimaced as he nodded. "I know. It's the last religious mistake I'll make as king."

The High Priestess smiled and came closer. Her scent was flowery and feminine, but with a sharp edge. She moved in a way Piair found appealing. From a distance he had always assumed she was much older than he, but now that he saw her up close in her sheer robe, he was struck by how young she was, and frankly, how alluring.

I'm the king now. Nothing is denied to me. What if . . .

The doorkeeper returned to the room, snapping Piair out of his thoughts. "Your Highness? Your tutor has come. He wishes to know if he may be of service."

"Yes, I would value the counsel of Brother Lewth right now. He may enter." The doorkeeper bowed. Piair glanced toward the High Priestess. "One of your monks," he said. She curled her lip and turned away.

Piair welcomed Lewth into his chambers. "Come in, Brother Lewth! We were just discussing religion. Astrebril is displeased with us. We must find a way to placate him."

Lewth shuffled his feet, apparently uncomfortable in the presence of two such powerful rulers. "I will serve if I can," he said.

"We don't need the opinions of lowly monks!" The High Priestess fingered the collar at her neck. "It's obvious what we must do. Does the surgeon dither about when a limb has gone gangrenous? Of course not! He sharpens his knife and cuts it off like the dead flesh it is!"

Piair was taken aback by the outburst, though he tried to cover his surprise. "What do you suggest?" He hoped he sounded confident, as befitted a king.

"Proclaim an edict at once! Send it throughout Chiveis under your royal seal. Anyone who serves Deu must renounce him or be executed on the spot. Citizens will be rewarded for exposing the heretics. A guardsman may draw his sword and carry out the execution immediately. We must rid Chiveis of this spiritual infection!"

The idea shocked Piair. "That's insane! Worshipping other gods isn't illegal, at least not according to the letter of the law. And we don't execute citizens without a trial. There's no precedent for this. The magistrates wouldn't stand for it."

"The magistrates!" The High Priestess's tone was contemptuous. She approached Piair and stood very close to him, as if she wanted to speak confidentially. The effect of her physical nearness excited him, making him breathless and jittery. "Is this the kind of king you intend to be?" she whispered in his ear.

"W-what do you mean?" Piair kicked himself. He knew his voice had trembled.

"Your father didn't rule like this. He didn't let bureaucrats and syco-phants determine his decisions. He did what had to be done. So I ask you, Piair: will you be a smaller man than he? Or will you—"

"Will I what?"

The High Priestess stared hard at Piair. Her eyes were painted black, and their green depths mesmerized him. "Or will you be as potent as I found your father to be?"

The suggestion of inadequacy bruised Piair's ego. He lifted his chin. "I am my father's equal."

"Excellent!" The High Priestess whirled away from him. "Then you must do what needs to be done! The blood of your father and sister cries out for retribution. It is your duty to avenge them." She walked to the side of Habiloho's casket, bowing her head for a long moment. "I mourn for her," she said quietly.

Piair felt a lump gather in his throat. "Me, too."

"She should not have died. The followers of Deu are to blame. Astrebril isn't one to be trifled with."

Lewth shifted nervously. "Uh . . . if I may . . . is that the only possible explanation?"

The High Priestess glared at him. "You dare to question my judgment?"

"No, Your Eminence. I only suggest we consider the matter from all angles."

"Your 'angles' do not concern me. Beware lest I consider you a follower of Deu." Lewth didn't respond. The High Priestess turned toward the king. "Your Majesty, assume the mantle of your father's rule. Avenge his death and that of your beloved sister. There is no greater threat to the security of Chiveis than the ancient superstition that has reared its head. You must eradicate it. Your people need you. Proclaim the edict!"

"But what about the magistrates?"

"I will take care of the magistrates."

Piair turned toward his tutor. "Brother Lewth, do you concur?"

The High Priestess crossed her arms over her chest. "Consider your response, monk. It will have many repercussions."

Lewth seemed uncertain. He started to speak, then stopped. At last he nodded, his eyes closed.

"It's decided then." Piair's voice was firm. "Send for the scribe."

◆　◆　◆

Ana awoke to the sound of a man snoring. At first it seemed strange, but then she smiled, recognizing that heavy snore. She was glad to hear its rumble again, as she so often had back in Edgeton. She sat up in her cot and nudged her father with her toe as he slept on the floor. He shifted, and the snoring stopped.

Her arrival last night at the cabin on Obirhorn Lake had marked a jubilant reunion with her parents. Stratetix and Helena rejoiced to see their daughter again, though the news of the failure at the duel had stunned them. Now a pervading sense of unease tempered everyone's joy. The future was uncertain. But at least they were together.

On the other side of the cabin, Teo slept quietly in his bedroll. Ana knew from their days in the Beyond that he never snored. A memory flashed into her mind: One night, she and Teo were awakened by a wolf's distant howl. The hour was late, and the campfire had burned low. Lying in their bedrolls, they had talked for a long time across the glow of the embers. She could still picture his face as the orange light flickered on his strong jaw. He had revealed some things about his upbringing in the orphanage that had made Ana sad. In the morning, however, nothing more had been said about it.

"Can't sleep?"

Ana glanced over at her mother in the second cot. "No, I guess not. Father woke me up."

Helena gave Ana a knowing smile. "Tell me about it. He's been doing it to me for years. Some men are just heavy breathers."

"I'm glad Teo's not like that." Ana felt sudden heat rush to her face. "I mean . . . you know . . . in this little room . . ."

"It's okay. I know what you meant."

Ana let it go, grateful her mother didn't press the issue. She sat up and leaned on one elbow. "I'm so glad to see you again, Mother. I missed you terribly."

"We missed you too, love." Helena sighed, closing her eyes and rubbing her temples with her fingers. "Somehow this all has to end."

"It will, very soon. Chiveis will turn to Deu."

"That's what we thought about the duel. But Deu didn't reveal his power."

"The people were deceived by tricks! Once they get a chance to hear the truth in a better setting, things will be different."

Teo sat up in his bedroll, lifting his hand for silence. "Shh! Quiet! Someone's coming!" He slipped from the blankets and darted to the window. For a long time he stared out, motionless.

"Are we in danger?" Stratetix was awake now too.

Teo turned back from the window. "No, it's fine. It's Lewth."

While Stratetix and Teo stepped into the morning sunshine to greet the monk, Ana dressed for the day. *What will it hold for me?* She didn't know, but she prayed for the strength to face whatever it was.

When the men entered the cabin, the look on Stratetix's face was grim. "Lewth says he has some bad news. Give it to us plainly, brother, and let's see what can be done about it."

Lewth frowned. "I'm afraid things have taken an evil turn, my friends. As you know, the king is dead. Now the crown prince has taken his place. Last night the High Priestess convinced him to issue an edict. All followers of Deu are to be executed by the Royal Guard unless they recant!"

The cabin was silent. No one knew what to say. Ana's mouth hung open as she tried to fathom the implications of this new development.

"That's illegal!" Stratetix stamped his foot. "The king can't do that!"

"He believes he can. I was in the room when it was decided. The decree is going out to the realm today."

"What about the courts?" Teo asked. "The magistrates may resist it."

"They won't. The High Priestess controls them."

Teo nodded in frustration at Lewth's reply.

Helena went to Stratetix's side and slipped her arm around his waist.

He looked at her, and the married couple communicated something with their eyes. She nodded almost imperceptibly, and he nodded back. Stratetix stepped forward and took Ana's hand. His eyes were tender as he looked at her.

"Little Sweet, I have some hard words to speak with you."

Ana's heart started pounding. *What will he say?* She steeled herself. "Yes, Father. I'm listening."

Stratetix glanced at Helena, then turned back to Ana with a sigh. "Your mother and I feared this day would come, and now it has. Anastasia, we're asking you to bury your love for Deu. Certainly you can love him in your heart. But outwardly—publicly—we must all deny him."

Ana staggered backward, so horrified at what her father was suggesting that her knees buckled. It was all she could do to remain standing.

No! Father! Mother! No!

Her mind reeled. *Deny Deu? How could her parents suggest such a thing?*

Lewth leaned toward her, stretching out his hand. "Anastasia, listen to your parents! There's no shame in it. We've been backed into a corner. We have no other choice!"

"He's right," Stratetix insisted. "You must do it. It's the only way to survive."

"Father, you can't ask me to deny the true God!"

Stratetix lunged toward Ana, taking her by the shoulders with an intense grip. His face was riven with anguish. "I *can* ask it! I *do* ask it! Listen to me, Ana! I lost you once in the Beyond, and you came back to me! Then I searched for you in the ashes of my own house and gave up hope, but you were found! I can't go through that again! Do you understand the depth of my agony? Do you know how much grief I endured? My little Ana!" He shook her, weeping as he spoke. "How well I remember the day you were born. All my memories are bound to you—my daughter, my only child! Yes, *you*, Ana! I bounced you on my knee and made you giggle. I taught your slender arms to draw a bow. How many times have I kissed your forehead while you slept? Do you even know I kissed your cheek last night and prayed for your safety? If you could see into my heart, you'd see how much I love you! Oh, Little Sweet, I know you love Deu! I love him too! But don't you also love your father? Don't you love me, Ana?" He stared at her as he held her shoulders.

"Yes, Father, of course I love you!" She had never seen him like this, and the weight of his distress bore down on her until it was more than she could bear. She hugged him tightly, the only man to whom she had ever given her heart.

Oh, Deu! What am I supposed to do?

Ana let go of her father. She gazed into his face. His beard was wet with tears. *How can I make him understand?* She spotted a water jug on the table and took it into her hand. "Father, do you see this? You couldn't call it a rock or a tree or an anvil, could you? No, because that's not what it is."

Stratetix looked at her uncertainly. "What are you saying?"

"I'm saying you have to call things what they are. Pretending doesn't change it. This is a jug. And likewise, I'm a follower of Deu. It's who I am and who I'll always be. I won't deny him, no matter what." She backed away, feeling more alone than she ever had.

"Ana, haven't you heard anything your father has been telling you?" Helena's desperation had made her angry. "He's trying to save your life!"

Ana looked from her mother's face to her father's. *I can't take them both on, not both!* She kept backing up until she felt something solid behind her. It was Teo.

He spoke with a calm voice. "You may think you're trying to save her life, but you're not. In attempting to protect her, you would destroy the essence of who she is. Who is Anastasia if not a woman more righteous and courageous than any other? What you're asking of her would be a death of another kind. Ana would cease to be the person you love so much."

"The person *we* love?" Stratetix shot back. "What about *you*, Captain? What's in this for you?"

"Father!"

Teo remained silent.

Down in the valley, a bugle sounded.

Everyone in the cabin exchanged glances, and then Teo bolted outside. Ana followed in time to see him mount Lewth's horse and gallop over a nearby rise. She hurried to the rim of the grassy depression around Obirhorn Lake. Already distant now, Teo raced across the meadow. He reined up at a vantage point overlooking the Maiden's Valley. For a long time he stood in the stirrups. Suddenly he wheeled his horse and came galloping back.

"What is it? What did you see?"

"An army's coming. We've been found."

Ana gasped, and Helena collapsed into Stratetix's arms. Lewth hung his head, shaking it back and forth.

Stratetix looked at Teo. "Can we get around them? Perhaps there's another trail out of the valley?"

"There are several, but they all lead toward those troops. The summits encircle us like a wall. Obirhorn Lake is a dead end. The guardsmen know all the approaches. They'll move up here and slowly tighten the noose. We can't get past them."

"Well, there you have it," Stratetix said. "We've all heard about the king's edict. We know what awaits us unless we deny Deu. Today is my fortieth day in exile at this cursed lake. No more! It ends right now. It's time to swallow a bitter pill and bend to the High Priestess's wishes. Then we can go back to life as normal."

Helena raised her head from Stratetix's shoulder. "In our hearts we'll still love Deu. He'll understand our weakness and forgive us."

"I have no doubt of that," Ana said. "Deu is that kind of God. But as for me, I can't deny him."

"So you'd rather die?" Stratetix asked bitterly.

"It hasn't come to that yet! The edict is just a piece of parchment. Deu is stronger than it! Let's wait and see what happens. Perhaps the king will change his mind when we show him the letter from Princess Habiloho. If we proclaim the truth to the army and the people, Chiveis can still turn to Deu. We must have faith!"

Teo shook his head. "I don't think that's what would happen. I know how the Royal Guard carries out orders. Before we could get anywhere near the king or the people, we'd be asked to deny Deu. Our faith would only lead to instant death."

Ana didn't know how to respond. She looked at Teo as he sat in the saddle. "Is this the end then? Is this how it's going to turn out for us, Teo?" She implored him with her eyes, needing his strength as her world came crashing down. He dismounted and came to her, laying his hands gently on her shoulders. She looked up at him, waiting for him to speak.

"Ana?" His voice was gentle. "I know of one more place we could hide until we find a solution. I'll take you there. Trust me."

❖   ❖   ❖

The dark clouds on the horizon suited the High Priestess's purposes. The day had already been declared a feast day to Astrebril. All work was prohibited, and now the rain would drive the citizens of the realm indoors. It was just what she wanted. Astrebril's victory in Chiveis would be sealed by the pleasures of the flesh.

The High Priestess lounged on an upholstered divan in her private rooms at the Capital Temple of Astrebril. Unlike her temple in the mountains where she manufactured her secret powder, the Capital Temple at the Citadel was open to the public. As a monumental building, its scale was enormous, though its architecture departed from the norm. Because the Citadel was built into the hillside to guard the fortified wall, the Capital Temple had to be constructed in tiers. Its lower levels were open to everyone, while the middle ones were reserved for the highborn. Only the eunuch priests were allowed on the uppermost levels, for the purpose of carrying out the rituals on which the god's favor depended. At the very top, a pointed spire jutted into the sky—the unifying feature of all Astrebrilian temples.

"What's taking the old fool so long?" The High Priestess drummed her fingers on the divan as she awaited word from the Warlord about the fugitives, who had fled to the upper reaches of the Maiden's Valley. It was a wild and remote region. They probably wouldn't have been found there without Astrebril's intervention. By the god's will, a peasant herder had mentioned it to a guardsman in a village tavern.

At last the doorkeeper knocked, and the Warlord was ushered in. The High Priestess didn't bother to greet her guest. "Well? What news?"

"I've just received a report from my commander in the field. The news is mixed. But all in all you should be pleased."

"Spit it out, soldier." The High Priestess was in no mood for ambiguity.

"My men canvassed the valley and closed in on the region of Obirhorn Lake. No one got past us, we are certain of that. Three people were captured—the girl's parents and an Astrebrilian monk."

"Did they deny the Enemy?"

"They did."

The High Priestess narrowed her eyes as a satisfied smile crept to her lips. It always pleased her when a soul was won for the name of Astrebril. "I'm glad to hear it. Let them serve as an example to their fellow citizens not to dabble in ancient superstitions. What about Captain Teofil and Anastasia?"

"We did not apprehend them."

The High Priestess exploded. She swept a flower vase from an end table, then kicked the table across the room. "What are you trying to tell me? I thought you said no one got past your troops!"

The Warlord remained impassive as he stood at attention. "The fugitives did not get past my troops, Your Eminence. Captain Teofil and Anastasia fled onto the glacier. It's a wasteland up there. Harsh temperatures, no shelter, nothing to eat. There's no fuel, so they can't cook or even melt ice for drinking. Perhaps you've noticed the storm rolling in. They simply cannot survive at that altitude. It was a desperate gamble on their part, but it will no doubt cost them their lives."

The rage simmering in the High Priestess's soul cooled somewhat at this news. She paced the elegantly appointed room, considering the possibilities. "Suicide, hmm? Perhaps we can use that. As I think about it, it's much better than some heroic martyrdom on their part. Instead they'll die like cowards, fleeing in terror." She tapped her finger on her chin. "Yes, that's it. Chiveis has spewed them out, unwanted in our land."

The Warlord cared more about facts than symbolism. "I've posted a contingent of guardsmen in the area. If the fugitives try to climb down, they'll be caught. All paths out of the valley are being watched day and night. If they don't descend soon, we can be certain they're dead. It's impossible to subsist for long on a glacier."

The High Priestess pointed her finger at the Warlord and drilled him with an intense stare. "If they are captured, I want them put to the question at once. They will curse their god on the spot or be run through with a sword. Is that clear?"

"Your orders will be carried out exactly, just as the king has commanded."

The High Priestess smiled coyly. "Remember, General, our teenaged king will not be pleased if I am not pleased." She waved the Warlord away with the back of her hand. "You're dismissed to your duties. Keep me apprised of any developments." He nodded, spun on his heels in good military fashion, and walked out with his back straight.

The High Priestess smiled as she watched him go. With the heretics now eliminated, she was ready to initiate the next phase of her plan. She summoned the doorkeeper and called for her personal transport. Four eunuchs appeared, carrying the sumptuous litter, and the High Priestess slid inside. "Take me to the assembly hall," she ordered.

All the girls were gathered by the time the High Priestess arrived. They milled around the hall, chatting idly as they awaited the big announcement they had been told to expect. Some of them were high-class courtesans, while others were common harlots, but they all had one thing in common: each wore an iron collar around her neck, for every priestess of Astrebril was also a temple prostitute.

The High Priestess walked to a dais at the head of the room. The waiting priestesses quieted when they saw their queen. She raised her hand in greeting. "The gods be over all!"

"Hail to the gods!" the priestesses cried in unison.

"I salute you, sisters, on this feast day to the lord Astrebril. I have ordained a special task for you, and only you can carry it out. It is unlike anything ever tried in Chiveis!" The High Priestess could see she had aroused the girls' interest. "Today I wish to bind the hearts of the people to their kingdom and their god. What better way to do it than through your holy services?" A cheer rose from the crowded hall.

The High Priestess smiled at her devotees. She knew what she was about to announce wouldn't go over well unless she expressed it properly, so she chose her words with care. "My sisters, I understand that for you some days are busier than others. What I have in mind will make today your busiest day ever. And for that I will personally triple your compensation!"

The priestesses had begun to groan, but the mention of extra money caught their attention. The High Priestess sensed their equivocation and seized the moment. "Messengers are now being dispatched throughout the realm. They are announcing that for today, and throughout this night, the normal fee for your services has been suspended. No money will be required for a visit to a temple prostitute. Instead the only payment required is an oath of loyalty and the sacrifice of a drop of blood. Censers will burn at the door of every temple in Chiveis. Any man who binds himself to the worship of Astrebril with a blood oath will be permitted to bind himself with you as well!"

The priestesses murmured and whispered as they tried to get their minds around the proposal. At first they were uncertain about it, but when a few of the senior courtesans began to smile and nod their heads, the High Priestess knew she had them. Her plan had worked to perfection, from start to finish.

In the distance, thunder rumbled. *Yes. Very good.* The rain of the highest god was about to fall on Chiveis.

◆ ◆ ◆

Teo stood at the edge of the glacier, resting one foot on the ice and bracing the other against solid ground. Ana was beside him. They were breathing hard from the uphill hike over the rocky terrain. Far below, Teo could still see Obirhorn Lake, a tiny blue gem on a piece of green velvet.

"Teo! Look!"

He followed Ana's finger as she pointed down the valley. Riders were coming up the trail—the Royal Guard in battle array. Teo shook his head. "You'd think we were revolutionaries trying to overthrow the kingdom."

"In a way we are."

"Hmm. Yeah, I guess so." He watched the troops advance. "Lewth told me that the reward for our capture is a thousand steel franks."

"A thousand franks! The High Priestess must really hate us!"

"Or fear us."

Ana glanced at Teo. "So what's next? Where are we going?"

"To a hut of the Ancients. Deu led me to it while I was hunting an ibex, though I didn't recognize his hand at the time."

"Will the soldiers follow us?"

"No, they won't deploy up here. There's no need. They can just wait until we're forced back down."

"What about my parents? Will they be okay?"

"As long as they curse the name of Deu, they won't be harmed."

Ana was quiet for a long time. "I just couldn't bring myself to do that. It makes me sad that Father and Mother would give in."

Teo put his arm around Ana's shoulder and pulled her to his side. "Your parents love Deu. Sometimes we're just not strong enough to do the things we wish we could."

"I know. I've prayed I'll be strong enough when the time comes."

"I'm surprised your father let you come up here with me."

"He knows how stubborn I am. He knew I wouldn't recant, so he saw it as my best chance at survival."

Teo frowned as he eyed the frozen wastes above. "We can survive on the glacier. It's what comes after that I'm worried about."

"Don't be anxious, Teo." Ana tilted her head and looked up at him. "Deu will show us a way through all this. His spirit can descend on Chiveis, and everything can change in an instant."

Teo met Ana's eyes without answering. There was something he had come to understand about their future, though he wasn't prepared to share it with Ana yet. He placed both feet on the ice, then turned around and offered her a hand. She took it and joined him on the glacier. "I don't like the look of those clouds," he said. "Let's move out."

Ana shifted her rucksack on her shoulders. "I'm right behind you."

They set out at a quick pace, climbing into a white world of ice and snow. At their first rest stop, Teo handed Ana a flask of water, then pulled a length of rope from his pack. The sky was dark with clouds, and the thunderclaps boomed with a nearness Teo found disconcerting.

"What's the rope for?" Ana asked between gulps.

He arched an eyebrow at her. "You don't want to know. Here, let me put it around your waist."

He tied Ana to himself, then asked her to lead the way. She maintained a steady gait while Teo brought up the rear. They had hiked for another hour through the desolate landscape when the first raindrops began to fall.

"It's getting colder, too," Ana observed.

"Cold air is moving in with the storm. Let's put on our cloaks."

The outer garments helped shed the water, but even so, it wasn't long before Teo felt chilled. Sweat soaked him from the inside, and the wind-swept rain managed to find its way past his cloak.

"You okay up there?" he asked.

"It's cold, but I'm making it. How much farther?"

"Not far."

A powerful gust blasted across the glacier, knocking Ana off her feet. Teo hurried to help her up. When he took hold of her hand, he was shocked. It was like a piece of ice. He rubbed her hands while she shivered against him. "Tuck them in your armpits while you walk," he instructed. She nodded.

They continued trudging as the storm's ferocity increased. Though Ana was only a short distance ahead of him, Teo found it hard to see her in the driving rain. It was late afternoon now, and it was quickly growing dark. Pellets began to strike his shoulders as the rain changed to sleet. He stared ahead, trying to get his bearings. With a sinking feeling, he realized it had become nearly impossible to find his way forward.

BOOM! The thunder's crash was deafening. Lightning flashed like the noonday sun.

"That was pretty close!" Teo called as the echoes died away. Ana didn't respond.

They plodded on. Through the sleet, Teo scanned the glacier for the small mountain that was his destination. A dark shadow loomed ahead. Maybe that's it—

Ana shrieked, and the rope went taut, dragging Teo to the ground. He slid across the glacier's icy surface. Dig in! He thrust his heels into the snow until his boots caught and he managed to arrest his slide.

"Help me! Teo! Help!" Ana's voice was distant, as if submerged.

"I've got you!" He tried to haul in the rope. It was too slick to get a good grip, and the weight on the other end was heavy.

"Can you drop your pack?"

"Get me out of here! Hurry!" Ana's cries were panicked.

"Drop your pack!"

As soon as the tension on the line lessened, Teo put all his strength into a massive yank. His thighs strained against the footholds, and his shoulders burned with the exertion of reeling in the rope. Ana's two arms appeared from beneath the glacier's surface, clawing for purchase in the ice. Just then, Teo's footholds broke loose, and he slid forward again. Ana plunged back into the crevasse with a scream.

A small boulder protruded from the glacier. Teo managed to catch it with his arm. The rope around his waist was tugging him hard, but he clung to the rock. It held firm. Wrenching himself around, he managed to get a leg behind it. Ana's cries were desperate and pitiful, but he ignored them and focused on the task of positioning himself against the boulder. Water ran in rivulets down his face, and sleet pellets stung his cheeks. He managed to wedge one foot against the rock, then the other. With a thrust of his legs, he threw himself backward, drawing the rope out of the crevasse. He wrapped the line around his wrists and pulled hard, ignoring the bite into his flesh. Like a man gone insane, he frantically hauled it hand over hand while pressing against the rock with his legs extended. At last Ana emerged from the crevasse. She collapsed onto the glacier, lying facedown, her cloak askew. Teo ran to her.

"Ana! I'm here!"

She didn't move, so he knelt beside her and rolled her over, covering her body as much as possible with his. Her drenched hair was plastered against her face, and her expression was numb. She raised a shaky hand. "T-Teo . . . h-h-help . . ."

Teo wrapped Ana's cloak tightly around her, then pulled the drawstrings on her hood until her face was completely hidden. He scooped her shivering body into his arms and staggered in the direction of the mountain that rose from the middle of the glacier. If he dropped into a crevasse now, it would be the end. Yet he knew if he waited out in the open, it would be the end regardless. He would have to take his chances.

Teo reached the base of the mountain and ascended its flank. A stone building materialized out of the gloom. He circled around it, laying Ana on a bench built into the wall. She moaned softly. The recessed windows had been sealed long ago with a crude stone-and-mortar job, but over time some of the larger stones had come loose. Teo cleared an opening, then crawled inside. After he had lifted Ana in as well, he wedged the stones back into place.

The room was dark, so Teo lit a candle and looked around. Two skeletons lay curled in the corner around a makeshift firepit, the colorful tatters of their clothing indicating they were Ancients. Pieces of broken furniture sat in a pile next to them.

Ana was shivering violently, but she was more alert now that she was out of the wind and rain. Her arms were crossed over her chest as she huddled inside her cloak. Teo knelt beside her, brushing water off her cheeks with his thumb. Her face was very pale, and her lips were blue. She smiled feebly. "N-n-nice hike. Wha-what's for d-dinner?"

Teo grinned back at her. "Hot soup. I'll get a fire going. You have to get dry right away. Are you able to change into some dry clothes?"

She nodded, then changed her mind and shook her head. "M-my p-pack."

"Oh yeah. It fell down a pretty deep hole, huh?" He considered the dilemma. "Okay, I have extra shirts in my pack. You can change into one of those, then warm up in my bedroll while I make some broth."

She poked a trembling finger out of her cloak. Her blue lips curled up mischievously. "N-no p-p-peeking!"

Teo burst into laughter at Ana's audacity. *Is there anyone else like her in the world?* He brought her the shirt from his pack, then laid out his bedroll on the floor next to her. Returning to the firepit with some cooking implements, he built a pyramid of sticks and lit the kindling. The cedar pieces took the flame readily. "Thanks for leaving it for me," he said to one of the Ancients. The skull stared back at him without answering.

When the broth was almost ready, Teo turned around again. Ana was reclining in the bedroll, wearing his oversized shirt and using the rucksack as a pillow. Her gown and chemise dripped from the ceiling. Teo was glad to see she was no longer shivering. He removed his wet jerkin and changed into a dry shirt. Holding the pot of broth in one hand, he motioned for her to scoot over inside the bedroll.

"Really?" Ana asked.

He waved reassuringly. "Don't worry, it's nothing personal. You could use the extra warmth. Besides, there's no other choice. Our other bedroll is at the bottom of a crevasse." Before she could protest, he handed her the pot and slid inside the woolen blankets next to her. They each had a spoon, and by the time the pot was empty, Teo knew Ana was going to be okay. At least for today.

With his stomach full and his body warm again, Teo started feeling drowsy, and he sensed that Ana felt the same. He yawned as he drew his thick bearskin cloak over the bedroll for extra warmth. For a long time, he lay still in silence, listening to the wind howl outside. Just as he was drifting off to sleep, Ana spoke into the darkness.

"Teo?"

"Uh-huh?"

"Thanks for spreading your wing over me."

"What does that mean?"

"I'll tell you sometime." Ana rolled toward him, and soon she was asleep at his side.

❖   ❖   ❖

Candles burned in Rosetta's chalet. The pouring rain darkened the evening sky, and she had drawn all the curtains. The members of the house community sat in a circle, just as they had many times before—except now Teo and Ana were gone, and Maurice wasn't standing in front to lead them to Deu. The times were indeed evil.

Shaphan braced himself for what lay ahead. The mood in the room was as gloomy as he had ever seen. He prayed a quick prayer for divine wisdom, knowing the words he needed to say wouldn't be easy for his friends to hear.

"Brothers and sisters," he began, "this is the last time we can meet like this. It's too dangerous now. Our journey together has come to an end."

No one responded. Stratetix slumped in his chair with his elbows on his knees and his forehead in his hands. Helena stared at the floor, her fingers intertwined in her lap. Everyone was mourning the death of a dream.

"Lewth, what's next for you?" Shaphan asked.

"Back to tutoring the new king, I guess. I denied Deu, so for now I'm safe." Lewth winced at those words, and his chin dropped to his chest.

"Deu will forgive you, brother." Shaphan gave Lewth's shoulder a squeeze, then glanced around the room. Since no one wanted to speak, Shaphan filled the silence. "As for me, I'll be moving to Vingin to help with the rebuilding. There will be lots of metalwork to do. And I can also keep an eye on Lina and Rosetta."

The community continued in bleak silence for a time, until Stratetix finally raised his head and sat up straight. He took a deep breath. "My friends, I too denied Deu today, as did my wife. We are deeply ashamed of it, but we felt we had no other choice. However, our daughter—" Stratetix's voice cracked with emotion. He squinted against the tears, covering his mouth with a fist.

Helena picked up where Stratetix left off. "Anastasia and Teofil refused to deny Deu. They fled to an unknown hut on the high glaciers. We await their eventual return, with some strategy for evading the edict's consequences."

"Captain Teofil is very resourceful," Lina offered. "He always finds a way."

Rosetta nodded. "There must be something he can do to change the king's mind."

Shaphan rose from his seat and lifted his hands to the ceiling. "Let us pray for that now."

✦　✦　✦

The people of Chiveis were celebrating Astrebril's victory, but the young King Piair II was in no mood for revelry. From his high window in the royal palace, he could see the rain-soaked men thronging the courtyards of the Capital Temple in the Citadel. With the fee suspended for the priestesses' services, he knew the same thing would be happening in all the towns and villages of the land. The men of the realm were offering their blood to Astrebril, cleaving to his cult prostitutes in exchange for a finger prick and an oath. Chiveis rejoiced to do so. Yet for Piair, it wasn't time for joy but for grief.

He walked to his father's casket, then to his sister's. People often referred to death as sleep, but Piair knew this was no sleep—at least not a sleep from which they would awaken. He pounded on the edge of Habiloho's casket. Hot, bitter tears stung his eyes. "Why? Why did she have to die?" Piair cried the words aloud, though he already knew the answer: Chiveis had incurred the wrath of Astrebril.

The doctors said someone had removed Habiloho's iron collar before her body was discovered. Captain Teofil must have done it while he was alone with her beneath the coliseum. Did he believe the gesture would cause his god, Deu, to save her? If so, he was wrong. Habiloho's cold, dead body was yet another confirmation of Deu's impotence. Piair clenched his fists and vented his frustration to the ceiling with an inarticulate groan. In the depth of his heart he vowed, *The name of Deu will never be spoken in Chiveis as long as I am king!*

Piair heard footsteps approaching from down the hall and assumed it was the High Priestess. She had requested a private audience in his chambers to discuss an urgent matter.

When she swept into the room, the young king immediately noticed her different attire. The High Priestess wasn't arrayed in her formal regalia. Instead of her usual white-painted skin and black lips, she had more color on her face, and her robe was similar to that of the temple courtesans. Only the collar around her neck indicated her status as a priestess of the Beautiful One.

She stared into Piair's eyes for a long time, silent and intense. Finally she held up a needle and a small censer filled with burning coals. "I've come to receive your offering to Astrebril," she said.

Piair's heart began to race.

❖　❖　❖

The sleet had changed to snow overnight, blanketing the glacier in a glittering mantle of diamonds. The sky was so blue, it wasn't blue

anymore, but a deep indigo that could only be seen at the highest eleva-
tions. Morning sunlight reflected off the snow and shone its warmth on
Teo as he stood outside the mountain hut. In the distance, the sky was
pierced by jagged peaks—the mighty banks of the ice river that flowed at
its timeless pace.

Wrapped in her cloak and wearing the boots she had borrowed from
her mother, Ana joined Teo outside. She laid her gown and chemise in the
sun to finish drying. Then, reaching into the hole in the hut's walled-up
window, she brought a steaming mug to Teo.

"Juniper tea?" She offered him the cup.

"Sounds good. Thanks."

"Mind if we share? I only found one mug in your pack."

"I don't mind."

Teo sipped the tea, then handed it back to Ana. His thoughts were
jumbled. He had some difficult things to tell her, but he didn't want to
speak them. After the trauma of yesterday, it was nice to relax in the
warm sun and pretend that nothing mattered. For a while, they drank tea
together in silence.

"How long can we stay here?" Ana asked at last.

He shrugged. "Does it matter? Eventually we have to go back down."

"If we wait, the soldiers might leave. We could sneak back to Edgeton,
keep a low profile, see what happens."

"A low profile? Is there anyone in the realm who doesn't know us? A
thousand franks is a lot of money. We would face the decision to deny Deu
immediately. And besides, guardsmen don't leave their posts."

Ana stared at her feet, shaking her head slowly. "I just don't understand. I can't believe we're here! Why didn't Deu reveal himself at the
duel?"

"Maybe he did."

Ana glanced at Teo with questions in her eyes.

"What I mean is, maybe Deu *is* leading us, but we've been unwilling to
see it. I'm afraid we tried to manipulate him at the duel—force his hand,
make him show up. He doesn't work like that."

"He's the All-Creator! Why wouldn't he want to come to the people
of Chiveis?"

"I'm sure he does, but when? On our schedule or his? Chiveis was around for hundreds of years before Deu led us to this." Teo held up the Sacred Writing from his morning meditations.

"That's exactly my point! Deu led us to the book so our people could know him. We have to bring them the truth."

"We already did. Clear as day. They didn't want it."

"They need another chance! We could go down there, and you could explain things again. They respect you. They would listen and turn!"

Teo didn't respond, and his silence made Ana grow more insistent. "What about the king?" she demanded. "He would turn if he knew about Habiloho. Look, we have her last wishes right here!" Ana removed the princess's note from the Sacred Writing and showed it to Teo.

He shook his head. "Before we could get that note to the king, we would face the choice to deny or be killed."

"Not if we showed them the letter first! Maybe they would let us appeal our case."

"That's not what would happen. The soldiers of Chiveis don't ask questions—they follow orders. We would be executed."

"Are you saying our only choices are to starve up here or go down to martyrdom?" Ana's voice had a desperate edge. "I thought you'd have a better plan than that! You're supposed to! You always do!"

It's time to tell her.

Teo faced Ana, wrapped tight in her woolen cloak. Despite all she had been through the past few days—or perhaps because of it—she was the most beautiful woman Teo had ever seen. He heaved a sigh and took the plunge.

"Ana, there is one other choice."

She searched his face, seeking an answer. "What is it?"

He turned his head and gazed into the distance. Ana followed Teo's gaze, then swung her head back to him with a look of horror. "No! Not the Beyond!"

He nodded gently. "It's either that or death."

"No!" She pounded her fist against Teo's chest. "There must be another way! You can give a great speech. The king will be moved with pity at our heroic testimony. Chiveis will turn to Deu!"

"Chiveis has made its decision. There's no place for us here any-more."

Ana was frantic. "I can't leave my parents! You have to think of something else!" She hammered Teo's body again and again, crumpling Habiloho's note in her fingers. Suddenly she lost her grip on it, and the wind snatched the slip of paper. "Grab it!" she cried, but it was too late. The note swirled away over the glacier and disappeared against the white landscape.

"Let it go, Ana. It's a false hope for us." Teo spoke as tenderly as he could. "Deu is calling us into the Beyond. Who can imagine what he has planned? There's a lot we don't know. What does the rest of his book say? Why is his symbol the cross? Who else might be out there, hungering for knowledge of the true God?" He paused. "Ana? Let's step into the future Deu has for us—not the future of our own creation."

Ana's face was distraught, and she breathed hard as she battled her conflicting emotions. She paced back and forth, looking north toward home, then south into the Beyond. Finally she returned to Teo and nod-ded weakly. "I'll go," she whispered. "But it's *so* hard."

Teo leaned forward and kissed her forehead. "I know. But you won't be alone. I came to you before, and I'll stay with you now. I promise. I always will."

❖   ❖   ❖

The world became green again as Teo and Ana descended from the gla-cier, heading south into the Beyond. Ice gave way to rock, rock to tundra, tundra to meadow, and meadow to forest. Under a late-afternoon sun, they paused to drink at a sparkling stream.

Teo cupped cold water to his mouth, then rose to his feet, wiping his chin. Ana stood apart, looking uphill to the north. Everything she loved lay on the other side of a glacier. Her head fell to her chest, and she covered her face with her hands. Teo's heart broke. He approached her, and she turned to him, allowing him to take her into his arms. For a long time she wept against his chest, until at last her shuddering ceased and she simply rested on his shoulder.

"Can I show you something?" he asked.

Ana separated from Teo and looked into his face with her blue-green eyes. Even though they were reddened by tears, they were deep and bright and lovely. She nodded. "Show me."

Teo retrieved the Sacred Writing from his pack. "I was reading Deu's words this morning before you awoke. He showed me this passage. I think it'll give you hope."

He led Ana to a flat rock, and they sat beside each other as the stream flowed beneath their feet. He found the text and translated it: "'For I know the plans I have for you,' declares the Eternal One, 'plans for peace and not misfortune, in order to give you a future and a hope. You will invoke me, and you will go away. You will pray to me, and I will grant your request. You will seek me, and you will find me, if you seek me with all of your heart. I will be found by you,' declares the Eternal One, 'and I will bring back your captives. I will gather you out of all the lands, out of all the places where I have driven you away,' declares the Eternal One, 'and I will bring you back to the place from which I have made you go.'"

When Teo finished reading, Ana didn't respond right away but stared at the tumbling water as if mesmerized. He waited silently, letting her sift her thoughts until she was ready to speak. Her words were confident when they finally came. "I'm going to accept that promise as my own. Even when Deu's plans are different from mine, I know he's faithful. I can walk whatever path he lays before me."

Ana raised her head and looked directly at Teo with a radiant smile on her lips. A sudden wave of admiration and love overpowered him, a feeling so intense he could neither move nor speak. All he could do was return Ana's joy with a smile of his own.

Downstream in the forest, a branch snapped. Ana inhaled sharply, and Teo bolted from the rock.

A short distance away, two men stood in the dappled sunlight, looking at Teo and Ana. Their clothing was foreign. They were outsiders from an unknown tribe.

Teo raised his hand in greeting. The men raised theirs in return.

Glancing down at Ana he asked, "Are you ready for this?" She nodded and stood up.

Deep in the woods of the Beyond, Teo approached the two strangers with the words of life in his hand. As he walked forward, Ana took his free hand in hers.

"Lead the way, Captain," she said.

Coming in April 2011

Book Two of the

CHIVEIS TRILOGY

For more information, visit www.Chiveis.com